Daria
(An Erotic Nightmare)

WOL-VRIEY

Burning Bulb
PUBLISHING

Novellas and Short Stories By Wol-vriey

Big Trouble in Little Ass

Forever Ago Sunshine

Daria
(An Erotic Nightmare)

WOL-VRIEY

Burning Bulb
PUBLISHING

Daria
By **Wol-vriey**

Burning Bulb Publishing
P.O. Box 4721
Bridgeport, WV 26330-4721
United States of America
www.BurningBulbPublishing.com

Cover photo © photoagent; used under license from Shutterstock.com; photo ID: 488815489.
Author Photo: Lolade Akinsowon © 2014.

First Edition.

Paperback Edition ISBN: 978-1-948278-03-4

Printed in the United States of America

PART 1:
ARRIVAL @ CROSSWAY

CHAPTER 1

Brie

The 5ᵗʰ of June. A Massachusetts evening. A quarter past six.

Brie Becker pushed open the glass door of the Crossway Diner and stepped inside. Her first impression of the place was uncomplimentary. The Crossway—announced outside by a red and yellow sign—was drab and a little run down, almost a dive. Stale air welcomed her. Air that smelt of greasy food. Air that stank of stale sweat and waitress perfume.

Brie didn't care what the place looked or smelt like. She was too tired and too hungry. She just wanted a bite to eat and then she'd be on her way again.

She had at least another hour of driving to do.

Brie had been driving for five hours now, initially coming up from New Jersey on the I-95, and afterwards (for most of the evening) on the I-91. She was on her way up to Bennington in southern Vermont. She was going to visit her older sister Kathleen, who'd just had twin boys. This Saturday afternoon she'd packed a suitcase full of clothes and shoes, leapt into her blue Volkswagen Golf and hit the road north.

Brie Becker was a slim blue-eyed brunette of average height. Thirty-eight years old. (A call center rep, she worked from home, loving her job's flexible hours.) She was wearing a short, sleeveless white dress. She caught a whiff of her armpits and grimaced: her deodorant spray had let her down again.

She'd intended to start out much earlier from Millville, but lots of little things had held her up. She'd also miscalculated the distance to Bennington. She'd finally left home at three in the afternoon, expecting to arrive at Kathleen's by seven in the evening. Only now it seemed like she'd be reaching her destination at 9 p.m. instead.

Brie *had* considered flying up to Vermont, but the distance hadn't seemed sufficient to her to justify the expense (her miscalculation again). So she'd driven up instead.

The trip had initially been fun going, watching the countryside pass her by. But Brie normally only drove to work and back, and to the shopping mall and beauty salon. After a while she'd begun feeling exhausted. And it wasn't just the concentration required to keep the car rolling in a straight line at 65 mph tiring her out. It was more the lack of other vehicles on the road. Sometimes there'd been only trucks on the highway, all going the other way, heading south. After a while it got disconcerting. In town, you were never alone. There were always people driving in front of you and behind you. The very presence of other traffic on the roadways kept you alert. Driving through endless stretches of countryside, however (particularly once she got to upper Connecticut), made you switch off your concentration. Especially if, like Brie, you'd stayed up late watching TV.

After three hours on the road, Brie had discovered in herself a tendency to relax behind the wheel. To *really* relax. And ten minutes ago, she'd found herself nodding off while the car sped north.

That was when she'd turned off the interstate. The I-91 continued up into Vermont, and once there she'd only need to make a single westward turn onto Route 9 to reach her destination . . . but she'd figured out a shorter route using the state highways. Her way should get her there a bit quicker. Maybe twenty minutes quicker. Even that though didn't seem quick enough.

All things considered, Brie felt lucky finding this diner here and now. Here was a place to unwind and relax her mind, if only for half an hour.

But . . .

Just as she took that first step inside the Crossway, she had a weird feeling. She felt she'd made a mistake by stopping here.

No, no, a mental voice warned her. *Not this place. Just turn yourself around, walk back over to your car, and drive off right now. Don't top up your personal tanks here. Just don't.*

Brie decided, however, that her sudden feeling of fear stemmed from her first sight of the man behind the service counter. The man was a giant. She felt he'd look more at home in a cage in a zoo. He was maybe six-foot-five in height, hairy as an ape, and with muscles that filled his striped blue shirt to the ripping point. He wore a deadpan expression on his ugly face, as if its muscles were engaged in a tug-of-war with the act of expressing happiness.

Don't do it! Leave now! Brie's inner alarm system shrilled again. *This is a bad place!*

This time Brie almost backed out of the door. Startled by her strange intuition, she took a good look around the diner. Over on her right, a single waitress was carrying two trays of food. One order she set down in front of a young couple wearing black leather. The other order she placed in front of a middle-aged man in a well-cut suit. He looked like a traveling salesman. He was a businessman of some sort anyway. Brie figured the young couple (who were now kissing) had arrived on the motorbike parked in the front lot. The middle-aged man most likely owned the white Mercedes SUV she'd parked her blue Volkswagen Golf beside.

Returning from serving the three customers, the waitress—a plump young brunette—gave Brie a look that asked: "Well, are you coming in, or what?" Then she turned away to get the customers' drinks from the fridge by the counter.

For a moment again, Brie almost bolted from the Crossway Diner. The waitress had been smiling, but Brie felt she'd seen something creepy in the woman's face.

She realized she was still standing in the doorway, one foot beyond the threshold, the other outside. She felt frozen in time, as if indecision had made an icicle out of her.

The waitress's smile had seemed like a cry for help. Which was silly, Brie thought. Who on earth begged you to save them from doing a routine, everyday job, when the front door was right open and there were no security guards in the place?

Leave! Brie felt again. This time though, the caution was weaker, almost as if her intuition was tired of warning her.

Or—she frowned—*Maybe my sense of worry is hungry too?*

She looked around the diner again. She saw no danger here. The young couple on her far right were playing footsie under the table. Clearly new love. The gleam in the girl's eyes spoke of an intense desire to get laid, and laid hard. Brie doubted her beau would be getting any sleep tonight. He'd better have enough rubbers handy. Across from the amorous pair, the businessman was eating his BLT sandwich with a look of placid boredom on his face. He also looked too out-of-shape to successfully assault anyone. So, rape was totally out of the question. Not that he'd be able to accomplish that in public, anyway. She figured she was safe here.

Finally (after a seeming eternity that had actually lasted only forty-five seconds), Brie took the plunge. Her stomach was nagging her as if they were married. She shrugged off the last of her shudders, stepped fully inside the diner, and let the glass door swing shut behind her.

Safety in numbers or not, Brie still wasn't taking any chances. She chose a table on the left of the restaurant, where she had a clear view of everyone, including the waitress who was now walking over to take her order. She ensured also that she was sitting near the front door. She no longer felt as jumpy as a rabbit, but she was prepared to bolt if the need arose.

Once properly settled, however, Brie wondered what her initial apprehension had been about. She revised her impressions of the place:

The Crossway looked exactly like a thousand other American roadside eateries. Opposite her was the service counter from which the waitress was approaching. A row of ten silver stools ran alongside the counter. The right half of the dining room was taken up by two rows of round tables—four on each side—separated by an aisle. On the left side of the diner where Brie sat, another four tables were arranged along the windows. Two small TVs hung suspended over the food counter: one facing the entrance, the other pointed at the right side of the room. The diner floor was a worn mosaic of silver and black tiles. The glass windows began halfway up the brick walls and gave a panoramic view of the outside. (Not that there was a lot to see: just the overpass, the parked cars, and a lot of trees.) Two corridors led to the rear of the building. One was on the far left of the dining room. The other was in its middle, between the service counter and the drinks' fridge.

All in all, a nice, homely place. Perfect to bring the family to on a weekend for some of that good American all-day-breakfast.

"I thought you'd never come in," the waitress said on her arrival at Brie's table. She held her little notepad poised ready. "What'll you have?"

Brie studied the menu. "Coffee for starters. Strong and black. I need something to keep me awake."

"Going far?" The waitress had on gray trousers, a short-sleeved blue top with white collar and cuffs, and white Nikes. Her green-and-white striped apron suggested that she also helped out in the kitchen.

"Up to Vermont," Brie replied. "Bennington."

The waitress smiled again. Again, Brie got the unsettling feeling that something unpleasant lurked behind her smile. The disturbing impression flickered through her mind and vanished. But, but for that moment, Brie had felt like . . . The best way she could explain it was to liken it to the sort of feeling one felt at times when watching a thriller or romantic drama—that period of fake gaiety which you just knew wouldn't last. Brie found the feeling especially poignant if she'd watched the movie before. Two happy lovers in a war film (maybe exactly like the pair across the room now) kissing and pledging eternal love to one another before the boy flies off to a foreign country and dies horribly in a explosion that blows both his legs off—dies with her name on his lips; or . . . or that scene where they're both so happy and then a gang of punks walks in, and on some contrived excuse, first break the boy's arms and legs with their baseball bats and then proceed to rape the girl to shreds.

This is the calm before the storm. The lull before the horror begins, the woman's eyes seemed to say.

Brie shuddered again.

The waitress returned to the counter. She'd realized that Brie needed some time to make up her mind on what she wanted. Brie heard her tell the giant, "Coffee, Gorilla. She wants it black."

Gorilla? What a name.

Gorilla turned to pour Brie's coffee. Like an infusion of gaseous vitality, the smell of the brew reached Brie across the room. From the window behind the counter, she heard the sizzle of the meat frying in the kitchen. Loud popping and sputtering. The meat's tantalizing aroma reached her too. It reminded her of her hunger. She studied the menu. She finally decided on a chicken pot pie and some salad.

The waitress was already returning with her coffee.

Just as the waitress reached Brie, another woman emerged from the corridor beside the counter. This woman was in her early thirties and very attractive, with pale gray eyes and bright red lips. She had long, strikingly white hair that fell down past her shoulders.

The waitress put Brie's coffee in front of her,

Brie was still watching the white-haired blonde by the counter. The woman was speaking to Gorilla. What was holding Brie's attention was the strange expression on the blonde's face. Brie thought it a very out-of-place expression for someone who worked in a diner.

The white-haired woman looked like she was starving.

CHAPTER 2

Shelly, with Craig and Erica

"How much further we got to go, baby?" Shelly enquired from the front passenger seat of the silver Ford Fusion.

"Dunno for sure," Craig replied, tapping the steering wheel.

They were presently driving through South Deerfield, MA. Following the GPS directions, Craig had taken the south-of-town exit from the I-91 onto Greenfield Road, and was now turning off of that onto Route 116 aka Conway Road.

He called back to Erica. "How close are we?"

The young woman seated in the back looked left and right. "About five miles," she replied. She pointed forward at the overpass they were about ascending. "Once over this hump, we're almost there."

The silver car climbed the overpass.

"You sure of that?" Shelly asked, staring down at the interstate highway as they crossed it. "It feels like I've been sitting in this car forever."

Craig laughed. "You should try driving *forever* sometime. And how is it that whenever there's a guy around, you women *insist* that he handle the wheel? Whatever happened to equality of the sexes?"

"Doesn't exist outside of the office and bedroom, darling," Shelly replied. "Everywhere else, we want *more* than you evil chauvinist pigs." She reached across and laid a hand on his thigh. "I'll make it up to you later, baby."

He smiled at her. "My ass aches, baby."

"Oh? Poor, poor ass. I'll massage it for you later. I'll take my time with rubbing each buttock cheek till it feels better."

"Hey!" Erica piped up from the rear seat. "What about *my* ass? It aches too."

9

Craig laughed again. "Uh, uh," he replied as they cleared the bridge, "find your own girlfriend. Shelly's mine."

Shelly looked back between the seats and winked at Erica. For a moment, as she watched her blonde friend's face, Craig's words floated through her mind: *Find your own girlfriend.* That might have been just what it sounded like, a joke-of-the-moment retort, or . . . or did Craig suspect the same of Erica as she did? That Erica was . . . sexually adaptable?

"Hey, ladies," Craig said, "here we are at the Crossway Diner. You girls still wanna stop for food? Or do we keep rolling on to Conway?"

Shelly turned from staring at Erica to look forward again.

"Ah yes, the Crossway," Erica rejoiced. "Guys, like I said, Conway's just five miles off now. But of course, Dr. GPS already told ya'll that."

The diner was on their right, in the angle between Conway Road and the southward turnoff from the I-91. The highway beckoned, but so did the building, with its promise of a hot meal. It was about 8 p.m. now, late spring evening. The sun was low in the sky, already saying goodbye to the day. They had thirty minutes of daylight left, tops.

Craig slowed as they reached the turn-in to the diner.

"So, which is it gonna be, ladies?" he asked again. "Turn off or drive on?"

Shelly decided. "Oh yes, we're stopping. Pull over, man. If I don't eat now, I'm gonna eat you instead."

"Oops," Craig said. He turned the car into the diner parking lot.

"Ugh," Erica said from the back. "You've no idea how that just sounded. Particularly after your earlier comments on how you're gonna squeeze his ass for him all night."

"Aw, Erica," Shelly said, "I'm so hungry I could eat *you*. Damn! My tummy's been rumbling for two hours straight now."

"Stop it!" Erica yelped, throwing up her hands in mock horror.

"Whatever," Shelly said. "Point is, guys—I'm frigging starving."

"Well, lunch *was* six hours ago," Craig said, pulling up beside a white Mercedes SUV. "So long as you two don't insist on burgers again."

He killed the engine and opened the car door.

Erica nodded. "Yeah, lunch does feel like it was forever ago." She made a face. "Even the buzz from the Cokes I had is gone now. Faded like last night's dreams." She yawned. "Besides, we already know

Marty's fridge is empty. Grocery shopping will commence tomorrow."

Shelly giggled. Erica sounded excited. *Carnally* excited. So maybe *she knew*. Maybe she suspected what Shelly was thinking. Maybe she even felt the same way.

***

Shelly Parker, Craig Michaels, and Erica Gelb were driving over from Lancaster, Ohio to Conway, Massachusetts for a weekend of fun and relaxation.

Shelly Parker was twenty-four. A pretty, bright-eyed brunette. Shelly worked as a waitress at Lancaster's Cherry Street Pub.

Craig was twenty-six. Tall, dark, and very handsome. He was a construction worker. He and Shelly had been dating for a year now. Shelly thought they had a good relationship. She loved him and wanted to marry him. He was her ideal man—loving and kind and never took her for granted. Their sex life was fun too.

Just like Craig, Erica Gelb was also twenty-six years old. Erica was tall and big-boned. Not fat, no. She looked like one of those olden day Wild West 'pioneer gals'—one of Slavic descent. One could easily envision her in ranch threads with a cowgirl hat on, crouched behind a wagon, long plaited pigtail dangling forward over her shoulder, and aiming a Winchester at a charging Indian horde. Erica had that rawboned look to her. She was a blonde, with boyish close-cropped yellow hair and pale blue eyes. She had an angular face, and thick lips that gave her a hard look. But in reality she was very kind. Shelly had personal experience of Erica's kindness.

When Shelly first started working at the Cherry Street Pub, Erica had taken her under her wing and steered her through her first fortnight of waitressing, explaining how to deal with rude customers, the even ruder bartenders and cooks, and, rudest of all, their boss Mr. Matthews. The dark, handsome, and arrogant Mr. Matthews roared like a lion all day long. Under Erica's supervision, Shelly had learnt to ignore him and just get on with what he'd hired her for.

Erica's kindness had made them firm friends.

***

This was a very cold evening. Very cold for late spring, that was. A wintry wind was blowing into the car. One expected better from the weather with summer knocking at the seasons' door.

The extended day was dying, settling into its grave somewhere. Sunset was merely an impression of transition from day to night states, a western sky of gray clouds with bleeding underbellies like the mountains were stabbing them to death.

**

Driving northeast to Conway had been Erica's idea. Her cousin Marty had invited her up for the weekend. Erica hadn't seen Marty in two years and had replied, "Yes, I'll come."

Then she'd remembered Shelly. She'd asked if she could bring a friend along.

"Sure," Marty had replied, "as many as you like."

So Erica asked Shelly. Shelly answered that she'd love to travel up north.

"Ask Craig too," Erica next suggested.

"You sure? Your cousin might not like it."

"Nah, Marty's cool. He said, 'the more the merrier.'" Then she winked. "Besides, we need a driver anyway."

Shelly laughed and asked Craig. Craig had instantly said to count him in. Yes, he'd *love* to get away from urbanity for two days. Away from the dust and sweat of a hard hats' life.

**

Shelly's main reason for accompanying Erica up north was so she could seduce her. As in *fuck* her.

Up till about four months ago, Shelly Parker had never once thought of herself as bisexual. She was *straight*. She did her heterosexual thing and the lesbian chicks did their homosexual thing. Live and let live; every woman had exclusive rights to how she used her vagina.

One of the Cherry Street Pub waitresses, Cassie, was gay. Shelly knew her girlfriend Maria. Four or five times now after work, Shelly had come upon Cassie and Maria kissing passionately in the waitress's dressing room. She'd just growl "get a bed somewhere," pick up her bag, and leave. Mr. Matthews had caught them at it too. He'd twice threatened to fire Cassie over her 'lowering the moral standards' of his establishment. But nothing had come of it. Everyone knew that so long as you didn't screw up on the job, the boss was all roar and no gore.

No, Shelly hadn't considered herself a sapphic seductress. She'd never thought of actually having sex with another woman. She did occasionally fantasize that it was a girl licking her lady parts when Craig was performing cunnilingus on her. But that was as far as it went. Girl-on-girl wasn't something she'd ever considered acting out.

Not until Erica entered her life, that was. Something about Erica turned Shelly on like a switch. Lit her up like a match. She'd liked Erica from their first meeting. Back then though, she hadn't known that her attraction to Erica had a physical component to it. Later, after they'd gotten to be friends, she'd often catch herself watching Erica out of the corner of her eye while she waited on customers, admiring how pretty she was, and wishing . . . she didn't know exactly what she wished existed between both of them, but she knew she wanted to be more than just work friends with Erica. And it had escalated. After a while, if she and Erica were standing together, she'd want to touch her, to stroke her arm or shoulder or hair. More recently she'd found herself wanting to kiss her. For the past two weeks it had been all Shelly could do to keep her hands and lips off Erica.

She had to have her. She had to hook up with her, or else . . . Shelly felt as though, if left unexpressed, her desire would corrode her from within.

Shelly could only guess at Erica's feelings in the matter of her impending seduction. However, she thought she had sufficient of a green light to proceed. When they'd first met, Erica had been going through a period of intense heartbreak—some heartless guy had totally shattered her heart. Erica had never told Shelly what had happened. Each time Shelly had asked, Erica had given her such a hurt look that she'd decided she didn't want to know anymore.

Erica seemed largely recovered now. At least recovered enough to fuck. Would she fuck another woman though? Shelly suspected she would. She'd already worked out that even if her crush wasn't actively lesbian, she wasn't entirely straight either. At the worst/best, Erica was herself bi-curious.

Shelly had deduced this from the 'overly appreciative' looks Erica sometimes gave female pub customers.

Another confirmation of her suspicions occurred one night after work, when she and Erica were hitting the bars as a foursome with Cassie and her girlfriend Maria. After three or four beers to loosen everyone's tongues, Cassie and Maria had begun discussing scissoring:

"It fucking hurts," Cassie said. Cassie was tall and thin, with short hair, a large nose, and large glasses. "I wonder how anybody believes they're gonna get off like that."

Maria, a small Panamanian girl with large breasts, had nodded. "It felt like using a hairbrush on my poor labia. Guys are crazy to think lesbians do that shit day-in day-out."

Erica had stopped sipping her beer and giggled. "You're going about it the wrong way, darlings. Scissoring's best if you both wax first. Like they do in porn? Or at least shave the vajayjay clean. And use some lube too. Then it's just skin-on-skin, and all pleasure."

Cassie and Maria had both looked at each other in shock. Then they'd nodded like lightning had struck them simultaneously. Shelly had pretended like she'd not heard anything. But she'd noted that. It wasn't just *what* Erica had said—anyone could have watched a porno vid and figured that out—but *how* she'd said it: Erica had sounded *experienced*; like she knew what to do because she'd done it.

Cassie and Maria had been about to grill Erica on how she knew that, but Erica had (conveniently, in retrospect) spotted an old friend of hers across the room and left to go catch up on old times.

So, Shelly was certain Erica wasn't about to *not* spread her legs if asked nicely by her best friend. She was certain too, that she'd correctly interpreted the lingering, longing stares Erica occasionally gave her. To Shelly, those looks screamed, "I want you!"

But still, she might be wrong. Well, she intended to find out for sure this weekend. She and Erica would likely be sharing a bedroom. Or, if they weren't, if she and Craig were in the same room, she'd visit Erica in the middle of the night. She'd hold Erica tight and playfully attempt to start something. A few kisses, and some fondling. If she was rebuffed, then she was. Her fantasy would have been proved to be just that—a fantasy. She'd tearfully apologize and forget about it.

And if she *wasn't* wrong about their mutual attraction? Well then . . . ha ha ha! . . . it was on!

But where did that leave Craig then? Shelly really, really, really loved Craig and wanted to marry him. But at the moment, she wanted Erica too. For a little while at least. Maybe she just needed to fuck another woman a few times and get the lezzie lust out of her system.

Most girls do that in high school. Me, I'm definitely a late bloomer.

But she wasn't selfish and only thinking of herself. If she and Erica worked out, she planned on including Craig too. Guys liked threesomes. They all fantasized about having two women in bed at the same time. And so . . .

Of course, Erica would have to agree to the threesome idea first.

But . . . Shelly realized she was getting ahead of herself. Well ahead of herself. First they had to arrive in Conway. Then, she had to seduce Erica. And only then, after she'd had *her* first dip in another woman's swimming pool, would she enquire if boyfriend could dive in too.

Oh, it was shaping up to be a massively fun weekend.

CHAPTER 3

Mostly Erica

They got out of the car and stared at the Crossway Diner.

Shelly shuddered. "Why am I getting a sudden creepy vibe about this place?" she asked.

Erica didn't reply. She'd noticed Shelly's sudden shiver. The late-evening air was frigid, but that clearly wasn't what was affecting her friend. Erica felt the same, as though cold fingers were stroking her nipples and the crack of her ass.

And yes, the spooky feeling had something to do with their stopping here at the Crossway.

Erica didn't see the connection though. She'd been here before with Marty on her previous trips up to Conway. Lots of times in fact. The ambience was good, the food fantastic. The service was fine. And Daria the proprietress was a sexy, cool lady.

The Crossway was like any other roadside place. This one was a two-story building that seemed to be right in the middle of nowhere. That was how it looked anyway. There were no tangible signs of humanity about. Just highways and the thick nearby woods now slowly taking on the threatening amorphous shapes of nightfall.

The diner's glass windows filled up the upper half of the front wall. Through the windows could be seen lots of chairs and plastic paneling, the checkered floor, and three or four customers.

In addition to the yellow and red sign by the road, another, similar, neon sign over the windows announced the restaurant's name.

Ugh! Erica felt it again: that same damn chill, this time mingled with a creepy feeling of utter powerlessness.

She snapped out of the eeriness. This was ridiculous. She looked at Shelly—pretty Shelly who she knew had the hots for her—and tried to smile. Shelly wasn't looking her way. She was instead staring back down the highway. Shelly looked like she was wondering why she'd ever thought it was a good idea to leave Ohio.

Shelly began rubbing her arms. "Damn, hurry up, baby. We need to get inside quick. It's colder than an icicle out here. As if spring's reverting back to winter." She was wearing shorts. The cold was raising goose bumps on her legs.

"Well, you know what they say here about the weather," Erica said.

"What do they say?"

"If you don't like it, wait five minutes . . ."

"Must be the wind coming in off the highway," Craig commented, picking his wallet off the driver's seat then straightening up. "With the trees so far back from the building, there's nothing to stop it."

As if to confirm this, an 18-wheeler rumbled past, heading west; honking, puffing smoke, and raising dust. The truck's passing blew an icy breeze across the parking lot, leaving scraps of paper dancing in the air.

Alright, Erica thought, *now this is getting creepy. I still feel weird about this place, but I don't see any reason why I should.*

She stared in through the diner windows. Behind the service counter, the house giant was having an intense conversation with Daria. Erica couldn't see Daria's face, her blonde hair was swept forward over it.

Erica returned her attention outside. She looked at Craig, who was now locking up the Ford. They'd met just once before. He'd come to pick up Shelly for a date after work and they'd each said "Hi." Craig was nice. He was a little cocky too, like he knew how handsome he was. She liked him a lot. A fact she was concealing from Shelly, who she knew liked *her.* And did Craig like her too? Things might get real interesting if he did.

He caught her staring at him and smiled back.

Shelly tapped an impatient foot on the ground. "Alright, you guys, let's go in and *eat.*" She took a step towards the diner entrance, then stopped and turned back to the others. She frowned. "Although, for some crazy reason, I've a feeling that's a bad idea."

Craig rolled his eyes, but didn't say anything. Shelly recognized the look on his face. It was the 'make up your mind, baby' one. She looked at Erica.

Erica shrugged. "We've no choice. Remember, Marty said he hadn't stocked up his fridge. Trust me—the guy never buys *anything.*

We're best having dinner here, along with buying takeouts and drinks."

Her cousin Marty was out of town tonight. His girlfriend's home desktop computer had suddenly blown up or something from her ten-year-old son playing video games on it. She lived over in Ashfield and Marty was over there now fixing the destroyed machine for her. He'd be spending the night there. He'd left the key to his house for Erica with his new neighbors Karen and Andy. Erica wasn't exaggerating about the state of her cousin's fridge either. Knowing Marty, there'd be literally nothing at home to eat. Nor beer or wine to drink.

"I sure could do with a beer right now," Craig said as if reading her mind. "At the moment I hate that damn 'no drink and drive' principle. My throat's so parched, I could—"

"Do we *have* to eat here?" Shelly persisted. "I mean, just look at that guy behind the counter: he looks like a frigging ape. I'm sure he's got hands for feet down there."

Erica laughed. "His name *is* Gorilla, if you must know." She stepped forward and took Shelly's arm. Then, on an impulse, she reached back and grabbed Craig's hand too. "Come on, you two. The food's great, you'll see."

Pushing Shelly in front of her, pulling Craig after her, she got them both to the front entrance.

She was about pushing in the door, when it opened outward. A fattish middle-aged man in a nice suit stepped out. He smiled and nodded at them, then walked past them to the white Mercedes SUV they'd parked beside.

Erica watched him slot his key in the car's door, then she grinned at her companions. "See, eating here didn't exactly murder him, did it?"

Shelly made a face. She had no reply to that. Craig shrugged.

The white Mercedes pulled out of parking and joined the highway, heading west.

"Oh, alright, lead the way," Shelly said.

As Erica stepped inside the Crossway, she had a sudden horrible impression. It was very brief, lasting just a split-second. She felt like she was being smothered with dirt, buried alive in a grave squirming with maggots. Yuck!

Then the door shut behind Craig and her sense of evil completely vanished.

Here inside the diner, there was a delicious aroma of frying onions in the air, with additional telltale sizzling coming through the kitchen window behind the counter. The air was warm; Erica already felt the outside chill leaving her bones.

Helen the waitress steered them towards a table on the right.

In this atmosphere it was impossible to feel moody. Shelly had already brightened up. They were here to eat. And eat they would.

Erica grinned to herself as they sat around the table. She studied Shelly as the brunette studied her menu. She felt a sudden rush of desire for her. Maybe later they'd both play kiss-kiss. And maybe they'd let Craig join in too.

CHAPTER 4

Brie

Brie Becker watched the three young people enter the diner: the tall handsome guy, the pretty brunette, and the tall rawboned blonde.

The trio were all dressed casually: Jeans and shirts for the man and the blonde girl, while the brunette wore a brown skirt, a black-and-white 90's rock T-shirt, pink socks and brown fabric sneakers. They all seemed relatively well educated. The young man wasn't a slob; the girls didn't look like sluts.

Brie watched them take their seats. The waitress took their orders. Brie studied the woman's fleshy body from behind as she wrote in her little notepad. The brunette girl ordered a corned beef sandwich; the blonde asked for "the meatloaf dinner with macaroni and cheese and mashed potatoes."

When the waitress turned around again, Brie studied her face. The waitress still looked haunted. Brie looked back at the three newcomers. They didn't look to have noticed anything unusual, though the brunette girl seemed to be cold. But that didn't mean much; Brie recalled that the girl had walked in shivering. It was likely quite cold outside.

Brie now felt much better about this place than when she'd entered it. The salesman she'd feared might assault her had left without so much as a glance in her direction.

And the food too. Now that had been a pleasant surprise.

She considered her plate. Dinner was over. She regretted not having space in her belly for more food. The meal had been delicious: the chicken pot pie and salad had both been expertly prepared. So much so that she planned on stopping here again for lunch on her way back south.

Ah, but it was time to go. What time was it anyway? She looked up at the clock over the counter and gaped in disbelief. That time couldn't be right! Oh no, it couldn't! Brie double-checked on her wristwatch. *My God, no! It's ten-past-eight? That can't be. I arrived here at a quarter-after-six, didn't I? How the hell can I have been sitting at this table for two hours and not have noticed the passage of time? It's simply not possible!*

She lowered her gaze to her tray again. She frowned. She was puzzled silent. *It isn't like I ordered beer or wine along with my meal. I had two coffees. Both black, the second without any sugars.*

She'd not snoozed off either. At the moment she felt more alert than on her arrival here. Caffeined-up and raring to go. *So how?* She stared suspiciously up at the restaurant clock again. The blue minute-hand was just arriving at twelve past the hour.

No, the clock can't be wrong. If it is it wouldn't synchronize with my wristwatch. But it has to be.

In a desperate final attempt to prove she'd not somehow daydreamt two hours away, she got her phone out of her purse and checked the time on it. 8:13, the display showed in white-on-black digital numerals.

Brie was stumped. Impossible or not, the truth had to be accepted. In the course of having a normal thirty-minute dinner in this place, she'd somehow used up two hours.

But . . . but it did seem like just thirty minutes.

She realized that was beside the point. Logical or not, she'd been more delayed here than she needed to be. She should have arrived in Bennington by now. By now her sister Kathleen must be worried about her.

But . . . she wondered, why hadn't Kathleen called to find out what was delaying her?

She checked her call log, then her messages. Nothing. And it wasn't like there weren't any signal bars on the phone either.

She realized she was getting worried again. *No need for that. I'm safe here.*

She looked around to confirm this. Across the dining room, the waitress was serving drinks to the three new arrivals. Root beers, and a Pepsi for the young man. Down in the far corner on her right, the amorous young couple were locked in a passionate kiss. Something about their passion, however, struck Brie as worrying: They'd been kissing when she'd arrived, and now, two hours later, they were still .

. . and the fries on their plates didn't seem to be any less in quantity than when she'd gotten here, as if they'd eaten nothing in the intervening time.

Now if that wasn't odd, Brie didn't know what was.

She felt a strangeness in the air. She looked across at the counter, at the giant standing there. Gorilla; how apt a name. The huge man was watching her; she was certain of it. The light around him was dim, but she imagined he'd winked at her. Damn, he looked evil, the kind of person just waiting to hurt a woman traveling alone. And something was wrong with his head, it was strangely flattened on the right side, like part of his skull had fallen off.

Gorilla was frowning at her. Scared by his attention, she looked quickly away.

Now her eyes locked onto those of the still-smiling waitress. Brie again read fear in the woman's face, dread and horror caged behind the forced upward curve of her lips.

Alright, that's enough, she told herself. *Stop panicking. Stop imagining that you're seeing things.* She gazed once more at the time on her phone's display. 8:16 p.m. No more time machine jumps to the future. *So maybe I did just doze off. Whatever the reason, by now Kathleen must really be worried about me. I'd better call her.*

She found Kathleen's number in her phone's Contacts and dialed. All she got was silence then a beep.

She stopped dialing and stared at the screen. She had full signal bars. *So what . . . ?* She tried calling again. More silence and another beep. A little static in her ears. She tried a third time. The same results. She lowered the phone and stared at it in disgust.

Something had to be blocking the signal. Best she just leave now. But first . . . She got to her feet and winced. Ouch. Her tummy was unsettled.

This must be the effect of my nervousness, combined with two coffees, and the engine vibrations from driving all afternoon.

She'd need to use the restroom before leaving, that was for sure.

It occurred to Brie then that maybe something in the restaurant was impeding the cellphone signal. She gestured to the dreaded giant behind the counter. Once she had his attention, she pointed to her phone and then to her handbag (which she was leaving on her table as evidence that she wasn't running off without settling her bill), then stepped outside into the settling dusk.

Hopefully, she'd be able to get Kathleen on the phone now.

CHAPTER 5

Craig

Craig watched the woman in the white dress step outside. The door shut behind her and she began pacing back and forth across the parking lot with her cellphone held to her ear.

"Hey, baby, I want some of your fries."

He turned and grinned at Shelly. The grin was automatic. He loved her and she loved him too. "Sure, baby, help yourself. You could just order more though."

"Uh uh. They'll take too long to arrive and I'm hun-greeeee!"

He watched her scoop the fries off his plate, amused at how both she and Erica's reservations about entering the diner had cleared up once they'd begun stuffing themselves. Erica had already completely demolished her meatloaf, and the macaroni and cheese wouldn't last long either. Shelly's corned beef sandwich was a monstrous culinary construct. It looked like a mountain of meat which the upper slice of bread had somehow managed to scale. (Craig had had a bite of the sandwich. The thin-sliced beef was utterly delicious). *He* was having a Buffalo Chicken Sandwich with fries. Root beers, orange juice, and sodas dotted the table. The serving portions were so huge. The table looked very colorful. Bread and meat and vegetables everywhere. Ketchup and tabasco sauce, three different dips, the white fluff of mashed potatoes on Erica's plate (the only part of her meal to so far escape the all-round oral ravaging), and three different salads.

The food smelt awesome.

Both girls seemed genuinely excited to be here now.

Craig intended enjoying this weekend trip with Erica. Most times either Shelly was working on the weekend or he was (he was working his way up to foreman with the construction company and sometimes had very busy weekends), but this time their schedules had coincided perfectly. He'd even managed to wrangle a free Monday out of his bosses. He needed the time off, a couple of end-of-spring days free from the tyranny of concrete piles, girders and rivets. This would be a good chance also to see some of the celebrated New England countryside.

Craig didn't know Erica very well, but he liked her. She projected vitality. She was sort of girl you didn't forget easily, like she'd been painted on your mind with watercolors and only repeated dousings of cleaner would wash her away.

So here they were.

Dating Shelly Parker was great. Craig thought she was wonderful. *Modern Liberated Female: Model 01*: Quick to laugh, quick to cry, quick to fight and accuse you of not loving her enough. Quick to forgive and forget. Fun in bed because she had few hangups. Pretty, sexy, passionate, and caring. Smart, but not eternally rubbing it in your face. The sort of young woman you didn't let go of except you were drunk or crazy. Nah, not drunk: Craig got drunk occasionally and he hadn't let Shelly go yet. Just crazy. Yeah, a guy had to be completely nuts—ready for the padded cell—to ditch Shelly. She was a keeper, that was for sure.

Yes, this weekend getaway was a good idea—no, it was a frigging *great* idea on Shelly's part. Craig had packed several bottles of whiskey to help the party along. They'd go sightseeing with Erica's cousin, get drunk, and have some great sex before both returning to the daily grind.

The waitress served Erica another drink, and put down a dish of pickles.

The food's delicious smell gave Craig an optimistic feeling about the world. He looked up at the woman who'd served it. The moment his eyes locked with hers, his compliments to the kitchen staff dried up in his throat.

There was something horrible in the waitress's face, something nasty that floated above her smile, something that lurked like a snake behind her brown eyes; something that scared Craig. His impression was of a woman suffering horrendous abuse, only this wasn't physical abuse, but rather a spiritual torment.

Troubled, he broke eye-contact with her. This waitress had a lizard eating her soul; a huge one. How the girls weren't noticing it, he had no idea.

The waitress departed. Craig felt an intense relief. Reading her eyes had been like staring at a person being roasted over a fire. A fire down in Hell.

The waitress vanished through the door between the service counter and the drinks' fridge.

Another woman stepped out of the same door and looked their way. This woman had long white hair that hung well below her shoulders. She was in her thirties—Craig guessed her age as maybe thirty-four. She was strikingly beautiful. She had lovely gray eyes and a perfect nose. And full red lips that were almost heart-shaped.

Her lips held Craig's attention. They were so red. For a surreal moment he imagined she'd used blood for lipstick.

Erica, her mouth packed with half-chewed pasta, looked up, saw the woman, and waved. The woman waved back and smiled. Her gray gaze met Craig's. Met and locked his eyes to hers. He felt like he was being sucked into her face, being blended into her beautiful expression.

Then she broke eye-contact with him and turned away. She started a conversation with Gorilla.

Craig was shocked. While they'd been focused on each other, he'd sensed a intense hunger in the white-haired woman. A hunger almost impossible to quantify. A hunger terrifying in its intensity, horrifying in its insatiableness. He'd had the impression that the white-haired woman was starving, starving down to the very core of her lovely being. Reading her soul through her eyes, Craig had understood that this beautiful woman would eat the entire world if she could.

But . . . *Eat the world?* He reset his mind to reality. *No, That's just ridiculous. Plain silly. I'm just freaking out. First the waitress and now this lady? I've been working too hard all week, been driving too long today. Get a grip on yourself, man. Soon you'll be seeing giant spiders on the walls.*

"That's Daria," Erica said. "Daria Simpson. She owns this place."

"Huh?" Craig asked. Erica had on a gold necklace with a heart-shaped pendant. Craig found himself staring at the glittering pendant like it was hypnotizing him.

"You were staring at her," Erica explained. She sipped at her root beer. "Daria's cool, really nice. And she's got great hair."

Shelly nodded. "Her hair ain't all that's great about her. I'd love to have her figure when I'm her age." She nudged Craig. "Hey, baby, eat up. Remember what Erica said: no grub at her cousin's place tonight."

"I'll ask Helen to pack takeouts for us," Erica said.

"Don't forget the beers," Shelly said.

"Who needs beer when you've got good whiskey?" Craig asked.

"We do!" both girls responded like they'd planned it. Then they burst out laughing.

Craig resumed eating. As if he was just beginning his meal for the first time, it struck him again that the food here was surprisingly good. So much so that he wondered why there weren't more customers in the Crossway Diner.

He asked Erica about that. She shrugged.

"Slow night, I guess. Though I do remember this place was packed full last time I was here. And Saturday is generally a good night for eateries." She gestured around the room with a forkful of corned beef lifted from Shelly's plate. "Now it's just the lovers over there in the corner, and the lady walking up and down outside. If I didn't know better, I'd say something was wrong. There should be more servers around too."

Craig glanced behind him, at the couple in the corner. The pair seemed incredibly in love. They were holding each other tight and French kissing. Then they'd separate for a moment and gaze into each other's eyes like they couldn't wait to jump into bed together.

But he kept thinking something was odd about the pair.

Dammit, here I go again, Craig thought moodily. *First it was the waitress, then the proprietress . . . now it's the customers. Dude, give it a rest already.*

Try hard as he might though, Craig couldn't shake the creepy feeling the pair gave him. They both looked normal. Very normal, but . . . but . . .

The young man again pulled the girl close. They resumed smooching.

Craig forced his mind off them and looked outside. The woman in the white dress was still out there pacing the parking lot, holding her phone up and staring at its screen from underneath like she was trying to magnify the sun through it. Then she'd hold it to her ear again and try calling. Then she'd stare at the phone as if mystified, then walk somewhere else and repeat the procedure.

Craig found her behavior disturbingly manic. *No, don't start that again,* he cautioned himself. *Not her too.*

He figured she had to make an emergency call. He turned back to resume eating, to find Shelly and Erica pushing their chairs back and standing up.

"We're off to the ladies'" Shelly explained. "We need to freshen up."

"As in—reduce the percentage of water making up our bodies from ninety-five back to a healthy seventy-five percent again," Erica added. "Gross water retention is only permitted during our periods."

"It's been a long trip, man," Shelly said.

Craig nodded and watched them walk off.

"This way," Erica pointed, and they headed for the passageway at the far end of the dining room.

It was now that Craig belatedly realized what seemed eerie about the kissing couple in the corner behind him. That had to be his imagination though; it had to be.

He turned to peek at them again, but quickly looked away. The boy now had his left hand inside the girl's top and was fondling her breasts.

Craig was annoyed by their overt public display of sexual intimacy. He hoped the pair shortly quit it. The proprietress was certain to take a dim view of their behavior.

But that was another matter altogether. What he'd seen? No, it had to be a trick of the light. Given the right shadows the mind easily conjured up illusions.

For the second time, Craig had gotten the impression that the amorous couple looked *thinner* than when he and the girls had first arrived at the Crossway Diner.

CHAPTER 6

Shelly and Erica

All the way to the restrooms Shelly felt a growing excitement. She felt lust. Intense lust like a fever burning her up. She wanted to make love.

The diner restrooms were reached via a long corridor. 'Ladies' on the left, 'Gents' on the right. Erica pushed the left door open. They stepped inside. The restroom was neat. White tiles, white walls, gray ceiling. Two pink toilet stalls with clean toilets. One of the washbasin taps was leaking, and likely had been for quite a while—a dark stain of wet rust lay under the slow dribble.

"Not bad," Erica commented, looking around. "Still clean after all these years."

Shelly nodded vacantly. She didn't care about that. The lust was high in her now, hot like raging fire. Her very intelligence seemed to be melting. She needed someone touching her. Stroking inside her or licking outside her, it didn't matter. She just needed intimate contact with someone else.

She looked desperately at Erica. She was possessed by the intense desire to grab the hot blonde, tear her top off, and suckle on her breasts. *But this isn't how I planned it: I wanted to seduce Erica slowly, calculatingly adding layer after layer of erotic foreplay, until . . . If I grab her now, what if she rejects me?*

She realized that Erica was staring at her. Erica was breathing hard and gasping. She looked sick.

"Hey, you okay?"

"You know, I feel weird," Erica said.

Shelly nodded. "Yeah, me too. It's this weird place." Breathing felt hard, talking felt even harder.

"No, not like that. I feel *weird*, if you know what I mean. I mean—I feel weird about *you*."

"Yeah, me too. That's what I mean. Really fucking weird, you know?" Shelly's mind was screaming: *Kiss me, you silly bitch, why don't you!? Can't you see that I want you!?* Though inwardly she felt about to explode, outwardly she feigned nonchalance. "Yeah, maybe we should just do our business in here. You know, just pee and leave? Craig's gotta be feeling lonely now." She peered into the left toilet cubicle. "Alright, you can have that one, I'll take—"

"Fuck, don't you play hard to get now," Erica growled. "I'll take *you*." Then to Shelly's surprise and delight, Erica was holding her and kissing her hard.

She kissed back equally hard, going at it like she wanted to empty the other girl's lungs of air.

Now that they were kissing, Shelly felt so much better. So, so much better.

They separated and caught their breath. They stared a moment into each other's eyes then both burst out laughing.

"Shit, I couldn't hold it back any longer," Erica said.

"Oh fuck, and here I was thinking you didn't want me. I thought I'd have to perform a striptease for you first."

"Oh yes, I do want you. I've wanted you for ages." Erica cupped Shelly's breasts and squeezed. "Time to free my little darlings."

Her legs trembling with desire, Shelly leaned forward and kissed her again. "Left or right? Pick one."

"Huh? Left or right what? I like both of your breasts."

"I mean the stalls, honey. If we're about to do what I think we are, we'd better get undercover in case someone else comes in here to drop water."

Erica giggled. "Right, babe, right. 'Cos things are definitely going right in here."

They slid inside the right-hand toilet stall. Erica locked the door behind them.

Shelly lifted her arms over her head. Erica pulled Shelly's T-shirt up and over her head, then reached around and unsnapped her bra. She bent and took Shelly's engorged nipples into her mouth. She sucked on them. Shelly dropped her arms onto Erica's shoulders and went, "Ooh, Ooh, Ooh!" Erica's hands slid up Shelly's thighs, under her skirt, and inside the waistband of her panties. The panties came down, Erica's fingers went *in*. The penetration felt to Shelly like she'd been shot up with love. Erica bent to see better. Erica began rubbing; Shelly did her best to keep from sobbing.

Fuck yes, I do like sex with girls! Shelly thought. At the moment she felt like her soul was in the wet spot between her thighs, a wet spot Erica was massaging with expertise. Caught like that, dangling between her fears of knowing herself too well and her desire for more of what she was currently getting, Shelly braced herself against the toilet walls with both hands and groaned and thrust her crotch against Erica's probing fingers.

In a gush of sensation that felt like she was dissolving, Shelly had her first ever lesbian orgasm. She bit her lip to keep from screaming as the pleasure surged through her. She moaned and trembled and looked down into Erica's blue eyes. Erica was looking up at her with a knowing smirk on her face, a look of satisfaction that said, "Yeah, you're my bitch now!"

Shelly's replying gaze said, "Fuck, yes—do it to me, give it to me! I need this."

The pleasure just kept on. Then finally, like the diminishing flow of water from a tap being slowly turned off, the pleasure subsided to a lingering glow of happiness, a memory she felt with her whole body. She sagged forward against Erica. She pulled her up and held her tight. She kissed her hard. *Oh wow! That was just mindblowing!* It had been as good as sex with Craig. *Yes, yes, yes!*

Erica hurriedly undid her belt. She hastily yanked down her jeans and thong. Then she bent forward over the toilet seat. Her gold necklace dangled free and swung in the air. Its heart-shaped pendant caught and reflected the light.

"Eat me!" she gasped back at Shelly. "Shit, I need you so bad, so damn bad!"

Shelly now found herself in a bit of confusion. She felt embarrassed.

Erica turned and stared at her. "What's the matter?"

"I've never done this before. I'm not sure what to do."

Erica was surprised. "You haven't?" Then she grinned. "Look . . . it's easy. Just stick your mouth between the cheeks of my ass and lick what you find there. Start with the upper hole, then work your way down to the lower one. Just hurry up. I need to feel you touching me! You've no idea how much!"

Shelly nodded. Now that that had been settled, the urgency of the moment reasserted itself in her mind. Erica had a look of intense sexual torment on her face, like she'd die if Shelly didn't immediately start making love to her.

Shelly remembered how *she'd* felt before Erica had kissed and fucked her. It had been a hellish sensation, like her arousal was an actual fire burning her flesh. Oh, she didn't want Erica to keep feeling that horrible! She quickly got down on her knees. The tiles were cold and gritty on her bare knees, but that didn't deter her any.

She sank her tongue deep into the crevice between Erica's buttocks. She was shocked at the effect her doing so had on Erica. Erica instantly stiffened, gripped the toilet seat extra-hard, and let out a growl that could have come from a wolf. She began shaking her butt in Shelly's face as if she was twerking.

I must be doing it right, Shelly thought gaily. She got right down to work licking and sucking on what she found there. It was hot, sweaty, sweet, musky, and above all wet, wet, wet. Damn, Erica had a wet vagina. After a little consideration, she stuck her right thumb inside Erica too. It fit snugly.

Now it was Erica's turn to do her best to keep from screaming out in pleasure.

CHAPTER 7

Brie

Brie made her brisk way down the passageway to the restrooms. She was pissed off.

She'd had zero luck with getting her sister on the phone. No matter where she'd walked to, her phone didn't work. She still had full signal bars, but the damn phone wasn't calling. Had to be something about this area. She didn't know what though. The nearby mountains were too far off to be the problem. Besides, there was a town right on the other side of the highway bridge, and another one eight or ten miles farther down the road. It wasn't like she was out in the boondocks where there weren't any cellphone towers nearby.

Damn, it's all such a mess. By now, Kathleen will definitely be worried about me.

The diner had a phone. It was at the right end of the food counter. Brie, however, was too scared of the hulking man behind the counter to ask if she could call from it. Something about Gorilla terrified her. She found the giant a nightmare figure.

When she'd reentered the diner, the waitress hadn't been in sight. It hadn't mattered that it felt like her insides were going to explode on her, Brie wasn't going to ask Gorilla the way to the ladies'. Oh no, she wasn't. She'd waited, waited until the waitress had reappeared from the back before asking the way to the toilets.

The corridor to the restrooms had gray walls. Almost at its end, she glanced down at her phone screen for a second. Maybe the damn phone was fucked up. She tried to remember if she was still within the device's warranty period. With her luck it had expired yesterday.

"How do you like our place?" a female voice enquired.

Shocked, Brie looked up. It was the white-haired proprietress. But how on earth had she appeared so suddenly?

33

"Oh, I'm sorry I startled you," the woman said. "It was thoughtless of me."

"No, it's alright." Brie now got her first proper look at the Crossway's owner. She was wearing a pale violet shirt, black pants and black sneakers. In the time since Brie had first seen her she'd also donned a blue plastic apron. Basic diner kitchen attire, certainly, but it fit her very well. The clothes cuddled her body like they loved her. They were both about the same height—5'6"—but the woman was infinitely prettier than herself. She had a much better figure too. But . . . there was also something sickly about her. She was wearing a lot of perfume—the expensive scent of crushed roses accompanying her formed an almost visible cloud in the corridor—but Brie felt she smelt something else under the pervasive floral scent. Something loathsome, something—the word dropped into her mind—*blasphemous.*

"Can't get a signal?" the woman asked. She had a soft, sweet voice. "Oh, I'm so sorry, I should introduce myself properly." She extended her hand. "My name's Daria."

Brie shook the small, delicate hand. Daria's skin felt eerily smooth.

She looked back up at Daria's face. The woman still had that aura of hunger about her, but it seemed slightly sated now, as if she'd just had a snack. On the whole, Brie found Daria very spooky.

"Is it a general problem around here?" she asked. "I mean—"

"Making cellphone calls? Oh, most definitely. It's something the phone companies say they can't figure out. They say we're a dead spot. Personally though, I imagine they see no point in putting up a tower this far out from the town." She looked concerned. "You've an important call to make?"

"I'm at least two hours late to meet with my sister."

"Oh, you could use our landline. That works most times. I'll ask Gorilla to . . ."

At the mention of the ugly giant's name, Brie gave an involuntary flinch. Daria noticed it, but misinterpreted the reason.

"Oh, my, my," she said. "I don't know why I'm being such a scatterbrain today. I stopped you on your way to use the toilet. You must be pressed. I'm so, so sorry." She smiled. "Look, you just go take care of your girlie business, and I'll tell Gorilla you'll be using the counter phone. Once you're done just stop by there."

Not on your life, Brie thought, repressing a shudder. *No way am I going near that brute.* She just couldn't help her feelings of revulsion towards the man.

"Alright, see you out front," Daria said. "I've got to check on the steaks in the oven."

She strode off past Brie. And then, just like that, the sound of her departing footsteps ceased.

Brie turned towards her. She figured Daria had remembered something she wanted to tell her. She wondered what that could be. Besides, wasn't the woman in a hurry?

She was shocked. The corridor was empty.

Brie took a moment to catch her breath, then she tried to figure the puzzle out. She'd heard maybe four or five footsteps before they'd abruptly stopped. They'd been normal-paced steps—despite her stated hurry Daria hadn't been running—and close by too, gradually receding from Brie. So where . . . ?

Brie did a quick mental calculation. The diner end of the corridor (she watched the waitress stride across it to stare out of the windows) was ten yards away. That was at least twenty more paces for Daria to have walked. The corridor did have two side exits, a short passageway on Brie's right and a staircase on her left. Both, however, were farther off than the five paces the diner proprietress had taken after leaving her. Besides, if Daria had taken either route, Brie should still be hearing her footsteps; and, other than her own rapid breathing, there was no sound in the corridor.

So, how had Daria left the corridor then? *This is absurd. The corridor can't have shortened itself, then lengthened again, can it? Why am I even considering such nonsense?*

Brie looked up, then down, then behind her as well. No, it didn't make sense. Her mind rang her a bell. Daria's vanishing act didn't make sense, just like her own losing track of time for two entire hours didn't make sense. Just like her phone not working with a full complement of signal bars didn't make sense.

Brie felt as if a cup of 'unease' had been poured on her.

She saw the giant bartender peering down the corridor. Was he smirking at her? *Oh shit! Why does he keep looking my way? Is he leering at me? Is he planning to abduct and abuse me?* She couldn't help herself that the man terrified her. She wished she had a gun on her. Then she'd feel safe.

The man was still staring her way.

She ducked quickly into the women's restroom. Screw making phone calls. She was going to poop and pee, and then she was leaving this creepy diner and driving fast-and-furious north. Her phone would work for sure once she was in the next town. She could wait that long.

The restroom had two toilet stalls. The right one was occupied. She dashed into the left and hastily hiked up her dress.

Brie was really scared and worried now. She prayed nothing nasty would happen to her before she left the Crossway Diner. She still remembered how Daria had smelt evil beneath her perfume. And now there was this second inexplicable happening to complicate things further: how the hell had the woman vanished like that?

Brie vowed that once she left the Crossway tonight she was never coming back this way again. Not ever.

She wasn't even driving on the I-91 highway. Next time she wanted to visit Kathleen, she'd take a detour through New York State. Better still, she'd overlook the cost and fly up to Bennington.

She'd just sat on the toilet seat when she became aware of strange noises coming from the next cubicle. Slurps and grunts. It sounded like a wild animal eating meat in there. Something bumped hard against the wall separating the stalls. Then suddenly, she heard a loud guttural howl that sounded like someone being murdered.

Brie was too scared by now to understand that the animal sounds she was hearing were merely two girls having sex, one of them having a violent orgasm. She forgot all about emptying her bowels and bladder. Not even bothering to pull down her dress first, she leapt off the toilet and dashed out of the stall.

Halfway to the restroom door, she realized she wasn't running as fast as she wanted to. It took her a second to work out why: her panties were still down around her ankles; each step she took was stretching their silk fabric to ripping point. She stumbled against the washbasin and pulled them up.

Another guttural, inhuman-sounding screech exploded from the shut toilet cubicle. The noise chilled Brie to her bone marrow. The other person in the cubicle was laughing insanely—to Brie's scared mind that second person was a serial killer with a bloody knife.

Looking up, Brie saw a frightened woman in the restroom mirror that she didn't recognize as herself. At the moment her reflection was merely another facet of her terror. Doing her best to not scream like crazy, she ran for her life out of the restroom.

CHAPTER 8

Craig

"Something wrong with the food?" a female voice asked.

"Uh, what?" Thinking it was the waitress, Craig looked up. No, it wasn't the plump brunette with the happy smile and miserable eyes. It was her boss. Daria, Erica had said her name was.

Daria looked curious. She pointed to his plate. "I was asking if something is wrong with the food. You haven't eaten much. If the chicken's off or anything I'll have Helen make you another sandwich."

Craig shook his head. "Oh, that. No, ma'am, your food's utterly delicious. It's just been a long hard week for me, and I need a huge amount of relaxation." He glanced down at his dinner. She was exaggerating, of course—he'd eaten more than half of what was on his plate. But he understood her: she was exhibiting normal restaurateur vanity; she wanted the customer to enjoy her kitchen creation.

She sat facing him. Craig was again struck by how beautiful she was. Yet there was pain in her face also. A deep, hidden anguish. Oddly, the pain seemed to refine her features, giving them a disturbing clarity. When she locked eyes with him again, he sensed the same ravenous hunger in her as before.

"Life's like that sometimes," she said, her voice as soft and alluring as her scent of roses. "Believe me, I've had crazy weeks too. You can just imagine what running a diner is like sometimes."

He was about replying to that when a moan from behind startled him. He looked back. He gaped, struck speechless. *What . . . ?*

It was the young couple in the corner. The pair had now taken their already explicit public display to the next level. Craig could see clearly what they were doing. The girl was half-naked, her cream-colored blouse undone and both her breasts out. Her black leather shorts were

down at her feet, completely off one leg and barely hooked around
the ankle of the other. Her boyfriend was kneeling between her legs,
using a tomato ketchup bottle as a dildo on her. She moaned again,
and smacked her hand on the formica tabletop. Her red hair was
scattered forward over her face. She was gritting her teeth to keep
from screaming out her pleasure.

Still speechless, Craig looked back at Daria.

He was startled. The Crossway proprietress was watching the
sexual action with clear interest. She was licking her lips and her eyes
had a strangely feral glow in them. Her face was flushed, but it wasn't
a coloring of lust. Nor was the expression of delight in her eyes that
of a voyeur having a thrill from witnessing something forbidden. No,
what Craig saw in Daria's face was more of that strange appetite he'd
noticed earlier.

Beyond her, Gorilla wasn't even looking in their direction. The
huge man was polishing the countertop with a cloth while whistling
to himself.

Behind Craig, the sexual noises continued, the girl's earlier moans
now augmented by the loud sucking sounds of the ketchup bottle
entering and exiting her vagina.

Craig found his voice. "They're . . . they're . . . !" He lost his voice
again. It was obvious what the couple were doing. Daria could see it
better that he could: her chair faced them.

She licked her red lips again, then seemed to come back to herself.
The excitement faded from her eyes, the color faded from her cheeks.

"I find sexual energy very satisfying," she said cryptically. "Sex is
one of humanity's two most potent drives."

Craig nodded. Behind him, the girl was clearly having an orgasm.
He didn't look back. He was disgusted.

"The other," Daria continued, "is violence."

"You mean *death*, don't you?"

"Not really. Death is an end; the final destination. Death only
releases a single explosion of energy. That explosion is certainly much
more intense than what you get from sex, but then it's over for good.
Violence, however, if properly managed, can be an eternal continuum.
Liken it to the satisfaction a torturer must get from hurting the same
victim every day of her life."

Again she licked her lips. Craig watched her tongue move. She both
attracted and repulsed him. He was both bemused and troubled by

her talk of sex and violence as sources of energy. An unusual concept for sure; almost a crazy one. And even if they were energy sources, how could one ever harness them? Attach light bulbs and batteries to people making love or fighting?

He began wishing Shelly and Erica were here. They'd be psychic protection/defense against Daria. What the hell was keeping them both in the ladies'? Had one of them suddenly started her period?

Behind him, the loud moans of the girl's orgasm had ceased, to be replaced by her rapid breathing. Craig still refused to turn and watch them. He didn't want to see the woman-smeared ketchup bottle.

He heard the boy say: "Alright, Tori, suck me off now."

"Yeah, yeah—pull that big thing out for me. I wanna wrap my lips around your lightning rod."

Oh no. This couldn't be happening in public. Craig no longer wished Shelly and Erica were here. He knew Shelly. This wasn't something she'd want to see. He looked pleadingly at Daria, whose face was once again taking on that glazed look. When she didn't respond to his stare, he reached across and tapped her arm.

The effect was like breaking a spell placed on her. "Oh," she said and was once more there with him.

He jerked his thumb behind him. "Do something about them. *Please.*"

"Yes, you're right. Of course I will."

She got to her feet and walked off behind him. He turned to watch.

The boy had his erection out and the girl was already kneeling to suck on it. From the entranced expression on their faces, they seemed to think they were alone in the diner. They didn't even notice Daria until she put her hand in front of the girl's mouth just as she was about sliding it over the head of the boy's engorged penis.

"Aw, c'mon, old lady," the girl protested angrily. "Don't be a party pooper."

"Alright, you two," Daria said in a tough, but clearly amused voice. "Stop it. That's enough. You're disturbing my other customers. Stop screwing or I'll have to call the police."

The young man replied, "Look, lady, we gotta have sex. We've just gotta. We're young, we're madly in love and we wanna fuck right now. We can't wait. Hell no, I ain't waiting. We gotta do it here, see? Alright, hey, how about this: you got a room we can use? We'll pay you."

"Yeah, we ain't bums," the girl agreed, standing up and wiping her mouth with the back of her hand. "Jimmy and me, we ain't bums. We just wanna fuck, ya know. And we wanna do it *here*. We like this place, see? It turns us on like crazy."

Jimmy flashed a handful of notes in Daria's face. "So, you got a room for us or what?"

Daria snatched the handful of notes from Jimmy's hand. "As a matter of fact, I do happen to have a room both of you can use. A large one, with a nice, soft bed. Follow me, it's upstairs."

She turned and walked back towards Craig. The young couple followed.

"Wow, now we can really get it on, Jimmy," the girl said.

"Yeah, Tori, yeah," Jimmy agreed huskily. "Once I get you in bed, I'm gonna do you like you're a blocked pipe."

"Yeah, that's my plumber!"

Craig tried to avert his eyes as they walked past him, but couldn't. (Now that he could see them better, that pair appeared to be around his own age—mid-twenties. Both had bony, angular faces. Craig figured that was why he'd earlier imagined they were getting thinner. The girl in particular did look a bit starved.) Dammit! The guy's fly was still open. The redhead was stroking his erection while leaning against him as they followed Daria. (All she had on now were her blouse and boots.) She was working the penis with such vigor that Craig began praying that the young man wouldn't suddenly ejaculate on the diner floor. There was no way he'd be able to cope with seeing that.

The redhead's breasts bobbed as she walked. They were large for her frame, juicy pink orbs with stiff brown nipples like cigar butts.

Oh no, Shelly and Erica, don't the two of you dare come out now!

Daria winked at him as she walked past. For the briefest of moments, her fingers brushed his shoulder and she smothered him in her rose perfume again. This time, however, he smelt something bad under her perfume. He couldn't tell what the bad smell was though.

She led the young couple to the corridor at the far end of the diner, the same one Shelly and Erica had taken to the restrooms.

Behind the counter, Gorilla wasn't even batting an eyelid as the pair walked past him, with the girl's hand still working furiously on the boy's erection. Her other hand gripped the ketchup bottle they'd been using as a sex toy.

Craig was perplexed. What sort of a crazy place was this? He didn't feel like there was any true danger here, but . . . he'd feel a lot happier—much, much happier—once he was well away from this Crossway diner.

Daria, gorgeous though she was, was definitely odd as well. And the way she'd just handled those two randy patrons? He'd never seen *anyone* behave that coolly before.

Vivid images of the redhead's vigorously bouncing breasts replayed in his mind. He visualized himself 'smoking' her cigar-butt nipples. The heady image tantalized him for several seconds.

He put the girl's bosom out of his mind and stared down at his food. Just like that, he suddenly had an appetite again. He even managed a smile.

Glad that the redhead wasn't presently giving her boyfriend a blowjob behind him, he began forking fries into his mouth.

Oh yeah, this food sure is good!

He was surprised by how hungry he felt now.

Then Craig was struck by a puzzling thought: *What's keeping all those women in the ladies' room for so long anyway?*

It wasn't just Shelly and Erica now; that was the real source of his puzzlement. He'd just realized that the other customer they'd met on arriving here—the woman in the white dress—hadn't yet returned from the restroom either.

CHAPTER 9

Brie

Two seconds after dashing out of the restroom to avoid being ripped to shreds by the imagined monster in the stalls, Brie realized she'd made a huge mistake.

She stopped in her tracks and stared in shock and horror.

There was no way she could have stayed in the toilet with all that bloodcurdling noise, but maybe she should have.

The corridor leading back to the dining room looked different from how she remembered it. For one thing, it had gotten wider in her absence. For another, its walls seemed darker and its ceiling higher. The left turnoff to the stairs was missing, as was the passageway on the right. The corridor lighting was also now flickering on and off like a strobe.

Brie fought to fit her mind around the changes. Her attempt to reason them out filled her with additional terror at the illogic of what she was witnessing. She just needed to escape this horrible place. The dining room was still right ahead, but it was far off now, a hundred yards away at least.

She turned back towards the restrooms.

"Oh no!" she gasped.

The twin restroom doors had also magically receded. Now they too were an impossible distance away.

She was stranded in the middle of an endless corridor.

Brie ceased wondering how this had all happened. She'd just realized she was in danger. She could a sound behind her—a slobbering, sucking, liquid sound that raised the hairs on the backs of her arms. The sound wasn't stationary. It was coming closer to her. Getting louder by the heartbeat.

She whirled back towards the dining room. There was nothing there. Just the flickering passageway with the light-rectangle of the entrance at its distant end.

Far, far off, the waitress was peering in at her.

"Hey!" Brie screamed. "What is going on!?"

The woman in the doorway didn't seem to hear her.

"Hey!" Brie yelled again. "What's going on here!? What is happening!? What's happening to me!?"

Still no reply. No sign the other woman had heard her.

Then she heard that liquid slobbering sound again. Once again it was behind her. Once again it was coming closer and closer to her.

This time she didn't dare turn around. She was certain that if she did, she'd see the terrible thing behind her, and once she saw it her mind would melt with fear.

Instead, she ran. Brie ran with every burst of energy in her for the far-off dining room. She was certain she'd be safe in there. She first ran in her shoes, then after stumbling twice, she kicked them off and ran without them. Barefoot towards safety.

Only, the far-off door remained far-off. Brie was running but it seemed like she was running in place, unable to flee in a dream with the monster breathing hot air down her neck. And Brie knew this wasn't a dream she would awake from just before the evil beast grabbed her. The monster *was* breathing down her neck—she could hear its liquid laughter behind her, feel its claws reaching for her.

She ran in strobe-fashion, like she wasn't moving at all. Even to herself in her frenetic breathless exertion, she seemed frozen on one spot. She was terrified. Her terror fueled her muscles.

Then, suddenly, the door up ahead of her vanished.

Startled by its disappearance, Brie stopped running. She didn't want to stop, but it appeared to her—struck her between the eyes like a flung rock—that she no longer had a destination to flee to. She leaned against the left corridor wall and breathed hard. Her heart pounded in her chest and her lungs felt like they'd burst from the ordeal she'd just put them through. She wondered where the dining room had gone. She was relieved, however, that the sound of the monster behind her had stopped. She appeared to have outrun it.

She peeped quickly over her shoulder and confirmed that fact. Yes, she had left the monster behind. There was nothing hulking and horrible in the corridor behind her.

She relaxed a little. The real danger was over. All she needed to do now was find her way out of here. But where was she now? She had no idea.

Then the overhead lights came on fully for a second and she realized her mistake:

The dining hall door hadn't vanished. Not at all. Nor had she outrun her pursuer. What had really happened was, the monster had somehow overtaken her. It was in front of her now, blocking off the light at the end of her tunnel.

Oh my God! NOOOOO!

The thing blocking the light stood from floor to ceiling. It towered over her.

The thing . . . it looked like . . . it was HUGE. Positioned as they were, with herself in the monster's shadow, she could make out very little of its face. But its head was massive.

Its mouth was open. It had very large teeth. She saw them because they shone silver in the darkness.

Just seeing its teeth made Brie want to wet herself. It was very hard not to start pissing on the floor; she was still carrying her load of waste water. The monster's teeth were the size of knitting needles. Each shiny silver projection was a foot long. These weren't canine fangs either: they filled both of the creature's jaws. The teeth dripped dark shimmering saliva.

She imagined its eyes as twin hollows over its gaping maw.

It seemed human. Did it have clothes on, or didn't it? She couldn't see well enough to tell.

Like a man, it smelt of sweat. In fact, it reeked as badly as her boyfriend Dave did after working out.

For a moment, Brie imagined that the ugly giant at the counter had left his post and come here to accost her. But this shadowy creature was much larger than Gorilla. (God, she wished it would stop blocking the light so she could see it clearly. But no, she didn't want that at all! She dreaded seeing any more of it than she already could. Better that it keep obstructing her vision.)

Then it reached for her. She began shivering. She was trapped in a paralysis of indecision. She wanted to turn and flee, flee back towards the toilet. But turning her back on it seemed like the wrong thing to do.

Now she could clearly see the monster's hands. They were massive. Each of its fingers was the size of her forearm. The scant light in the corridor glinted off its horny claws.

She let out a scream as it grabbed her. Her scream was a tiny, pathetic shriek, something a startled kitten might make. She was too scared to even properly express her fright.

Brie quailed before the thing. It was monstrous and disgusting, a primeval fear taking on humanoid form just to terrify her.

The lights began flickering sickly again. Brie was trapped there with the monster. And now she'd run herself out of energy.

The monster. The monster. Oh God! It seemed like the giant shadow of the giant behind the counter that had somehow come to evil life.

"Help me, somebody!" she screamed. "HELP ME!"

The monster had her now. Oh, it had her good. Right where it wanted her. Right where she didn't want to be.

Brie felt its teeth sink into her body. They sank deep into her flesh, like they were rooting themselves in her heart and lungs. The teeth were as cold as icicles. She felt her blood spurt out around them and run down her body and splash on the floor. She felt her life pour away, felt herself going to waste.

She howled out her agony. She was dying and she knew it. She felt cold and helpless and utterly violated. Violated both physically and spiritually.

The monster squeezed her tight and sucked her dry. It slobbered cold spittle all over her.

And oddly, as Brie Becker died, she could hear a woman's laugher. A woman's happy laughter echoing from far away, maybe even from the unreachable dining room.

And Brie was certain that the voice she heard belonged to Daria, the Crossway proprietress.

CHAPTER 10

Erica and Shelly

Oh, my God! Erica's orgasm had been so intense that she'd not even heard Brie first walk in, then flee from the toilets. *Oh, my God! Oh, my God!*

This was so good. Oh yes, it was. Erica was perched on the edge of the toilet seat with her legs spread wide while Shelly fingered her vagina. She'd long ago kicked away her jeans and shoes. She tensed up. She was about having another orgasm, and if anything, this one was going to be even more mind-blowing than her first.

The orgasm hit her. She went rigid. Her thigh muscles clenched tight and her arms and legs trembled. She gasped down, her eyes locking with Shelly's as the other girl slid fingers in and out of her dripping sex, while at the same time rubbing her clitoris with her other hand.

"You like this, bitch?" Shelly asked with a lust-filled grin and shining eyes. She reached up a hand and smacked Erica hard across her breasts. "You like me fucking you like this, huh? Tell me that you like it!"

"Yes, fucking yes!" Erica moaned. "Yeeessssss!"

The fingers inside her body moved faster still. The other hand smacked her breasts again. "Say it! Say it like you mean it! Tell me that you *love* what I'm doing to you!"

"I-I-I . . . li-li-like it!" Erica managed to gasp. Those two hits on her breasts—now it felt like her nipples were having orgasms of their own. "I fucking love it! D-d-don't stop-p-p, pl-pl-please!"

Shelly didn't stop. Her hand was now creamed with Erica's vaginal juices.

47

Erica rode out the orgasm for as long as she could. Then she grabbed Shelly's hand to stop her thrusting. Shelly tried to go on, but Erica held on firmly.

"No, stop!" she gasped. "No more now. Later, later." She'd overloaded on pleasure; she couldn't stand any more of it.

She pulled Shelly's face up to hers and kissed her passionately. That was when the toilet lights began flickering. It was also when her gold necklace snapped. Erica noticed the first, but not the second. For the moment, with her loins simmering with satiation, she ignored the flickering lights and drank her fill of Shelly's sweet lips. She sipped Shelly's saliva as if it were a rare wine. Her gold necklace and pendant slipped unheeded from her neck to clink softly on the floor behind the toilet bowl.

Shelly finally pulled away from Erica and sucked in several sharp gasps of breath. Erica was surprised: Shelly looked like she wanted to make love some more.

She was even more surprised by how good this sexual episode had been. For a woman who, by her own admission had never had a lesbian experience before, Shelly had done great. No, she'd done *fantastic*. Erica's vagina was very impressed by the handling it had received.

And here I was, thinking I was gonna be the dyke in this relationship.

She grinned at Shelly. "You've no idea how good you were. C'mon, don't lie to me now. Sure this is really your first time?"

Shelly nodded back, her expression slowly turning from a ravenous to a demure one. "Yes, except we count the fifty or more times I've eaten your pussy in my daydreams. Damn, baby, if lezzie sex is this much fun, sign me up for the bi club!"

The lights were still flickering erratically. Shelly kissed Erica again, then looked around for her panties. "We'd better get back to Craig. He'll be worried about us by now."

Erica picked her shirt off the floor and pulled it on. "Yes," she agreed while buttoning it up, "we've spent quite a while in here." She found and pulled on her jeans. "You really care about Craig, huh?"

"Like crazy. I'm gonna marry him for sure."

Erica nodded. Shelly sounded serious; she always did while discussing her boyfriend. While fishing around in the on/off darkness of the cubicle for her purse, she wondered what Shelly had planned for Craig now that *they'd* hooked up with one another. The 'bi club?'

It was a possibility; though maybe not a good idea if you planned on marrying the guy. *And me? What do I want?* Well, she knew for certain that she didn't want to break up Shelly's relationship. True friends didn't act selfish like that. Both their bodies, however, seemed to have different plans.

I'll just have to wait and see, won't I? she mused.

The lights stabilized for about a minute, then began flickering again. That minute was put to good use wiping lipstick smears off their faces and hands and each applying fresh makeup.

Then, both their legs still weak, they stepped out into the corridor. Immediately they did so, the lights stabilized for good.

"Damn, this is a weird kinda place," Shelly remarked.

Erica concurred. She felt inexplicably drained, as if she'd not just loved Shelly with her body, but with part of her soul as well. Then she smiled. Well, that—the 'soul' part of the sex—was a good thing. It meant they were meant for one another. Hole mates.

"Damn, do I feel winded or what?" Shelly said as they set off for the dining room.

"That's lesbian sex for you," Erica joked. "It's a real pussy workout."

Shelly giggled and leaned against her for support. "I feel like I could eat a whole plate of roast beef and gravy, mac and cheese, and chop suey, along with yet another corned beef sandwich." She wasn't exaggerating. The smell of food coming from the Crossway's dining room had her practically salivating.

"Me too. I'm ravenous. In fact, baby, I wouldn't mind eating Craig as well, if you'll share."

"Really, darling?" Shelly grinned like a cat. "Oh, we'll definitely see about that. On the hunger side of things, though, we really do need to get takeouts now."

Already, however, both young women felt their hunger pangs reducing. As they walked on, their bodies quickly normalized again, till all they felt was refreshed. Eating could wait.

Their eyes on Daria, who was walking from the stairway ahead of them to the dining room entrance, neither young woman noticed the pair of blood smears on the floor of the corridor. Both smears were in the angle where the left wall met the floor. Both looked more like shadows anyway. Both shrank and vanished as Erica and Shelly approached and stepped past them.

Completely unaware of anything amiss, both girls walked past the liquid remains of Brie Becker.

CHAPTER 11

Craig

Craig felt disoriented. A minute ago he was certain he'd heard a loud shriek coming from the corridor down which Shelly and Erica (and later the woman in the white dress) had gone to pee. He'd been startled and worried. But then, before he could get up to go investigate—barely five seconds later—Shelly and Erica had both walked out of the corridor entrance, laughing and waving at him.

The woman in white hadn't yet reappeared, but then she'd gone in *after* them, so she could logically be expected to exit later too. And his girlfriend and her girlfriend (he saw no irony in thinking this) didn't seem flustered or upset or scared, so everything had to be fine on the toilet front.

He checked the time on his phone. 8:32 p.m. They'd only been gone about five minutes. Just five minutes? That was the thing disorienting Craig. The time that had passed in their absence had appeared to be much longer. It had seemed closer to half an hour. In that time, he'd chatted with the diner's proprietress, had watched her deal with the couple who'd been having sex out here in the dining room, and had finished his supper.

How exactly had he fit all that into just five minutes?

Still, he was relieved. His love and her lovely friend were back now. Time to leave. Next stop was Erica's cousin's pad. There, they'd break out the beer and Jack Daniels and relax.

Shelly and Erica were currently over at the counter collecting their takeouts and buying beer and crisps and whatnot. Craig was paying for everything, but he didn't feel up to the hassle of actually handling the purchases. He'd given Shelly $200 and told her to get whatever the hell she liked. In his opinion, women were way better at buying groceries anyway; they tended to remember all those little things a guy would forget. Stuff like fruit and vegetables and . . . Craig didn't know any of his male friends who ever remembered to buy apples and oranges and cherries and pears and broccoli etc. when they went shopping. It was all six-packs of beer and sandwiches and cheese and Doritos and 2-liter bottles of soda and loaves of bread—dry stuff you didn't have to worry about how to prepare. Even microwavable food seemed a problem for guys to select in supermarkets. As far as Craig could tell, the average young adult male would starve to death if McDonald's and Subway and KFC ever went out of business. It was just like how bachelors never seemed to own pots and pans until they got a girlfriend, because they never cooked anything.

Still, Craig figured, watching Erica and Shelly pointing to something arranged behind the counter, maybe that was because he wasn't married yet. He'd seen older guys in stores pushing carts loaded with a variety of raw edibles. Almost all of those guys usually had wedding rings on though. (Half of them had their wives picking out the edibles and loading the carts too.) Most likely, when a guy got hitched (like he hoped to be soon), then he understood that there was life beyond fast food. Or maybe, you didn't understand that really. Maybe that wasn't how it worked at all. Possibly what happened after marriage was that you simply got used to seeing the sort of stuff your darling filled your fridge with, and once something was missing on the shelves, you automatically felt a subconscious need to please her by replacing it. Or maybe, you didn't feel anything. Maybe what happened was that when you told your significant other that you were going down the road to buy smokes and some Bud Light, she simply handed you a long list of stuff you didn't have at home and said, "Honey, please buy these too," and that was how you wound up pushing a piled-to-overflowing cart through the supermarket as well, possibly without even knowing what half the stuff you were buying was used for.

Yeah.

Craig realized that Shelly and Erica were gesturing to him from the counter. The giant cashier (damn, was that guy ripped or what?) was handing Shelly change from the till.

Craig got to his feet and walked over to join them. He duly noted that the girls each had two bags full of food. No, it didn't look like they'd be starving to death before morning, or whenever Marty got back from Ashfield.

"Here you are, baby." Shelly handed him a bag filled with sodas. "And I'll keep the change if you don't mind."

Craig grinned at that. It was a good joke.

"Where's Daria?" Erica asked the giant. "I want to say goodbye to her before we leave."

"I think she's somewhere out back," Gorilla replied. "You'll have noticed how it's just us three around tonight?"

Erica nodded. "Yeah, we did. What gives?"

He frowned. "Half our staff didn't show up today. Some kinda Canadian flu bug that's goin' round. Helen and I are immune, it looks like; so we gotta do everyone else's work for 'em." He had a deep voice and spoke with a slight drawl.

Erica nodded. "Sorry to hear that, man. We'll likely drop in again on our way back south."

"Look forward to seeing ya," the giant replied.

"Yeah, maybe tomorrow evening or Monday morning."

"Maybe even earlier than that," Gorilla said with a crooked grin. "You never know when the craving'll hit ya."

"Yeah," Shelly agreed. "'Craving' is definitely the right word. You guys cook something awesome here."

"I'll tell Daria that," Gorilla said. "She'll be pleased to hear it. Oh, and thanks for patronizing us."

"Thanks for the great food." Erica waved. "Be seeing you then."

Craig felt Shelly tugging on his arm and turned away from watching the exchange. One thing he was certain of: he never ever wanted to get into fight with this Gorilla chap, or even meet him in a dark alley. The guy was a literal wall of muscle. And he didn't give one the impression of being a 'gentle giant' either. No, this dude seemed the sort of guy who liked to hurt people. There was something about his face—already an ugly face to start with—a mean look in his eyes that gave one the shivers. Yes, this was one bad hombre alright. One bad hombre.

***

It was dark outside now. The wind whipped in from the road. It felt to Craig like being cut with razors.

Not so Shelly and Erica apparently. They seemed warm with life.

"Literally the worst thing I can imagine happening to me," Erica was saying, "would be getting raped by that guy Gorilla."

"I can imagine way worse than that," Shelly said.

"You can? I find that really hard to believe. What could possibly be worse than a guy that ugly forcing himself into you?"

"Being married to him and having to willing spread your legs to let him in every night?"

Craig laughed at that. That was just classic Shelly. Part of why he loved her so.

He was glad that the girls were having fun. He was looking forward to having a few drinks and making love to his super-hot girlfriend.

Shelly and Erica had reached the Ford and were waiting for him. Craig looked in the diner windows. Gorilla was nowhere to be seen. However, Daria was back at the counter. She looked out at him and their eyes met again. She smiled but didn't wave. He smiled back. Somehow, she didn't seem as hungry as previously.

An empty diner that serves some of the best food I've ever eaten at a road stop. Great, but . . .

"You okay, baby?" Shelly asked, stepping forward from the car.

"Yeah, I'm fine." He kissed her. "I just need to get to a bed and lie down. Maybe it's the great food they serve here, but I feel just oh so tired all of a sudden."

"Must be the food," Erica said. "After meals, the blood tends to rush from your brain to your stomach to help you digest what you ate. That's why you feel drowsy now."

Shelly nodded. "Yeah? Just ensure you stay awake till we reach Conway. I'll be mad if you crash the car and kill us."

Suddenly, Craig felt bothered again. Something about Shelly and Erica didn't seem right anymore. He didn't, however, know what it was. They both looked exactly the same as before—young and sexy— yet were both somehow different as well. (This evening's continual noticing of disturbing things was itself becoming a disturbing thing, he thought.) Out here in the parking lot, illuminated half by light spilling out from the diner and half by the building's exterior lights, Shelly and Erica looked somehow *altered.* But *what* was odd about them both? His subconscious had automatically tagged a difference in both young women that his eyes were yet to recognize.

"I'm fagged out too," Erica said, breaking his train of thought. "Good thing Conway is only a short drive away." She looked up at the sky. "Damn, I hope it doesn't rain tonight."

"It won't," Shelly said. "The clouds have all blown over towards Boston."

Craig shifted his bag of drinks to his left hand and unlocked the Ford. The girls dumped their shopping bags in on the rear seat. Erica climbed in beside them. Shelly walked round and got in the front passenger seat.

After a final brooding stare through the diner windows, Craig also got into the car. He reversed. As he curved the Ford backward prior to driving out, he looked into the rearview mirror. In the rearview he had a clear view of Erica examining her fingers. The look of concentration on her face sparked the realization in Craig's mind. Now he knew why she looked different.

Spooked, he looked right, at his girlfriend. Yes, *it was* true: both she and Erica looked *thinner* than before they'd left to freshen up in the ladies' room.

But that's impossible! No one loses weight in just five minutes!

Shelly placed a loving hand on his arm. "Are you sure you're okay, baby? You look really bothered."

"Yeah, yeah," he replied softly. "I'm cool. Just clearing my head before we head down the highway again."

He forced a smile. Shelly looked unconvinced but didn't press it. Still in her 'good humor' zone, she looked forward and grinned. Behind them, Erica had begun humming a ballad to herself. Sounded like *Dirty Diana*. Craig peeked at her in the rearview again. She had the same 'satisfied' look on her face that Shelly did. Which was similar to the last expression he'd seen on Daria's face.

Craig just refrained from smacking his head in confusion. That would have alarmed Shelly. *But . . . what is going on here?*

He put the Ford Fusion in 'Drive' and pumped the gas pedal. The silver car rolled smoothly out of the Crossway.

Craig spent the five-minute trip to Conway pondering Shelly and Erica's sudden weight loss. Or did the Crossway Diner actually serve a miracle diet?

He finally decided he was merely suffering from 'overdrive,' the cross-country version of jetlag.

Both girls still looked great. In fact, if anything, they both looked even hotter than before. And besides, Shelly had often remarked to him that she needed to lose a few pounds anyway.

He decided there was nothing to worry about.

PART 2:
BEAUTY AND THE FIST

CHAPTER 12

Erica . . . mostly

Marty Kolbek lived in a duplex on Baptist Hill Road. The split building (two three-bedroomed cottages) was quite large, white and blue in color, and close to the road. Marty lived in the right half of the duplex. The division between both sides of the house was a flimsy blue picket fence that seemed unlikely to survive even the weakest of thunderstorms.

To minimize noise leakage between the tenants on either side, the duplex was constructed with its twin garages in the middle.

"Nice place," Craig said appreciatively as the Ford drew up the short driveway. The roll-up garage door was beige in color. Craig parked up close to it and cut the engine.

"And yesss, we're here," he said. He turned to look at Erica. "Time for your magic key-fetching trick."

Erica opened the left rear door. "I'll be right back." She swung her feet out onto the gravel. A cool wind welcomed her to the night.

She shut the car door behind her. Then she walked back down the driveway and made the turn up into Andy and Karen's drive. The picket fence between the duplex halves seemed more of a territorial demarcation than anything else. Erica was surprised it was still standing. The line of weather-worn blue pickets had always seemed to her something she could kick over without even trying.

The lights were on in the left house, glowing warmly behind partially open blinds. Erica thought she heard a television.

Erica still felt ecstatic about finally hooking up with Shelly. But now she felt moody too. In a way it was like discovering one had superpowers and then realizing the heavy responsibility that came with possessing such exceptional abilities. Every new relationship brought anxieties mingled with its thrills. There was no such thing as certainty. Particularly not in a case like this, where the woman she liked was already dating someone else whom she claimed to love.

She looked right, over the fence. Craig and Shelly were discussing something and laughing. On seeing their happiness, Erica felt a mild pang of jealousy. Shelly began giggling then, her teeth glinting like tiles in the lit vehicle interior.

Oh, romance is so damn complicated! Erica thought. *Why can't humans be like animals, or bugs?*

Still, she walked with a bouncy tread. Even if complicated to unravel, a love package was great to have. And for her, a new romance like this was the perfect tonic after the intense heartbreak she'd recently suffered. This love affair was exactly what she needed. Her lips turned down at the horrible memory of all that had happened with John Parks. She felt her customary sadness about to return, but then she resolutely forced all memory of John from her mind. She wasn't ready to hurt again. She'd hurt enough; now she was determined to be happy. She'd lived in that painful past for too long. She needed to leave it behind or it would drown her for good.

And Shelly held the key to her happiness.

Erica's hands unconsciously felt her chest for the pendant she always wore there. It wasn't there—in its usual position close to her heart—but she didn't notice. She didn't notice at all. She'd worn the pendant non-stop for six months, and now didn't even realize it was gone. Her mind filled in the gap the necklace had occupied with the delicious memory of Shelly's soft lips pressed on hers.

Erica completely forgot about her pendant. Her questing fingers moved up to tug on the ends of her blonde hair instead.

The wind blew around her. Up above, the stars were out. It was a clear spring night. It was warmer here than at the Crossway. She also noted that Andy and Karen's lawn needed mowing. Talk about overgrown grass.

Smiling to herself, she left the neighbor's drive and strode towards their front porch. She felt vigorous and inspired. The rejuvenated vim Erica felt now was as intense and as complete as the draining she'd earlier experienced after she and Shelly had made love.

Erica's original plan had been to get Shelly tipsy before seducing her. But everything had worked out better than she'd hoped for. Even though she'd understood for two months now that Shelly wanted to get into her pants, Erica had been terrified of being rejected when the moment of truth finally arrived. One never knew with girls.

Erica had been frightened, knowing she needed to protect herself. Twice bitten; thrice shy. Her heart was still fragile from her recent heartbreak. No way could she have stood rejection. Shelly rebuffing her advances would have knocked her back down to the bottom of her emotional recovery ladder.

But . . . the question perplexed her as she climbed the porch steps *. . . how come I was so forceful back there at the Crossway?* That part of the sexual encounter still surprised her. Usually, when seducing someone, she was all demure and coy, girly and flirty. Sometimes she even needed to get a little drunk first to give herself courage. But tonight? She'd felt possessed by lust. Hot damn! When she'd grabbed hold of Shelly that first time and kissed her, she'd felt almost like she was someone else. Like she was acting out the part of a great seductress. She'd been full of confidence, both of her own desirability and also of her sheer irresistibility. Failure in her romantic conquest of Shelly had seemed impossible.

She wasn't complaining though. It had been fantastic—she'd always wanted to be that sexually aggressive. But it had also been immensely sapping. Each orgasm she'd had in that toilet cubicle had felt like she'd been losing a part of herself. Like something had literally been taken from her.

For a moment Erica felt scared. Now that she was remembering the experience, she recalled sensing at one point, a dark presence around them both, an invisible aura that had both fed and fed off their ecstasies.

She shrugged the fear off. *C'mon, that's just crazy.*

She smiled. *It was fun though.* She looked over from the porch steps back at the Ford, where Craig was kissing Shelly's ear while she giggled like mad. This time she felt no jealousy, just a surge of expectancy. *And there's more to come where I got the first lot from. Maybe I'll even have both of them to myself. This is sure gonna be one sweet weekend.*

On that happy thought, she rang Andy and Karen's buzzer.

***

The door opened almost immediately.

Karen Losey was a tall woman, wearing a loose white cotton blouse over brown baggy trousers and slippers. She had long black hair, dark eyes, and seemed to be about thirty years old.

"Hello," she said with a smile, "you must be Marty's cousin Erica."

"Yeah, I am," Erica replied. "We just got in from Ohio. Marty said he left his house keys here with you?"

Karen stepped back from the door and held it open for Erica. "Oh yes, please come in. You'll need to wait a bit: Andy's misplaced your keys somewhere and is looking for them."

Erica stepped inside. Karen shut the door behind her. Erica followed her into the living room.

Karen smelt like she'd been drinking. Indeed, when they arrived in the living room, there were bottles and glasses on the coffee table.

Karen gestured to the chairs. "Please have a seat; Andy shouldn't be long. We've been expecting you for hours now. Almost thought you weren't coming anymore."

"We stopped for dinner on the way." She was looking around the house. Its interior shape was of course a mirror image of Marty's place, but this house both looked and felt better. It was more feminine. Seeing as his girlfriend lived out of town, Marty's place just screamed testosterone overload at you. This living room, however, with its soft colors, its patterned throw rugs and its throw pillows on the two couches, and its flowered drapes and lovely hung landscapes, spoke of a woman's gentle touch. Erica liked it. She began warming to Karen.

"I'm really sorry to keep you waiting like this," Karen apologized. "What happened was—"

"I found 'em!" a gruff male voice interrupted her. "I found the damn things. I told you they were in my jeans pocket . . . Oh, hello there. You must be Erica."

Andy Watson was quite handsome. He was a little older than Karen—mid-thirties—and had short brown hair and moody blue eyes. Clean-shaven. His nose was a little crooked and his jaw a little square, but overall he was good-looking.

Andy was also visibly crippled. His right leg was fitted in a steel brace running from hip to heel. The brace held the leg stiff, so he swung it in a sideways arc while walking. He was barefooted, and his right foot had a slight curl to it, like the nerves were malfunctioning. He was tall and muscular, dressed in faded denim pants and a black

'Ozzfest' T-shirt. Andy wasn't anywhere near as huge as Gorilla at the Crossway, but he was large enough to make you take notice of him. Erica could easily visualize him as a biker.

He walked over and handed her the keys. "Sorry to keep you waitin'. Damn things slipped outa my pocket and under the bed when I was changin' my pants." He was slurring his words. He'd clearly had more to drink than his girlfriend.

"That's okay," Erica said. She jerked a finger over her shoulder. "I'd better be getting back to Marty's—I'm here with friends."

"Say, how 'bout a drink?" Andy offered, pointing at the coffee table with its array of bottles. "Karen baby, fetch a glass for our beautiful young guest, wilya, hon."

Erica shook her head. "Thanks, but I'd better not. If I'm any longer my friends will think I've forgotten about them."

Andy looked upset, then he nodded grimly. He sat carefully in an easy chair and picked up a half-empty glass of whiskey. "It's good booze too. Shame you ain't sharing it with us."

Karen escorted Erica back to the front door.

"About what Andy said about drinks?" Karen said. "Please, consider this a proper invitation. I'd love for you and your friends to come over and share a few glasses with us once you're settled in."

Erica hedged. "I'm not sure . . ."

Karen pulled the door almost shut behind them both. She lowered her voice. "Please do. Andy's a bit upset tonight, so it'll be great to have company over."

Erica felt impelled to ask: "Does he get . . . you know . . . violent when he's been drinking?" She didn't want to get involved in any domestic abuse scenarios. But then, if that *was* the problem, it would be best if they were there, so as to prevent Karen getting beat up.

Karen read her concerns on her face. She shook her head. "No, it's nothing like that—I'm in no danger at all. Drunk, he's as gentle as a bear with a pot of honey. I'm more worried that he's going to start crying, and I'll be unable to calm him down. Tomorrow's a really sad anniversary for him, but he tends to start drinking early. Sort of a 'Blue-Years-Eve' thing, if you catch my drift."

Erica sort-of did. "I'll invite the others," she promised. "We'll be sure to come over."

"Thanks," Karen said. "I'll really appreciate that. We both will."

***

"Oh, but I wanna sleep early," Shelly protested when Erica relayed Karen's invitation to them.

"We're drinking!" Craig announced. "We're going over there and drinking, and that's that!"

"But I don't want to."

"Sorry, baby. I'm going and you're coming along with me for alcoholic support."

"Why?"

"Drinking is great for a guy after a long day's driving. It helps loosen up his cramped muscles. His road rage dissolves into the heavenly brown liquor. It also helps him forget how unappreciative of his motor-handling skills his two female passengers were. Also—"

"Okay, okay—we'll go drink then."

"For real?"

"Yes, yes, I'll do it. But it's only 'cos I love you. Okay, let's get the car unloaded and get over there."

"Yeah!"

The three of them got out of the Ford. Erica and Shelly got the shopping bags off the backseat. Craig got to work unloading their travel bags from the trunk.

"Welcome to Franklin County, folks," Erica said as they headed for the front steps.

CHAPTER 13

Erica and Shelly

Marty Kolbek used one of his spare bedrooms to keep his computers. Erica, as family, got that one.

A long PC desk extended the entire length of one wall. The desk held two desktop machines, three monitors, a printer/photocopier, six bulky external hard drives, two PlayStation machines and stacks of CDs/DVDs. Two adjustable chairs on castors were parked beneath the desk, beneath which one could also see a mass of dangling PC cables.

On the other side of the room a large mattress lay on the rug.

"Home sweet home," Erica said, dropping her bag on the mattress. She slipped out of her shoes then lay on her back and shut her eyes to wait for her friends. After a while she began humming contentedly.

***

The other bedroom, the one beside Marty's, was properly furnished, mainly because this was where his girlfriend's son slept when they came over. Erica had ushered Shelly and Craig in there before going to check out the computer room.

Thankfully the bed wasn't kid-sized too, Shelly noted with relief.

"So here were are, babe," Craig said.

"Yeah." Shelly sat on the bed's edge and pulled off her sneakers. She got out two pairs of black flip-flops from her bag. She slipped one pair on and threw the other to Craig who was bent over his rucksack. "Now we relax."

Craig pulled out a fifth of Jim Beam bourbon from his bag.

Shelly wagged a finger at him. "Oh no, you're not."

"I'm just taking our new friends a gift."

65

"Hey, don't you dare drink too much tonight," she warned him. "I want you hard inside me later."

He grinned. The grin got her feeling hot. She got to her feet, made her way across to him, and grabbed his crotch. She squeezed it lightly. The fabric-clad penis swelled in her grasp. She felt a thrill between her legs. She actually wanted him now, not later. This wasn't any carryover lust from the Crossway toilet either; it was her honest desire for her man.

She sighed. But they had to go next door, didn't they? Erica had promised.

Craig was really hard now in her hand. His penis was bent like a hoop. Damn, that had to be painful. She looked up at his face. His eyes were shut. She considered quickly sucking him off. She decided against it. She wanted him ready for later, when she introduced him to the pleasure of his first threesome. Well, the pleasure of *her* first threesome anyway. Craig might have had one before—she'd never asked and he'd never ventured the info. Dammit, men were so secretive. But a threesome it would be tonight for sure: Erica had practically agreed that she was up for it. But would Craig agree? Shelly wasn't really bothered on that count: few guys ever turned down an offer of free no-strings-attached vajayjay. Lots of them were constantly trying to convince their women to let another woman into their bed.

Craig was squeezing her ass. His eyes were still closed. His expression was grim, focused on the sensation. He was breathing hard. His fingers were trembling, as if he was drawing energy from her buttocks.

The grip of his hands—those firm masculine hands, so large and powerful—was getting her more and more aroused.

Shelly decided she'd better cut this short now. If she didn't she was certain to shortly find herself flat on her back with Mr. Penis inside her. (Inserting the penis into her would be made very easy by the short skirt she was wearing. In teasy situations like this, it was better to be wearing tight pants [those usually took some pulling off], not a skirt you could just flip up like it wasn't even there.)

She ducked out of Craig's grasp.

"Aw, babe, please don't go-o . . . !"

He tried to pull her back to him, but she pushed him away with firm hands on his chest, then retreated to safety across the room.

"Later, darling." Then to rub it in, she added, "After all, it was your idea to go get cozy with the neighbors."

He looked miserable, which she actually liked, seeing him standing there with his penis hard and no avenue of relief (except her Pussy Avenue, which she wasn't letting him drive through).

"Bring that ass back here right now!" he growled.

"No." But it hurt seeing him like that. That boner looked like it might snap in two. Once again she considered fellating him. She shook the erotic impulse off. Sucking a penis would mess up her lipstick. And besides, Erica was waiting for them. Erica was certain to be getting impatient now.

"How do I look?" she asked, striking a pose for Craig.

"Unspermed."

"Unspermed?"

"You'll look much better with my dick ejaculating inside you, that's for sure. C'mon, baby, please . . . ?"

She rolled her eyes. "I've told you to forget it. Later." She rushed across and kissed him. "And if you're a good little boy and don't drink too much, I've a special surprise for you—one you're certain to love."

"Surprise? What?"

She ducked out of reach of his amorous arms. "I ain't tellin'. Wait and find out."

He pointed down at the bulging front of his jeans. "What am I supposed to do about this?"

She laughed at him. "That's a good question, baby. Hey, and please wait for it to go down before coming outside. Erica will likely faint from fright if she sees you with a woody."

"What's the deal with her anyway? She a lez or something? A beauty like that with no guy?"

Shelly gave a slight start. *Oops!—he's getting rather close to home*, she thought. She didn't want that. She didn't want Craig suspecting a thing. She wanted to really surprise him when she introduced Erica into their bed. She wanted to see the utter shock in his eyes when Erica walked through the bedroom door naked with her breasts and ass swaying.

"No, no, no, baby," she said, waving a reproving finger. "Don't change the subject, huh? You've asked me about that before, and I've told you: she's had her heart broken. I don't know the details either, but I know it was really bad. The guy must have been an absolute scumbag. She just needs time to get back on her feet."

"Changing the subject would have helped me forget this hard-on you've given me."

"Oh, that." A major understatement on her part; the penis was still hard. "Yeah, and don't you dare wank it off either. I want you really hard later. And I want a full load of your love cream. I'm gonna drink down every squirt of your love milk. Trust me, you're gonna be doing a whole of stuffing tonight, lover. I'm horny like you won't believe."

The problem was, her words were getting him even more aroused. She noticed this and headed out the door. She saw him coming after her with ravishing intent written all over his face and went fast. His hand caught the left sleeve of her T-shirt, but then she slipped free and out into the hallway.

"Damn tease!" she heard him call.

"Who loves you! Never forget that part. I *love* you, baby." She lowered her voice to a loud whisper. "And remember what I said: don't you dare jerk off! I ain't joking 'bout that, man!"

"Yeah sure, I won't. This surprise of yours had better be good though. My balls are already aching."

"Oh, poor, poor you. And there's really no time to take a cold shower, is there? Think of something sad or horrible. Like a car accident or a funeral. That should work."

"Thanks, prick-tease."

However, thirty seconds later, Craig stepped out of the bedroom with his pants flat in front again. "Thinking about a funeral worked."

He gestured down the hallway with his free hand (the other clutched his whiskey gift for the neighbors) and said, "We'd better get Erica. She most likely thinks we've been doing what we've not been doing."

They walked to Erica's bedroom. Shelly knocked. "Hey, Erica! We're ready."

"Door's open."

Shelly pushed the door open and peeked in. Erica was sitting up on her mattress with her cellphone in hand. She dropped it and began pulling on her shoes. "I just got through calling Marty to let him know we've arrived. He sends his greetings. Says he looks forward to meeting you both."

"Cool." Shelly walked halfway into the room and struck a pose. "We're both ready for our tour of the neighbor's bar."

Craig peeked in too. "Cool pad this," he remarked admiringly. "What's your cousin do?"

Erica gestured dismissively at the long computer desk. "IT stuff— lots of software coding. I think most of it has to do with games now." She slipped her heel into her second shoe and stood up. "Alright, let's go drink ourselves silly."

Shelly stole a wink at her. "Not that silly, silly." Then she pushed Craig, who'd begun staring at the PlayStations with interest, out of the room. "Hey, move it, baby! You and Marty can talk *Call of Duty* and *Grand Theft Auto* tomorrow."

Craig went ahead of them. Behind him, Shelly and Erica held hands, but separated when they got to the front door.

Shelly stepped out into the warm spring night. A moment later she felt Erica's soft lips on the nape of her neck. A kiss, then a whisper: "Later, honey cake. And boyfriend makes three."

Shelly tingled deliciously. Later tonight couldn't come fast enough for her. *Oh, Craig, sweetheart, you've no idea what I've got planned for you!*

She looked up at the moon. It was full. In its light she could see clear down to the end of the street.

She stepped up to Craig's side and slipped her arm through his, then looked back to ensure Erica was following. Erica was locking the front door, after which she hurried to catch up with them. She did so just as they reached the sidewalk and turned the fence.

"Strange night this," Craig said as she joined them. "First it's freezing, then it's merely cool. Then all of a sudden it's warm. Let's hope the weather doesn't suddenly turn furnace-hot, like we're in a desert."

"We'll survive," Shelly said. "Though if tonight heats up any further, we may all need to sleep in the buff. But then, that's never hurt anyone. Sometimes it's even fun."

They all laughed.

Shelly decided having some drinks was an excellent idea. The alcohol was certain to loosen everyone up for what she had planned.

CHAPTER 14

Karen & Co.

". . . so that's what happened to Dwight," Andy finished. "By the time his daughter Elsie found him the next morning, his damn cows had damn near smeared him into the barn floor. He was alive, but just barely . . . Nah, Dwight won't ever ride a Harley drunk again in his life."

They all laughed. Karen could never hold back the giggles when Andy related this tale. It had been a funny story, particularly the bit (narrated post-incident to Andy by Dwight [Andy's older brother] himself) about how he'd gone literally flying through the air after his bike hit his farm fence, and through a open barn window and into the cows' feed trough. The trough had tipped over. The feed it contained had spilled out. Dwight, miraculously alive after an airborne trip that had lasted some thirty yards, had unwisely tried not to topple over along with the trough. As a result he'd spilled out of it last and wound up on top of the cows' feed. That had been his real undoing. Unable to reach their food, the usually placid animals had resorted to kicking and stomping him to get him out of the way. In a matter of course, one of those kicks had knocked Dwight out. Several calves had then used him as a pillow to chew the cud on.

It was about ten-thirty now, an hour or so after the three travelers had joined them for drinks. The visit had been fun so far. Karen was pleased the three were around. She was already tipsy. It would have been hard comforting Andy once he got to reminiscing with her.

With company present, however, that was unlikely to occur. At worst Andy would drink until he fell asleep in his chair.

They were seated around the comfy living room: Andy on his recliner (best for his game leg), the two girls on one couch, herself and Craig on opposite chairs between the others. She was in charge of keeping everyone's glasses refilled. Whiskey, brandy, and the Jim Beam bourbon the kids had nicely brought over.

She raised her glass to their guests. "So, are you three still in school?"

"Nah, we're all finished and working," Erica replied. A pretty, tough-looking girl she was, Karen thought. Then she felt a little dizzy. *Dammit, I've drank more than I should.* But she sipped some more of her brandy.

"Yeah? So what y'all do for a living?" Andy asked, waving his glass at them. He had a high alcohol tolerance, but his eyes were part-crossed now. Shouldn't be long now before he was out for the count.

"We're waitresses," Shelly replied. She giggled. "Erica and me, that is. We work at the same restaurant, place called the Cherry Street Pub." She pointed to her boyfriend. "Darling here, he's a construction worker."

The young man was already very tipsy. For the past hour he and Andy had been matching one another shot for shot. Karen didn't think drinking this much was good for a man. Sure, lots of women were into the so-called 'bad boys', but Shelly here didn't seem that type. But then, one never knew: the girl's wholesome exterior might mask a vixen who thrived on being roughed up. The other girl—Erica—looked more the sort to be into rough guys.

The two girls weren't drinking much. Which was good: neither of them seemed to have a head for booze anyway. They were already giggling like mad and slapping each other on the thigh at the slightest comic provocation. They were hugging a lot too. If she didn't know Shelly was dating Craig, Karen would have gotten the wrong impression about them.

Andy stared pointedly at Craig. "So, tell me, man, how are things in the construction business?"

"So, so. It's a good job, but it's long hard work."

"Yeah, man, so it is," Andy agreed. "It's a man's work, for sure."

Karen began feeling hungry. Then it occurred to her that their three guests might be hungry too. That was quite a long drive they'd had over from Ohio. She figured she'd better make sandwiches for everyone. Everyone except Andy, that was. Give Andy food in his current state and he'd just puke everywhere later. She wasn't even letting him near the beer nuts and potato chips in the fridge.

She decided to enquire about appetites and food before she was too drunk to serve it. Andy had however just begun telling a new story. Knowing how he hated being interrupted, she decided to wait till he was finished.

In the meantime, she picked up her glass and drank some more brandy.

***

"See, I got a hardware place on the other side of town," Andy said ruminatively. "Business is slow but steady. We're okay, making a reasonable living. Karen helps me out sometimes. Other times, she's a secretary to . . . but forget that bit. See, the story I wanna tell you has to do with before I began running the hardware store. Now, before I hurt my leg, I used to drive a truck between Boston and Omaha, Nebraska. So see, this one time I'm hired drive a load of frozen pork out that way. Really, it came about quite weird, ya know? I got my own rig, but see . . ."

Craig grinned to himself. Yes, this was a good idea coming over. This couple were just great. This guy Andy, he certainly could tell a grand tale!

"Well," Andy continued, "now see, Tommy Shawcross who shoulda really handled the truckin' contract couldn't be found. Now it's Tommy's truck and my older brother Dwight is desperate to get that load of dead hogs out west to Somerset in Pennsylvania. . . . So, well, he calls me to help him deliver it. Tells me they can't find Tommy anywhere, but the key's in the ignition. Can't say no to my older brother when he's in straits now, can I? So I agree to drive Tommy's rig over there for him. Now it's a full-day trip out there and back, and it falls on a Sunday, when by all rights I shoulda been resting."

He sipped some whiskey. "Alright, now for some reason, I'd driven off of the interstate—the I-84 which is the straight road down south to Pennsylvania. I think there'd been a bad accident—a pileup of some kind—on the Yankee Expressway around Waterbury and the traffic cops had diverted everyone along the state roads instead . . . but, for whatever the reason, I find myself drivin' through some small towns . . . Middlebury and Southbury, looking to rejoin the freeway south of Southbury . . .

"Now, see, so I'm a drivin' through Southbury and who do I see walking into a church there? Dammit if it ain't Tommy Shawcross."

"He's walking into a church?" Shelly asked. "How the hell did he get out there?"

"Don't know," Andy replied. "But see, I'm getting ahead of myself. What I actually see at first is Tommy walking up the road towards the church and he's carrying a dead pig over his shoulder."

"A dead pig?"

"Yeah. And not just dead, the fucker had been *skinned* too. It was bloody as . . ."

Karen laughed drunkenly. "That's not even the worst of it. See, according to Andy, Tommy was naked himself as well."

"C'mon, you guys, that's hard to believe," Erica said. "You're telling us you saw a naked guy carrying a dead, skinned pig along a main road . . . on a Sunday morning? Aw, c'mon, man."

Andy shook his glass at them. Half the remaining whiskey splashed out of it. He stared apologetically at the waste, then philosophically handed the glass over to Karen. "Fill 'er up for your man, babe."

Karen topped the glass up and returned it to him. In the interim no one said a word. The expectancy was high in the air, taut like you could cut it with a knife.

Andy took a sip of his booze before continuing. "Now I'm sure you three are gonna ask me how a guy can walk naked through a town on Sunday morning with a dead animal on his shoulder and not get arrested, right?"

"Yeah," Craig said. "How'zat even possible, man?"

Andy waved his glass again. This time, to avoid spilling its contents, he was more careful. "Believe me, folks, that's what I asked myself too. I'm driving through the town kinda slow for some reason—I think maybe Anna-Marie Bevis, my lady at the time, was callin' me on the phone or somethin'—and next thing I know, I see Tommy pulling this stunt. And I'm certain it's him—same long black hair and long beard, same antichrist tattoo or whatever it was he's got on his left bicep—I could tell that asshole from half-a-mile off even if I was blind. We were drinkin' buddies too, and dammit, Tommy could drink. So I don't think too much of it—I just figure he's having a drunken blackout and I'd better rescue his drunken ass before he embarrasses it. So I park the truck by the side of the road, and start yelling his name outa the side window. And then—"

"And he stops, right?" Shelly interrupted breathlessly. "And you catch up with him before the cops get there and spirit him off to jail? And he later doesn't remember anything about what happened? Wow, what a cracker of a tale!"

Andy wagged a finger at her. "Nah, missy, nothin' like that happened. It was much worse."

Shelly and Erica both gaped at him. "You're telling us that he made it inside the church, naked and with the pig!?"

"Somethin' more like that. Now stop interrupting and let me finish telling ya this story of mine." He waited till they were all silent before going on: "Now, when I call to Tommy from the window of the truck cab, he don't either stop or reply me. He looks up at me once, then just keeps walking. And that's when he turns off the road into the church. It's a small Presbyterian place with a short driveway bordered by flowers and trees leadin' up to it, and a graveyard planted off to the rear. A nice sunny place; the sort you'd like to be buried behind when you die. Now I know Tommy's gonna go to jail forever and ever for both indecent exposure and desecration of a place of worship, not to mention creating a public disturbance, if I let him carry on with this crazy stunt of his—I mean, his wiener's on public display—so I leap down from the cab of the truck and run into the churchyard after him. By this time, Tommy's almost at the church entrance. How he's walking so fast I couldn't goddamn figure, but I'm running after his ass as fast as my lungs'll permit. I ain't yelling his name: I'm trying to get this over with *silently*. But he's well ahead of me and gaining distance on me."

Andy stopped speaking and took another sip of his whiskey. This time too no one said anything. He went on: "Now, I know what you're thinkin', but you're dead wrong. No, Tommy didn't enter the building. Just when it looked like he was gonna—he's already got his left foot up on the front steps—he vanished." He grinned at their surprised faces. "Yeah, vanished. Now how do you like that, huh? The son-of-a-bitch just up and disappeared on me."

"He was a ghost?" Shelly asked with a hint of fear in her voice.

"Sure as hell he was," Andy said. "Of course, I didn't know that at the time. I just thought my eyes were playin' tricks on me. Hangover hallucination. I'd been drinking a good amount the night before. Well, once Tommy vanished like that, I got out of there fast. I could see the parson and an usher already lookin' at me weird from inside the building, like I was a sinner runnin' to the Lord for the saving of my soul. I didn't wanna get wrapped up in any explainin', and I figured I had too many sins to repent from anyway—it'd likely take the Lord all day long to cleanse my soul and I had a delivery to make—so I just legged it out of there again, fast as I could. I got in my rig—sorry, I mean it was actually Tommy's rig, weren't it—and I pumped the gas outa there. And I drove out of Southbury thinkin' hard."

"Wow, man, now that's just downright scary," Craig said.

Erica and Shelly looked awed. "That *really* happened?" Erica asked finally. "I mean, you're not fooling with us?" A really spooky kind of atmosphere had fallen on the drinkers.

"Sure as hell did happen," Andy said. "Swear on my mother's grave."

"Tommy Shawcross *was* dead," Karen continued. "He was in the back of the truck Andy was driving. They found his corpse while offloading in Somerset."

"What!?" Shelly yelped.

"Yeah," Andy said. "Now, don't you people ask me how, but Tommy had somehow locked himself in the truck with the load of pigs he's supposed to deliver. Frozen to death in there. He'd apparently been drinking heavily. He was stiffer than a board when they unloaded him." He laughed sadly. "And, see, that's not all that was weird. Remember that church where I saw him?"

"Yeah, what about it?"

"Well, it turned out later that Endicott La Rue, founder of La Rue Meat Processing, the meat company I was making the delivery to, was buried in the graveyard at the back of that little roadside Presbyterian church in Southbury." He tipped his glass to his lips then finished off his tale: "Tommy apparently stopped off to drop him one last load of pork: They found deep bare male footprints beside Endicott's grave."

"Damn," Craig said, turning to look at Shelly and Erica, "that's weird as hell."

"And it's all as true as you see me sittin' before you here now," Andy said. He adjusted his bad leg as if it was hurting him. "Chills me no end each time I think about it—that a man could die, and yet still be intent on carrying on his business. I sure hope Tommy's not still deliverin' ghost pigs to old customers in the afterlife. That'd be Hell for sure." His voice now took on an unsettling poignancy. "Strange things happen when you drive a rig for a living. Of course, since I broke my leg I don't get around much for that kinda excitement anymore. It's a pity, a real pity—a man has some really good times out there ridin' the highways."

Karen looked sympathetically at him when he said that. She patted his arm, then took his empty glass. The room was silent while she poured him some more whiskey. As silent as if Tommy Shawcross's ghost was delivering a skinned pig to their front door. Everyone stared into their glasses and looked moody.

"All this talk of dead meat has gotten me hungry," Karen interjected into the silence. "Does anyone care for some sandwiches? We've got ham, turkey, tuna spread . . . pickles and cheese . . . or should I just do giant BLT's with mayo for everyone?" She looked around the room, her eyes finally settling on Craig's face. "What of it? I'm sorry I forgot to ask you earlier. It just completely skipped my mind. You guys have to be hungry after the long drive over."

"Nah, we're alright," Craig said dismissively. "We ate on the way into town."

Karen looked to the two young women for confirmation of this.

"Yeah," Shelly agreed tipsily. "Marty told Erica his fridge was empty, so we turned off into a diner just outside of town. Great eats too."

"Are you guys absolutely certain you're full?" Karen asked just to make sure. "It's no bother at all to me, if that's what you're concerned about."

Erica nodded. "Yeah, we're all as stuffed as peppers. We stopped at Daria's place. The food was still as fantastic as I remembered from last time I was here. We bought some takeout food and drinks as well."

Then Craig realized that Karen was gaping at them. "You stopped at the Crossway Diner?" she asked in a confused voice.

"Yeah, sure we did," he agreed. "The old two-story place right where Route 116 crosses the 91 interstate, right? Hey, what's wrong?"

At his reply, Andy had suddenly sat bolt-upright in his recliner, in the process spitting out his latest mouthful of whiskey. His eyes gaped wide. Shelly and Erica wondered what the matter was. Craig worried that the guy might be having a seizure from too much drinking. Still, he sympathized. This was some great whiskey Andy had.

"The Crossway, ya say?" Andy finally enquired. "You're tellin' us you three saw Daria . . . Daria Simpson *tonight?*"

"Yes we did," Erica replied. "At her diner."

"She even spoke to me, man," Craig added in a slurred voice. "There was this couple there who were . . ." He decided no one needed to know about the in-diner porno show.

"I don't get it," Shelly said. "What's the big deal about us seeing Daria?"

Karen let out a long exhalation of breath; it sounded almost like she was deflating. "Guys, Daria Simpson died two years ago."

Now it was Erica's turn to gape. "Died?—but that's impossible! Last time I was here *was* two years ago. She was still alive then. I know that for sure."

Karen smiled, but it didn't reach her eyes. She was visibly troubled. "When exactly were you here?"

Erica sipped her drink and tried to remember. "Late March, or maybe April. Yes, I think it was the middle of April."

"That's why you didn't hear about it then."

"Hear about what?"

"The Crossway burning down. Daria was inside it when it was torched."

"It burnt down?" Craig asked. "Then it must've been rebuilt, right?"

"Nah, it never was," Karen said. She'd been standing, but now retreated and sat heavily on the second couch. "Daria's brother Gorilla was gonna rebuild the place, but he died in a car crash two months later; on the day before he was supposed to ink the contract with the construction folks. Helen, one of the waitresses, was in the car with him."

Andy had recovered from his shock now. "Yeah, Helen Brooks. Gorilla Simpson was sweet on her but she was still holding out on letting him between her legs. I saw Gorilla that night. He told me he thought he'd finally sweet-talked his way through Helen's chastity belt and was gonna get lucky." Andy laughed. "Well he sure did get *unlucky*: car burst a tire over on Elm Street, spun off the road, hit someone's fence and shot 'em both through the windshield. Freak accident for sure, the cops said. For one thing, the fence that stopped the car in its tracks was mere pickets, as flimsy at the one separating our side of the house from Marty's side. For another, neither of the vehicle's front airbags worked. Neither of 'em was wearing a seatbelt either. Gorilla—God rest his soul—was shot straight into a wall, damn near pulverized his head to mush. I remember our undertaker Ephraim Snitsky telling me how he'd had to build a plaster model of Gorilla's skull and stretch the skin of his head over that so it'd look normal enough for his ma to view during the funeral. He said Gorilla's skull and brain were a mush of paste—like they'd been run through a grinder. The skin was okay, but the head's *contents* . . . Shit! Helen fared a bit better, or worse, depending on how you wanna view it: she'd been gutted by a tree branch. When the cops arrived she was down on the lawn with her intestines reeled out above her like red skipping rope."

"Eww!" Erica looked like she'd puke. Karen too.

"Now you mention it," Shelly said, "there did seem to be something wrong with Gorilla's head while we were buying takeout stuff. It looked flattened on one side."

"Yeah, on the right side," Erica tipsily agreed. "I was gonna ask him how that happened, but just like that, I forgot to."

"For God's sake, stop it, wilya!" Karen gasped. "You *didn't* see him tonight; I was at his damn funeral!"

"But we did," Erica protested.

"We did, we did!" Shelly protested too.

Craig said nothing. Seeing as Karen seemed to have quit serving everyone, he leaned forward and poured himself some more whiskey.

Andy shook his head sadly. "Nah, you didn't see her; I know that much. Guys, I was there when the Crossway building went up in flames. Get it?—I was there in person. You never did see such a blaze in your damn lives." He shook his head again and finished off the last of the whiskey in his glass. This time he didn't look to Karen for a refill, nor did she offer to replenish the glass for him.

"Oh, I get it," Craig said suddenly, a wise look stealing over his features. "You're trying to scare us again. Ha ha ha!" He slapped his knee. "This is just another ghost tale like the one you told us about Tommy . . . what was his name again?"

"Shawcross. Tommy goddamn fuckin' Shawcross." Andy shook his head emphatically and with more than a hint of anger. "Nah, I already told you three: that happened as sure as I'm sitting here. I swear on my dead ma's grave it did." He wiped a tear from his left eye. "But this fairy tale of yours sure as hell didn't." Then he laughed. "I'll admit though, it was a good try, you three tryin' to scare me like that.

And it almost worked too." He looked right, at Karen. "What'cha think, baby, huh? A good try, yeah?"

Karen nodded. "Yeah, it was scary alright. But I think it was in bad taste, seeing as how you and Daria were so close."

"But we're not . . ." Shelly started saying, then gave up on seeing the reproving look in Karen's eyes. She got the message: *Stop it, just stop it right now.*

Shelly resolved to keep her mouth shut on the matter henceforth.

Unfortunately though, the damage was already done.

Just like that, out of the blue, Andy gave a loud groan of, "Oh, Daria baby, why!? Why!?" and began weeping. He wept profusely, the tears spilling down his cheeks. "Oh, honey! Oh, honey! Oh, Daria, how could you leave me all alone like that!?"

Shelly, Erica, and Craig just stared. It was painful to watch Andy weeping like this. Still, a drunk was likely to get emotional at the slightest provocation. At the moment Andy seemed totally inconsolable. He just cried and cried on like a baby, his boozing completely forgotten.

Karen had instantly leapt to her feet and hurried over to Andy's side. She leaned over him and cooed, "Now, darling, take it easy. Just take it easy, alright? It wasn't your fault that it happened like that. Everyone knows it wasn't your fault."

Erica felt relieved on one account. Just like Karen had earlier said, she clearly wasn't in any danger of being abused here. Swaying slightly, she got up and addressed Karen's back: "Say . . . I think it might be a good idea if we left now."

Karen turned and nodded. "Yes, I think so too." She straightened up. "Wait, I'll see you out."

"There's no need," Erica protested. "We'll be fine on our own." Craig, however, was taking so much time with getting to his feet, that she decided they might as well wait for Karen.

Karen poured Andy a stiff double whiskey, then escorted the three of them to her front door.

"We're all really sorry about that," Erica apologized. "We didn't mean to . . ."

"It's alright," Karen said. "You didn't know, that's all. It's what I was telling you about. Tomorrow's the second anniversary of Daria's death. Andy's all cut up over that. He's usually fine, but—"

"You're serious about that?" Craig asked tipsily. "Then how . . . ?" He stopped asking at a stern glance from Erica and hard pinch in the side from Shelly.

"Please stop it!" Karen pleaded. "As a joke it's in appallingly bad taste. The Crossway was never rebuilt. It's just ruins down there by the overpass now. If you stopped on the way for dinner, you're most likely mistaking the Crossway for some eating place in South Deerfield." Her expression turned softer. "Look, you guys, I gotta go back in and see to Andy. You do understand that?"

"I'm sorry," Craig said.

"Hey," Erica said brightly. "Are we still on for the picnic tomorrow? We really wanna get into the woods and away from it all while we're here."

Karen thought a bit. "Yeah, sure. Don't you worry about Andy. He'll be fine. A trip through the great outdoors will be great for him too; it'll help take his mind off Daria." She looked hard at the three of them in turn. "Only, you guys have gotta promise me you'll not mention her at all."

"We promise," Shelly and Erica said immediately. Then they looked sternly at Craig.

"Baby, say something," Shelly prompted.

"Huh? . . . oh yeah. Sure. I promise not to mention anything about the Crossway." He squinted at Karen. "Sorry, I think I've had too much to drink. I might be a little drunk right now, see?"

Karen smiled tightly. "I think we've all had a bit too much to drink." She made a shooing motion. "Alright, now run along, all of you. I've got to go attend to my boyfriend before he starts talking of shooting himself again."

She stepped inside and shut the door. Outside, Craig, Shelly and Erica heard her footsteps recede. They started off down the driveway for their own quarters.

***

"That's one really kooky pair," Erica said as they turned the fence and were well out of earshot. "Really, really bonkers. I wonder how in the world Marty manages to live next to them."

"They've given *me* the weirdies tonight, that's for sure," Shelly agreed. "First, Andy's crazy tale of his dead compadre and that damn pig. That was bad enough; I almost peed myself on hearing that. The one about the Crossway was even worse. They had me doubting my sanity for a while."

"Yeah," Erica said. "That tale about the Crossway was taking it too far." She burped then farted. "Way too far. How in the world can anyone claim a place that's still standing burned down two years ago?"

"Sour grapes," Craig said knowingly.

He was holding on to Shelly for dear life now, leaning on her shoulder like he couldn't see where he was going and he'd collapse to the ground if she got away from him. Making them both sway left and right. He was heavy and she was quite annoyed with him for getting drunk when she wanted to make love.

Still, she managed to ask, "Sour grapes? Baby, what in the world do sour grapes have to do with tonight's crazy stories?"

"Yeah," Erica added. "We're all rather drunk, but that's fermented grapes, not sour ones . . . or maybe it's fermented wheat or barley or hops or what-the-hell-ever." She squinted at Craig. "Shoot, man— whatever are you talking about?"

"Romantic fruit gone bad. That's the sour grapes I mean."

"Huh?"

He swayed on Shelly's shoulder. "Lemme explain what I mean. According to Karen, Andy was once dating Daria, right?"

"Yeah, so?"

They'd just reached the front porch. They sat on the steps, absorbing the night air, which was now several degrees cooler than when they'd earlier set out.

Shelly figured they'd need to get up soon and go inside. She intended on having her threesome tonight, no matter what. Erica wasn't too drunk for sex. And she hadn't forgotten either. Just now, Shelly had felt Erica caress her butt, slowly and meaningfully, a clear indication that she wanted the treasure buried there.

Craig *was* drunk though. But she'd get him primed. Shelly didn't imagine it would be too difficult; he was already safekeeping that hard-on from earlier. A cup of coffee should suffice to get Craig alert enough to perform. She wasn't willing to wait till morning. They'd all likely be too hungover then to screw. Besides, she had an intense feeling that their magic coupling had to happen tonight. Maybe because the sex at the Crossway Diner had been so mind-blowing, she felt that if she had both her lovers caressing and penetrating her tonight, they'd launch her out into sexual orbit. It was simply going to be fantastic; she already felt the splendor of the fuck in her bones.

"Yeah, so?" Erica repeated on her behalf, reminding her that Craig hadn't yet finished his explanation.

"Okay," Craig said. "Now you both saw how gorgeous Daria was, right?"

"Yeah, so?" Shelly felt a bit jealous at that. Yes, Daria had been breathtakingly beautiful, with that long pale hair, ivory-like face, and large red lips, but Craig should know better than to mention that. Still, she forgave him. Both because she was horny and because he was drunk.

"Now, you imagine a guy like Andy. Rough-looking as a bum, drinks like a fish, and has a bad leg to boot. Shit, I need to pee soon. Anyway's, Andy ain't much of a catch for a chick that beautiful, right? So Daria most likely dumped Andy for some Book Boyfriend type— movie-star good-looks, Dave Bautista physique, etcetera—and Andy can't handle the fact that he's now stuck with Karen. I ain't being nasty, but did either of you notice that Karen can't ever have won any beauty queen awards in her life?"

"Yeah, so what?" Shelly said. "I haven't either."

Craig burped. "That's only 'cos you've never competed, hot pants. Karen on the other hand . . . Listen, I'll put it nicely . . . hic . . . whatever Andy sees in her, it ain't her looks."

"You're a nasty, horrible man to describe a nice woman like that, Craig baby," Erica said. "But still, I like ya a lot."

"Craig, frigging make sense dammit!" Shelly growled.

"What I mean is—shit, girls, I really gotta take a pee."

Shelly grabbed a firm hold of the waistband of his jeans. "Finish explaining this first, or you're gonna end up wetting your pants."

"Alright, alright. All I'm sayin' is, Andy's *jealous*. He wishes Daria's dead because he can't have her. Sour grapes."

"And Karen? So, yes, she is rather plain, but she isn't an erection-killer. Besides, she seems really nice. So what's *her* grudge?"

"More jealousy. She's nowhere as good-looking as Daria. She wishes Daria dead too. Then the competition's eliminated."

"Craig, you're a horrible person."

"It's hard to be dishonest when you're drunk—alcohol is a truth serum. Look, we gotta be careful dealing with those two. They're psychos. Or, more likely . . ." he burped again, "Andy went psycho when Daria dumped him and Karen's humoring him so he doesn't dump *her*, 'cos she's scared she won't get anyone else."

Erica made a face. "And the anniversary of Daria's death that Karen was so serious about? Hey, drunken genius, how d'you explain that?"

"Simple. Tomorrow's the anniversary of their breakup. That's why he's so upset that we reminded him that we saw her. He's trying to forget his ex and we show up and open our big mouths."

Now it was Shelly's turn to grimace. "That's just so frigging pathetic, baby. Wow, what a pair of losers. And we're going picnicking tomorrow with 'em? I can't wait."

"For a drunken fuck, you're certainly making a lot of sense," Erica told Craig. "I'm frigging deeply impressed."

"Say, can I go piss now?"

"Yeah, go water the flowers. . . . Hey, man, move further along the flowerbed. Move along, dammit! Don't you dare turn and wet us!"

"Yeah, shift right down . . . down to the end. Don't you dare unzip till you're away from here. I don't wanna see it!"

"But you're both such pretty blossoms. You need some of Craig Daddy's yellow sprinkler system. Help you grow up all nice and strong."

"I'm already all grown up nice and strong, you . . . you . . . Craig, I frigging mean it, if you dare pee on me, I swear to God Almighty that I'll never suck you off again. Not ever. I ain't jokin'."

"Hey, baby, why d'you keep threatening me like that? You know my dick can't take those threats."

"Just go! Hey, further away, turn the corner!"

"Yeah, turn the damn corner before taking your dick out. I've seen a gust of wind blow pee over someone before."

"Bye bye, stud. Out of sight equals no airborne fright."

Once Craig had vanished around the corner of the house, Erica leaned forward and whispered in Shelly's ear, "Hey, I'm curious. How big is Craig's dick anyway?"

Shelly giggled. "It depends."

"Depends?"

"Yeah. On whether or not I'm naked."

They both burst out laughing, then sneaked a couple of kisses before Craig lumbered back around to the front of the house again.

Then it was time to get up and go inside. Oh, Shelly couldn't wait!

CHAPTER 15

Shelly & Co.

Five minutes later, threesome preparations were in full swing.

The only thing hampering an instant falling into bed together was Shelly's insistence to Erica that she wanted to *surprise* Craig.

She wanted to present Erica to Craig as a 'gift.' Well, sort of.

Her reasoning was simple. It was based on her desire to preserve her relationship with Craig: *If I let things appear to happen naturally, I'll lose control of the situation. He's my boyfriend, not hers. As much as I like Erica, I'm not putting myself in a situation where I stand to lose out. And that could happen if Craig gets the impression that she's just coming onto him spontaneously and I don't mind. Then what happens if on another occasion another girl suddenly gets 'spontaneous' with him while I'm there? I'll likely be expected to go along with that scene too, even if I'm not turned on by the girl. And I'm definitely not up for that . . . So, I am going to present Erica to Craig. That way he'll understand it was my decision to include her in our relationship . . . at least for a while.*

Such was her reasoning. It was hard thinking after drinking so much.

Of course, she didn't tell Erica any of this. How she explained the waiting to Erica was to kiss her, fondle her breasts, and say, "Go make us some coffee, darling. I'll tend to Craig. I'll come fetch you once he's good and hard."

Erica sighed against Shelly. Her breath—both their mouths—smelt of good whiskey. Her breasts felt all tingly and her nipples felt like hot rocks. She wanted to melt into Shelly, wanted to become one with her again. "I'm just worried that he's gonna fall asleep on us before we . . ." she giggled, "you know."

Shelly was in the living room with Erica. Craig had already wandered off to their bedroom. They heard the thud of him falling heavily onto the bed.

84

Shelly kissed Erica. Her tongue slid inside the receptive mouth, making their contact a deep French kiss. When they separated she said, "If he does, it's to our benefit, isn't it? Then you'll be all *mine* tonight. And I'll be all *yours*. He'll get his in the morning." She cupped and squeezed Erica's breasts again, harder this time, then pinched her nipples. "Alright, get us that damn coffee, darling."

"Coming up, boss." Erica turned and sashayed off. Shelly watched her tight ass sway for a moment, then headed determinedly into she and Craig's bedroom.

Craig lay in bed with his eyes half-shut. She sat beside him and began undoing his belt. Sensing what she had in mind, he reached down to help her.

She pushed his hands away. "Just relax, let me do it. I just wanna check that you kept that hard-on for me like we agreed."

"Oh, I kept it alright. But you were really horrible to do that to me. Oooh, easy, easy."

She'd gotten his penis out and was stroking it. It responded quickly to her touch. She soon had him hard. She grinned down at the throbbing manhood in her hand, then grinned up at him.

"Now let's get you fully undressed."

He was already taking off his shirt. She quickly stripped off his pants and briefs. Once he was nude, she pulled her T-shirt up over her own head, then reached back and snapped open her bra. She saw the excitement in his eyes as her breasts fell free. Her own excitement rose too. He now had himself in hand, was stroking himself slowly while watching her undress. She admired his strong masculine physique as he lay there; from his powerful shoulders and biceps and the just-hairy-enough chest, on to the flat abs with the chiseled six-pack, to the dark and curly pubic hair, and then, like a tree growing amidst dusty grass, the stiff penis. She took her eyes off the lovely erection. She let her gaze rove down his shapely muscular legs to his ankles and feet, then back up his legs again to his penis. Now, as she dropped her skirt and stepped out of her panties, she focused on the stiff manhood, feeling her breasts swell with desire as Craig stroked himself.

She kicked her panties aside and went to him. She pushed his hands away, and took over stroking him. His penis delighted her.

Craig burped loudly then yawned. "Hey, what's the surprise you promised me?"

She squeezed his scrotum, then giggled. "Be patient; good things come to those who wait."

She silenced his protests by taking his penis in her mouth. Her lips closed tight and warm and wet over his glans. He let out a long gasp of air.

She worked the penis expertly, licking and sucking on the swollen shaft, running her tongue up and down the organ's underside, lifting her eyes to stare at him as her mouth caressed him, forming her thumb and index finger into a ring around the stiff rod and stroking it up and down as she sucked on its engorged head.

Craig thrust his hips off the bed and gasped. "You're killing me, baby. Just sit on it. Please?"

Ha ha ha! Now she had him exactly where she wanted him: raring to go. Instead of fulfilling his request, she unlocked her lips from his glans, squeezed his balls once, then got off the bed.

He stared at her groggily. "What're you . . . hey, come back . . ."

His eyes were red. She could tell he was barely awake. All that was keeping him awake was his erection. "Relax, I'm just going to get us some coffee."

Craig was bleary and baffled. "Coffee? At this time of the damn night?" He yawned. "Shelly, let's just screw and kiss goodnight, huh?" He yawned again. "It's been a hell of a long day."

"You shouldn't have drank so much booze. Just wait and I'll be back to give you all the loving you need."

Craig nodded. "Yeah, alright. Damn prick-tease."

Giggling, Shelly slipped out of the room and went looking for Erica.

Erica had three cups of coffee steaming in the kitchen. "How is he?" she enquired eagerly.

"If he's any more ready than he is now, we'll both get preggered with triplets tonight."

Erica slipped a hand between Shelly's legs and rubbed her genital fur. "Oooh, I can't wait."

Shelly shuddered with delight at the caresses and sagged against Erica. Erica's touch felt so nice. While Erica fingered her, she sipped her coffee. It was strong, creamy, and sweet. She didn't drink a lot though. Craig was right, it *had* been a long day. They were all long overdue for some shuteye. She didn't want to finish having sex and afterwards find herself unable to fall asleep, her eyes propped open by caffeine.

Meanwhile, her vagina felt like a bowl of cream being licked.

Erica lifted her fingers from Shelly's vagina and licked them clean. Her blue eyes sparkled with lust. "I really can't wait to fuck Craig. I mean it."

Shelly groaned. "Neither can I, baby. Let's get in there and do it." Then she laughed. "Remember I'm his girlfriend—I get first pick of the dick."

"Hey, that's pulling rank."

"Your fault, lover. Touching me like that, you've got me so hot, it feels like I'm baking bread down there."

Erica laughed. Carrying Craig's cup of coffee, they headed for the bedroom.

***

What awaited them there was an utter anticlimax.

"I don't frigging believe it!" Shelly gasped.

Erica began laughing. She found the sight so hilarious, she almost spilled hot coffee all over herself.

In Shelly's brief absence, Craig had fallen asleep. He lay snoring gently with his mouth open, his chest rising and falling.

What Erica found so funny was that Craig still had his erection. The penis stood up stiffly in the middle of him like it was a separate entity, an organism powered by something other than his brain.

"Ooh, that's a nice one," Erica said. "I like the way it curves up like a unicorn horn."

"Yeah, yeah," Shelly said testily. "Sure it's pretty, but what are we gonna do now? He won't wake up now no matter what we do. Trust me, I know that from experience—except for the boner. He rests sweet in the bosom of Queen Booze tonight."

"We'll leave him alone, I guess. We'll do it like you said—go to my room and be breast friends for a while."

"Breast friends. Yeah, I like that."

"Ooh, baby, kiss me."

"I like your tits too. No, I frigging *love* those milk factories of yours. Hey, you know what?"

"What?"

"Well, seeing as he's *already* hard . . . let's . . . you know."

"Er . . . well is that, you know, legal? Isn't it rape?"

"He's a *guy*. They *can't be* raped by us chicks. Once they're hard it means they *want* to do it. An erection implies male consent. Ask any jury."

"You sure about that?"

"No, baby, I'm just horny. And I'm fucking my boyfriend whether or not he's aware of it."

"Yeah, I guess, yeah . . . but are we sure it's ethically cool?"

"Why are we both just standing here like a bunch of nerds staring at a naked man's penis anyway? It ain't like we've never seen Little Richard before. Are we making use of it or what?"

The two young women stared at Craig's erection. The meat pole seemed to bewitch them. It called to them, begged them to touch it. They wanted to touch it. They wanted to feel its stiffness between their legs. But (mainly because of all the alcohol in their bloodstreams) both young women really felt it was a bad thing to do.

"Shelly, we're wasting time here. Let's fuck him like this. We'll be doing him a favor."

"A favor?"

"Yeah, I read it somewhere that it's dangerous for a guy to have an erection for too long. After a while they might need surgery to deflate it."

"True?"

"True."

"You sure of that?"

"For real."

"Wow, Erica, that just makes me feel so much better. Yeah, let's help Craig out then. Alright, I'll go first. No, Erica, you have first dibs; all this debating's turned my arousal burner down."

"You sure? He's your guy."

"Yeah, I'm frigging sure! Go to it, girl. I wanna watch you ride that fat dick like it was your first bicycle. Remember how you rode that machine—hard, hard, hard, all over the yard?"

"Babe, I think this coffee we're drinking's a complete waste of throat. We're both still drunk."

"So what? Who cares? It's the middle of the night, bitch. Now get up on the bed and . . . hey, wait a minute."

"What? But you said . . . You don't want me to fuck him any more?"

"No, girl, just frigging wait. I *want* you to fuck him. I *really want* you to fuck him. I just don't want you getting *pregnant* for him. I'm looking for the rubbers. You wanna get pregnant for him? Do you? Do you?"

"Nah, 'cos I'm so not into abortions. I love babies, but not before I'm ready. I'm really liberated and all that shit, but . . ."

"Yeah, I know. Contraception's a real lifesaver. Here's a rubber. First, I gotta rip the pack open. Now, I'll just slip it on the dick like this, see? See how you do it right?"

"Wow, you're real good at doing that. You could be a hooker for sure."

"Practice makes perfect and I practice a lot."

"And that's a whole lot of condoms you've got there."

"We're madly in love—we fuck a lot."

"Craig's erection looks lonely. I'd better get on it."

"Yeah, I think so too. Alright . . . yeah . . . Yeah, girl, squat over him like that and slip it in . . . Oooooh! Now, how's that feel, huh? How's that dick feel inside you, bitch? Ha ha ha! Tell me, come on, tell me!"

"Ooh, Shelly darling, it feels so *big* inside me. So filling, so deep, so niiiiccee! Oh, Shelly—I just love you. This is so . . . ooh! Ooh! Ooh!"

***

Erica bumped and ground herself over Craig. At first she bounced up and down on his penis, then she lay flat and still on him. She pressed her lips on his and stuck her tongue into his open mouth and licked his tongue. Positioned like that, her only motion was that of her hips as she rolled her crotch on his.

She came.

She gasped as the orgasm ravaged her. She gripped Craig tight. Craig meanwhile, moaned. Erica imagined it was a moan of excitement. Despite the orgasm, her vagina still ached. She couldn't understand how she felt so sexually ravenous tonight. The sleeping man's penis was still hard inside its rubber sheath inside the flesh sheath of her juicy wet sexual tissue. She sat up again on him. She placed her hands on his chest and rode him hard. Her muscular thighs jerked her soft shapely buttocks back and forth over him. Her sex tightened and loosened around his. She stared at his face, imagining his eyes were open and staring back into hers. He twitched and moaned again. This moan sounded as though he was having a bad dream.

Shelly watched bright-eyed. Contrary to the jealousy she'd imagined she'd feel on seeing Erica make love to her boyfriend, she was excited. She was surprised by how aroused she was. One hand held her coffee cup to her mouth; the other spread the lips of her sex so could finger herself. She rubbed her clitoris in time to Erica's violent risings and fallings on Craig's erection. She felt sad that Craig had fallen asleep. *Some surprise this turned out to be, huh, baby?* She considered getting her phone and making a video to show Craig what he'd missed by nodding off. Then he'd be able to get his wank on. Then she giggled. There was no point filming it. They still had Erica. Tomorrow—it was almost midnight now—there'd be more than enough time for an encore. Several encores in fact.

Erica began coming again on top of Craig. She gasped breathlessly in her orgasmic throes. She sounded like she was choking.

Feeling suddenly empowered, Shelly put down her unfinished cup of coffee on the floor. She walked over to the bed. She leaned over the bed. Erica was still gasping, her mouth open, sucking air with her tongue out. Shelly grasped her by the back of her short blonde hair and turned her face sideways. She pressed her lips hard against Erica's and pushed her tongue into her mouth. Deep inside the wet oral cavern, as far as it would go. Erica stopped moving on Craig and clung to Shelly. Still kissing her, Shelly grabbed Erica's breasts with a hand, then slid the hand down further and rubbed circles on her clitoris.

She separated her lips from Erica's. "Wow, girl, you're so wet. You're dripping like you're pissing yourself. Tell me, is the dick that great?"

"Oh yes!" Erica gasped again. "Yes it is!"

Shelly made a face. "Hey, what about me, huh?"

Erica was still gripping Shelly tightly. Now she pulled back a little and looked embarrassed. Then she laughed. "I'm being really selfish, hogging the dick like this, aren't I?"

Shelly giggled. She wasn't really upset. She'd gotten a huge kick out of watching. She was about coming herself.

Erica sagged against her. Their bare flesh, their naked breasts, rubbed together, sparking tremors of additional excitement throughout their bodies.

Shelly's desire for penetration seemed about to drive her crazy. "Alright, it's my turn now," she told Erica huskily.

Erica got off Craig's erection. At first too weak with satisfaction to stand up, she sat on the edge of the bed. Her thighs were trembling. She pulled Shelly down to her for another wet kiss. "Yes, it's your turn, baby."

Shelly eyed Craig's penis. It still seemed wood-stiff, probably the result of all that whiskey he'd drunk. Most times, when Craig was drunk he couldn't come. And with a condom on? Craig's erection twitched in its wet rubber covering.

Shelly knew she was going to orgasm the moment she got Craig into her body. She got up on the bed. She slid her right leg across his thighs. She prepared to fit his sweet organ into hers.

Then, staring at Craig's face, she froze. There was a look of intense horror on Craig's face. He looked like he was having a nightmare.

Shelly didn't think their 'raping' Craig was what was bothering him. No, this was something different. His face went back to normal again. She decided his dream horror was over. She settled herself over his crotch and grasped his penis.

Erica, meanwhile, had slipped off the bed. She now lay on her back on the floor. Sweat was beaded all over her skin. One of her hands fondled her crotch, the other caressed her breasts.

"This is crazy, Shelly," she gasped as her fingers slid back and forth through her pubic hair. "I don't know what's got into me tonight. I'm not normally this horny. I know I've wanted to make love to you for ages, but . . . It's like there was an aphrodisiac in the food they served us at the diner. The more we do it, the more I wanna do it."

"Yeah," Shelly agreed. "I feel just like you do."

Lying there on the rug, Erica couldn't see Craig's face. Shelly could, and it was putting a major damper on her sexual ardor. She had Craig's stiff member in her hand (the organ slick with Erica's juices), its fat tip poised at the entrance to her body. But she couldn't go through with it. Craig looked like he was being tortured in his sleep. She felt it would be cruel to subject him to the dubious pleasures of an unknown fuck when it already looked like he was suffering.

With deep regret, she let go of his penis.

Erica, fingers deep in her sex, heard the released penis slap wetly against Craig's belly. She looked up at Shelly. Shelly was climbing down off the bed.

"What's wrong?" Erica asked.

"Oh, nothing," Shelly lied. "I want *you* tonight, not him."

She pulled Erica to her feet. She was careful to block off Erica's view of Craig's face. She herself looked back and grimaced. His face was distorted with angst. Whatever Craig was dreaming about had to be really horrible.

One hand on Erica's buttocks, she steered the blonde to the bedroom door. "Let's go be breast friends in *your* room. No point waking him up with our moaning."

Erica kissed her. Erica was kissing her a lot. Shelly liked that.

"Don't you think we should take the condom off him?" Erica asked when they were outside in the hallway.

Shelly considered it. "Nah, let's just go. I'll tell him he fell asleep while we were doing it. Drunk as he is, he's not gonna remember a thing about tonight."

They laughed.

Shelly pulled Erica after her. "Hurry. I'll go mad if I don't feel your tongue between my legs soon."

CHAPTER 16

Craig

Craig was having a nightmare.

Two things were exactly the same in his dream as in the real world. First, he was naked, and second, he had an erection.

In fact, his dream erection was the source of his real-world erection.

In his dream he was knocking on Death's door. Literally. Death lived in a mansion built of ancient decaying stone. Craig was knocking on its front door.

A corpse opened the door and let Craig in. "Welcome to Enlightenment," it said.

The house smelt musty and old. The corpse servant smelt musty and old as well. Craig couldn't tell if it was male or female. It was too rotted and shriveled for gender differentiation.

The corpse pointed to Craig's erect penis. "Hard, huh?"

He nodded. "Yes, hard. Very."

"Follow me," it said. "Death is waiting for you."

They walked through the house, which was filled with gothic furniture. Craig was worried. Death killed people and here he was going voluntarily to meet it.

The corpse sensed his fears. It turned to him and smiled wryly, drawing its dry and cracked lips over its equally dry and cracked teeth. "Don't worry," it said, "you're not going to die. Death just wants to tell you something."

On that cue, it pushed open the red door they'd just reached.

Craig stepped inside.

He was in Death's throne room.

The room was large, with a black floor and more gothic furniture, mostly chairs arranged to form an aisle to Death's throne. Its walls were obscured in shadows.

Craig walked towards Death.

Death's throne was made from human bones and skin, bound together with dried human guts. She was naked. She had the most incredible body Craig had ever seen in his life—even porn stars came nowhere close. Her bosom, hips, behind, legs, all were perfect down to the tiniest detail. Just like Daria the Crossway proprietress, Death had long white hair.

But Death also had the most horrible face Craig had ever seen in his life. A face that could literally kill one with fright.

Seeing her face, Craig felt every fear he'd ever known come rushing in on him at once.

"Welcome, Craig," Death said. She gestured to the corpse. "Leave us, Henry." Her voice was old and raspy, the blowing of a winter wind through the trees in a graveyard.

Her eyes bulged like those of a frog. They were yellow, with slit pupils like a serpent's. Her nose looked like an erection—a fat, six-inch-long tube. However, her mouth was the worst of all. It seemed to be an unhealed wound, a horrible gash in her lower face, with broken glass stuck in it to serve as teeth. She had no lips. Her tongue looked like a cut of raw liver. Her whole face—tubular nose and all—was covered by an ugly network of fat and knotted veins. She looked utterly revolting, a nightmare sculpted in dead white flesh.

Craig just managed to overcome his natural impulse to throw up. If Death wasn't about to kill him, he saw no need to give her a reason to want to.

She got down from her throne and walked towards him. The perfection of her body struck him speechless. Never had a screen goddess in all of Hollywood's history had a body like Death's.

But, oh God, that horrendous face!

She reached him and licked his cheek. She licked him from cheek to forehead. Her breath was rotten. It reeked of dead things and shit.

"You're hard," Death said, gripping his penis.

"Yes!" he gasped and almost ejaculated. Her touch was obscenely magical. She was obscenely desirable. The body of Venus amplified and the face that sank a thousand ships.

"I'm the original hot-body model for the Love Goddess," Death said. "But then, just like Medusa, at some point I pissed the Almighty off." She laughed. "No, that's a lie. The Old Guy In The Sky just thought my job would be easier with a kisser that scared people to death."

She let go of his penis. "Come with me," she said, turning and walking the opposite way, past her throne of bones and skin. "There's a woman here who wants to talk to you."

He followed her to a black door. Death pushed the door open then pushed him through it. "She's in there. Goodbye, Craig—I'm sure I'll be seeing you soon."

Frightened by her words, he turned back. "Hey, what do you mean by that?"

She frowned. "You'll see. Now if you'll excuse me . . ."

The door shut in his face.

"Turn around." The request was female.

He turned around.

It was the woman from the Crossway Diner, the one in the white dress who'd spent twenty or so minutes walking around the parking lot trying to get a cellphone signal. Her dress was red with blood now, as well as ripped-to-shreds. Her body was similarly torn up. Flaps of her skin hung through her dress, revealing her broken ribs and savaged innards. As if a maniac had attacked her with a drill, her neck and breasts were perforated through by a multitude of holes.

Craig stated the obvious. "You're dead."

"Yes, I am dead," she agreed. "And Death brought me back to undeath to warn you." She pointed to his crotch. "You're hard, man."

He nodded. "Yes, I am. It won't go down."

The dead woman giggled. "Erica loves it, you know."

"Huh?" Her comment made no sense to him. "You said you have to warn me. Warn me about what?"

"About Daria and the Crossway Diner. About the food there."

"What about the food there?"

"Come closer," she said meaningfully.

He closed the distance between them.

"Give me your hand," she demanded. It was an order.

He gave her his hand. She lifted it to her mouth. He expected her to bite him, but instead she began gagging as if she were going to throw up. Then she spat something into his hand. Something that squirmed with life.

"Look," she said.

He looked. There were three maggots in his hand. Big and white and glistening with the dead woman's saliva.

He stood looking at the maggots. "What are these?"

"The eternal worms—minions of the Maggot King; he who dares to feed upon the flesh of the living. They're in you too now. In you and the two girls as well, now that you've eaten Daria's cooking. They infect everyone who eats Daria's food. They're growing in you, coming to maturity in your body. Soon they'll be looking to come out of you into the world. It's going to be very embarrassing."

Craig's unease and fright, both of which had reduced considerably since the corpse butler had assured him that Death didn't intend to kill him, now returned magnified. He gaped at the dead woman. "You're saying that there are grubs growing inside me now?"

"Yes."

"How do we stop them? How . . . ?"

She winced. "I don't know."

"You don't know? Wh-why ask to see me then?"

She laughed. With all the holes in her neck, the laugh sounded fluty. She pointed to his erection. "To tell the truth, I really just wanted to see what your dick looked like hard."

"What?"

"I noticed you over in Daria's place and thought you looked rather cute, with your hard construction-worker body; and now that I'm dead . . ." She licked her lips. "Nice, nice cock. I like it very much. It's neither too big nor too small, and isn't too veiny either. Most penises are only acceptable to a woman because she loves the man they're attached to, see? I like how yours tapers from root to head, and it's nicely curved too. You'd fit nicely into my penis Hall of Fame—I mean, into my pussy."

He was very confused. "You mean . . . you pulled me into your dream, I mean, you entered *my* dream . . . whatever . . . just to look at my erection?"

She nodded coyly. "Us dead women gotta have some perks now and then. "Ooh, I'd love to suck you off, get messy with your sperm all over my face." She scowled. But Death won't allow it."

"No, I won't." Death's voice was coming from somewhere overhead. "Look but don't suck. That was our agreement."

The dead woman shrugged at Craig. *See?*

The maggots were still squirming on Craig's palm. One of them was biting him. Disgusted, he made a fist and squashed them, then opened his hand so she could see their white mush. "Ah, so *this* is just a joke, right?" He flipped the mess off into the darkness.

She'd begun to melt into black liquid now. Like a votive candle shoved into the flame of a blowtorch. The right side of her face was already flowing down over her breasts. Her left arm dropped off and fell to the ground where it turned into bubbling black jelly.

"Answer me!" he demanded desperately as she dissolved. "This stuff about the maggots and Daria's cooking—you're joking, right? We're not really all full of grubs now, are we? You were just joking!?"

She smiled with what remained of her mouth. "I might be lying, kiddo, and I might not be. Don't worry. You'll find out soon enough."

Which was almost exactly what Death had earlier told him. Intense fear flooded his mind. "Please, tell me! Please! . . . Please?"

"No, it'd be a waste of time. Believe me, baby, it really doesn't matter. You're not going to remember any of this when you wake up anyway. You won't remember a thing, so why should I waste my breath telling you? Besides, I'm almost completely melted away now."

Then she giggled. "But I gotta tell you one last time, that's one hell of a nice penis you've got on you, boy."

Then she was all gone, a frothy black jelly that flowed to merge with the tiles on the floor. He dully noted that the tiles were arranged like a chessboard, black and white, and that the dead woman had merged with the black tiles.

He stared down at his erection. It was still as hard as stone. Despite his horror, he felt a twinge of pride. No woman had ever praised his penis to him like the dead woman had.

Then he was seized by a sudden fit of coughing. Violent spasms racked his chest and he was forced to bend over.

Something flew out of his mouth and dropped to the floor. He bent to stare at it.

He was horrified. It was a maggot. A large abnormal maggot that had Daria Simpson's face.

Staring at the maggot (with Death's mocking laughter echoing all around him), Craig felt paralyzed with fear. He was so terrified he imagined his muscles were turning to water. He looked down at himself. It was true; he *was* becoming liquid. He was melting like a candle, becoming a pale translucent goop. He was flowing away and merging with the checkered floor's white tiles.

He began yelling for help, while the maggot with Daria's face laughed at him with Death's hag voice.

CHAPTER 17

Shelly and Erica

"Welcome to advanced Dykesville, slut. You're about to be handballed. Hope you got a big pussy—you're gonna need it."

Erica's words rang through Shelly's head. Erica's right hand slid an inch further into Shelly's vagina. Then it entered even further. Shelly felt stretched to her utmost already, and yet her body was stretching even more to accommodate the penetrating hand, greedily yawning ever wider.

She gasped. They were on Erica's mattress. She lay on her back with her legs spread wide and her head lifted by a pillow so she could watch what was being done to her. She followed Erica's actions with interest, entranced by the hand that was opening her up. The hand was slick with a lubricant Erica had had in her bag. Erica seemed prepared for everything. Shelly wondered if Erica had a strap-on in her bag too.

She felt . . . she didn't know how she felt. At first the hand in her sex had hurt a little and she'd bit her lip in protest. She'd considered asking Erica to stop. But then she'd felt an aftershock of pleasure, as if the nerves in her stretched sex had initially been scared of the unfamiliar vaginal invasion and had only just realized that it was actually something to enjoy.

Now she gasped again, this time with delight and wonder. Wonder that her body could accomplish this. She was filled with expectancy for whatever came next.

"Wow, you're tight," Erica said. "I don't think you can take me. Some girls just can't. Hey—you want me to stop?"

As her response, Shelly grabbed hold of Erica's right wrist with both hands. Slowly but surely, she pulled the fist fully into herself. "I *can* take you, darling," she grunted. "I *want* to take you."

And now here I am, she thought dreamily, *with another woman's hand stuffed past the wrist inside my pussy. And I thought extreme stuff like this only happened in porn.*

Being filled like this—topped to the brim, fully occupied—was so overwhelming that she froze for a moment. Once again it felt like her nerves needed to adjust to her vagina's new sensations. Once she was over 'the hump' as it were, she collapsed back and let her body go limp. She made certain to relax her sexual muscles. Erica had already warned her that this was key.

She worried for a moment: *Will I ever enjoy Craig again after this?* She dismissed her worry as silly. Erica said she'd herself been fisted often, and yet she still enjoyed men. In fact, she claimed, if you did it right and worked on your kegels afterwards, fisting could even help tighten up your vagina. Shelly doubted that—widening wasn't tightening by a long shot—but tonight she wasn't going to protest.

She felt . . . she felt . . .

Erica spat on her hand to lube it up some more. Slowly and gently, she began moving it in and out of Shelly's body.

"How do you feel?" she asked.

Shelly grabbed her breasts. "Like I'm floating!" she gasped. "That's the only way I can describe it. I don't feel like I'm going to come, but . . . Oh, oh . . . Yeeessssss! Do it like that!"

Erica licked her lips. "Yes, I knew you'd enjoy being fisted. I could taste it in your kisses."

"Stop talking and do it. Kiss me some more."

Grinning Erica got down to really sliding her hand in and out of Shelly's vagina. The orifice spread in delighted welcome around her fist as she slid it in, then sucked at it in dejected farewell as she drew it out again. In, out, in, out. Every now and then, she'd twist her wrist and Shelly would groan like mad.

Shelly felt as though she were dreaming. The fist in her sex was a force to be reckoned with. It was an energy that couldn't be ignored. The irresistible force and she a very movable object. Erica's fist controlled her. It dominated her. It took her to places she'd always wished to go, but had lacked the courage to explore. As it slid in and out of her wet passage, it lifted her, lifted her, lifted her. She gasped and moaned and jerked and trembled and kicked and . . . The fist owned her. It controlled her body—she was its sexual puppet.

"Just relax and enjoy yourself, girl," Erica instructed as she fisted Shelly. "Don't pressurize yourself to have an orgasm. Me? Sometimes I come during fisting, lots of times I don't—it's more about the journey than the destination. If you don't climax, I'll eat your pussy again. Alright?"

"Yes, oh God yes! Yes!"

And that was when it happened:

Shelly almost swooned in surprise. Suddenly she was no longer in Marty's spare bedroom. Instead, she was in a shadowy boudoir, spread-eagled on a queen-sized four-poster bed that was covered in black velvet sheets and canopied with black drapes.

She was still being fisted, but now it was Daria, the woman from the diner, who was pleasuring her.

Oh, the feeling was so good!

Daria was herself naked except for a thong. Her white hair covered her breasts, concealing her nipples. Shelly was jealous: In the buff, Daria was truly gorgeous.

The woman had a worryingly intense look on her face, however. The intensity of her gaze scared Shelly. She seemed very hungry. She looked very angry. Most frightening of all, Daria looked nasty, like she intended to do Shelly grievous bodily harm during or after their lovemaking.

Her small hand slid in and out of Shelly's vagina.

"Feed me! Feed me!" she said.

Shelly didn't understand the woman's demand. She was scared stiff of Daria. Despite which, she was about to have an orgasm.

Sensing this, Daria fisted her faster and faster.

"Feed me! Feed me!" Her eyes were colder than a corpse in a morgue locker. She licked her lips. Her teeth were strange now, gleaming and longer than they should be. They were shiny silver like tiny knives.

Shelly thought Daria might be thinking of biting her. She had to get away from her, get away from here, from this dark room of shadows and this dangerous white-haired beauty. But the beauty's fist was inside her and, oh God, it felt like it *belonged* inside her.

Shelly came. She came like she'd never come before. She came like a cloistered virgin being ravished by the pirate lover she'd always fantasized about.

All she saw during her orgasm, however, were Daria's gray eyes. Lovely eyes that seemed to suck the marrow from her bones. Beautiful eyes that seemed to drain the blood from her veins with their ghastly glance. Seductive eyes that seemed to greedily tear the flesh off her body . . .

But her terror did nothing to halt her climax or lessen its intensity.

At the acme of her orgasm, when it felt like she'd been vacuumed up into Daria's cannibalistic gaze, she passed out.

As she fainted, she heard Daria demanding, "Feed me! Feed me!"

***

She awoke to find Erica kissing her. She still felt some terror and dread, but now she understood that it had all been just a dream.

"So how was it?" Erica enquired. "You fainted when you came."

Shelly giggled. "Were you scared?"

"A little. When you came, your pussy squeezed tight on my hand, I mean, *painfully* tight. Then your eyes rolled back in your head and you were out cold. I was worried, but then I saw you were breathing normally. So I just pulled out of you and waited."

"Damn!" Shelly exclaimed. "I don't think I've ever come that hard in my life." She relaxed. Erica lay alongside her, leaning up on an elbow to peer into her eyes. Erica's eyes were pretty, Shelly thought, but nowhere as pretty as Daria's. Daria had utterly stupendous eyes. Eyes that ate you up. She felt her dream terror returning—her fright at Daria's demand to be 'fed.'

She forced herself to stop thinking about the lovely woman.

Shelly felt herself between the legs. She felt normal there. Her vagina wasn't the gaping postpartum hole she'd expected would result from fisting. She felt expanded but normal. She wasn't overly wide.

She ached though. She didn't know if she was aching because she'd been overfilled, or if she ached to be filled some more. Whichever was the case, it felt very nice to be sated but able to go on. She stroked Erica's face. She felt like they could keep making love all night long if they wanted to and their desire for one another wouldn't lessen, no matter how many orgasms they each had.

But she was tired in a non-sexual way. She glanced at a clock over on Marty's computer table.

She kissed Erica. "It's half-past-twelve. We'd better get some sleep."

Erica nodded. "Where do you wanna bed down—here or with boyfriend?"

Shelly giggled and snuggled close to Erica. "I'm staying here with you, girl. Tonight, there's no place else in the world that I'd rather be."

"And here I was, thinking you were straight."

"I'm *still* straight. Well, okay, I'm partly straight and partly gay now, if that makes sense."

"It does. Alright, darling, enough yapping. Go to sleep, both of us."

"Goodnight, slut."

"Goodnight, slut."

***

Twenty minutes later, they were both still as clear-eyed as ever.

"It's the damn coffee. We shouldn't have drank so much."

"Seemed like a great idea at the time."

"Yes, it did."

"You wanna make love again?"

"Nah, let's just talk. Tell me about yourself."

"Hmmm, what do you wanna know?"

"Your heartbreak. What happened to you? I know it was *really* bad, but you've never told me what the jerk did to you. . . . Yeah, so what did happen to hurt you so much? Did he abuse you? Did he screw your best friend? Did he get her pregnant? Did he get you pregnant and run off? Did he give you a disease? . . . Oops—sorry, I didn't mean that last one like that."

"No, no, no! Nothing like that. John *wouldn't ever* do that to me."

"What then?"

"He died."

"He died? Oh my God. Oh, Erica, I'm so sorry. I'm so, so sorry. I had no idea. I-I-I I shouldn't't've—"

"Look, stop apologizing. Do you wanna hear what happened or not? I feel like I can talk about it now with you. I can tell you *now*. I might not be able to do so in the morning."

"O.K., I'm all ears."

"It happened eight months ago. His name was John Parks and I loved him with all my heart and he loved me with all his heart. We were gonna get married and live happily ever after and have a million kids. And then one horrible Sunday morning, as he was leaving my house . . .

***

Erica and John had agreed to meet that night for dinner, then kissed their goodbyes.

John Parks was a Canadian Business major at Ohio University. He was tall and muscular, with happy green eyes and blonde hair. He and Erica had been dating for a year and a half and things were going great between them. Their future together looked bright.

Departing from Erica, John hadn't been watching where he was going. Still waving to her, he'd stepped backward out into the road, straight into the path of a swerving black Honda pickup truck. John tried to jump out of the way, but it didn't do any good.

The driver of the pickup had been having a heart attack. With his heart feeling like it was tearing apart, the man had pumped on the brake to slow the truck, then, when another spasm hit, pumped on the gas again. Then the brake, then again the gas. He could hardly breathe and was having crazy spasms and was so dizzy that he couldn't see where he was going or even control his arms and legs anymore.

The black truck smashed into John. Unfortunately, it wasn't going fast enough to knock him out of its way. John Parks had a single view of the guy behind the wheel throwing up his hands as if to ward off death, then he was under the vehicle, unconscious and with half the bones in his legs already broken. Then his real bad fortune hit: His belt got snagged on a piece of metal jutting from the pickup truck's undercarriage, so that instead of simply running over him, the vehicle dragged him along over the blacktop for over a hundred yards.

The truck skidded left and right across the road, riding the curbs and scattering traffic in the oncoming lane as its driver finally slumped down in his seat and died. The runaway vehicle stopped ten yards later. At a speed bump.

Behind the pickup truck was a long line of blood and intestines from when John Parks had burst open.

Erica had screamed when the pickup truck initially hit her boyfriend. When it passed her by and John didn't reappear on the ground behind it, she'd begun running after the vehicle, yelling at the dying man behind the wheel to stop, for God's sake. The trail of blood the departing vehicle was leaving on the road had unnerved her with its implications.

Once she'd had to duck out of the way of a blue Nissan SUV driven by a blonde with two kids in the back. The blonde mother, herself terrified and shrieking, had swerved left to avoid the black pickup truck and was now driving on the wrong side of the road. She swerved back into her own lane again just before she'd have hit the USPS truck turning off the street corner.

When Erica reached the stalled pickup truck, she saw no sign of John. What she did see was a large ball of meat on the ground, just under the rear bumper. This large ball of meat had two littler white balls stuck in it, and some hair at one end.

Then Erica realized that what she was staring at was John's severed head. His face had been completely ripped off; the two white balls were his eyes.

At that sight, the universe collapsed around Erica. She fainted.

The ambulances arrived.

What was left of John Parks by now was hardly recognizable as human at first glance. It was hard to tell even if he'd been black or white. In addition to bursting open like a squashed blood sausage, while trapped under the truck the young man had been skinned. He'd been pulverized into homo sapien mush. (The skin on his head and face had apparently been ripped off because, after his head had been severed, it had gotten 'stuck' in a cranny under the vehicle where it had begun bouncing like a basketball.)

His liquefied brains were dripping from the undercarriage like oil spillage.

The two male paramedics to first arrive on the scene had leaned over puking. Their female colleague took one look at the stripped head and immediately joined Erica in her faint.

Erica's faint was the only reason she'd not instantly gone crazy. Heartbreak didn't even begin to qualify what she'd felt. She'd felt dead, like she'd burst and been emptied along with John. She'd felt like *she* was the one strewn along the road, her heart and liver and soul ground up in that gory mess that could never be reassembled into a whole person again.

She'd felt like killing herself.

She'd been in hospital for a week under intense sedation. And once out, it had been two whole months before she could leave home unsupervised. During that first two-month period, each time she'd see the road in front of her house, she'd relive the whole horrible experience and slump again.

***

"For four months, I was a total wreck," Erica finished. "My psyche was so bound up with John's that I kept seeing him in my dreams. I'd nod off in a chair and he'd be there with me . . . holding me and kissing me . . . telling me how I shouldn't worry, that he was going to talk his parents over into approving of me . . ."

She began sobbing on Shelly's shoulder.

Shelly held her tight against the night of her memories. "That's really horrible," she said. "I never even suspected you were bottling all that up inside of you."

They'd dimmed the lights now, and yet, somehow, the night felt like it had just gotten darker. Everywhere Shelly looked were pools of shadows. The vague illumination coming in through the drapes made Marty's PCs and accessories look like an invading alien force.

Erica wiped her eyes. "I'm better now. A whole lot better."

"But to go through so much pain! I couldn't ever stand losing Craig that way; I'd kill myself for sure. It'd be easier if I wasn't there, or if he got shot by someone. But watching him die like that . . . just listening to you makes me wanna start crying myself."

Erica smiled sadly. "When John died, I felt like I'd died along with him. That's why I wear this necklace." She felt her neck for the gold pendant. "John gave it to me for Christmas. It has a locket and I keep his picture inside it so . . ."

Then she sat bolt upright and gaped at Shelly. She looked horrified. "Shelly, my gold necklace is gone!"

Shelly sat upright too and gaped back at Erica. "But how? You never take it off."

Erica leapt up off the mattress and began ransacking her bag. "No, it's not here! It's not here!" She turned and stared at Shelly again, worry written all over her face. "How could I possibly have thrown it away? Where in the world can it be now?" She pointed towards the bedroom door. "Do you think it snapped off in Craig's car?" She got to her feet and grabbed her pants. "You can wait—I'll go check."

Shelly watched her pull her pants on for a moment, then said, "Stop. The necklace isn't in the car."

Erica stopped pulling her pants on. She gave Shelly her full attention. "How can you be so sure?"

"'Cos I know both *when* and *where* it came off your neck."

"Where? When?"

"In the ladies' toilet at the Crossway, while we were . . ." She couldn't resist chortling.

At first Erica looked both bothered and unconvinced. However, after a few seconds she visibly relaxed. An inquiring look entered her eyes. "You're *sure* you saw it?"

Shelly nodded. "Sorry, it's my fault for forgetting. It happened around the time when the restroom lights began flickering." She grinned. "And you'd just come and we were kissing and it felt so damn good that . . . Well, I filed it in memory—I figured I'd get it for you afterwards."

Erica slid her jeans off her feet again. "Where exactly did it drop to?"

"It's behind the toilet bowl. Remember your head was pressed against the cistern and your butt was out on the rim of the toilet. Positioned like that, the necklace fell straight down."

"Someone might find it and claim it for their own. It's pure 24-carat gold, damned expensive."

Shelly waved off the comment. "Don't worry, it'll still be there in the morning. It's well hidden where it is. I think one reason I didn't remember to tell you was because I didn't see it again when we stood up. That and the flickering lights, of course." She pulled Erica down to her again. "Don't worry about it—come morning, we drive over and pick it up. It'll still be there, you'll see."

Erica sighed. "We'll have to go real early though, before the cleaner starts work. I don't want it getting tangled up in the guy's mop."

"Okay, we'll leave as early as we can. Now just *relax*. You're so stressed out, I'm thinking I'll have to make love to you again to relax you."

"I just feel so . . . incomplete without it, that's all."

Shelly watched her in the half-darkness. Erica's face was strained. She looked sad, lost. Shelly's heart went out to her. She couldn't imagine what Erica had suffered, seeing the love of her life being shredded to pieces in front of her like that. She utterly sympathized with Erica. "I understand. It must be really hard for you. But we'll get it back. Once the sun's up, we'll jump in the car and drive over there. And if they aren't open yet, we'll go back later. Thank heavens it's just outside town. Imagine if we had to drive all the way back to that greasy spoon in Harrisburg, Pennsylvania to get it."

Erica pulled herself up on her elbows. "There's something unsettling about all this," she said. "Something I can't understand."

"What do you mean?"

She frowned. "Shelly, I've worn that necklace for six months without taking it off. I laminated John's tiny picture so it's waterproof—I have my bath with the necklace on. It's almost a part of me. So how could I have not noticed that it came off my neck? Okay, yes . . . I *have* taken it off a few times—each time I felt naked until I put it back on. So how could I . . . ?"

"That's easy enough to answer: It's because you were already naked then and had my fingers tucked up your vajayjay. Reason with me, darling; you honestly can't feel more naked than that, can you?"

"Yes . . . no, I mean no. Okay, I'll concede that. But how do you explain the rest of it?"

"What rest?"

"Well, for one thing, I didn't notice my necklace's absence all the way here." She raised a finger to forestall Shelly's grinning comment. "No, don't say it."

"I wasn't going to say anything."

"You were about to say I had afterglow amnesia, right?"

"Not really."

"Yes, you were."

"Oh, alright, I was. It could be that."

"O.K., so let's say I agree with that too: that my delight at finally getting in your pants made me forget John's gift to me. Let's also say that my amnesia was made worse by my anticipation of bedding you again?"

"Yes, that's reasonable enough. But what're you getting at exactly?" Shelly yawned. "Oh, thank God. The damn coffee is wearing off." She reached out a hand and tweaked Erica's left nipple. "Yeah, girl, what's bothering you? You're so wrinkled with thought, you're beginning to look like a raisin."

"The third problem," Erica said, "is this: Okay, even leaving out all the time we spent over at Karen and Andy's place . . . we can excuse that too by saying we were drinking and talking, right?"

Shelly yawned again. "Darling, just say it—we need to fall asleep before the sleep thinks we're uninterested in it and leaves again."

"O.K. O.K." She looked worried again. "Baby, we've both been naked for two hours straight now. How is it possible that in all that time—through all that sex—I never noticed the necklace was gone? And please, don't you dare say it's because the sex was utterly mind-blowing."

"But it was; it really was. The ghost of your fist still haunts my vajayjay."

"Oh, how our swollen private parts affect our silly hearts. Biatch, stop thinking with your snatch and just answer my damn question: How did I not notice all that while? That's what I need to understand."

Shelly furrowed her brow in thought. "Hmmm, that's a good question. . . . Maybe you've subconsciously gotten over your loss? If that's the case, then your not noticing the necklace's absence would be completely natural."

Erica frowned at that, so Shelly quickly added, "No, don't retort yet—I'm not finished. Or, if it's not that . . . well there's this documentary I once saw about a person's subconscious blocking or filtering out things that might offend them or cause a relapse or whatever . . ." Yawning again, she turned her full gaze on Erica. Erica was yawning too, but she also had a stubborn look on her face, a look that said she'd solve this mystery even if it kept her awake all night long.

"Okay, tell me. Have you really gotten over losing John? I mean, *really?*"

"I . . . I think I have. I'm sure I have. I'd like to think so. But . . ." she sighed. "I don't know. If I lose that pendant, I'll feel like I've once again lost a part of myself."

Shelly pounced on Erica's admission. She was really tired now and also tired of discussing this. So Erica had forgotten she had a necklace on. So what? Once the vagina was suitably inflamed the brain shut down operations. Many times when a woman was in that aroused state, bad decisions were made, some of which lasted a lifetime.

Merely losing a pendant was hardly a criminal offence. "That's it then," she said triumphantly. "Because you wanted to fuck me and Craig and not feel guilty that you were betraying John's memory, your subconscious mind simply blanked memory of him out. That way you could have fun with us and not feel bad about it."

Erica looked unconvinced. But thankfully (so far as Shelly was concerned), she yawned again, long and loud. Shelly peered deep into her throat. Erica still had her tonsils.

Erica kept yawning. Shelly took this interval to look across the room at Marty's banks of computers, and beyond them, out at the soft spring night. She couldn't see the moon, but a large tree in the back yard reflected its silver glow off its leaves. Somewhere an owl hooted.

"You really think that's it?" Erica asked when she was through yawning, her eyes now close to nighttime shutdown. "That I forgot about it because I *didn't want* to remember? But that's just horrible."

"You forgot it because you didn't want to hurt yourself," Shelly gently corrected her. "Because your subconscious or unconscious or whatever the shrinks call it didn't want you going nuts over post-orgasmic guilt. You haven't been with anyone since John died, have you?"

Erica shook her head. "I've been too scared."

"See? So that's definitely it. Well, I think it makes more sense than the alternative explanation, which would be that you forgot you had a gold necklace and pendant on because 'something' (she made quote marks with her fingers) or 'someone' (more finger quote marks) made you forget about it." She grinned at Erica. "Or do you prefer *that* explanation?"

Erica smirked sleepily. "You're too smart for your own good. You should be a shrink, not a waitress on her way to becoming a desperate housewife." She snuggled close to Shelly and drew a duvet up over them both. She was suddenly very tired, in addition to which Shelly's overelaborate answer had achieved its intended aim of confusing her. She no longer cared about how/why she'd forgotten her most prized possession for four-and-a-half hours. It was enough to know that they'd retrieve it in the morning. At the moment, she just wanted to sleep, sleep, sleep. The sleep felt like peace welling up inside her.

She leaned over and kissed Shelly on the lips. She kissed her for a long time. Shelly moaned and groaned beside her and her nipples hardened. Then she yawned, breathing into Erica's mouth. Erica didn't mind. Their lips touching, she yawned back, equally long and hard into Shelly's mouth. They each breathed the other's exhaled air back and forth for a while.

"Oh," Shelly said when they separated, "and, don't you dare wake me up in the morning with your hand inside my pussy."

"If that's a fisting invitation, you slut, I'm not biting the bait. Now go to sleep."

"Love you, slut."

"Love you too, slut."

CHAPTER 18

Craig

It was just past seven in the morning when Craig woke up. The sun was high, the air was warm. Sunday had begun in earnest and was waiting for him to join it.

He yawned and sat up. He had a bad hangover. He rubbed his eyes. He saw that he was naked and remembered why that was. He and Shelly had been about to . . .

Then he noticed the condom on his penis. His penis was flaccid and the condom was halfway off it.

He pulled the condom fully off himself then sniffed it. It smelt musky, and more revealingly, had a thin dry 'lady crust' on it. Also, the rubber was empty of semen, meaning he hadn't come. He didn't feel like ejaculating at the moment anyway. Maybe later, when his head had stopped ringing its church bells.

He dropped the condom on the floor by the bed. *I must've fallen asleep right after she came,* he thought grinning. He searched his aching brain for the memory of Shelly's soft sexy body sliding over his. He came up empty. He couldn't remember zilch about their lovemaking last night. He figured he'd remember later, when his mind was in better shape to think. He sighed. *Did she give me her 'big surprise' or not?* He'd have liked to recall that at least.

And, he wondered, *where is Shelly anyway? Oh, she's probably outside on the front porch with Erica.*

He needed to pee. Urgently. He leapt down off the bed and staggered into the bathroom. The bathroom had light-green wall tiles. He leaned on them to steady himself. He felt weak, like he should really still be sleeping. While urinating, he stared out of the bathroom window, at the back yard. The cottage grounds extended fifty yards back, to a border of ferns encroaching over a blue picket fence.

Birdsong rang out from the single tall tree out there. He couldn't see the birds. It sounded like they were all up on high branches.

Craig finished peeing. He found the happy bird chirping depressing. It wasn't helping his hangover any. He flushed then washed his hands. A little more stable on his feet now, he made his way back into the bedroom. Might as well pull on his pants and go sit with the girls.

That was when he saw the note on the dresser. Brown cosmetic pencil on pink paper, Shelly's cursive handwriting:

Baby, I've gone with Erica to look for her necklace at the Crossway Diner. She lost it there yesterday. We took the Ford. Be back shortly. Love you loads. P.S. I told you not to frigging drink so damn much. You ruined my surprise!!

The message was signed with a lipstick kiss and two hearts.

Erica lost her necklace at the diner? Craig shrugged. Well, no need to hurry outside then. He crossed back to the bed and sat down again. He was still trying to wake up, booting his mental PC. Damn, his head ached. And now he also felt a bit sick.

In addition, he felt troubled. Shelly's mention of the Crossway in her note had reminded him of his nightmare. Or rather, reminded him that he'd had a nightmare: he couldn't remember anything about it other than that he'd been terrified in it. Even now, as he searched his memory for strands of the nighttime vision, the dream's terror returned. But that was all that came to him. Beyond that, all his questing brain encountered was a blankness populated by an ethereal psychic disquiet.

He was certain, however, that the dream had had something to do with the Crossway Diner. The diner . . . Had he dreamt about Daria? It was quite possible that he had. But then, they'd been drinking with the crazy couple next door, who'd told them that creepy joke about Daria Simpson having died two years earlier. Which was most likely *why* he'd had the nightmare in the first place.

Craig smirked now. *Yeah, sure, she's dead. And we ate dinner at the Cemetery Diner.*

But he still felt uneasy, illogical as that was. His stomach felt unsettled too. He felt close to throwing up.

Craig reasoned matters over for a moment. Andy and Karen's tale was clearly B.S., but still, he couldn't shake his odd feeling. He was worried about Shelly and Erica. He hoped they'd not run into trouble on the way to the diner. He figured he'd better call them. He looked around for his phone, but couldn't see it.

Aw, c'mon now! Where'd I drop the damn thing?

Then he saw the cellphone. It was poking out from under the dresser shelves. One of Shelly's brown canvas sneakers was half-covering it.

The moment he got up to get the phone, his unsettled stomach did a double flip. Puke alert! Craig hurried into the bathroom again and bent over the toilet vomiting. The nausea seemed to be coming from inside his head. It was so intense that, dizzy, he sank to his knees beside the green ceramic bowl, shut his eyes, and trusted to the heavens that he'd survive the massive surge of regurgitation.

Finally, the vomiting stopped. He spat out the last bitter chunks of vileness, then stood up with his brain throbbing and a horrible taste in his mouth, and peered blearily into the toilet bowl, his vision temporarily hampered by a splitting headache. He dully acknowledged the disgusting pink and white mess in the toilet bowl. Last night's dinner revisited, along with a whole lot of wasted whiskey.

Craig blinked and flushed. The mess vanished. He was relieved: for a moment there it had seemed as if part of the vomit was alive and squirming.

(Had Craig taken the time to properly examine what he'd just thrown up, he'd have been shocked to discover that there were indeed live maggots in his vomit. The pale larvae actually comprised about forty-percent of the puke.)

His stomach felt settled now. His hangover had also given up trying to kill him. He rinsed out his mouth at the sink, then gargled fiercely with some Listerine he found in the medicine chest. He was still unsteady on his feet, but the headache was receding; he no longer needed to keep his eyes shut to maintain his balance.

While he'd been throwing up, his dream had come to his mind again. But once again, he couldn't remember the details, only that it had been nasty.

Feeling his way like a blind man, he walked unsteadily back into the bedroom. *Yes, I need to call Shelly.*

He stepped towards his phone, miscalculated his step, and almost trod on a half-empty cup of coffee.

Where'd that come from?

Nonetheless, he was glad of his good fortune in finding it. He picked up the cup of coffee and took a sip from it. Not bad, even it was cold: lots of sugar, lots of cream. His stomach heaved in protest as he drank it, but it was merely a reflex. He wouldn't throw up again. He'd purged himself for the moment.

He finished the coffee, retrieved his cellphone, then noticed another cup of coffee. Still full, this one was on top of the dresser, concealed in part by Shelly's purse. It had to be sweet too: six or seven ants had died while trying to drink it. Their little maroon bodies floated on the drink's mocha surface.

Craig already felt better after the first coffee. He decided he'd drink this cup too. It had most likely been intended for him anyway. But first, he had to call the girls.

Immediately he thought of them, his inexplicable worry returned.

Quickly, he dialed Shelly's number. He had a heart-stopping moment when she didn't pick up. But then she did and he relaxed.

"Hi, baby," her sweet honey voice came over the line, soothing as a cup of chamomile tea. "You just got up? . . . Wow, fancy that! It's not five minutes since we both left the house. . . . Nah, it's okay. I can talk, Erica is the one driving. . . . Nah, she's not hungover, she's as clear-eyed as the robins in that tree at the back of the house. . . . No, baby, we're not at the Crossway yet. Darling, what's with all the questions? . . . Oh no, don't worry, we're fine. . . . The road's mostly empty. Remember it's Sunday morning—it's too early even for most church folk to be out yet. . . . Yeah, love you too. I'll always love you, Craig . . . I *really* love you. . . . See you in twenty or thirty minutes. Oh, and you missed your surprise. . . . What was it? Ain't telling you, but don't worry—I've still got it. Ha ha ha!" (At this point Erica laughed too.) "Alright, bye, baby, we're about reaching the Crossway now."

Craig hung up, feeling relieved. The women were okay. He cleared the dead ants off the second cup of cold coffee, drank it down, then lay back on the bed and concentrated on breathing normally, waiting for his mind and body to normalize.

In the adjoining bathroom, a single unflushed maggot crawled around the rim of the toilet bowl. Then it dropped to the floor and wriggled out of sight.

CHAPTER 19

Erica & Shelly. Erica, mostly

The wind poured in through the car window. It ruffled their hair.

Promise made in the delicious beauty of afterglow or not, Shelly had initially protested that half-past-six was too early to wake up on a Sunday morning.

Erica had insisted that they immediately set out for the Crossway. She'd felt compelled to set out. As if her beloved necklace would grow legs and run off if she didn't.

Shelly had protested. "Girlfriend, they can't have opened yet. We're both waitresses; how early do *we* ever get to work on Sundays?"

Erica, however, had doggedly pulled her to her feet, kissed her, and pushed her into the bathroom to tidy herself up.

"Hurry up and wash me out of your pussy!" she'd growled.

Now, as the silver Ford Fusion rolled smoothly along Massachusetts Route 116, Erica tapped on the steering wheel. Shelly had the stereo on. It was a new band, Kimchi Chocolate Stereo. Two half-Korean sisters and three American guys. The girls sounded like they gargled with battery acid. Raw voices like their vocal cords were shredded and bleeding. Drums like sledgehammers crushing baby skulls. Bass that buzzed like monster bees coming to kill you. Guitars like the crumpling of a fatigued suspension bridge.

"They're really great, you know," Shelly was saying.

"Yeah." Erica wiped her face with her left hand. The town of Conway was behind them now. Left and right of the car was thick woodland. Lots of tall trees. She could just about make out their destination ahead. Say about half a mile away.

"My brother Stevie knows both sisters and their manager, who's also their sister."

"Hmmm," Erica acknowledged. She really wished Shelly would stop talking so she could enjoy the song. Her crotch had been feeling tingly for a while now. The music was helping her ignore her arousal.

And damn, did she feel aroused!

The song finished. The DJ said, "Well that was *Enema Conscience*, the first single off the band's debut *Social Messiah* CD." He laughed. "Wow, now was that loud or what? Alright, folks, you know where you are: This is Slick Rick Foster on station WAAF. It's Rock 2 Wake U Up—the early morning hotspot. Stay tuned to 103.7 FM. Don't touch that dial, people. East to west, we're the heaviest; don't *settle* for soft metal. I'll be right back after the commercial break with the new Slain Jane single."

"I can't stand Slain Jane," Shelly grumbled. "That Janet Orgasm is such a phony."

"C'mon, they have some good songs," Erica countered. *"Antidote For God* was great. Most of that album was just killer. Like that song *Starship Cowgirl*, for instance." She began singing: "I'm gonna eat up the moon with my diva spoon, 'cos it'll be lunchtime soon. Drink up the Milky Way today, bay-bee. Mars is my home, clear my landing dock, you worker clones, I've got a terminal overload of Cosmic Bitch Syndrome. Hey, Scotty, beam me up some universal fuzz tones. It might take me light-years to come,"—she made the Devil's hand sign—"So, in the meantime, we'll rock on into the sun! Yeah!"

Shelly shook her head. "Nah, they utterly suck. They're just ripping off The Astral Leftovers, the guitarist's former band. Jane O practically admitted as much in their last interview on MTV. She didn't mean to let the cat out of the bag, but she was higher than the Trump Tower when Bebe Rock asked her about their influences."

Shelly began changing stations. Ten seconds later, she gave up. She flicked the radio off. "We're already there anyway."

They were. They could see the Crossway clearly now. A two-story construct of brown stone, sparkling glass, and shimmering plastic that seemed to abruptly rise up out of the ground. This impression was an illusion of course. The building had been visible on the horizon for a while now. Another illusion was the dark outline the building appeared to have, almost like it was an illustration.

Seeing the nearing building made Erica feel really good.

They cruised forward in silence.

Erica was focused on the road, but then a moan made her glance sideways. She whistled. Shelly was clutching her breasts with one hand and rubbing her crotch with the other. Her skirt was up, her panties pulled to one side. She was licking her lips.

"Oh, so you're feeling it too?" Erica asked. "I thought it was just me. I've been getting hornier and hornier since we set out from Marty's."

Shelly nodded back. She shifted the hand pinching her nipples to point through the windshield at the approaching diner. "Fuck yeah, Erica, I can feel it! I feel like I'm on fire."

"Me too," Erica admitted. She took her right hand off the steering wheel and rubbed herself between the legs also. Doing so felt so natural. "What is it about this place that gets us both so hot?" she asked.

Shelly was back to pinching her nipples. In the interim, the fingers caressing her crotch hadn't stopped. "I dunno, but I like it."

Erica liked it too, but she fought to remain objective. "Yes, yes, but it isn't normal for us both to become as horny as rabbits just on seeing it."

"I think the reason it works like this for us is 'cos that's where we first declared our passion for each other."

"Do you really think that's all?" They were now pulling into the Crossway's parking lot. Erica slowed the silver car. She made ready to circle out again if the diner wasn't yet open. But they seemed open. Yes, they were. Through the front windows, she saw Helen the waitress wiping tables.

Still, she parked the car just inside the entrance to the parking lot. She turned to Shelly, then for a moment was distracted. Her belly rumbled like she'd need to shit soon. She grimaced. At first the 'poop coming' feeling was urgent, but then the discomfort passed; the urge to defecate settling into something she could manage for a little while longer. She returned her attention to her companion.

Shelly looked desperate. "I need you, baby," she said miserably. "I need your mouth on my breasts. I need your fingers inside me." She leaned across the space between the seats and grabbed Erica's shoulder with vagina-wet fingers. "I need you *right now*."

"Out here in the car park?"

Shelly's replying gaze was defiant. "Why not? If possible, yes."

Erica scanned the parking lot. There was no one else around. The only two vehicles on the premises were the same ones they'd met here yesterday—the blue VW Golf and the motorbike. (Her lust blocked off her brain from questioning why the two vehicles were *still* parked here.) She wanted Shelly too. Every nerve in her body, every fiber of her being, every component of her soul was screaming for Shelly Parker's body.

Such an intense desire should have felt wonderful, but it felt all wrong.

This isn't me, Erica thought. *And this isn't Shelly either. Neither of us behave like this. Neither of us did until yesterday.*

"I don't like this," she told Shelly. "I feel like we're being used. I feel like something has a hold of us both and is manipulating us for its own dirty ends."

She pointed over at the Crossway diner, where Helen was now done wiping tables. No, this waitress wasn't Helen; she didn't recognize this one. Erica blinked. For a moment she'd seen a giant shadow—much larger than the giant Gorilla—walk across the dining room. Shivers fell through her, dropping like spilled ice from her temples to her ankles. She rubbed her eyes to see better, but the shadow had already vanished.

Shelly had meanwhile resumed masturbating. She moaned deliciously, "Manipulation? C'mon, don't be silly. I want you, you want me. Manipulation? I want womanipulation—I want your fingers womanhandling my clitoris. What's wrong with that? What else is necessary?"

Erica was surprised that Shelly didn't get it. "The *intensity* of our desire for each other is what's wrong."

Shelly paused long enough in her masturbation to look hurt. "You don't like my pussy that much? I know I *love* yours."

Erica smiled back. "Shelly, I love *everything* about you. At the moment, I want you even more than you want me."

Shelly looked about to cry. When next she spoke, her voice was plaintive with yearning. "That's hard to believe. Why won't you make love to me now, then?"

"Oh, it's true. I feel as if . . . as if . . ." How Erica felt was hard to put into words. She felt as though she'd die if she didn't immediately hurry Shelly into the Crossway Diner and start licking her vagina and anus. She wanted to stick her fist up Shelly, wanted to push it in elbow deep. She felt like a tree of lust planted in erotic soil. Now was like yesterday evening in the diner toilet. Once again she felt strong and brazen, the irresistible seductress she'd always fantasized she was. She felt as sexually potent as Cleopatra—a goddess of . . .

She gripped the steering wheel hard with both hands. She was scared that if she took her hands off the wheel for even the briefest instant, she'd grab Shelly instead and begin sliding her fingers up her.

Shelly grimaced. "No matter how hard I rub myself out here, I can't come. But I'm a hundred percent convinced that once we enter the diner I'll orgasm like crazy."

"We *have* to go inside," Erica huskily agreed, "to recover my necklace from the toilet." She turned and looked pleadingly at her friend. "But, Shelly, I'm scared to go inside there now. I'm really, *really* terrified of going inside there. Please, *please,* don't make us."

"Scared? You're scared, darling?" Shelly lifted her wet hand from her crotch again and stroked Erica's cheek with it. "But why? There's nothing dangerous here. Baby, I'm desperate to get inside. I need to come. If I don't orgasm soon, I'm gonna die."

Erica felt the same way. She said nothing though. There was nothing to say. She started the car up. She drove across the front lot to park up beside the diner building. As the vehicle rolled forward over the concrete, Erica again thought she saw a monstrous shadow walk through the dining room. Again, once she'd blinked, she saw nothing odd in there. Again she felt bathed in shivers. Again her tummy rumbled its toilet warning. Again the rumbling abruptly ceased. She felt like wheeling the Ford around, burning rubber out of there, and never returning.

But she had to have her necklace back. It was now her only real memory of her dead darling John Parks. She couldn't give that up. Not yet, anyway.

She parked. "Alright, here we are. Look, Shelly, how about if *you* go in and pick it up? I'll wait out here."

"Uh uh," Shelly immediately objected with a violent shake of her head. "If I go in there alone, I might never come out again. I need you to remind me that I've a boyfriend to return to."

Why did Shelly just say that? Erica wondered. *It's such a eerie comment for her to make, because . . . well, because I feel exactly the same way. I feel that if I enter the Crossway Diner this morning, I may never leave it again. But why would that be? How could that possibly even happen?*

She didn't know. Peering through the front windows now, the place looked normal enough. A pleasant, slightly old-fashioned restaurant that served exceptional fare.

She saw Gorilla walk out from the kitchen passage and look towards them. Today he had overalls on.

Alright, everything looks fine . . . but . . .

"Let's go!" Shelly insisted. "Come on, come on! Gorillas eat bananas not pussy!"

The joke was a sufficient goad. Erica opened the car door. Yes, Shelly was right. They'd just go inside, find the necklace, perform cunnilingus on one another, again have two or three of the best orgasms of their lives, then leave.

Oh yeah . . . and they'd also buy a takeout breakfast for Craig.

So why then do I feel so damn apprehensive? Erica asked herself. *And not in any kind of a good way. Yes, I do feel that fantastic lust. But underneath it all, there's something yelling at me to run for my life.*

She wouldn't be running anywhere though. Shelly had walked around the rear of the car and linked arms with her.

Shelly pulled her towards the diner entrance.

***

"Hello, girls," Daria said. "Good morning."

"Good morning," they both replied.

She'd met them the moment they'd stepped inside the entrance.

Daria was exactly as Erica remembered her: medium height, a little fleshy but gorgeous nonetheless, with a longish face, a perfect nose, and those red, red lips. And that knockout white hair that fell halfway down her back. Oh, that hair was to kill for.

Or to die for, Erica thought grimly. She had a sudden vision of Daria plaiting her albino tresses into a pair of nooses and hanging she and Shelly.

"I said you'd be back, didn't I?" Gorilla called from behind the counter.

They ignored the giant, all too preoccupied with the heat of the moment. Daria was plainly delighted to see them both. Shelly seemed enthralled with Daria. Erica was both wary of Daria and hungry for Shelly.

Now that they were inside the Crossway, Erica felt dizzy. Entering had been a mistake. On that score she had no doubts. The erotic force that had been pulling their strings outside now had them firmly in its clutches.

We need to get out of here fast!

"Last night . . ." she began. It was hard to focus on speaking. Very hard. The diner air was doing something wonderful to her. Each breath she took inflated her with passion.

Feeling helpless, she turned to Shelly, who stood on her left. Her breath rapid, Shelly was looking up over Daria, at the clock on the counter. (It was 7:08 a.m.) She had her hands in her pants again and was rubbing herself for all she was worth.

Erica sympathized with her. She felt the same way. She wanted to tear her clothes off and bend Shelly over one of the dining room tables and ram her fist up her vagina till she punched a hole through Shelly's cervix and gave her a fist baby. That was how violently turned-on she was.

She returned her attention to Daria. Daria was smiling at Shelly. She was licking her lips. She looked pleased. She also looked hungry. Erica didn't understand the hunger in Daria's gray eyes. It scared her. It seemed almost cannibalistic.

Hey, I sure hope they ain't been serving us human burgers here! The thought came weakly, sluggishly. Thinking was difficult. What she really wanted to do was rip Shelly's panties off with her teeth and then suck on her clitoris.

But . . . The thought stalled unborn.

But . . . I . . . Dammit! Thinking was a pain in the ass. Sex—violent and sweaty sex—was all she needed.

But . . . She forced the thought through. *I came here for something else. My necklace. Johnny's last gift to me. I've gotta get it back!*

Beside her, Shelly was having an orgasm. It was loud. She turned to watch. Shelly's eyes were rolled up in their sockets, just the whites showing. She was stabbing herself with three fingers while thrusting her crotch forward. She was drooling at the mouth like an idiot. Sex juice was pouring from her crotch to the tiles. The translucent drops splattered the checkered floor like yoghurt rain.

"You're supposed to wait for me," Erica said reproachfully. She didn't even realize that she'd spoken aloud. She was very upset that Shelly wasn't sharing her orgasm with her.

Around them, the diner walls approached and receded. The squares on the checkerboard floor floated over and under each other. The shadows in the room intensified. The walls became transparent, then turned black as night, then faded again.

Shelly exhaled long and hard as her orgasm wound down. Erica felt even more upset. She felt jealous of Shelly. She desperately wanted to come also. But she wasn't going to play with herself in public. No, she wasn't going to masturbate in front of Daria and Gorilla. She might be more aroused than a bitch in heat, but she had some decency left.

"A sexual climax is such an edible sensation." Daria's voice restored the room's solidity. Suddenly everywhere was normal again, the diner's dimensions restored.

"W-we c-came here for m-my necklace," Erica stuttered. "I-I-I fo-forgot it here la-last ni-night."

Daria nodded understandingly. Oddly to Erica, the woman seemed more solid now. Also the earlier hunger in her eyes seemed slightly appeased. As if, as if . . .

Erica stared at Shelly. Shelly looked somehow 'less' than before. Something ineffable about her was missing. In contrast, now Daria looked 'more' than before.

Erica was horrified. Her panic was razor-edged, blades of terror that sliced through her cloudy thoughts. *We've gotta get out of this place! We've gotta have sex here! No, we've gotta leave here! We gotta leave here! I gotta hurry Shelly out of . . . this public dining room! We gotta find a place where I can come as much as I want without being scared that a cop's gonna walk in the door and bust me for indecent exposure!*

"We found the necklace last night," Daria said.

"What?" Erica asked in confusion. "What necklace?"

"The one you came here for, of course. You just asked me about it. Don't you remember?"

"Huh? I asked you?" Then she remembered driving over here because she'd lost the necklace. Wow! And it had seemed really important just a short while ago. She wondered why. "Oh. Yeah. That. O.K. Alright. Sure." Erica didn't care about the damn necklace anymore. That was old history. John Parks was dead and gone. His locket had just been dead weight dangling between her breasts, the past preventing her from enjoying the future. She was really much better off without it. Losing the necklace had freed her to have sex again. Sex was the real thing. Sex was the only important thing now. The necklace wasn't even secondary.

However, it wouldn't be proper to act like a horny bitch here. Shelly was the horny bitch. Shelly was already fingering herself again.

Cool it, you slut! Wait till we get a bed!

"The necklace is upstairs," Daria said, curling her white hair around a finger. "I'll have the waitress fetch it for you. Oh no, sorry—I'll have to get it myself. I just remembered I asked her to clean the toilets." She frowned. "We're very understaffed at the moment; everyone's doing triple duty. Please wait for me. I'll only be a minute."

"We'll go with you," Shelly said. "That way you won't have to come back downstairs again just on our account."

Daria licked her red lips. Those lips the color of fresh blood. "If you say so . . ."

"Yes," Erica agreed. "It's best that we go upstairs with you."

Daria licked her lips again then nodded. "Alright then, both of you. Come along."

They followed Daria into the corridor on the left of the building, then up the staircase to the upper floor. Shelly was right. Erica understood that. It was important that they accompany Daria. She didn't know why that was, but following her instincts felt much better than trying to be rational. Her head felt full of vapors. Her crotch felt liquid with desire. Decent young woman or not, she was gripping her crotch now. She was squeezing herself deliciously. She was very wet down there—her love juices had visibly seeped through her jeans.

They climbed the stairs. Shelly was in the middle. A few steps lower than Shelly, Erica wanted to flip up her friend's skirt and lick her anus into wet ecstasy. She wanted to stick her tongue deep into that smelly hole until Shelly's poop blocked its further progress. But she controlled herself. Oh, she controlled herself! It took all her willpower, but she managed it.

On the upper floor, they walked along a corridor with doors left and right. From behind one door they heard a young woman moaning, "Oh, fucking kill me with your penis, Jimmy! I wanna die like this!" The emotion conveyed by the girl's soft voice was a mingling of equal amounts of intense pain and pleasure. It was just so silkily erotic. Hearing it, Erica almost climaxed on the spot.

"Yeah, Tori baby, I'm gonna fuck us both to death!" the young man replied. His voice was weak and trembling. He sounded very close to death indeed. Like the young woman's, his voice also conveyed the impression of mixed ultimate delight and despair.

They stopped. Daria opened a door. They entered.

The room was large and windowless. Despite the light overhead, its walls were dim, as if it had been painted with shadows. It had a large bed with gray sheets. There was definitely something scary about the room.

"This is my bedroom," Daria said, walking off into a corner and vanishing amongst the shadows. Her voice floated back to them. "I'll only be a moment. Please make yourselves comfortable on the bed."

Erica needed no further invitation. She began undressing. Shelly was already naked on the bed, her spread thighs glistening with lubrication, her arms outstretched towards Erica.

Daria wasn't yet back from her sojourn into the room's shadows.

Erica's panties dropped. She stepped out of them. She reached back and undid her brassiere. She flung the bra away—it vanished into the shadows. She stepped towards the bed. She fell onto Shelly. She wished she could fall *into* her girlfriend and merge completely with her.

Shelly rolled Erica over and stuck three fingers into her sex. Her other hand rubbed Erica's swollen clitoris. Erica instantly had an orgasm. Like a dam crumbling before the pressure of an overfull reservoir, her body gave way to the backlog of sexual angst it had built up since leaving Marty's house.

Erica's orgasm went on and on. Her world contracted to Shelly's hands and the magic spell Shelly's fingers wove on her flesh. On and on and on. Every now and then during this endless climax, she saw Daria's face. Daria smiling and licking her lips in delight. And then she'd feel like something was vacuuming a part of her away. Just a teeny-weeny part. Not something she'd really miss. Just a little donation to Daria in payment for such ecstasy.

And Erica wanted more of such delightful pleasure. She wanted a whole lot more of it. She was prepared to pay for it with her life it need be. So long as the ecstasy didn't stop.

The pleasure did stop for a while. Her orgasm ended. Shelly loomed over her.

"My turn now," Shelly said.

Erica wanted to keep climaxing, but again, Shelly was right: Shelly needed to orgasm too. Great sex was give-and-take.

Though Erica felt drained, she also felt energized. She understood *that*: this bedroom—Daria's bedroom—was powering her up so she could fuck more and come more. Daria was herself energizing Erica, so she could feed more . . .

This last thought was muddled in Erica's mind. It came with huge overtones of horror, with massive suggestions of mortal danger. But that wasn't really important. No it wasn't. What was important was the ecstasy. Nothing mattered but the *feeling*. Her entire body a single sensual organ. Her vagina: a wet mouth singing a primal song of physical love. She knew now what the couple in the bedroom they'd passed were experiencing.

She flipped Shelly over. She licked two of her fingers wet then stabbed Shelly in the anus with them. Shelly yelped and squirted in her face.

Digging her fingers deep into Shelly's ass, Erica began slapping her clitoris with her left hand: *Pap! Pap! Pap!* Shelly shrieked and went limp. Her brown hair fell forward over her face. She kept on squirting. Erica bent to catch the jets of female ejaculate in her mouth. She thrilled to feel them warm on her tongue. She began twisting her fingers around in Shelly's butt.

Shelly whimpered. She also visibly *shrunk*. Erica was both terrified and thrilled to watch Shelly *shrink*. Really, it was an imperceptible shrinkage. A miniscule reduction in Shelly's 'shelly-ness,' for want of a better description. This reduction would have gone unnoticed by an 'outsider,' but Erica was now part of the 'in-club.' She understood what was going on. Shelly had just paid the price for her pleasure. Daria had taken something from her: she'd just *eaten* a part of Shelly. Only a little part, mind you. A tiny part. But Shelly was going to have more orgasms—a cascade of multiple orgasms—and those little parts would soon add up.

And Erica too was going to have many more orgasms in quick succession and her own 'erica-ness' would shrink also. And if it shrunk too much, there'd finally be no Erica left at all, just the shadows. Nor would there be any Shelly left either. Daria would have eaten and drunk them both to death. (A vivid vision of Daria, bloated fat on them both, flashed before her eyes.)

But even though these scary thoughts terrified Erica, they thrilled her too: *The pleasure, oh, the delicious pleasure! Anything to again feel . . . to continue feeling, these priceless sensations!*

"Oh, the pleasure is so damn intense!" Shelly gasped under her. "Add another finger in my ass! Stretch me a little more! Please, darling! Hurry up!"

Erica added a third finger to the two already in place in Shelly's anus. She leaned forward and sucked on Shelly's clitoris. Shelly began coming again.

Erica lifted her head at a sound.

Daria was stepping out of the shadows. She seemed exceptionally solid. She'd been solid enough before, but she was more so now. Erica tried to imagine the chunk of herself that she'd lost during her orgasm slotted somewhere in Daria's body. Or maybe it didn't work that way. Maybe Daria physically ate what she extracted from them. If so, did she poop it out later? (Which reminded Erica—she still felt that need to defecate. Nauseatingly, it felt like the excrement was alive and squirming in her guts.)

Daria stepped up to them. She looked solemn, her gorgeous face calm as a moonlit lake. Her eyes were silver pools amidst the dark forests of her eyelashes. She smiled at their tangle of limbs on the bed. Shelly was moving her arms and legs across the gray bedcovers as if she was swimming. Her eyes were shut and her mouth open. An endless syrupy groan spilled from her lips like erotic audio molasses.

"Feed me," Daria said. "Yes, my pretty darlings, feed me."

She held out her hands to Erica. Her right hand dangled Erica's lost gold necklace with its glittering heart-shaped pendant. Her left hand gripped a strap-on dildo and harness. The dildo was flesh-pink and nicely realistic.

Erica whistled with delight. The dildo was absolutely perfect. Exactly what she needed right now.

"I knew you'd like it," Daria said.

Erica snatched the dildo harness from Daria.

"Where should I put the necklace?" Daria asked.

"Flush it down the crapper," said Erica impatiently.

Not waiting for a reply (actually, she immediately forgot the other woman was in the room with them), she turned back toward the bed. She flung the dildo down on Shelly's belly. "Hurry up; strap on that plastic cock and stick it in me. Quick—I gotta come again real fast."

"Yes, FEED ME! FEED ME! FEED ME!" The insistent female drone seemed to echo from the bedroom walls. Like the shadows were demanding sustenance. The voices' excitement was plain to hear.

Shelly slipped into the strap-on harness. She tightened it around her hips. Erica lay back waiting. Her entire body throbbed with expectancy. Lust tingled in her fingers and toes.

She peered beyond Shelly. A shadow was stepping out through the bedroom door. No, it wasn't a shadow—it was Daria. But the woman looked so huge and shapeless all of a sudden.

Once again Erica felt terrified. *Is this really worth it?*

Shelly sank the dildo into Erica. She slid it in down to the harness. She completely filled Erica with the plastic phallus.

Erica forgot about Daria again. She began coming again. Her switch from arousal to orgasm was instantaneous. Her sex clenched tight around the dildo. Her fears vanished. Her worries became phantasms like the room's shadows. *Hell yes, it's worth it!*

Shelly began thrusting hard.

"Harder," Erica moaned. "Make me bleed if you can."

Shelly, her eyes suddenly manic, did her best to oblige. Her breasts bounced violently as she thrust into Erica as hard as she could.

"Harder!" Erica gasped. "Haaaardeeeeer. . . ." She felt a chunk of herself detach and slip away again, and for a moment was scared shitless. But then, another orgasm began and her loss of herself no longer mattered.

Oh, for fuck's sake, she instead pondered angrily, while gritting her teeth and curling her toes and balling her hands into fists as her vagina destroyed her with ecstasy, *what the hell is the matter with Shelly? Doesn't she understand what HARDER means?*

"Screw me harder, darling," she pleaded. "Please, please, you're not doing it vigorously enough. I said—fuck me *hard*. HARD, HARD, HARD!"

"I'm going as hard as I can," Shelly grunted back. She slammed the dildo in as violently as she could, then again and again. She was excited too. She was sweating. Her vagina dripped with juice. It wasn't just Erica feeling that they needed to up their sexual game.

"DO IT HARDER, BITCH!" Erica screamed as a crazy cocktail of fear, pleasure, and intense joy hijacked her mind again.

As she screamed her delight, three white larvae squirted out of her anus. The maggots were instantly pulped when Erica's thighs slammed down on them, but that didn't matter. There were more—many more—where those first three had come from.

Outside her bedroom, Daria paced her corridor and fed on both lovemaking couples.

CHAPTER 20

Andy & Karen

She was gorgeous and at the same time utterly repulsive. Lovely but also horrible beyond description. Familiar yet completely alien.

Her white hair fluttered behind her in an unseen breeze.

Her face . . . ! Her eyes were alert and merciless, the eyes of a lioness on the prowl. Her long, sharp teeth dripped something that wasn't quite meat and wasn't quite blood. It wasn't saliva or fat either. It was liquid but chunky; a mush like ground beef, blood sausage, and canned tuna mixed up with bone marrow.

The dark sludge of extracted humanity ran down over her red lips, then down over her chin. Down her neck. Into the deep cleavage between her alabaster breasts. Dripping through that erotic valley, down over her belly . . . down . . .

***

Andy came awake to a pleasurable sensation. It took him a moment to realize that he had a hard case of morning wood and that Karen was sucking hard on it.

He raised his head and peeked down at her. She was kneeling on his right side, her face obscured by her hair. Her head bobbed up and down as she fellated him.

He was hungover. That was to be expected after last night. His brain was throbbing almost as much as his penis was in Karen's mouth. He was also naked. He didn't recall taking off his clothes before going to bed. Karen must have undressed him. She'd even taken the brace off his game leg. The leg didn't really hurt anymore, it just didn't work right anymore either.

Andy didn't recall much about last night . . . period. The three kids coming over, him telling them a story . . . them telling him a story . . . him getting all worked up . . . them leaving. Had he wept or not?

Karen gently scraped his penis with her teeth. Andy groaned. He forgot as much as he could remember of last night. Karen performed great fellatio.

Like she could read his mind, at that moment Karen tightened her lips around his shaft and drew her mouth slowly up it. All the way up to the glans.

He groaned loudly and grabbed at her buttocks. He kneaded the soft round cheeks, then pushed his fingers in between them and stroked her lightly-furred sex.

She pushed her hair back over her shoulders and looked his way. Her mouth glistened wet with saliva. "Wakey, wakey, hon."

There was love in her eyes. A whole lot of honest love for him. As much as his hangover would allow, Andy felt a sudden intense gush of emotion for Karen. He felt love and friendship for this woman who wasn't pretty but whom he wouldn't ever exchange for any other. Not even for Daria, if she ever came back to him.

He smacked her buttocks lightly. "Bring your ass over here, baby. Let me eat you too."

She quickly repositioned herself so her vagina overhung his face. The cleft glistened above him. Her beautiful white thighs enclosed his head like marble pillars of pleasure. He lifted his head slightly and began licking her. She gasped and stiffened when tongue met clitoris. She was as wet as a river. Her juices flooded out over his lips. He couldn't really taste her because of his hangover, but he could smell her musk, sweet and pungent, the lovely smell of a lovely woman. Her smell filled his mind like his penis filled her mouth.

Her body felt nice and warm positioned over his like this; her nipples were stiff points pricking his belly. Her sucking on him became more irregular now that he was eating her too. Each time he made her spasm with pleasure, she lost her rhythm on his penis. She stalled like a car. Then, when she recovered herself again, she compensated for the downtime by sucking harder and faster than before. It was a wild, if lazy ride. A Sunday morning erotic matinee. Andy kept licking her, moving from clitoris to vagina proper and then up to her anus. When he felt he was about to come, he stuck a wet finger deep in Karen's ass, clamped his mouth over her clitoris, and sucked like a vacuum cleaner on the swollen bud.

It was going to be a close call, this one. He could tell. She'd had a good head start on him. She'd been sucking on him for maybe five minutes before he'd woken up. All that while his penis and testicles had been storing up the pleasure. It looked like he might come before she did. But then also, she'd likely already been horny before she'd begun fellating him. (Or maybe, she'd just noticed that he had a piss-hard and decided not to waste it?) So they just might make it together.

He got her off first. Just when he felt like he couldn't hold back any longer, she stiffened and gasped. He kept on licking her, paying good homage to her clitoris. Now her juices really flooded his mouth. As if the cunnilingus had purged his tongue of the alcohol, he could taste her now, that taste that wasn't exactly clean and yet wasn't dirty. That unique female blend of vaginal spices that had no liquid parallel. He just loved how she tasted.

He couldn't see what she was doing down there, of course, but he could feel that she'd stopped sucking him and was now jerking him hard with her little spit-slippery fist. She was moaning loud and fast. It was sexual instinct more than anything else making her keep working his phallus during her own orgasm. Her persistence paid off. A moment later, Andy felt his testes twitch and the sperm traveling up his penis. The first squirt of semen went high into the air. The next one went into Karen's mouth. Her own orgasm was fading into afterglow now and she concentrated on sucking him. She didn't stop till he was drained empty. Then she collapsed on him. Her limbs gave out and she lay on him like a starfish. He'd wiped her out. She'd wiped him out.

He lay there with his chin in her crotch and grinned.

***

Later, while Karen lay beside him curling his pubic hair in her fingers, he remembered his dream. Daria. He'd seen Daria. But not the Daria he'd loved. This had been a nightmare version of Daria.

But then, today's the goddamn anniversary, ain't it? I'd be expected to dream crazy shit like that.

But . . . but last year he'd not dreamt about her. And also, each other time he'd dreamt about Daria, she'd been sweet and lovely, not the monster he'd just seen with its mouth dripping liquefied human essence.

With an effort he forced Daria Simpson out of his mind. He'd moped too much already. He needed to face the past like a man. What was done was done. All that drinking last night wasn't worth it. His moping wasn't going to bring Daria back to him.

Besides—he pulled Karen close and hugged her tight—Karen deserved better. A whole lot better. She was a wonderful lady.

Andy determined to do whatever it took today to make Karen happy.

***

After they'd kissed a bit, Andy went into the bathroom to pee. Karen watched him go. He walked funny without the brace on. His right leg simply refused to move straight ahead. It tried to go left instead. The brace fixed that, but when he wasn't wearing it, Andy had to be very careful not to trip himself up. He had to walk with his legs well apart.

Listening to Andy pee, Karen felt relieved. Yes, their early morning lovemaking seemed to have done the trick. Andy seemed calm; much calmer than last year. Last year had been just horrible. Andy had spent the entire day sulking and grumbling at everyone at the Losey Hardware Store. He'd treated old Mr. Jenkins so nasty that the old man had sworn he'd never be back to the store again. And Mr. Jenkins was a longstanding Losey customer of almost thirty years. Then later, when they'd gotten back home from the store, Andy had begun drinking . . . No, last year had been just horrible.

But so far, today's anniversary had begun better.

Karen looked down at her breasts. Her nipples were still hard. She grimaced. This thing with Daria was very complicated. Really, really complicated indeed. Karen understood it was best to play it cool. It only happened once a year, on June 6, Daria's birthday. Today. Then Andy was inconsolable.

Karen knew Andy loved her. There'd never been any doubt about that. She knew it like she knew her middle name was Edna. It wasn't that Andy was pining for Daria, or that he wanted her back. It was just the bad taste of memory. Karen understood that too. She also understood that the memory would fade. Someday, maybe soon, maybe far off, Andy would stop hurting.

Andy hobbled back out of the bathroom. He was scratching the mess of scar tissue over his right nipple; a souvenir of his romance with Daria.

Karen pointed at his crotch. "You wanna go again? I could do with a little more of you."

He nodded. "Yeah, honey. Sex seems to be helping my hangover this morning. How do *you* feel, by the way?"

"I'm alright, but then I didn't have as much to drink as you did last night. It was hell on two legs getting you undressed for bed. I'm delighted you didn't puke all over us."

He grinned. "Me too."

With that slow careful walk of his, Andy made his way back towards the bed. His penis was already getting hard again. Karen reached out and took the swelling organ in her hand. It got even harder as she stroked it. She stared at Andy's face as he climbed into the bed.

"Baby?"

"Yeah, sweetheart?"

"Baby, are you okay? I mean, you ain't thinking about . . . are you? It's okay, I'll understand if you are. I just want you to know . . ."

He dragged himself through the space between them and kissed her. He kissed her a long, long time.

"No, honey," he said when their lips parted, "I'm gonna be happy today. We're both gonna be happy. In fact, to prove how happy I am, I'm gonna mow the damn lawn today after breakfast like you've been after me to do for the past fortnight."

"That'll have to be next weekend. We promised the kids next door we'd take 'em out on a picnic before Marty gets back."

"We did?"

"Don't you remember? We planned a mid-morning trip into the woods."

"All I remember are your ass and tits." He grabbed at her.

Giggling like mad, she fell back on the bed and spread her thighs wide. "Alright, come in the front door, you naughty man." She was wet; ripe with anticipation.

He slid over her and into her. They resumed making love. It was wonderful. She was very pleased. She didn't know what had come over Andy this morning, but she was delighted that it had.

Karen figured there would be no nonsense about Daria Simpson today. None at all.

CHAPTER 21

Craig

Shelly and Erica should be on their way back now, Craig thought.

He called Shelly's phone. No reply. Her number rang and rang but she didn't pick up.

Nothing to worry about there, he figured. *Maybe they stopped off at a store to buy some groceries. They'll both be here soon enough. But they need to hurry. I think I recall talk about a picnic last night.*

He wondered again about the surprise Shelly had promised him.

***

Craig pulled on a pair of shorts. He felt like making himself a fresh cup of coffee. The cup-and-a-half he'd already drunk seemed to have smothered his hangover. Coffee worked sometimes; at other times you just started drinking again, tricked the hangover into thinking you were still drunk and it wasn't yet time for it to hit you.

So more coffee it was then. Black and sugarless this time. Just the pure lifesaving liquid.

Ignoring his flip-flops, he left the bedroom barefoot and headed for the kitchen.

On entering the living room, he smelt something rotting. To his mind, the bad smell was completely out of place here. For a bachelor pad, Marty's house was very clean and neat, so Craig assumed the stink was coming from outside the cottage. As he neared the kitchen, however, the smell intensified. Craig was puzzled.

Then he stepped inside the kitchen and just gaped. That was all he could do; stand staring with his mouth open in disbelief.

The top of the kitchen counter was awash with maggots. It hadn't been awash with maggots last night. Back then Craig had helped Shelly carry in the stuff they'd bought at the Crossway Diner and the kitchen counter had been sparkling clean. The whole kitchen had been in pristine condition. They'd put the drinks down on the counter and put the food in the fridge.

The grubs were spilling over the countertop to the kitchen floor. Craig gagged at the sight and smell of them. Then he saw that the maggots were all spilling from the three Crossway purchase bags. The bags themselves now looked both old and soggy.

Again, for some reason, he remembered his dream that he couldn't remember.

Craig was puzzled by what he was seeing. He looked around for something to poke the paper bags with. He settled on a long wooden spoon. He poked the nearest bag. It punctured inward. The maggots swarmed out of the bag and up the spoon towards him. He shook them off and resumed poking. Yet more maggots poured out. Finally, Craig used the wooden spoon to shred the bag completely so as to clearly view its contents.

When the bag was destroyed, Craig was even more puzzled. The paper bag, which he knew had contained cans of soda, was now full of moldy earth. In fact, Craig wasn't even sure the lumps he was looking at were actually sod, they seemed more like rotten meat. They *smelt* like bad meat too. Destroying the bag to expose its contents had merely made the stink worse.

Feeling shivery, Craig turned his attention to the other two bags. Both, on being ruptured, revealed a similar smelly mess, each one riddled with holes from which the grubs spurted.

The maggots had by now filled the kitchen sink. They were all over the microwave oven and knife rack. They were climbing the kitchen walls and leaving icky gray trails of slime. They were spilling thickly over the countertop, and were crawling down its sides. The pale larvae moved blindly, in all directions.

Craig just managed not to throw up. He kept peeking at the floor to ensure that none of the maggots were close to his feet. He wished he'd not left his slippers in the bedroom.

What he was seeing made no sense to him. *We bought . . . How in the hell? . . . What the . . . ?*

Then he remembered the fridge. *We put the food in the fridge. I wonder what's in there now?*

Between himself and the castle of the fridge door, however, lay a two-foot-wide moat of maggots. The spread of the hideous larvae was widening toward him by the second. Though scared of what opening the fridge would reveal, Craig nonetheless felt compelled to make the discovery. He had to know what was in there now.

The encroaching pool of white larvae was almost at his feet. It was going to be now or never.

He pinched his nose shut with his left hand, then leaned forward and opened the fridge with his right.

His morbid expectations were not disappointed. If he'd had slower reflexes, he'd have been buried in the deluge of maggots that poured from the fridge. As it was, the force of the larval spillage wrenched the fridge door from his grasp, flinging it fully open. Craig was already leaping away at the time; the pressure on the opening door shoved him to the right.

He landed smack-dab in the middle of a squirming pile of maggots that instantly began climbing his legs. They climbed very fast. He yelped and began stamping and knocking them off. Amazingly, he felt some of the tiny horrors biting his shins.

They were *biting* him? Did grubs bite?

He ran out of the kitchen and banged the door shut.

He stood outside there panting. What the hell was going on this morning? How did . . . ?

It occurred to Craig that he was merely hallucinating, that the previously pristine kitchen wasn't really full of maggots spilling from the food-and-drink bags they'd brought in last night.

He tentatively opened the kitchen door for a quick peek. No, he wasn't hallucinating. Marty Kolbek's kitchen *was* indeed full of maggots.

Then Craig yelped in pain again. He looked down at his legs. Several maggots were still climbing his legs. They'd reached his knees. Some of them hung from his skin like leeches, biting him.

Horrified, he began plucking them off his legs then pulping them with his heels. Other of the larvae he simply squashed in place. When he was through, there were trails of blood and white exploded messes on both his shins.

Gasping in shock, he stumbled across the living room, first back to the bedroom, then into the bathroom to wash the blood-and-maggot mess off his legs. There, nausea once more got the better of him and he bent over the toilet and vomited.

This time he threw up much less than before. However, he once again made exactly the same mistake as earlier, in immediately flushing the toilet (while groping blindly for the sink to rinse out his mouth) and not paying any attention to what he'd thrown up. Had he studied the coffee-tinted mess in the green ceramic bowl, he'd have seen the five or six living maggots he was flushing away.

When his nausea subsided, he returned to the bedroom and broke the seal on a bottle of Jack Daniels. He took a long sip. He was completely shaken and needed to calm his nerves. Making coffee was clearly out of the question now anyway.

We gotta do something about that damn kitchen before Marty gets back, or he's gonna throw us all out of his house!

It was a rational thought, albeit a desperate one. It was also a much less stressful line of reasoning than trying to figure out where all the maggots had come from in the first place. How they'd just bloomed overnight. Craig had no answer to that question.

He had himself another drink of whiskey. He wasn't yet ready to go near the kitchen again. He'd wait till Shelly and Erica returned, then hopefully, they'd all figure something out. Craig could still clearly visualize the maggot swarm. Just the thought of them made him want to puke again.

And his belly felt oddly unsettled.

CHAPTER 22

Karen, mostly . . .

After breakfast, Karen and Andy stepped outside.

Karen was relieved. Andy still hadn't started brooding over his lost love.

They stood on the stoop watching the street. There wasn't much to look at: just the Whitman's house opposite. And closer to home, their own front yard, which was rather overgrown.

She grimaced. Andy always put off mowing their lawn. Karen didn't consider lawn-mowing a ladylike occupation, or else she'd have done it herself. Andy, on the other hand, found it hard to do because of his damaged leg. The real problem though, wasn't Andy's leg, but the steel brace he wore on it. They had a push/'walk-behind' mower and the vibrations it made while cutting grass made Andy's brace shake in a peculiar way. Andy disliked the feeling so much that he viewed the lawn mower with dread. But if he tried mowing the lawn without supporting his right leg, the leg gave out on him after a while and he invariably wound up flat on his ass on the grass.

The solution they'd hit on was to buy a riding mower, one that Andy could drive around with his brace off. For this, however, they had to get a customized 'left-footed' model. Andy had protested that their lawn wasn't large enough to warrant such an investment. Karen had insisted. Andy had ordered the new lawn mower, but it hadn't arrived yet.

Young Lucy Fitts rode past on a red bicycle. Lucy lived four houses away and played high school soccer. She waved and called, "Hi, Miss Losey!" Karen waved back.

They stepped down from the porch and walked towards the road. Karen leaned on Andy and linked her arm in his. This was a pleasant morning. She was with the man she loved, and she intended enjoying herself today. The sun was bright and warm.

Karen hoped it wouldn't rain and ruin their planned outing. She'd already thought the picnic out. They'd drive up to South Sugarloaf Mountain. The observation tower up there gave one an incredible view of the countryside and the Connecticut River. She was sure Marty's blonde cousin and her friends would love the view.

She'd of course have to seriously caution the trio again to not mention either the Crossway Diner or Daria in Andy's hearing. She wasn't having a repeat performance of last night. Last night she'd used up almost all the Kleenex in the house before Andy had stopped bawling his eyes out.

"Their car's gone," Andy said, pointing.

She looked across the fence and saw what he meant. Yeah, the city kids' vehicle wasn't there now. She hadn't noticed. Or rather, she'd noticed but thought nothing of it. They were halfway to the foot of the drive now, so Andy must just have realized it himself. She still didn't think it odd.

"They likely went grocery shopping," she said.

"It's too early in the morning for that," Andy replied gruffly. "Most folk sleep in late on Sundays." He turned towards Marty Kolbek's side of the duplex. "See, there's that young man from last night. What's his name again?"

She looked. The young man was sitting on the front porch. She shoved Andy playfully. "Shush! His name's Craig. And next time don't drink so much. Next thing now you'll be telling me we had *six* visitors last night—Superman, Batman, three humans and a wookie."

Craig noticed them. He waved, then got up from the porch steps and walked over. Karen noticed that he looked worried.

They stepped up to the blue fence to meet him. Karen smelt the alcohol on his breath. Damn, the kid had started early today. At this rate he'd be drunk before they went on their picnic.

"Hi, man," Craig said, extending his hand to shake Andy's. "Thanks for making us so welcome last night."

Andy shook his hand and laughed. "Hope you enjoyed yourselves. Personally, I don't remember too much about your visit. But there, that's good whiskey for you." Then he noticed the expression of disquiet on the young man's face. "Hey, what's bothering you? You look like someone stole your car."

Karen hadn't considered that option. "They didn't, did they? I mean, no one's stolen . . . ?"

He shook his head and made an effort to smile. "Nah, it's not that. We've got a grub infestation in the kitchen."

Karen shivered. "Grubs? You mean as in, maggots?"

Craig nodded. "Yeah. I've never seen anything like it before in my entire life." He winced. "I'm trying to figure out how to clean the place up before Marty gets back, or he's sure to be pissed."

Andy shook his head. "I'll come have a look at it. See if I can help out any."

"I don't see why Marty'll be upset with you though," Karen added. "It's *his* house—the grubs are his problem, not yours."

Andy laughed. "Yeah, or did you truck up a load of maggots from . . . sorry, where're you guys from again?"

"Lancaster, Ohio." Craig looked perplexed, then said, "No, man, and that's the really crazy thing about this. The grubs—and I don't know how this is possible—all came out of the takeout food we bought last night at that Crossway Diner."

He saw that they were looking at him in shock and added, "Karen, Andy, I'm not making this up. The kitchen's *full* of damn grubs. Come see for yourselves."

Karen finally got a hold of her shock. "Say that again."

"Say *what?*"

"The bit about where you bought last night's dinner."

He looked confused. "The Crossway Diner. The old-fashioned place by the overpass over I-91 as you're driving up from South Deerfield. We mentioned it last night. We stopped there to eat 'cos we were hungry and . . ." They were still gaping at him, so he asked, "What's the matter? Do they sell expired food there or . . . ?"

Karen said quietly. "It's not that, not that at all. Craig, we already told you yesterday—the Crossway Diner burned down two years ago."

He looked at them both in shock. Then he laughed. "Aw now, come on; not that joke again. It was funny last night, but don't you think it's a bit old now?"

"Craig, we *ain't* joking," Andy said, and his voice came out all kind of funny now. "The Crossway *did* burn down two years ago. Two years exactly today. That's why I was getting so drunk last night, 'cos I was dating the proprietress and she went up in flames along with her damn building. There's only concrete floor and charred earth there now.

Now please, dude, for God's sake stop foolin' with us about this. It hurts."

"But I'm *not* fooling, man." Craig gestured to the empty driveway behind him. "That's where the girls went. Erica forgot her necklace at the Crossway yesterday. She and my girlfriend Shelly drove back to get it."

Karen was about to dismiss Craig's words but couldn't. He looked dead serious, that was the thing. She asked him softly one more time: "Craig, are you sure about this?"

He nodded. "As sure as I'm here talking to you both right now. I even spoke to Daria, the woman who runs the joint. She's got long white hair, gray eyes, and her face is kinda long, right? And she's curvy and not too tall?"

The previously lovely day now turned cold around Karen. Saying she felt chilled didn't even begin to describe it. No, this wasn't happening. It couldn't be happening. She looked left, at Andy. Andy wasn't saying anything. She couldn't read the expression on his face either.

She was about to reply Craig when Andy said, "See, man, something's sure wrong here, for sure. I'm not saying you're lyin', but believe me, I no longer know what to believe. Listen, we're not jokin' either. Daria Simpson did die in a fire two years ago when the Crossway burned down. *I know.* I was Daria's boyfriend—I was there the night the damn thing happened."

Now it was Craig's turn to look less-than-sure. "You're serious about this? For real?"

"Yes," Karen said. "Dead serious. The damn place did burn down. The fire department had one hell of a job putting the blaze out."

"But that's *impossible.*"

Andy nodded grimly. "Well at least that's something we all agree on."

Craig was looking really confused now. "And no one rebuilt it since then?"

"Nah. Daria's brother Gorilla was going to, but then he got killed in that accident along with Helen. That entire triangle of land bordering the interstate and Conway Road up to the turnoff belonged to her family. Daria's ma died last November, so the title now belongs to her cousin, some rich Boston lady named Grace Barbanell. She though, don't seem to have any interest in doing squat with the land. So, till she sells the lot to someone else . . ."

"You just said Daria, Gorilla and Helen are all dead," Craig said slowly, as if he were picking out the words scalding hot from a bubbling cauldron of thoughts. "But we—the girls and I—saw all three of them alive last night." He looked really worried now. "What this means is that Shelly and Erica just drove off to somewhere that doesn't exist. How is that possible?"

"I got a bad idea 'bout that," Andy replied grimly. "A real bad idea. Do you believe in magic, man? I mean *black* magic?"

Karen watched Craig's face. She was frightened herself and thought she saw a similar reaction in him. He was doing his best to hide it though. The way he looked now, there was something about him that she really liked. He was young, handsome, and horrified. She enjoyed his vulnerability; she wasn't that much older than him but it made her feel motherly towards him. Or maybe it was just because the kid was so good-looking.

"Black magic?" Craig snorted. "C'mon, that's preposterous." But then he added in a bothered voice, "But still, I don't like this at all. My girlfriend is over there now and I can't get her on the phone."

"You can't get her on the phone because . . ." Andy turned to Karen. "Get out the car."

She knew what he had in mind and it alarmed her. "Andy, you're not thinking of . . ."

He nodded. "We'd best head over there and see for ourselves what's going on. And fast at that. Those girls might need our help." He spoke to Craig now. "Lock up your house. We're heading over to the Crossway right away."

Karen didn't argue with Andy. There was no point. She could see that his mind was made up. *We're going to the damn ghost café and that's that. And because Andy's bad leg doesn't let him drive anymore, I'll have to come along too.*

Craig had already left them and was climbing Marty's front steps.

Andy turned to her. "You don't have to come along, sweetheart. It might be dangerous for ya."

"Baby, you can't drive."

"No, but the kid can."

"*I'll* drive. *He* both looks like he's got a hangover, and I can smell fresh whiskey on his breath. I don't want him crashing our car and totaling your left leg too. Sure I love you, but I don't wanna spend the rest of my life pushing you around in a wheelchair."

Her excuse/reason was complete bullshit. Karen recognized that as surely as she knew Andy did: *I'm going along solely because this business involves Daria. If she really is somehow alive over there, who knows what madness she'll pull once Andy turns up. I ain't losing him to her! Hell no, I ain't!*

"I hate this shit," Andy said as they headed back into their house. "Why the hell does it have to start up again after so damn long?"

"Just get the guns, man," Karen replied, knowing that that was what he was going to do anyway.

***

Ten minutes later they were on their way to the Crossway. Karen was driving the black Chevrolet Cruze, with Craig seated beside her. Andy was in the back.

Andy had broken out the gun case. They had four guns with them: Andy had a shotgun and a heavy-duty pistol. Craig and Karen each had revolvers.

The guns made Karen uneasy. As far as she could tell, you couldn't shoot a ghost. But Andy had said he wasn't taking any chances. Neither was she then. If she had to shoot someone to keep Andy safe, even if it was Daria herself, then so be it.

They were half a mile from the intersection when they saw it. From here on the road was straight and vision as clear as freshly-washed windows.

"Look!" Karen said, pointing while her heart leapt up to block her throat. She felt a sudden cramp south of the border, like she'd wet herself from sheer fear. "Look!"

Behind her, Andy didn't say a word. She hadn't really expected him to. She pulled the car over to a handy shoulder and parked it.

They sat there looking down the highway at the two-story building. It was over a minute before any of them was able to comment. Even Craig was struck speechless. Karen knew why he was speechless. The bright light of morning—it was about 7:40 a.m. now—had revealed something the previous night had likely covered.

Yes, the Crossway Diner was there, right where the overpass ended. It shouldn't be there, that was for sure. Hell no, it definitely shouldn't be there. But the damn thing *was* there. Up ahead in plain view.

Karen's head hurt, her brain felt squeezed. In a weird, weird way, the Crossway looked like a painting. In addition to seeming overly vivid like it was leeching color from the morning, the building had a thick black outline around it. Like in a kindergarten drawing made with thick black crayon. Even at this distance the black outline was startlingly pictorial. In some ways it seemed more real than the building itself.

"What the hell is that all around it?" Craig finally asked.

Karen was glad of the question. The silence was permitting her fears to overwhelm her. "I've no idea. None whatsoever. All I know is that that damn building wasn't there yesterday, and hasn't been there for two years now. As for why it has that outline around it, I've no frigging idea. And honestly, man, I really don't wanna know." Even to herself, she sounded close to panic. She gripped her revolver—a snub-nosed Airweight—and stared at the steering wheel. She didn't want to look at the Crossway any more than she had to.

Andy spoke up from the rear of the car. His voice was calm but eerily subdued. "Alright, Craig, before we go any nearer to that place, I'd better let you know the background gist."

Karen was grateful he'd said that. She felt like kissing him 'thank you.' She'd dreaded him asking her to restart the car. She wasn't in any hurry to meet the force that had brought the Crossway Diner back to 'life.'

"Yeah, sure," Craig said, turning to look at him. "But you'll need to be fast, man. I need to get my girlfriend out of there."

"Yeah, don't worry, I'm keepin' that in mind," Andy replied. He peered ahead between the front seats. "I just need you to understand that I wasn't joking earlier when I mentioned black magic."

Craig gulped. "Yeah, okay. If you're right that that building . . ." He shut up and Karen knew why: that thick outline around the Crossway Diner wasn't anything natural. It wasn't anything from this world, that was for certain. (When she squinted at it, it seemed to flicker with black flame.) She'd given up on staring at the steering wheel. Now she was instead gazing forward through the windshield with scared eyes.

She felt a magnetic pull from the distant building. Something there—possibly even the dark outline itself—was tugging on her mind, filling her head with an urgent command to draw near to the danger ahead.

Rather than obey that unvoiced instruction to put the car in motion again, she instead forced her mind onto what Andy was saying. She turned and gave him her full attention. She felt cold in the car, as if the heat had all been sucked outside.

". . . Alright. Now the reason I keep mentionin' black magic is 'cos that's what's at the root of this mess."

"But how?" Craig enquired.

"Some asshole named Xander Mood, is how." Andy spat out the man's name with intense bitterness. Karen had heard the story more than once before. But still she shuddered now.

Andy got over his anger. He sighed deeply, then composed himself.

"You see, Craig," he said with an audible lump in his throat, "Xander wanted to open a gateway to Hell."

"To Hell," Craig repeated. He stole a quick glance over his shoulder at the distant building before turning back to ask, "Why the hell would anyone want to open a gateway to Hell?"

Karen shrugged and said, "Most evil people wait until they die to meet Satan, but Xander Mood was apparently impatient."

"I daresay the crazy son-of-a-bitch was impatient," Andy said impatiently. "Look, baby, let me finish telling the guy my story. I'm gonna keep this short and bitter. I just want him to understand what we'll likely be gettin' ourselves into when we get over there."

"Yeah, sure," Karen quickly agreed.

"O.K.," Andy continued in a grim voice, "now what happened was . . ."

Karen listened. Andy seemed serious about keeping the tale short and bitter. The version of events he told Craig merely summarized everything. Karen, however, knew the whole tale, and it really was a horrible one.

Real, real horrible:

PART 3 (FLASHBACK): THE EVIL MR. MOOD

CHAPTER 23

Andy & Daria, mostly . . .

I

Andy Watson had met Daria Nicole Simpson four years ago, while he was working as a trucker.

The Crossway, though not really a truck stop, occasionally lay along Andy's route. Also, seeing as he lived in Conway anyway, he'd quickly formed the habit of stopping at the diner for breakfast or dinner.

The proprietress had quickly caught his eye. But then she caught just about everyone's eye. Daria Simpson was beautiful. Her kind of beauty was the undeniable kind that other women envied. She had the sort of good looks that literally took your breath away. Daria was the sort of woman one expected to see on TV shows, not running an eatery. She looked completely out of place overseeing the Crossway.

But she made a good job of it. She was hardworking and driven by the desire to succeed. And succeed she did. The Crossway Diner prospered, and the clientele—a motley crew of truckers, bikers, motorbike teens (teens who were not bikers but loved bikes), and just everyday traveling folks or folks from the surrounding county towns who appreciated good cooking—kept coming back for more.

Andy hadn't really thought he'd stood a chance with Daria. Not with all the other good-looking fellows always hanging around the place. But for some reason she'd liked him better than all the others, and their romance had begun.

It was a normal enough romance. Love with the occasional dose of bickers. Never any serious arguments.

Like most women in love, Daria would tolerate just about anything from her man except other women. Just the thought of infidelity drove her nuts. To his credit, Andy had no interest in any other women.

Just like how she ran the other areas of her life, Daria was typically no-nonsense about romantic competition from other women.

When Karen Losey, whose father Lew owned the Losey Hardware Store, began stopping by the diner and taking an interest in Andy, Daria called her aside into the Crossway's kitchen one day. There, with a razor-sharp carving knife in hand, she 'explained' to Karen exactly what she'd do to any woman who tried to take Andy from her.

She emphasized her 'explanation' by ceaselessly hacking into a long cut of meat that was just the right size and shape to have come from a human being.

Karen got the point and stayed away thenceforth—from both Andy Watson and the diner. (Karen knew she couldn't complain to the police about being threatened. They'd been standing in the diner kitchen and the cook had had a knife. Cooks in kitchens were expected to have knives.)

The fact that Daria had assured her that the 'romantic offender' would disappear—vanish without trace into the soup and burgers the Crossway served—had given Karen nightmares about what the diner's everyday cuisine *really* consisted off. Despite all of waitress Helen Brooks' amused protests to the contrary, Karen could well imagine the giant Dave 'Gorilla' Simpson murdering people so his older sister could cook them.

***

Fast forward two years.

June 6th. Daria Simpson's thirty-second birthday.

Andy had come over the previous evening so they could spend the next day together. Gorilla (who lived with Daria) had gone off with some friends. (Gorilla was sweet on Helen, but Helen wasn't giving up her body yet, so he was hanging out with her crowd till she decided to let him have a taste of her female goodies.)

Once it was just Andy and Daria left in the diner, they'd locked up then retired upstairs. They'd stayed awake till midnight so Andy could give Daria her birthday present—a 'carved heart' art canvas with both their names inscribed on it. Then they'd undressed and made passionate love. Daria had insisted that she wanted thirty-two birthday orgasms but had fallen sound asleep after orgasm number four. Andy had flossed her pubic hair out from between his teeth then joined her in bed. He'd quickly fallen asleep too.

2 a.m. in the morning:

All of a sudden Andy Watson jerked awake. Immediately he woke up he sensed danger. He'd perceived the danger even before waking, if that was possible.

There's someone in the bedroom!

There was a man standing at the foot of their bed. He must have climbed in through the wide-open window behind him, the west one that faced the town of Conway. The north window was only partly open.

Moonlight streamed in through the fully open window. The wind whisked the curtains in and out. They'd switched off the lights, but the moonlight framed the intruder clearly. He wasn't tall, five-eight at most. He wasn't muscular either. He was wearing some kind of flowing cape which the night breeze blew around his legs.

Andy hadn't yet given the man any sign that he was awake. He was still analyzing the situation. He lay there quietly, thinking.

Who the hell is this guy? Is he a burglar, or a rapist?

Neither possibility seemed right though. And, something about the man's poise as he stood there motionless additionally bothered Andy: he had a strange air of 'specific purpose' to him. The intruding silhouette appeared focused rather than manic.

And, just how exactly did he get up to our window? Andy wondered. *There ain't a ladder on the premises.*

"Dammit," the man said finally. "I should have expected you'd have company."

With that, he strode over to the wall and switched the lights on.

When he turned back around, Andy sat up.

"What the hell are you doing in our bedroom?" Andy growled. "Now, just you climb back down out of that window over there like the lizard you are . . . before I throw you out of it."

The intruder smiled. It wasn't a nice smile. He had a thin face, with a long nose and sunken black eyes. Rocker-length oily black hair. He was clean-shaven except for a pencil-thin mustache.

Two thing *really* bothered Andy about this guy. Two things that prevented him from immediately attempting to show the asshole the door:

The first was the man's dressing. He wore a red cape over a white suit and white shoes. Andy could forgive the man's white suit and shoes, but that damn cape was taking bad fashion sense too far.

The other thing—the *really* worrying thing—was the fact that a large part of the front of the man's white suit was splattered with red. Andy had no doubt that the red was blood.

So though this guy didn't appear to be armed, he was dangerous for sure. Maybe even deadly.

"Who the fuck are you?" Andy enquired. "And what the hell are you doing in our bedroom?" His voice was louder this time. He was really regretting that Daria didn't have a gun in here. Gorilla might have one, but Gorilla's bedroom was at the other end of the hallway. No way to get there fast, even if he knew where Daria's brother might have stashed a firearm.

"My name is Xander Mood," the intruder replied simply. Then he pointed at Daria. "And I'm here to sacrifice *her*."

"What?"

"I'm here to sacrifice Daria Simpson to open a gateway to Hell," Xander Mood repeated in a matter-of-fact voice.

"Huh?" This guy *was* dangerous. Worse, he was crazy too. "Did you just say *sacrifice?*"

Xander Mood continued speaking in an emotionless voice. "Your girlfriend is the reincarnation of Erin De Mornay."

"Reincarnation of who?" Andy wasn't really interested in knowing. He'd already gotten the deal figured out. This guy Xander believed himself to be a wizard, and planned on killing Daria in some black magic ritual. Hell no!—that wasn't ever happening. Andy's plan now was to keep the man talking until he found a suitable weapon to attack him with. He didn't want to just rush this guy unarmed. The blood splattered all over Xander's clothes meant he was armed. Andy also didn't know if Xander had friends in the house. So he figured he needed to err on the side of caution.

"Erin De Mornay," Xander explained patiently. "She was a famous witch who lived in California during the middle of the last century. She died about forty years ago." He spoke as if he were lecturing a high school class. "She was a disciple of Anton La Vey. Erin was right there with Anton when he opened the original Church of Satan in San Francisco on the thirtieth of April, 1966. A wonderful, powerful woman, and through her books, my spiritual mentor too."

"Yeah, man, I mean, that's really enlightening for sure. But . . . what's any of that got to do with Daria?" Andy's patience had just paid off. Partly hidden by a paperback novel, there was a pair of scissors on the nightstand beside him. Silver and gleaming and sharp. Dangerous enough. They'd have to do. He had to get this psycho out of the bedroom. Hopefully before Daria woke up, so she didn't start screaming. He stole a glance at her. The duvet was off her breasts. He watched her superb chest rise and fall. Damn, orgasms sure did help a woman get a good night's sleep.

Xander, meanwhile, had pulled two photographs from inside his suit and tossed them at Andy. "That's Erin De Mornay," he said. "I think the pictures'll answer any other questions you might have."

Andy picked up the pictures and examined them. Both were old black-and-white 4 × 6 inch glossies. Yeah, Xander really was nuts. The top photo showed Daria. But . . . no, no, no—Andy caught himself—this wasn't *his* Daria. This was *another* Daria. This Daria was dressed in 1930's clothes. This Daria had wanton, evil eyes and a debauched smile.

The second photo was even older. The same 'Daria' in Jazz Age dress and hat posing against the hood of a vintage Ford Model A.

Troubled, he looked up from the photos.

Xander nodded. "Convinced now, man? I assure you that your girlfriend's a dead ringer for Erin De Mornay in more ways than one. They even share the same date of birth: The sixth of June. Today."

Daria woke up then, before Andy could reply. Neither man spoke while she rubbed her eyes. Then, when she was properly awake, she gaped at the intruder.

"Xander? Xander, what are you doing in my bedroom?" She noticed the pictures Andy was holding. "And where did you get these pictures of me? Hey, this *isn't* me . . . who . . . who . . . how?"

Andy turned to her. "You guys actually know each other?"

Daria nodded. "Yeah, Xander's a warlock. He does magic tricks and stuff for kid's parties." (She was still sleepy. She clearly hadn't heard the part about herself being sacrificed.) "He also runs a nightclub called the Hole Faith down in Portsmouth, Virginia."

"But . . ." Andy said, "Daria, where do you know him from? I mean, how'd you two ever meet?" The question of their association honestly puzzled him.

She yawned. "Where else but Facebook?" She scowled at Xander. "Man, you got the time wrong. My birthday party is *tonight* . . . not this morning."

"Yes," Xander agreed, pulling a long knife from inside his cloak, its blade smeared with blood. "Yes, the party *is* tonight."

Daria screamed.

Andy grabbed the scissors off the nightstand and lunged at Xander.

Andy's main worry as he went flying through the air concerned his nakedness. All he had on were his light blue briefs. If this asshole slashed him anywhere sensitive . . .

But was I supposed to go to bed wearing Kevlar underpants? How's a guy to know that Psycho Joe was gonna turn up tonight?

Then he was all over Xander Mood. He was much bigger than Xander and with the scissors in hand, had the initial element of surprise. Before Xander knew what has happening, Andy had smacked the knife out of his hand.

That took care of that. At least he wasn't about getting his manhood sliced off.

But after that, things went downhill.

Back in the bed, Daria was seated upright and staring, with the duvet now pulled up over her breasts. She'd stopped screaming, but that was only because she'd remembered she lived well outside of town and the only persons likely to hear her yells at this hour of night would be folk driving by the intersection, of which she doubted there would be any. So she watched the two men, believing her lover would easily overpower the intruder.

Andy, though, *couldn't* overpower Xander Mood. He had the scissors raised near Xander's throat to frighten him, but Xander looked anything but frightened. Instead, he just looked irritated, like he had an office deadline to meet and Andy was wasting his precious time.

Then, suddenly, Xander flickered black. For a second he became a black statue, one that glinted wetly like it was freshly painted. Then he was himself again, exactly the same crazy asshole as before. The strange transfiguration was over almost before Andy realized it had even happened.

But the balance of power in their contest of strength had now shifted. Xander got a viselike grip on Andy's right wrist and squeezed. Howling with pain, Andy dropped the scissors; it had felt like Xander was breaking the bones in his wrist. The scissors fell on the bed by Daria's feet.

Then, next thing, Andy was being lifted off his feet. It was ludicrous—this guy who was maybe 5'8" in height and couldn't possibly weigh more than 150 pounds tops, carrying Andy (all 6'1" and 250 pounds of him) like he weighed nothing.

"I think it's time you left the building," Xander said, in that insanely calm way of speaking that he had. "This is supposed to be a private party."

He turned and carried Andy towards the open window.

Andy fought against Xander, but it felt like there was more than one set of hands carrying him. Unseen hands were grasping his arms and legs. One set of unseen hands was even covering his mouth so he could yell out.

Seeing Andy's straits, Daria flung away the duvet. She grabbed the scissors and leapt naked off the bed.

She stabbed Xander in the back but the scissors didn't penetrate. She dropped the scissors and picked up Xander's fallen knife instead. She stabbed him again. The effect was the same. The knife simply would not cut the magician.

Then Xander backhanded her. She flew across the room, ending up in a heap on the bed. She lay there breathing noisily, all fight for the moment knocked out of her.

Andy saw all this, but couldn't do a damn thing about it.

"Bye, bye, boyfriend," Xander said. "Thanks for leaving us!"

And then Andy was flying out of the window and through the air. He was twisting and turning and flailing wildly, trying to somehow stop himself from crashing into the approaching concrete. It felt like he'd been thrown by all the 'hands' that had carried him, not just Xander's.

Andy slammed into the ground below and was knocked unconscious.

II

Up in the bedroom, Daria had gotten her breath back. She attempted flight. She grabbed her cellphone off the nightstand and leapt off the bed again. She didn't care that she was naked; what mattered was getting away from Xander and calling the police. And calling an ambulance also for Andy. She couldn't hear him down there; he had to be hurt really bad.

Xander moved with catlike agility to stop her. One moment she was opening the bedroom door, the next moment he'd spun her round and was slapping her face.

By the third slap she was almost unconscious. She hardly felt her phone fall to the floor. She felt Xander drag her over to the bed and lay her flat along its bottom edge. She felt him tying her down there, binding her wrists and ankles with ropes.

She felt him smearing something on her belly.

He walked over to the window and peeked out. "It doesn't look like you'll be getting rescued tonight, Daria."

She found her voice. A weak one. "Why . . . why . . . ?" It was the only question in her mind.

He was taking off his clothes. "Remember when you told me on Facebook that you were born at 6. a.m. in the morning?"

She didn't reply, so he went on. He was naked now and had an erection. "You don't? Well I certainly do, Daria. You said you were born at six o'clock in the morning on the sixth day of June, which is the sixth month of the year. That was something you should have kept your mouth shut about."

"Why?" she repeated. She was doing her best not to stare at his stiff penis. She prayed he wasn't going to sexually assault her.

He picked up his knife and twisted it so it caught the light. "See, Daria, I know we joked about your date of birth and all, but in actuality it's no laughing matter."

Daria remembered now: It had been an innocent gag, that was all. The info was correct, but who in the world took that kind of thing seriously? She'd laughed when he'd suggested that maybe she was the Antichrist.

I can't be, she'd written back. *I know the Antichrist is a 'he' not a 'she.'*

To that, he'd LOL'd and replied: *Well, be careful when you're gonna have kids then. You just might be the Mother of the Beast.*

That had been hilarious. She'd LMAO-ROTF'd it.

Now, however, it didn't seem funny in the least.

Xander sat beside her on the bed. With his knees raised like this, she couldn't see his penis, which she was grateful for.

"Now, see," he explained while stroking her breasts, "what you didn't get was that the 666 coincidence in your birth makes you a perfect 'goat' for a magic ritual. All blood sacrifices work, but some work better than others. Anyone with that 666 coincidence—doesn't matter how the sixes occur, whether you were born on the sixth of whatever month in a '66 year, or on the sixth second of the sixth minute of the sixth hour of whatever day, you get the point—can be used—"

"That's great," Daria mumbled. The slaps still had her dazed. "Why use me then? There's got to be thousands of other people just as suitable. Xander, we're friends. Let me go, find someone else."

Xander grinned then. It wasn't a pleasant sight. His grin was that of a gator about to bite off someone's leg. "There are *millions* of suitable people. 'Sixers' we call 'em. Walking, breathing supernatural 'batteries' we can use to power our occultic needs." Squeezing her left breast painfully, he laughed. "In fact, right now there's a dead woman downstairs in my car."

At that information, Daria's eyes bulged wide. "Dead? A dead woman in your car? "Dead?"

"Yes. A prostitute born on the sixth of June, 1986. See? Another sixer like yourself. By the way, I met her on Facebook too. Social networking can be very dangerous, if you start giving out personal info to people you barely know. You might pick up a serial killer, or . . . a warlock."

She ignored the taunt. "Why use me then if you've already killed *her?*"

Before replying, Xander picked up something from the bedroom floor. He held it up for her to see. It was a large transparent jar filled with red liquid.

"The hooker's blood," he explained. "For seeding. Preparing the ground as it were." He uncorked the bottle and slowly poured the blood over Daria's body. She began screaming. Xander poured the dead women's blood into her open mouth. Horrified, she stopped screaming and began sputtering instead. Xander kept pouring the blood into her mouth. He clamped her nose shut so the only way she could breathe was to keep her mouth open. She had to either swallow the horrible red liquid or choke on it. Then she decided to shut her mouth. She wasn't a goddamn vampire; she wasn't drinking any more blood and that was that. She clamped her lips tightly shut and refused to open them even when she began seeing black dots before her eyes.

Xander left her. He stood up and crossed to the side of the room. She watched him. He bent over a bag and began rummaging through it. When he stood up again he was holding a rag and a roll of duct tape.

"Time to shut you up, baby. You'll utterly hate what's going to happen to you next and I'm really sensitive to female noise. So . . ."

He stuffed the rag into her mouth.

She bit him while he gagged her. She knew she'd bitten him—she could feel his fingers clamped between her teeth—but he didn't appear to notice. And then two of her front teeth snapped off. One tooth in each jaw. They shattered against Xander's withdrawing hand. Just like that.

Her mouth was filled with blood again. Her own this time. And the damned pain!

Xander raised her head and looped the duct tape around it twice to hold the gag in place.

She stared at him in additional horror. She'd never before heard of teeth breaking off when you bit someone. A throbbing ache now filled her mouth.

He correctly read the confusion in her eyes. "It's a spirit shield. Nothing natural can get through it." He tapped his left wrist with his right index finger. A black plume flared up around the finger. "There *are* some benefits to worshipping Satan, you know."

He picked up the bottle of blood from where he'd placed it on the floor. He'd poured half of it on her. "More than enough left to draw the pentagrams," he noted.

She noticed then that he had an intricate tattoo on his right hip. It was an 'A,' but upside down. She'd never seen its like anywhere before.

She watched him place the bottle of blood somewhere else on the floor, then return to the bed and pick up the two black-and-white pictures of the woman who looked exactly like her. She was utterly terrified now. Here she was, gagged and bound and drenched in another woman's blood, and Andy had been thrown out of the window. She hoped with all her heart that Andy was okay.

Xander sat on the edge of the bed again. He waved the photos at her.

"Okay," he said, "I already explained this to your boyfriend, but you were sleeping then so I'll do it again. . . . It's like this: This lady in the pictures is Erin De Mornay. She was a powerful witch who died in 1975. *You* are Erin De Mornay reborn. It's ironic then that I'm here to kill you again, I guess. But then, it's largely your fault that you're about dying again. Next time you reincarnate, Erin, be more choosy about your online friends." He dropped the pictures on her blood-smeared belly. "And *why* am I killing you? Simple: There's this realm called SADE—Yes, like the French marquis, though that's just a coincidence. SADE is a wonderful place, a place of magical power and evil glory. SADE is a place of transcending sexual ecstasy and also of incredible opportunity to cause pain to others . . . or to experience such, if that's your thing." He paused and ran his hand in the crack of her crotch, digging fingers into her vagina so she thrashed and squirmed. He went on: "Sacrificing a witch who's also a sixer will open a clear gateway into SADE." He laughed. "Most witches know this, so the sixers amongst us tend to keep such information about themselves very private . . ."

Listening to him rant, Daria's thoughts returned to Andy again. He was her only hope now. She began praying desperately that he wasn't dead, and that if he wasn't, he'd be able to get to a phone and call the police. Xander struck her as being quite egocentric. He liked spouting at the mouth. She prayed he'd continue talking until the police arrived to save her.

III

Andy opened his eyes to the agony of a shattered leg. There was a bleary second when he took in the fact that it was still the middle of the night, then the pain woke him up fully.

He sat up. He almost fainted from the agony of doing so, but he needed to have a proper look at the damage he'd suffered during his fall.

Oh shit! His right leg was broken in at least two places. White bone projected from the flesh above his knee. Below the knee, his lower leg was bent at almost a right angle. His right thigh and the concrete around it were covered with blood. The pain couldn't be described. It was amazing to him that he'd ever been unconscious at all with this sort of injury.

Cursing Xander Mood, he looked up. It was ridiculous how far he'd been thrown. He was at least thirty feet from the west wall of the Crossway building, almost out into the turnoff road that came from the interstate. He blinked. *What?* For a moment the house had seemed to have a thick black outline, as if someone had traced its photograph with a giant Sharpie.

An eerie light flickered in Daria's bedroom window. Purple fluorescent light in which black shadows danced on the ceiling. He couldn't see either Xander or Daria. He couldn't hear them either; which bothered him. Yes, Daria wasn't screaming, which meant Xander wasn't hurting her. On the other hand, she might be silent because she was dead.

Oh no, baby, don't die!

With that thought in mind, Andy began dragging himself around to the front of the building. With his leg broken and twisted like this, there was zero chance of him being able to stand up. He couldn't raise himself on his hands and knees either. All he could do was crawl on his belly. As he inched forward, the pain shot up into his brain, threatening to short-circuit him. He couldn't go on and he couldn't stop. Worst of all, he couldn't yell out each time the shattered ends of bone scraped either his muscles or the parking lot floor. If he made any noise Xander would remember him, and he was in no condition now to fight the wizard again.

He made his slow progression forward. With just his briefs on, the rough concrete chafed his skin. It was almost as bad as being worked over with a cheese grater. Still, this was mercy a lesser pain to complement the major one.

He had a simple plan: to somehow break into the diner and use the phone on the service counter to call the police. That was the only chance he had of stopping Xander from killing Daria. Once again he hoped she wasn't already dead. He'd die if anything happened to her!

Andy kept pulling himself forward. The pain was excruciating, as though his leg was being sawn off. He could feel himself bleeding out onto the parking lot floor, but the blood didn't seem to be too much. His biggest worry now was *how* to break into the diner. There was a steel shutter over the main entrance. That ruled the door out. All he could do was hope one of the windows wasn't properly latched. Or else, he'd have to resort to shattering a window to get in. That wasn't the real problem though. The real problem was, that even if he did break a window, how the hell was he supposed to climb up to it when he couldn't even make it to his hands and knees?

Still he kept going. Inch by agonizing inch. He couldn't—wouldn't—let Daria down. He *mustn't* let Daria down. He loved her. He had to save her.

He'd now reached the side of the diner. There were two windows here. But he intended to turn the corner to the front of the building. He didn't want Xander peeking out of the window and seeing what he was up to. Or hearing him.

Xander. Thinking was helping Andy ignore his broken leg. He pondered the case of the 'blackness' that had come over Xander for that moment, and the impossible strength the man had exhibited afterwards.

Black magic, black magic, black magic! The words thrummed in his brain like Spanish guitar chords.

(Like a lot of people, Andy Watson had never leant much credence to tales of supernatural occurrences. Though deep in his heart he believed God did exist, for credulity's sake he tried to state as fact only what he could prove to others. The case of dead Tommy Shawcross and the skinned pig had been one exception, and tonight was another. Andy had no doubts that what Xander had demonstrated to him upstairs was real magic.)

He got around the side of the diner only to discover there was a car in the way. The car, a red Nissan Sentra, was parked between the front entrance and the windows he wanted to reach. It had to be Xander's ride. (His own silver pickup truck was parked farther along the side of the diner.) The red Nissan was dusty all over, like it either hadn't been washed in a long while or had been driven a far distance. *Where the hell did Xander come from anyway?* Daria had mentioned it, but Andy had forgotten. A sudden twitch of pain made him abandon the question. It didn't matter anyway. Not now. Who the hell cared where the shithead had come from so long as he went away again, and preferably in police custody.

Andy felt a sudden burst of hope. There was someone in the car. He could see the outline of a head on the front passenger seat. If he could alert the person to what Xander was up to . . .

But then he realized the futility of his hope. Whoever was in Xander's car was clearly Xander's ally. They weren't about helping he and Daria. They'd most likely try to kill him.

And to get to the windows (one of which did seem to be open), he had to crawl around the rear of the car. Which would almost certainly result in him getting a bullet in the back of his head.

Momentarily defeated, Andy rolled over onto his back. Doing so twisted his right leg. Dammit! It felt like the leg was coming off Andy's body. He wanted to howl his lungs out, but didn't dare.

He lay there with Daria on his mind. *Daria, Daria, Daria. Don't die on me, sweetheart. I'm gonna figure this out. I gotta figure this out.*

That was when the front door of the red car opened and the woman stepped out.

Andy heard the sound of the car door opening over on the passenger side. Still flat on his back, he turned to look. He saw bare feet touch the floor. Female feet. So Xander's accomplice was female. The feet walked towards the rear of the vehicle. When they'd passed the rear tires he looked up to see if the person coming around the Nissan's trunk was armed with a gun.

It seemed it was time to die.

Only it apparently wasn't.

Andy was shocked when he saw that the woman walking towards him was already dead.

She *had* to be: her neck was gashed open from ear to ear. (The parking lot was well lit; he had no difficulty seeing the damage.) Her slit esophagus was a white-rimmed cavity in the meaty upper half of the cut. The wound was so deep that the woman's head wobbled precariously as she approached.

In addition to this, she had several long and deep slashes across her bare belly, cuts which formed the rough shape of a five-pointed star— the kind that usually filled a pentagram. He could see her guts in the depths of the cut.

She walked like a reluctant puppet on strings. Like she'd topple over at any second. A damned zombie walk it was.

Black magic, Andy again thought dully. That was the only 'logical' explanation for what he was witnessing. The only theory that fit the facts of the case. *Yet more of Xander's goddamned black magic.*

He couldn't take his eyes off the gaping hole in the dead woman's neck.

Her face was expressionless. But then, corpse's faces usually were. Also, her eyes were rolled up inside her head, so for the most part only the whites of her eyes showed. She was a blonde, though her short hair was mostly red now, dyed by the spillage of her blood. Her bright pink lipstick was smeared all over her cheeks and chin.

The 'dead' woman was dressed in a criminally-short black skirt that screamed "Hooker!" and fishnet stockings that seemed to confirm her profession. She was also wearing a pink tube top, but that had been slashed open all the way down the middle to allow Xander access to her belly to mark it up with the five-pointed star. She'd clearly not been wearing a bra—she had large breasts—and had no panties on either. Yes, definitely a hooker.

But none of this was really on Andy's mind as she wobbled her way towards him. Tough guy or not, you didn't want to hang around dead women. Not at 2:30 a.m. in the morning (he assumed he'd not been unconscious for too long). Especially not when the love of your life was about being murdered upstairs.

Andy levered himself up on his elbows and began dragging himself back the way he'd come. Oh no—he didn't want none of this.

Then he saw that the dead woman was holding out a cellphone to him.

"You'd better hurry up and dial 911," she said. "This place is gonna blow—we gotta get out of here fast."

Her voice was a harsh whisper. It seemed to come from the hole in her neck rather than her mouth.

Andy just gaped at her. How could she even talk at all? It shouldn't be possible with her throat ripped open like that. Didn't one need a voice box and trachea (or whatever it was called) to speak?

The horrible answer filled his mind: *More black magic.*

She remained like that, bent over him with her pink cellphone extended. "Stop gawking at me and take the damn phone, man. Yeah, I'm fucking dead. So fucking what? You got something against dead women? Huh?" To Andy, it sounded like she was snorting the words out. Yes, like they were powered by air from her nose, not her lungs.

Andy was real confused now. But he was grateful too. He took the phone from her hand.

"Hello. . . . 911? . . . I've got a situation here; someone's trying to murder my girlfriend. . . . Yes, yes, and my leg's broken . . . We're over by—"

The phone cut out. Andy redialed. It didn't connect. He kept redialing. Finally, he gave up and stared at the dead woman.

"Forget it," the dead woman said. "You won't get through again."
Now he was certain her voice was coming out of the hole in her neck.
Her lips and tongue moved as she spoke, but her mouth made no
sound.

"Time to go," she said. She grabbed his right wrist and pulled him
up to a sitting position. A burst of pain in his leg made him drop the
cellphone. He leaned over to pick it up, but she held him back. "Leave
it." Her breasts bounced against his face. There was a faint decaying
smell to them as if she'd recently started to rot. Blood from her slit
neck dripped in his hair.

"Ouch!" he yelped as his broken leg scraped the concrete. "Ouch!
Stop! . . . Hey—Who are you?" he asked.

"Piper Harris. An unfortunate prostitute who got in way over her
head with that asshole Xander." She was staring at him, but her eyes
were still rolled up in her head, so all he saw were their whites. The
semicircles on their top curves were either blue or green.

She began crying. The tears rolled down her cheeks.

Andy really felt for her. "I'm Andy Watson," he said. "Look, Piper,
I'm damn sorry that Xander killed you—"

"You can fuckin' well say that again." She wiped the tears from her
dead eyes.

"—But I gotta rescue my girlfriend."

"Forget it," she said. "Try to get up instead. We gotta get away
from here."

"Stop!" He almost screamed the words as she tugged on him, but
caught himself in time. So long as Xander didn't know he was alive,
there was hope. He explained: "Piper, there's no way I'm walking away
from here. I can't put any weight on my leg. You can see it's broken
in two places."

"Yeah." She let go of him for a minute. She stood over him, hands
on hips. He figured she was thinking. She looked utterly ghastly.

"Hey, Piper," he said after a while. She seemed to have frozen, and
he wasn't sure if she'd re-died on him or not, if that was the right
expression.

The almost-severed head wobbled down to face him. Her eyes
were still total blanks. "What, man? Hey, wait, I'm thinking."

"So am I. Listen."

"Okay, I'm listening."

"Piper, *you* can move around. Can you pleeeaaassse try to get into the house and stop Xander from murdering my girlfriend?" He pointed across the front lot, beyond Xander's red Nissan. Try that window over there; the one that looks open."

"It won't work."

"Why not?"

There were tears rolling down her dead cheeks again. "'Cos Xander's the one powering me up, that's why." She frowned and shook her head at Andy. "No, he doesn't know it—he doesn't even suspect that I'm reanimated down here. But if I go upstairs to interrupt him . . . do you get it?"

Andy got it. If she went upstairs Xander would most likely zap her with a wizard wand and that would be it for her. Nothing accomplished. The pentagram carved into Piper's belly had begun dripping a black liquid that didn't look anything like blood. If anything, it reminded Andy of the 'black' that had covered Xander upstairs for the split-second before he'd suddenly become superstrong.

He nodded grimly at her. "Yeah, I guess. Alright, how 'bout if you climb into the diner instead and call the cops using the phone on the counter?"

She shook her head, which made it look like it was going to fall off. "The phone won't connect."

"It won't? Why?"

"Magic stuff. Just take it from me that it won't. You're lucky you managed to get through on my cellphone. I think that's 'cos it was near my body so the magic couldn't immediately turn it off."

"Piper, I gotta do *something!*"

She hung her head just so. He could see the white links of her vertebrae inside her neck; they looked like fat worms crawling through the meat of her throat. "You already called the cops," she said. "They'll be able to trace the call to here . . . . Well, not immediately, they won't, but they'll get here later than sooner."

"Damn! . . . I need them here now!" Then he calmed down. "Listen, I got a better idea. We can take Xander's car and drive to Conway police . . . no, no—the Deerfield police station is closer; it's only a mile away. Did he leave the keys in the ignition?"

"He didn't. And even if he did, that wouldn't work either."

Andy was curious: "Why the hell not?"

"'Cos we'd not be able to drive off anywhere, that's why." She wagged a finger at the wounded man. "You're missing the point here: I'm being powered by Xander. Once I get a certain distance away from him—I think the range is about a hundred yards—I'll shut down and *really* be dead. As in *stone cold* dead. Then you'd be stranded."

"Shit!" Another door to rescuing Daria had just slammed shut in Andy's face.

The dead prostitute scowled at him. "You don't get it, do you? Xander's gonna succeed in what he's trying to do. He's gonna open a route into SADE and there's nothing that you or me or anyone else can do about it."

He squinted. "How d'you know that?"

"I'm *dead*, man. I know lotsa stuff." She grimaced at him (well it looked that way to him). "Most of it's really bad stuff though— murders and rapes and child and animal abuse and . . . evil icky things that are gonna happen no matter what. Hey—do you wanna know where you're gonna die?"

"*What?*"

"Do you want to know *where* you're gonna die? And when? And how? I know—I can tell you if you like."

No, Andy didn't want to know that. "Tell me this instead: Is Daria gonna survive this?"

Piper laughed. "You're one dedicated lover man, ain't you, trucker? Listen, forget Daria, she's as good as dead." The black stuff was now really oozing out of the devil-symbol on her belly. It dripped down her thighs like hot tar.

Andy forgot the pain in his leg. "Don't make crummy jokes like that."

"I ain't joking, Andy. She's not getting out of this alive. You got my word on that. Believe it."

He was going to protest again, but the fight had left him.

"Alright, time to save your life," she said.

Then she was behind him. She hooked her hands under his armpits and hauled him halfway to his feet, until his head was pillowed on her breasts. More of her death-liquids dripped down on him. Her death-smell was in his nostrils. Part of it was a smell of vomit, as though he were smelling her last meal through her slit throat.

She pointed in front of them both, out across the parking lot, at the moonlit road. "Now, Andy, we're both just gonna take a little stroll across the road."

She set off, dragging him along with her. She'd turned them around; they were moving with their backs to the road, their faces towards the Crossway building. Andy was a large man. He knew he was mostly dead weight in Piper's grasp, but she wasn't complaining. She just hauled him along with her while grunting through her neck.

His weight was telling on her though. They went slowly and it was a bumpy ride. The dead woman's big breasts cushioned his head. He needed their solace. His bad leg constantly bumped up and down on the concrete, firing pulses of agony through him. He'd begun bleeding again, leaving fat red drops on the gray stone. He was sweating from the pain of motion. He tried doing a 'hopping' sort of step with his left leg, but every now and then he'd mistime it and his heel would scrape the concrete. He gave up and just let Piper drag him along. He concentrated on not screaming out. It was clear that both his heels would be skinless by the time they'd crossed the road.

There was a wet heat against his back which had to be the demon-liquid spilling from the pentagram sliced into her belly.

"Alright, Andy," Piper said while pulling him up onto the sidewalk on their side, "I'm saving your life now, right?"

He grunted a reply. He couldn't think straight. And it wasn't just the pain either. His eyes were focused on the receding diner. His thoughts were focused on the rectangle of purple light spilling from that upstairs west window.

Daria . . . Daria . . . Daria!

They started out across the highway. Piper didn't, however, take Andy across Conway Road like she'd initially suggested. Instead, she pulled him into the grassy triangle formed by the splitting of the interstate turnoff into 'to' and 'fro' branches where it met Conway Road. This intra-route space (large enough to park four or five 18-wheelers in), was, on Andy's retrospective consideration, a much safer destination. (Opposite the diner, Conway Road had no sidewalk. It was bordered by a metal railing, beyond which the land dropped away steeply into the tree border. So if she'd taken him there, he'd actually be sitting in the main road.)

The grassy triangle also afforded Andy clear view of Daria's bedroom window.

"You know, Andy baby," Piper told him as she pulled him along, "I shoulda listened to my ma and never become a prossie in the first place."

Andy didn't reply then either. This time he didn't even grunt. He just wanted the pain to stop.

"It's a shitty job," she went on. "The hours suck, the pay sucks, and you keep sucking too. You've no idea how much fellating a working girl does. It's practically our calling card. We suck and suck and suck and . . . damn! And then there's the cops too. The law just sucks—lotsa times I gotta give cops blowjobs to not bust me . . . and then there's shits like Xander who're gonna kill us hookers just 'cos we're easy prey. . . . Nah, I shoulda never become a hooker . . ."

Andy couldn't be certain since he couldn't see her face, but it sounded like the dead woman was crying again. Then she bumped his right leg again and he let out a long loud groan.

Piper didn't seem to notice his discomfort. Or maybe, she just didn't care; a mere broken leg clearly didn't compare with being dead.

"And, Andy, you wanna know what sucks worst of all, man? The goddamn afterlife, that's what. You've no idea how horrible being dead is. It's just nasty. I'd pick being a meth-brain STD-riddled truck stop junkie whore—the lowest of the low—over dying any day. I mean it. Being dead just sucks, man. . . ."

While she'd been speaking Andy had been gazing up at the moon. It was almost full, with only barest wisps of black cloud marring its gleam.

He began praying that the cops would arrive quickly. It shouldn't take them too long to trace his call, should it?

IV

Daria gaped and struggled but it was no use. Xander's penis came closer and closer to her face.

No, he'd not raped her like she'd expected. But he'd been masturbating for five minutes now, all the while ogling her like she was a porn video. His lecherous gaze felt as bad as if he *was* raping her.

The wizard stroked himself faster and faster. He was kneeling on the edge of the bed, his erection right by her head.

And then—*splash, splash, splash*—he ejaculated all over her face. Some of the come got in her eyes. It stung. She blinked rapidly, trying to get it out. She flapped up and down, feeling utterly degraded.

***

Xander flicked his final drops of semen off on her nose, then straightened up.

"And now it's time for you to die," he said.

He gazed around at his preparations: The woman tied down on the bed, the bloody pentagrams inscribed on the wall and on her naked body, his semen glazing her face like dissolved pearls . . . The semen was important because it determined which gateway he opened, which part of SADE he went to. The SADE acronym stood for Sex, Agony, Detention, and Enlightenment. Until Xander knew more about the realm, he was only interested in visiting the Sex area.

(The ejaculation had also helped Xander clear his head. He'd not screw up the spell now, for sure.)

There were some other little touches to the sacrificial scene: a multitude of black candles burning everywhere and a severed goat's head on the dresser next to Daria. Then there was the fluorescent purple light. The purple light had nothing to do with the ritual. It was just a wizard trick; a personal touch. Being a showman of sorts, Xander felt the light gave his ritual a touch of class. He smirked. Thank Satan he was done with holding parties for crappy 10-year-olds who had no idea that what they were witnessing wasn't sleight-of-hand but actual demonic manifestation.

The book with the sacrificial spell—the Necromantica—lay on the floor inside one of his pentagrams. Its pages of dried human skin were open. Its letters of human blood glowed in the candlelight as if the blood were once again fresh and wet. The book had an eerie black outline to it. He'd placed the Necromantica close enough to the bed that he could read it if he forgot part of the spell. It wouldn't do to mispronounce one of its cryptic words and end up in the Agony or Detention area of SADE.

Xander nodded, everything was in place. He'd been worried that the goat head might not be fresh enough, but it wasn't smelling too bad. The prostitute's blood was nice and red everywhere.

He smiled at Erin De Mornay's reincarnation. She looked so lovely with the blood-pentagrams on her breasts, belly and thighs. The final pentagram was drawn over her crotch, with her sex at its center.

Xander moved back to beside her head. He turned and stared at the Necromantica. He concentrated on the book's evil text. He filled his mind with its evil words. The book's skin pages flickered with death and murder.

He picked up his ritual knife.

"It's time to begin," he said, a demonic gleam in his black eyes.

***

Daria thrashed and groaned against her bonds, but it was no good. She stiffened as she felt the huge blade press against the right side of her neck. Then the blade was through her skin and inside her body—she could feel the pain of her severed neck muscles and the wetness of her blood escaping her. There was nothing she could do. She was dying.

Her blood jetted out from the deep slit and splashed Xander's naked chest and belly. In horror, she saw that he was erect again.

Her already complete horror increased ten-fold when Xander bent towards her, inserted his penis into the hole he'd ripped in her neck, and began fucking her there.

Pump, pump, pump! She felt his hard penis moving up and down inside her throat, stabbing through her torn muscles, violating her in a way she'd never imagined was possible. The warlock fucked her neck violently as the blood poured out, his penis widening the hole his knife had made. He pulled out his erection once and the blood gushed out after it. Then he again plugged her neck with his manhood and resumed the violent assault. And while doing so, she could hear him reciting an incantation in a language she'd never heard before:

"*Natas, natas . . . Bruzz . . . SADE . . . SADE . . .*
Katua, Erin De Mornay . . . Nakus koos nigi!
Kadana liva liva, tiva kuus,
Lleh, Natas, lleh Natas,
Erin De Mornay, bruzz SADE . . ."

As she died, she stared up at the madman who was killing her. Fucking her to death. Yes, he was *fucking her* to death, his erection lubricated with her spilling blood. She didn't understand it. No, she didn't understand it at all. How could her life end this way? How could a good woman like herself expire in such a nasty, repulsive fashion?

Daria really could feel her life ending. It was over for her. She wasn't going to be granted a last-second reprieve.

As she died, she wondered where Andy was. She wondered why he hadn't saved her. She hated him as she died. He was supposed to protect her from madmen like this one. He was expected to protect his woman from people like this crazy man who was now ejaculating into her neck like it was a vagina. From this man who as he came had picked up his knife again and was stabbing it into both of her breasts, while screaming, "Koo-oo-op Erin De Mornay! Jaka SADE, lleh Natas SADE!"

You were supposed to protect me, Andy, Daria raged in thought. *But you didn't. You didn't, you didn't! I hate you! I hate you! I hate you!*

And then she died.

V

Across the road, Andy sat in the grass triangle. He was facing the diner, gripping his right thigh, and groaning.

At least three inches of bone now stuck out from his skin. He wasn't bleeding, but the leg was now wrenched sharply to the side. His right leg now seemed to have three joints between hip and ankle. He didn't dare try to straighten it out. The best he could do was brush away the coating of dirt on it. That hurt bad enough.

He stared across the road at the Crossway. There had to be something he could do to save Daria. Piper had said she was destined to die—but he didn't want to believe that. Nothing was *destined* to happen. He had to save her!

Piper, meanwhile, was standing on his right, watching the moon. The satellite shone bright and unobstructed, the night black velvet behind it.

The purple glow from Daria's bedroom window had now turned to an intense red.

Red like spreading blood.

Andy winced. He felt like shit, sitting here while Daria might be getting killed.

"Dammit, Piper, ain't there nothing we can do to save her? I gotta do something. I can't just sit it out like this!"

Piper turned to face him, a ghastly smile on her dead face. "Actually, Andy, there is something you can do for me."

"Yeah? What?"

"I saved your life, right? You do appreciate that, don't you?"

"Yeah, sure." He had no idea where this was leading.

Piper stepped up close to him and bent over him. Her reek of death had now intensified. Or maybe she'd just farted.

She squatted facing him with her hands on his shoulders. Her blank-eyed stare gave him the creeps. And that horrible gash where her neck had been torn open . . .

Then she dropped her right hand from his shoulder to his crotch and began fondling him there.

He instantly jerked back, which merely poured agony through his right leg again. "What are you doing?"

"See, Andy," she said, her voice gushing like air from her neck, "I want one last fuck before I'm gone from here for good. I just saved your life; you're definitely gonna remember me for that. Now give me something to remember *you* by." Her smile spread into a grin. "And, baby, this one's on the house." She was still fondling his penis. He knocked her hand away. She responded by sliding her fingers inside the waistband of his briefs and really taking hold of him.

Andy laughed. This was utterly ludicrous. *She wants to fuck? Now? A dead hooker wants to fuck?*

"My leg's broken," he protested. "And my girlfriend's getting murdered opposite us. Besides which the cops'll be here soon. You're real pretty, Piper, for sure, but I assure you I'll never get it up."

She leered at the unintended compliment.

Next, Piper produced a condom from a skirt pocket. He stared at the rubber. He found her action ridiculous, seeing as she was already dead. Did she actually think she was going to catch a disease? Or maybe she was doing it for *his* protection? Maybe Piper had an STD?

"Oh, you'll get it up, baby," she cooed. "I do this for a living. Yeah, man, just watch me work."

He relaxed back. He saw nothing to worry about. This wasn't going to work. He'd never get an erection for her. It couldn't happen. She'd give up shortly and he could go back to worrying about Daria.

He got it up.

Crazily, once Piper began stroking him again, his penis got hard. No, he wasn't aroused at all. He didn't even feel his erection. Not at thing. What he actually felt was horror. Horror at his penis inflating with blood despite his disapproval. He stared speechless at the swollen organ. He was struck dumb by its betrayal of him. Hard as it was, it didn't feel like part of him. It felt as if Piper had 'magicked' it erect. It felt frozen and unreal. Like some arcane supernatural force was working on that part of his body. He was scared it was going to start flickering with black light.

Giggling with delight, Piper rolled her condom on him. "See, Andy, I told you you'd get it up for me."

"Piper, please. I don't want to."

"Your dick says otherwise. Talk to my tits, hon, 'cos your dick sure ain't listening."

That was when Andy realized that the gut-wrenching pain in his right leg had vanished too. *How the hell did she do that? And if she can it now, why didn't she do it earlier and stop me hurting like my damn leg was being amputated without anesthetic?*

He was still pondering this when Piper squatted over his thighs and slid down on his erection.

"The cops'll be a while yet," she said as she took him completely into herself. He felt the pressure of her crotch on his, but had no sensation of his body being enclosed inside hers.

"Now just relax and let me do all the fuck."

He was still sitting up, leaning on his arms. She held him tight, wrapping her arms around his muscular chest, squashing her cold breasts against him. His one relief in this position was that he couldn't see her face with those disgustingly blank white eyes.

He made a final protest as she began riding him. "Please, Piper . . . If the cops arrive now, they're gonna think I'm having sex with your corpse. That'll get me in world of trouble. I'll likely even go to jail for it."

She gasped through her neck. "Andy, baby, deal with it—*you are* having sex with my corpse. But, but don't . . . Ooooh, that feels real nice, baby. I was gonna say . . . don't worry, man . . . ooh, ooh, man that's just so *deeeeep*. Your cock feels so fat and big in my juicy pussy . . . Oh yeah, the police won't be here anytime soon. They've screwed up the triangulation on which cellphone tower caught your call." She sighed with feeling. "And, besides, they'll be too late anyway."

Then she really began humping him. HARD, HARD, HARD! Andy just let her do it. Her almost-severed head kept bouncing up and down. And really violently too. Her head whipped back and forward. He feared it would snap off her neck and roll away. He was certain that if her head did pop off she'd continue screwing him regardless.

"Wow, Andy," she gasped in delight after a particularly violent pump of her hips, "I'm the dead one here, but it's your dick that feels like it's got rigor mortis!"

He honestly couldn't feel himself inside her. He kept staring moodily over her shoulder at the Crossway Diner. The red light in Daria's window looked like fire. Like there was a lake of boiling sulfur inside the room.

Piper bounced on him, squealing and moaning, groaning and gasping, and making loud varts. The hot black goop spilled from the cuts in her belly. The goop dripped down between their bodies to their joined crotches. There it acted as lubrication to their necromantic sex act.

Andy now became aware of a danger: Piper's relentless bouncing on him was wrenching his damaged leg all over the place. True, he couldn't *feel* his right leg anymore, but he could damn well *see* it. The leg dragged left and right over the roadside grass with each twist and turn of her body on his. It looked horrible now. At the moment it was bent almost in a semicircle.

He grew scared: *That broken thighbone inside has gotta be tearin' my muscles and nerves to shreds in there. I need my leg to be okay to drive my truck!*

Andy found his situation impossible. The dead prostitute was clutching him tight. He felt the desperation in her grip. This was her last fuck, and she was definitely making the most of it. He imagined she was crying again. She was making little squealing noises, either from pleasure or pain. Her feet were behind him, helping keep him upright, so he held her too.

Comforting her seemed the only thing to do. That and hoping she'd be done with him soon, before the police got here.

VI

Though dead, Daria discovered that she could still sense the world. Just not in the way the living did. Her body was limp and lifeless and already cooling, but her spirit hadn't departed it. Her spirit hovered over her corpse like a vulture. Her spirit was like a massive eye, a spectral telescope ranging far and wide.

Dead, Daria also knew things. Things she couldn't see. Just like Piper Harris outside, Daria now knew a lot of weird stuff.

She knew, for instance, that the police were on their way over. Coming as fast as they could. Fast enough to cause an accident. Better late than never, right? Besides, their lateness was all Xander's fault. His magical shield had screwed up all the telecoms for miles around. No nearby telephone was at the moment working right.

She 'turned.' On her right, Xander was getting dressed again. The horrible warlock was smeared with her gore. But that didn't matter. Not where they were headed.

Daria knew that too: where they were headed. She knew Xander had succeeded. He'd opened the gateway to SADE. All around them her bedroom had altered in appearance. Its windows and doors had vanished. Each of her pretty cream walls now had an ominous black archway in it. Each of the four archways led into a dim space beyond. The archways had inscriptions carved over them—in four languages, one of which was English: SEX, AGONY, DETENTION, ENLIGHTENMENT.

SADE, an utterly horrible place. Xander had been more successful that he'd intended. He'd wanted to open just one route out of the human realm, but the sheer brutality of his murder of her had unlocked the others also.

SADE. A part of Hell.

Xander was dressed in his blood-spattered suit again. "Time to go, Erin," he told Daria's abused corpse. He picked up his knife, then walked over and cut her bonds.

SADE. Daria knew their destination was a bad place. She didn't want to go there at all.

Suddenly, flames poured out of the AGONY gateway and filled her bedroom. The hellfire squirted in like it came from a flamethrower. It flowed red like lava without substance. Her bedroom furniture began burning. Her bed burnt, but she didn't burn along with it. Neither did Xander.

As the room combusted around them both, Xander packed up his wizard gear. She watched him pick up his horrible book—the Necromantica, she now knew it was called, ageless evil inscribed on human skin, using as ink the blood and feces of those murdered in the vilest of ways.

She turned from him to 'look' outside the Crossway again.

177

Andy.

She could see her boyfriend as clearly as if he was inside the burning bedroom with her: Andy by the roadside having sex with that butchered hooker Piper. Or rather, being fucked by her. Piper had herpes but had thoughtfully put on a condom first so Andy wouldn't catch it. She needn't have bothered though. The magic reanimating her had killed all her sex bugs.

Andy who'd not saved her. Daria couldn't forgive him for that. She just couldn't. She *hated* him.

Piper was coming for the sixteenth time now. And still going strong. She was going to keep on screwing Andy until she died for good. And that would only occur once Xander entered SADE and his backflow of reanimating energy was cut off. Poor Piper. Hell sucked. Piper was desperate to enjoy as much ecstasy as she could before the Agony demons got her again.

Piper had frozen Andy's penis harder that steel. All Andy could do was hold on and hope for the best. Hope Piper didn't snap his manhood off.

Yes, yes, yes—Daria *knew* it wasn't Andy's fault. She could feel his worry and love for her . . .

But still she hated him. (Her horror was so absolute that it needed a definite object to focus on; someone to take the blame.) If only Andy had saved her from this asshole magician . . .

The flames were ceiling-high around them now. Daria looked away from Andy and instead looked through her house. Her diner. The business she'd labored to build into a success. The fire was spreading downstairs now. This wasn't just any normal kind of fire. This fire was alive. It had a head and arms and legs and eyes. A fire-beast from Hell. It moved with purpose. The fire had a destination. It was walking downstairs to the Crossway's kitchen. It was headed outside, for the 1000-gallon propane tanks that fed the diner's gas ranges. And once it reached them . . .

Despite how much she utterly despised him now, Daria was relieved that Andy was well away from the diner.

"Alright, Erin, time we were leaving."

(She wished to God that this jerk would stop calling her 'Erin.' She wasn't his goddam witchy high school crush Erin De Mornay.)

Xander picked her body up. As easily as he'd picked up Andy and thrown him out of the window. Like she weighed nothing. She almost expected him to tuck her under his arm. He slung her limp body over his shoulder in a fireman's carry.

Then she was sucked back down into her body. Reentering herself was as bad as dying all over again. It was ghastly, going from being a free spirit to being squeezed and compressed into a cage of dead meat.

Afterward she felt horrible. She was still dead, but a living kind of dead.

She could feel again. She could move again.

Suddenly, Daria was really, really scared again. She was terrified. With the foresight of the dead, she understood that there was worse to come for her.

Xander strode towards the SEX gateway into SADE. The words over the doorway flickered red in black stone. She beat and kicked against him, trying to free herself from him. It was useless. She knew it would be useless.

But she didn't want to go into SADE. Not even into the SEX gateway to the realm, which promised intense erotic gratification. There was real ecstasy in there, despite which she didn't want to venture into the place. She knew what Xander would do to her once she got in there. She didn't want the bastard ever touching her again, not even to make her orgasm.

She tried screaming, but she'd forgotten that her mouth was still taped over. The noise she attempted making whistled from the gaping hole in her fucked-open neck. Her intended screams merely blew drops of semen out of her throat. In frustration, she beat a tattoo on her captor's chest.

Xander Mood laughed as he walked through the fire.

VII

Andy miserably watched the flames billow out of Daria's bedroom.

Damn! It looked like Piper had been right. Daria *was* going to die in there.

Piper, meanwhile, was still riding him hard. Andy had lost count of how many orgasms the dead woman had had by now. Might have been thirty or forty. Or fifty.

"Ooh yeah, baby, give me that deep hard dick! Oh, I gotta come some more like—!"

Then, all of a sudden, Piper stopped moving and talking. She didn't give any warning. She didn't slow to a halt. She didn't gasp and stiffen and tell him how fantastic the sex had been. She didn't say "Thanks!" or "Call me?" She just stopped moving. She was rising to ram her ass down on his erection again when she froze.

She hung there in space for a second. Then she collapsed on him.

At the same moment his penis magically unstiffened. It went limp and he could feel it again.

Then he heard the first police sirens. Coming fast from the east. That would be the Deerfield cops responding. Sounded like at least three squad cars coming.

Andy thrust Piper off him. He shoved her violently and she collapsed left. She hit the ground hard. Her neck vertebrae snapped. Her head detached and rolled off her shoulders. Her head rolled sideways into a ditch. Her body lay beside his in a crumpled mess. All the black goop that had spilled from the pentagram on her belly vanished. Once again he could see her guts in the cuts.

The pain in his right leg returned. The pain hit him like a punch to the head. It was so excruciating now, it almost knocked him unconscious.

But not yet, he knew. He had something to do first. Something of the utmost importance to his future reputation: Working fast, he pulled the condom off his penis and flung it behind him with all his might; as far as he could. Then he pulled up his briefs again.

The lights of the first police car showed in the distance, up on the overpass. Andy leaned back on his elbows and watched the diner.

There was a whole lot of fire over there now. Like monster tongues, the flames were licking along the building's outside walls. It looked like the flames had a mind of their own, the way they were crawling along the side of the building like fat orange centipedes. The fire gave him the impression that it was alive and intelligent.

Watching all that, Andy didn't know what to think. The now unceasing pain in his leg chopped up his thoughts into little bursts of regret that he'd been unable to save the woman he loved. *Maybe the cops will . . . no, they won't*. The thought had a horrible finality to it. He stared at Piper's body. *She said . . . she said Daria was as good as dead.*

Watching the Crossway burn, Andy felt like dying himself. He wished he were dead. Yes he did. Daria was dead. So what was *he* living for? Why the hell had he survived?

The diner exploded the moment the police arrived.

One moment it was this crazy monument writhing with centipedes of fire, the next: **Kaboom!**

Andy shielded his eyes against the glare as the Crossway went sky-high. He fell onto his back as he jerked his elbows off the grass. The heat seared his naked body. Red light penetrated his fingers and palms. He shut his eyes as tight as he could. Without daring to look, he was aware of the entire building disintegrating into a massive cloud of fire and mangled debris that floated overhead. The sounds reaching his ears told him more than he wanted to know. He knew that along with Xander's Nissan, both his own pickup truck and Daria's Mazda convertible had been blown up too.

***

The arriving policemen gaped in their vehicles as the two-story building erupted like a volcano. None of them knew what to make of the spectacle of watching a house break apart like it was built of matchsticks. Then the pre-dawn air was filled with a flaming cloud— a cloud that visually obliterated everything ahead of them.

The three patrol cars had screeched to a halt the instant the explosion happened. Now, as it began raining particles of the building everywhere, they made a series of tight U-turns and got out of there fast, heading back up the overpass.

Once they were a safe distance away, the driver of the front car got on the radio and called the Fire Department. No one wanted a fire burning out of control here. Not with all surrounding woods.

***

Andy was aware of an intense heat floating over him. Tongues of flame licked at him. The fire was an infernal mouth that wanted to eat him. He heard loud noises; things hitting the ground around him.

His right leg was now a throbbing agony he'd become used to. The pain was part of him. Unable to either ignore or end it, he'd been forced into accepting it.

The heat subsided a little. He opened his eyes. There was dust and smoke everywhere. He peered up and down the highway.

Where the hell did the police cars go? They were approaching a moment ago . . . just before the Crossway blew—

He leaned up again and stared across the road. *DARIA!!!! NOOOOOO!!!*

There was precious little left of the Crossway to see. The building's entire top floor and roof were gone—likely up in pieces in the sky somewhere. The lower walls were all flattened, blown outward across the parking lot. Little mazes of brick that had once protected people from the elements. Whatever still remained inside the erstwhile building was currently being blown sky-high. It really looked like a volcano was erupting under the place. Red fire, yellow fire, orange-mingled-with-blue fire. The fire raged everywhere. A hellish hill of flame that once again seemed horribly alive.

Scariest of all, though, was the cloud overhead. That cloud of bricks and furniture. Andy was puzzled. What was holding the damn thing up there? It wasn't like it was comprised of drops of water.

But the cloud clearly wasn't going to be up there long. It was already raining debris everywhere—half of a chair, an axle with tire attached, a half-melted pane of glass, a flaming mattress, Daria's portable hairdryer . . . He made those out as they whizzed past him, dropping out of the sky like air-to-surface missiles. A car steering wheel spun past his head. Then bricks began dropping around him.

I'm living a charmed life, he thought. *Well, I'd better be. With my leg fucked up like this, there's no way I can move anywhere.*

Then, he had a strange recollection: what Piper had said concerning his place and time of death. She'd offered to tell him both if he wanted to know. He considered: *That more or less means I ain't about dying here and now, right? Well I sure as hell hope that's what it means.*

He stared at Piper's headless corpse. She'd already been hit by three or four bricks (which had made large dents in her), and a long shard of glass was stuck in her belly. He felt a sudden massive twinge of pity for her. She'd saved him. Even if it was only because she wanted one last fuck. He owed her a lot. He grew sentimental. *If I ever have a daughter, I'll call her Pi—*

A whirling metal bar fell from the sky then and hit him in the chest. The bar went right through his right lung. He howled in pain and blood erupted out of his mouth. *So much for living a charmed life!* Andy looked down at the metal rod that had pierced him. *What the hell?* It was the tire iron from his pickup truck. He couldn't believe it. The damn thing was sticking out of his chest and blood was seeping out around the wound. He could feel its exit wound in his back too.

He coughed again and blood poured out over his lips. All of a sudden it hurt like hell to breathe. He began worrying about the amount of blood he was losing. Just how much blood did folks have in them anyway? He had to be down to his own reserves by now. In fact, he was certain of it.

Then a brick dropped down from directly overhead and knocked Andy unconscious.

***

Across from Andy, the diner finished burning down. The ravenous blaze ate up the building's remains like they were breakfast.

The fire trucks arrived five minutes after Andy was knocked out. Two hours later, when the sun rose, the firefighters were still trying to extinguish the fire.

VIII

Andy woke up in hospital, in intensive care. It was four days later. He was bandaged from head to toe and more doped-up than a heroin addict. His right leg was up in traction. In addition to the tire iron through his chest, while he was out unconscious a kitchen knife had stabbed him in the belly, and Daria's home theater DVD player had broken both bones in his left forearm when it dropped on him from the sky. And then there were all the first-degree burns from the fire.

Andy was in hospital for a month.

There was nothing the doctors could do to properly fix his right leg. The nerves controlling his right thigh muscles had been ripped apart in more than one place. There simply wasn't enough nerve tissue left to splice together. Some of the muscles themselves weren't much better than chopped meat. The doctors did the best repair job they could, but Andy would wear a brace on the leg for the rest of his life.

There goes my damn truck drivin' career, Andy realized. Knowing that he'd never drive a rig again, he was unsure whether or not to curse the late Piper Harris. All the shredding to his leg had clearly occurred while she'd been having her 'last ride' on him and dragging it left and right everywhere.

***

The police visited. Andy told them what had happened: How Daria had met Xander Mood on Facebook, only she hadn't known he was crazy; how Xander had broken into their bedroom and thrown him out of the window. When they asked him how he and the headless prostitute had gotten across the road, Andy replied that he didn't know. He lied that he'd been knocked unconscious by his fall from the window and had woken up inside the grass triangle. He'd stayed awake long enough to see the diner explode, then been knocked out again.

He was already injured enough; he wasn't ready for the added insult of being thought insane.

The cops nodded in sympathy.

Then the cops told him that they'd not found Daria's body.

"We didn't recover a thing, not a single piece of either of their corpses," Detective Rob Farrell told him. "No bones, nothing."

"Nothing?" Andy asked, keeping his real thoughts to himself.

"Nothing," Detective Farrell confirmed. "All we can assume is that the fire got so hot that it incinerated both their corpses. And then, that crazy cloud—no one can explain that either—scattered their ashes all over the state. That's the only explanation that makes sense." He looked bothered for a minute. "Just 'tween you and us, Mr. Watson, there's really a whole lot to this case that makes little sense."

Andy pretended innocence. "Like, what else?"

"Like why the propane tanks out behind the diner kitchen exploded in the first place. There was utterly no reason why they should have. Or even, when they did, how the fire leapt across the backyard to the house. And also, we've the mystery of why the fire itself raged for so long. You were unconscious so you can't possibly know this, but it took the fire boys four hours to put it out. Four damn hours. And when they finally subdued the blaze, they couldn't find what had been fueling it. The Fire Chief said it was almost like the ground itself had been burning. Or the air."

Andy nodded. It wasn't important. What was important was that the woman he loved was gone, murdered by that wizard asshole Xander Mood to open his portal to . . . where had Xander called it?

The police left. Andy lay there in bed wondering. They'd not found the bodies? Had Xander actually succeeded in . . . ? Yes, Piper had said he would. And he'd taken Daria's corpse along with him, to wherever it was. But what use was a corpse to him? Or had he left it behind for the flames to consume; those flames that had to have come from Hell itself?

Andy wouldn't ever forget the moment when it had seemed to him as if the fire consuming the Crossway was a living, breathing beast that was eating the building.

Andy wept for a long while over losing Daria. He wept for a good long while.

IX

Once out of hospital, Andy found himself faced with the dilemma of how to earn a living now that he could no longer drive a truck.

He could no longer *drive*, period.

***

Enter Karen Losey. Again.

Karen Losey had always had a thing for Andy Watson. She'd cooled that thing off after Daria had pulled her into the Crossway's kitchen that time and threatened to make her part of the diner menu. But now, Daria was out of the way for good. Karen wasn't pleased that Daria was dead, but then she wasn't shedding any tears for her either. She just no longer needed to fear that someone was going to make womanburgers out of her.

Karen didn't care that Andy was now a cripple. The way she saw it, his being crippled worked in her favor. It shaved off a good amount of the romantic competition. Most ladies she knew only wanted properly bipedal men. She also knew she wasn't the prettiest woman around. It was nice that the man she wanted wasn't perfect either. It evened things out.

She'd visited him while he was in hospital. After he got out, they'd taken to sitting and drinking together. They weren't an item yet, but Karen wasn't in a hurry. She wasn't worried. Before Andy's accident, women had flocked around him; he was tall and handsome and fun to know. Now, where were all those girls?

So they sat and drank and laughed. Occasionally Andy reminisced about what had happened that night. But he never told her everything—Karen could tell that he was holding back some details. She let it go. It was enough to just be with him. And, so far as she could tell, he enjoyed being with her too.

They discussed his plans for the future—he still had some money, but it wouldn't last forever and he really needed employment. But of what sort?

Then one day, Karen's father Lew told her he wanted to sell his hardware store. The old man had prostate cancer and couldn't cope anymore. He'd have let Karen have the hardware store, but she'd never shown herself to have much of a head for figures and he was certain she'd run the place into the ground in no time. (That was how Karen had begun working as a secretary in the first place: she'd screwed up the old man's bookkeeping one time too many and he'd been terrified she'd put him in the red. So he'd 'fired' her.)

"Hold on, daddy," she'd replied him. "I'll sound Andy out about it."

She'd told Andy. Andy had been more than interested. He'd sold both his truck and his house to raise the cash. The money still hadn't been enough, so he'd taken a small loan from the bank. He'd bought the store and temporarily moved into the little room at the back.

Karen had moved into the little room with him. He'd looked surprised but had said nothing. In fact, he'd seemed pleased.

In bed that first night, she'd been pleased to discover that it was just his leg, not his penis, that had gotten broken. And he'd seemed to delight in her body too. She'd been worried about that—that he might compare her unfavorably to Daria in bed. But he hadn't and the sex had been as satisfying and rewarding as she'd expected. His bad leg caused them some bedroom limitations. For one thing, it meant no doggy-style; but then she'd never liked dogs anyway—cats were more her scene. They also couldn't make love with him lying on his right side. But then, spooning on the left was fine too.

And so, they'd been together since then. Andy had a good head for business. She worked for him occasionally, but bearing in mind the reason her father had lovingly 'sacked' her, she insisted on not doing the books.

Karen was well aware she was living in another woman's shadow. Daria had only been dead six months when she and Andy had hooked up.

Sometimes Andy drank too much. When he did, she knew why. Sometimes also, he was moody and short-tempered with her for days on end; she knew why then too. She was patient. She had faith that time healed all wounds.

They lived and loved and were happy. And slowly but surely, the dead woman's shadow faded from over them. After a while it was as though Karen and Andy had been dating for years. As if Daria had never existed.

But of course, this illusion was shattered on the next 6th of June. Then she'd been scared Andy might commit suicide. She hidden his guns. She taken all the knives and razor blades out of the house. She'd let him drink as much as he cared to. She'd sat 'au naturel' across from him all evening—legs spread, her pink womanhood on display—just in case he wanted her. She'd been shocked when he'd begun crying. That night he couldn't get it hard for her. She'd been more relieved than annoyed. She'd been worried that if they did have sex, he might start calling her 'Daria.' She'd been relieved when he'd fallen asleep.

These damn anniversaries are gonna be hard to get through, she'd thought glumly, lying in the darkness of their little room and listening to him snore. Then she'd smiled. *But it doesn't matter. I love Andy enough to get through 'em.*

***

The pain faded. Andy slowly responded to Karen's love for him. What had begun for him as merely a fling to tide him over his grief—because a man always needed a woman—became true love.

As his love for Karen deepened, so did his longing for Daria fade.

Not entirely though. One never forgot a significant romance. Andy always carried that sadness—that knowledge that he'd lost an important part of himself when the Crossway burned down. It was an emotional chip on his shoulder.

If only I'd been able to save her, he never ceased thinking. *If I could just have prevented that son-of-a-bitch Xander from . . .*

It was a regret he knew he'd never outlive. Even when (not if) he married Karen (he hadn't told her, but he was merely waiting for the store to make a bit more money before proposing, so she could quit her job if she wanted to when [not if] he knocked her up) that regret wouldn't ever leave him. *If I'd just been able to save her . . .*

But whenever Andy passed the junction where the diner had stood, he couldn't help but remember Detective Rob Farrell's disturbing words: "We didn't recover a thing, not a single piece of either corpse."

Andy didn't like thinking about that. He'd stare at the expanse of neatly-stacked rubble and wonder. If the detectives hadn't recovered the bodies . . . who was to say that there'd ever been any bodies to recover to start with?

Is it possible, he'd wonder, *that Daria ain't actually dead? Is it possible that Xander took her alive with him down into Hell?*

Andy never thought like this for long. The implications scared him.

PART 4:
THE CORPSE WHO LOVED ME

CHAPTER 24

Andy, Craig, & Karen

"Black magic," Craig said in a horrified voice when Andy finished his tale. "Shit, man, I get what you mean now." He looked back, at the reborn Crossway Diner. The building's black outline flickered again in the morning sunlight.

The young man looked scared. Andy didn't blame him. He felt scared himself.

Although he'd relived the whole experience vividly while telling it, he'd of course left out all the details about him screwing Piper Harris. But that was all he'd left out.

Craig wasn't the only one horrified. Karen was gaping at him too.

"Andy, you never told me that the hooker's corpse came to life and dragged you across the road."

"I know, sweetheart. But would you have believed me? You'd most likely think I was crazy and break up with me." He grinned. "And then, where'd I be once you left me?"

She stared at him for a while longer. It was a good reason; a wise one. She accepted his concern for their relationship as a valid excuse for his not telling her about Piper Harris. He was right: she'd not have believed him.

But hearing that aspect of the story for the first time now doubled her fright. She'd already been scared, but now . . .

No one spoke for a full minute. You could have heard an atom fall. The universe inside the car was static.

Andy figured they both needed a little time to digest what they now knew. He relaxed back and let them. The shit was going to hit the fan anyway; there was no point in insisting on flushing the toilet.

Craig and Karen stared at each other with a 'what the fuck?' look in their eyes.

***

Craig's belly began rumbling again. He pushed open the car door. "Excuse me, I think I'm gonna throw up," he said.

He got out of the black Chevrolet and hurried off a few steps into the grassy verge bordering the shoulder.

Craig puked long and hard again. This time, though, he saw what he'd just thrown up: There was very little food in it, and a whole lot of maggots.

The world swum before his eyes.

For a moment he tried to convince himself that the squirming pile of horror he was looking at hadn't just come from inside his own body. Maybe he'd thrown up on a roadside deer turd. But the puke wasn't done with him yet. Another, smaller mass of it was coming up his throat. This time when he vomited, he felt the grubs alive on his tongue. One of the little shitheads even bit him on the tongue.

He stood staring at the mess. There were red streaks amidst the white larvae. Blood. Like the maggots were already eating him up inside.

He tried to think, but his mind drew a blank. His subconscious had erected a protective wall around his mind. Unable to reason, he instead turned and stared down the highway at the Crossway Diner. That didn't help much; his brain doggedly refused to connect the horror without to the horror within.

After a while, conscious of the others waiting for him, he got back into the car again. He sat quietly, saying nothing, trying to come to terms with the foulness that currently resided inside himself.

"Are you alright?" Karen asked.

He nodded at her. She looked scared enough without him adding to her fears. He had the sudden clear knowledge that he was going to die. It scared him immensely.

"Craig, are you sure you're alright?" Karen asked again. Her question seemed directed back at herself. He felt suddenly as if the continuation of their expedition hung on his reply.

"I'm alright now," he said without conviction, crunching down hard on his terror. "I guess ghost diner food don't really agree with me."

I don't know what's going on anymore, he thought, *but we've got to go on. I've got to get Shelly out of that terrible place.* With everything he'd just heard and what he'd just seen outside in his vomit, the bottom seemed to be falling out of his world. *What else can I do but go on? I've got to rescue Shelly! I doubt if she and Erica have any idea of the kind of danger they're in!*

Andy hadn't yet said anything. He was looking past them and stroking his chin meditatively.

Craig could feel Karen's eyes searching him, probing the wrinkles on his forehead, looking for cracks through which to read his mind and see what was wrong with him. *Hell yes, lady, there's a whole lot wrong with me, but what use will talking about it do?*

He gazed resolutely into Karen's eyes. Then, like Siamese twins sharing a single mind, they turned simultaneously to Andy.

"So what are we gonna do now?" Craig asked in a troubled voice. "The girls are in over there in that reappeared Crossway Diner. And from what you just told us, that building isn't somewhere that anyone planning on a long life expectancy should be at the moment.."

Karen nodded her agreement to his statement.

Andy grunted and tapped his shotgun. There was grim resignation in his voice when he replied, "Well, baby, the diner and Daria are over there, and we're over here. I suggest we shorten the distance before we all get too scared to kick any ass."

CHAPTER 25

Poppy and TJ

The chocolate-brown Bentley SUV approached north-to-south down Interstate 91. Just before South Deerfield, it turned off the I-91 to join Conway Road.

"Well, honey bun, here's one," TJ Murphy said on sighting the Crossway Diner.

"No," his wife Poppy immediately objected. "Let's keep on. You can eat in Cheshire."

"Poppy darling, honey sweetcakes, we're stopping here and that's that."

"Don't you ever think of anything but your belly? All you ever do is eat."

"If you took more time looking after my belly and not your appearance, maybe I wouldn't eat so much."

"If I take less time looking after my appearance, you'll be jumping into bed with your secretary."

It was an old back-and-forth argument, acted out so many times that the venom had long since gone out of it. Yes, TJ loved food—he liked his T-Bone and Ribeye and Porterhouse steaks, and his fruit-and-nut-and-vegetable omelets, and triple-decker burgers with enough cheese in them to make a Charlie Chaplin movie, and massive submarine sandwiches, and quadruple portions of fries with everything fatty on the side, and massive tubs of ice cream and waffles. But he loved his wife too. Really loved her. It was too bad he couldn't eat any part of her other than her delectable pussy.

TJ Murphy was a short obese man of fifty, with dark hair and eyes. He'd both inherited money and made more through shrewd investments. Dressed in a white suit, driving a Bentley Bentayga that cost a quarter of a million bucks. TJ had once been handsome, but the food and beer had long ago destroyed his looks. That didn't matter too much though. He was rich, and if you were rich you didn't need to be Tom Cruise or Denzel Washington. The women went for your money. Women were great like that: they didn't need to like *all* of you, you just needed a little something to hook them with. Some of them (the literary ladies) might like your brains, some (the romantics) might like your looks. Some (the socially conscious) might even like your altruistic self-sacrificing personality.

But best of all was money. Cash worked best with women. Money bought comfort and women grew best in comfort soil. The female of the human species was never designed to live in hardship. So, the more money you had, the more love you got from the ladies.

TJ was walking proof of this. Here he was, fifty years old, unrepentantly obese and yet married to a smoking hot bombshell (so hot that if they'd dropped her on Libya, the war would have ended in a day). Poppy was 33 but looked 24. So pretty he had no need of Viagra. Breasts, butt—body perfect. His money of course. He was good at making it, she was good at spending it. She was also smart enough to realize that she mustn't spend all of it.

Best of all, she wasn't stingy with herself in bed. But then, he figured, why should she be? What else did she have to do all day except watch TV, get her hair done, and screw him?

He looked over at her from the driver's seat of the Bentley and grinned. He hadn't done too badly for himself there. No sir, he hadn't. Staring at his young wife, in her expensive blue dress, with those pneumatic breasts and those long, long legs . . . Damn, he'd better concentrate on the driving.

Yes, but his belly was rumbling and, gorgeous wife or not, TJ Murphy never messed with his food.

***

Poppy knew TJ was appraising her. She preened herself and settled back in the seat. She knew he loved watching her act all girly and feminine.

Poppy was extremely high-maintenance. From a very early age, she'd understood that she wanted the good things in life. After doing her best to earn those good things—spending most of her twenties working a variety of low paying Boston jobs—she'd decided to marry them instead. She knew she looked good. It was just a question of waiting for the right man to come along. Poppy hadn't cared how old he was, her only criteria was that he had to be loaded. She put a very high price tag on herself. (To her mind, marrying a rich man you didn't like wasn't a crime: it was a job. It was like prostitution; only you were fucking the same person for your money. And society praised you for it.)

Initially, she'd dated several rich brats. Ivy League heirs. The rich brats had all decided she was too old for them. She'd begun getting desperate. She needed to marry money before her looks faded. Then TJ showed up. With his oily skin and stout non-athletic figure, he definitely wasn't anything to look at. But he was rich. He was swimming in it.

It took Poppy took exactly thirty seconds to decide that TJ's obesity didn't make the slightest amount of difference to her.

Her romantic equations were simple: She loved money; TJ = MONEY; therefore, she loved TJ.

Once she'd decided that, she got hard to work loving him. She worked hard at falling in love with TJ. Falling in love with him was of supreme importance. Most important, she'd begun taking classes in gourmet cooking so she could surprise him with big meals. And she'd made a point of showing him how great sex with her could be. She didn't lie about how great he was in bed. She'd instead concentrated on making him feel as fantastic as she could.

It worked. Once TJ realized she was head-over-heels crazy about him, he'd proposed.

Poppy considered herself lucky. TJ never treated her bad. He'd never once gotten physical with her, had never slapped her around or anything like that. In fact, the only times he was ever snarky with her was when dinner was late.

His only offence was that he was *really* fat. Okay and he liked food, which was why he was so fat.

Most times in bed she had to do all the work. But she was philosophical about that. All she had to do was spread her legs and she got a mink coat? And whenever TJ made it before she did, she had her faithful vibrator.

Poppy had twice had affairs with younger, better looking men, but she'd quit on them. They were too much trouble; both the men and the affairs. While screwing around on TJ, she'd always had it in the back of her mind that she was skating on paper-thin ice. TJ might love her but he wasn't a pushover. If he found out she was cheating on him, he'd divorce her. He'd replace her. She didn't deceive herself that she was irreplaceable. She also knew lots of women who'd love to have her life. She and TJ had a pre-nup agreement. (TJ had insisted; she'd resisted then conceded once she'd considered her lack of alternatives.) She wouldn't do too badly if they split. She'd get a half-a-million dollars and their holiday cottage in Westerly, Rhode Island. Yes, that might be enough for some women. But those women weren't Poppy Annabelle Murphy née Crenshaw. With Poppy's kind of expensive tastes, she knew she'd blow through that money in two years flat. Maybe less even. And then what?

So no more affairs. Poppy had made a firm decision to reserve her body for TJ's use alone. It was better to be married to twenty million dollars, with the prospect of making even more through your man, than to be cut adrift with a fraction of that amount.

***

The Murphys were traveling from Boston to Cheshire (a little town in the western part of the state) to see TJ's younger sister Cece. Cece Krail had been ill for a while now. She'd been in and out of hospital with various complaints. Neither her doctors nor her husband had any idea what to make of it all. TJ and Poppy were scheduled to fly to Hong Kong tomorrow—he for business (and to sample the Asian cuisine), she to raid the stores of the latest Orient fashions—so they'd decided to hit Cheshire today.

They had a chauffeur, but TJ had insisted on driving. He liked driving himself. Poppy wasn't looking forward to spending four hours watching the woodlands, but what harm could it do? In any case, an extra bout of Hong Kong shopping was certain to ease any stress she accumulated during the cross-state trip.

So TJ had given their chauffeur the day off.

This morning, though, Poppy had woken up feeling grumpy. Her bad mood had led to her making the unforgivable mistake where TJ was concerned: They'd set out from home too early for breakfast, and in the rush, she'd forgotten to pack any sandwiches.

Hence TJ now insisting on pulling into the diner up ahead.

Strangely though, Poppy didn't remember this place from the last time they'd driven by here. And that had been just two months ago. But then, that time they'd had breakfast before leaving home, so TJ hadn't thought of stopping.

And, she figured, *I most likely wasn't looking out of the window either.*

***

The diner was an old-fashioned two-story place with a yellow and red neon sign vaguely reminiscent of the McDonald's one.

Poppy winced when she saw it clearly. But then, she accepted that this was all her fault for not packing that vital road breakfast: *After four years of marriage, I really should know better. TJ runs on his damn belly.*

But all wasn't well here. She just knew it. Something about the Crossway Diner instantly filled Poppy Murphy with a sense of dread. She just couldn't put her finger on *what* that thing was. Still she felt chilled.

She rationalized it away as just her usual dislike of dives and low-class eating joints. *Ugh, just look at this damn place. Whatever will the girls think if they hear we stopped here?*

She turned to her husband. "Hon, I really don't feel good about us stopping here." She pointed right, down the wide stretch of Route 116. "Can't we just go on, please? It's only about forty minutes more to Cece's, right?"

She got the answer she expected: "Hell no, sweetheart. Cece's ill, see? She ain't able to cook. And I'm so hungry right now I could eat that Gucci handbag you're carrying."

She let it go. They were already turning left into the diner's parking lot anyway.

There were three cars parked outside the Crossway: a blue Volkswagen Golf, a silver Ford Fusion, and away from those, a police squad car. There was also a motorbike parked near the front entrance.

Rather than reassuring Poppy, seeing the police car made her feel additionally nervous. It was a silly feeling, she knew, just like her previous chill over their stopping here had been.

She smirked at the squad car. *TJ and I aren't crooks. Whatever are the cops going to hassle me for? A fashion violation?*

TJ swerved towards the diner entrance. He eased the Bentley in between the Volkswagen and the Ford.

Poppy slipped on her shoes and they both got out. They seemed to be the day's first customers. Through the diner windows Poppy could see a solitary waitress wiping tables. So where were the cops? She looked right, across the hood of the Ford, at the parked squad car. The policeman she saw seemed to be asleep in the driver's seat. She shrugged. Maybe he'd had a hard night chasing felons.

She turned back to their SUV.

Next, Poppy had a sudden moment of total unreality when the entire building facing them seemed to flicker. Flicker and vanish so that she could see past it to the highway beyond.

Then it was all there and solid again.

She blinked, then rubbed her eyes. *What just happened?* She blinked again, but the building was still there, as solid as a mountain. That would mean she'd just imagined it. But how did one imagine a building vanishing? And if she'd imagined it, how come she'd seen the white Chevrolet Camaro now passing the diner *before* it arrived?

Once again she felt the same creepy feeling as before. She looked sideways at TJ. He was locking up their car, whistling in anticipation of his hot roadside breakfast. No, he'd not noticed anything.

Poppy looked in through the diner windows. The waitress frowned back at her. Poppy instantly looked away. She didn't like the woman's face. The waitress had a hassled look, like she felt cleaning tables in a diner was beneath her and she'd rather be an office executive.

Someone has to do it, girl, Poppy thought back at her. *Better you than me.* She remembered back when she'd been twenty-one years old. She'd had a waitressing job too then, at a busy Back Bay restaurant. Talk about dreary work, hours when her life had consisted of an endless back-and-forth trudge between tables and kitchen, and tables and counter, taking and delivering orders to a motley array of different individuals who, after the first hour or so all blended into one Transamerican, transgender, transracial, transsized and transage person. Once Poppy got to that point, it had seemed like she was serving an army of clones, just the same person duplicated over and over again. Not an experience she'd ever care to repeat.

She looked in again at the waitress. The woman was back to wiping the tables. She worked with a nervy efficiency that struck Poppy as psychotic. It didn't matter. She wouldn't bother talking to her; she'd let TJ handle the moody bitch. After all, he was the one who was hungry.

"Alright, honey bun," TJ said, taking her arm, "let's go."

She went with him. She didn't speak. She was remembering how, just half a minute ago, this building they were about entering had flickered like it wasn't really here. She was sure it was going to vanish again. Maybe right before they stepped inside it. Vanish for good this time. The Crossway Diner would flicker out of existence and she and TJ would be left staring at the empty countryside beyond.

But the diner didn't vanish. Poppy was more worried than relieved by this.

She looked back at the squad car. The policeman was still napping.

Then TJ propelled her forward with a hand on her buttocks. "C'mon, honey bun, move your tight ass—my stomach's killing me."

She moved her tight ass. She was glad he appreciated her butt. It had taken a whole lot of TJ's money to mold it into its current callipygian ideal.

That aside . . .

The moment they stepped in through the front entrance of the Crossway Diner, Poppy Murphy had the crushing feeling that they'd both just made the worst mistake of their lives.

But by then, it was too late to flee. TJ was loudly squeezing in through the diner entrance behind her, and the nervy-looking waitress was coming over to show them to a table.

And then, just like that, Poppy found she was horny. Without warning, she was suddenly more aroused than she'd been in ages. But this was no ordinary arousal, not the sort that could wait till they were comfortably settled in one of Cece's Cheshire bedrooms. No, what Poppy felt now was a desperate craving for sex. Her lust felt bloodthirsty, like a wolf out to shred her flesh.

Without questioning her actions, she instantly dropped her expensive Gucci purse on the floor. Next, she kicked off her shoes and began pulling her dress up.

Once her dress and bra and panties were covering her purse on the floor, she looked around. TJ had better be ready to give her what she had to have.

TJ *was* ready. His pants and underpants were already down around his ankles. He was stroking his erection with one hand. His other hand was fumbling to get his jacket and shirt off. TJ's fat face was flushed. His eyes bulged like they'd pop from his face. He was breathing as fast as she was. He looked as desperate as she felt.

"I need you, honey bun!" he gasped. "Oh, I need you so damn bad!" To a loud tearing-off of buttons, he wrenched his jacket and shirt off and flung both down on the checkered floor.

They were still standing by the diner door. It didn't matter. At the moment Poppy Murphy had no inhibitions left. She saw nothing wrong with having sex in a public place. She was merely about fulfilling many women's top erotic fantasy. She went down on her knees and grabbed hold of her husband's hard penis. She loved how it throbbed in her hand. She wanted it in her mouth right away.

The waitress pulled her back upright. Poppy hadn't even been aware of the woman's presence. Irritated by the interruption, she turned to the waitress. "What is it?" she asked in an icy high-class voice. "Can't you see that we're busy?" Her words made perfect sense to her.

The waitress smiled. At any other time, Poppy would have found her smile creepy, but not now. Now, only the feverish heat in her groin mattered.

"Not here, ma'am," the woman said. "Someone else may want to get in through the door and then they'll only disturb you."

That made sense to Poppy. The policeman in the car outside might want to come in for coffee and donuts.

"Where then?" TJ asked from behind her. He sounded as if he was in pain.

"Follow me," the waitress replied. "I've got just the table for you two love birds."

She led. They followed. She led them to the far end of the room where a pool table waited.

Perfect, Poppy thought. *Just perfect.*

Poppy climbed up on the pool table, lay back and spread her legs. "Eat me!" she demanded of her husband, her voice so hoarse with lust, she hardly recognized it as her own.

TJ, now as naked as the day he was born, stuck his head between her thighs and began licking.

She exploded in orgasm almost immediately and the orgasms just kept on coming.

But there was something wrong. Poppy realized this after a while. The more TJ stimulated her, the more she came; but after each orgasm, the hungrier for him she felt. There was no final satisfaction, no relief, no comedown into a delicious afterglow—her desire for him merely spiraled exponentially upward. Up, away, and out of her control. Also, each sexual climax she had seemed to 'reduce' her in some way that she didn't understand.

When she could unhook her mind from the pleasure consuming her, Poppy felt as if a demon of lust had possessed her and was using her as a weapon against herself.

CHAPTER 26

Daria

Daria smiled as she fed. Eating the foodstreams. Sexmeat and violenceflesh. The only things that satisfied her endless demonic craving.

First the young biker couple. Then the two girls in her own bedroom. And now this married couple downstairs. The flow of food was unceasing.

The nourishment entered her from all directions. She felt it both in her mouth and in her anus. It tingled in her fingers, scented in her nose, rang in her ears and was vision to her gray eyes. It caressed her pale hair, stroked her engorged breasts, smacked her buttocks, penetrated her wet sex. It seeped through her skin into her blood.

Daria licked her lips with pleasure. Then she frowned. She felt hatred, hatred for someone close by. She could sense the man she hated. He was in a car coming to her. He was with other people, all of them drawing nearer by the second.

She felt confusion about this man. She remembered him. But her memory of him was of how much she despised him. He'd hurt her in some horrible way.

But she also recalled that she loved this man who was on his way to her. She loved him a lot. No! She *hated* him. Her hatred smothered then ate her love.

Daria didn't remember very much now that she was dead. She remembered once being alive, being human and having the capacity to love other humans.

And then Xander had come to her and destroyed her.

She hated Xander Mood.

Xander had murdered her and taken her into SADE, into that sideworld of Hell itself. SADE: Sex, Agony, Detention,

Enlightenment. He had taken her into its Sex zone. There he'd shown her overwhelming pleasure, ecstasy that had broken her mind.

She utterly despised Xander Mood.

She'd first hated him for murdering her to open his portal. Then she'd hated him for using her body and making her enjoy being his toy. Then, finally, when Xander had tired of her and left for an unspecified destination, she'd hated him for deserting her. For leaving her alone and empty of anything but lust and degradation.

Xander Mood disgusted her.

And once Daria found herself alone, without her tormentor to confirm her identity, she'd become one with SADE's darkness.

And even in its Sex zone, SADE's darknesses were many.

Daria the Once-Human had become Daria the Amalgam of Sex and Violence. She'd merged with the Evil that survived beyond death, and it had merged with her. It had sucked out part of her to feed itself. In return, it had made her like itself.

As she fused with the darkness, she'd become HUNGRY. The hunger had grown in her like a cancer.

She needed food. Xander had fed her sex and violence in SADE and now she needed its nourishment to continue to be.

Without sex and violence, Daria would fade. She would become weak. She would become a shadow, food for the other nightmare creatures that inhabited SADE's dark spaces. And Daria had no intention of becoming nourishment for any of SADE's abominations.

She herself was abomination enough already. She was the phantasm and the darkness and the predator. She was the ghoul and the nightmare and the desecration. She was the all-consuming horror. She was the harrowing leech that suckled on the hapless, helpless soul.

Now, Daria waited like a lioness and fed on the unwary. All who entered her diner were prey. Each of them would surrender a part of themselves to her. Some would get away. Most wouldn't . . .

But . . . she was limited here. For instance, she'd known for a long time now that she had the power to make this building materialize on Earth. She'd worked out the rules of the crossing: The Crossway could appear, but mostly at night. And only in specific places—gateways— where the walls between Hell and Earth were weakest.

Where she'd died was one such place.

She'd tried many times before to cross over to Earth. Each attempt had failed. She'd kept on trying, growing ever more frantic as she weakened further and the monsters that wanted to feed on her grew ever bolder.

And then she'd succeeded. Only yesterday, in the hours approaching both her birthday and her death-day, had her hunger and desperation been strong enough to breach the walls between the worlds.

Now she was here. Back from SADE to Earth. Making the trip had proved more than worth it. She had everything she'd hoped for. Everything. The human world held so much promise, so much possibility. So much *food!*

But even now, Daria's grip on the human realm was weakening. She couldn't hold the paranormal door open much longer. Maybe an hour or two at the most. And then she'd be sucked back into SADE. Once again queen of her personal pocket of darkness.

To return when? To feed again when?

But at the moment, the menu was excellent. And, oh, she lusted for much more to eat.

The woman with the fat husband had another orgasm. Daria ate her pleasure. The blonde girl in her bedroom got a rectal tear from a too-violent dildo thrust. She screamed. Daria ate her pain. Pain was a product of violence. Violence was delicious. (Violence produced more food per occurrence than sex. But violence also quickly destroyed its object: the higher the amount of foodstream released, the shorter-lived the nutritional value of the persons involved. Sex, however, was easily repeatable; people craved pleasure. In the long run, sex provided more food than violence.)

And there were still those three approaching in the car. Amongst them, the man she hated more than anyone else; more even than she hated Xander Mood.

Maybe, when she saw the man again she'd recall the horrible things he'd done to her.

CHAPTER 27

Craig

The car slowly drew near the diner. Slowly. It moved at the pace of a tortoise with a tummy ache. Karen wasn't in any hurry to arrive at the Crossway and Andy and Craig didn't rush her. It was harrowing enough to see the 'ghost café' up ahead; none of them was eager to step inside it.

That 'ghost food' we ate infected me with grubs?

As much as it was possible to do so, Craig was coming to terms with this fact. He'd have loved to rubbish Andy's tale about Daria and the diner, but clear evidence to the contrary resided in his own body. *I never heard of anyone puking up live maggots before—worms, yes, but . . .*

Even now he could feel his belly squirming. He'd soon need to crap. He didn't imagine that that was going to be pretty. He still felt death hovering over him. Death within, death without.

At least the damn things aren't chewing up my insides. Or are they? There was blood in my vomit.

His legs still ached where the grubs from Marty's kitchen had earlier bitten him.

Oh shit—Shelly and Erica must have the same grub infestation too! How'd I ever forget that? Once they're both safe, we all need to head for the nearest ER and get our guts flushed out!

Like it or not, they were rolling ever closer to the diner. They were now up to the Whately Road turnoff on the right. Then it too was past them.

Or . . . maybe . . . maybe Andy's entire tale IS a load of horseshit after all. It could be that all that's going on is simply that Daria is selling contaminated meals to everyone! But if that's the case, how come the food in the shopping bags transformed too? No . . . if the food is polluted you'd expect it to transform. It's the drinks that are the problem. How did the soda cans become flyblown meat? How does metal transform into rotting flesh?

The questions perplexed rather than helped him. He found no 'logical' explanation that trumped the paranormal one.

He turned in his seat to face Andy. "Don't you find it odd, though, that with this building just materializing from nowhere, the police haven't noticed while driving past? It's not like this is some backwoods, deep-country place. It's in plain view on the highway, walking distance from the interstate, man."

"That's a good point you raise," Andy replied. "I dunno, maybe the place is only visible to certain folks. Folks like me and Karen, who knew Daria personally, or . . ."

"Folks who aren't from around here," Karen finished for him. "Folks that won't be missed."

Craig didn't ask any more questions. 'Folks that won't be missed' clearly meant he and the girls.

Snail-crawl forward or not, their car was nearing its undesired destination. The Crossway was now less than a hundred yards away. Craig just hoped Shelly and Erica were still alive and well in there.

"Be alive, baby," he whispered to himself. "Please, be alive."

CHAPTER 28

Shelly & Erica

Their orgasms went on and on and on. Each was the greatest climax of their lives. Then the next one topped that one. And the next one was better still.

Each orgasm creamier than the last. Each orgasm flinging them higher into ecstasy than they'd ever dreamed possible. Each orgasm leeching something vital from them.

Shelly and Erica could no longer deceive themselves that they were having fun however. This wasn't fun. It hadn't been fun for over twenty minutes now. Now they were merely two sex addicts compulsively feeding the crazy craving that was going to kill them.

Yes, this sex would kill them. There was no chance that it wouldn't. Already both young women were little more than flesh and bones. Shrunken down as though in the middle stages of anorexia nervosa. Their faces were skeletal, their breasts shrunken and flaccid. Their ribs and hipbones jutted.

And still they kept having sex . . . in Daria's room of shadows. Around them, the shadows were as dark and as thick as ever. Between the shadows, the walls dripped blackness. Evil was palpable in the air. Evil that both fed on them and fed their lust. Evil that built up their lust like someone adding logs to a fire. Evil that manipulated their hormones and nerve endings.

At the moment Shelly lay on her belly with her legs spread wide, while Erica sodomized her. Erica worked relentlessly, sliding the bloody dildo fast and deep into Shelly's shriveled body.

There were live maggots on the bed. Large, pale, squirming fly larvae crawling about everywhere. They'd both excreted the maggots. In their horror they interpreted the maggot presence to mean that they were both decaying inside. (Their horror barely dented the surface of their arousal, however.) There was also some excrement smeared on the bed sheets, but much less that might be expected. In fact, considering the amount of grubs they'd each shat from their anuses, they found it uncanny how there was so little feces on the bed; almost as if the maggots had eaten most of it up (for sustenance) inside their bodies before being ejected.

There was a lot of blood on both their bodies. Bright crotch-blood from ripped vaginal and rectal tissue. Neither young woman had escaped the rough wear and tear of the dildo's use. Neither had been gentle with the other's body. At times their passion had had the violence of a brutal rape. At times it hadn't felt any different from sexually abusing each other. But they'd gone on—their constantly shrinking bodies demanded the orgasms from them. Despite hurting themselves worse each time, they regularly swapped positions and spread their legs again, accepting the horrible pain that led to the glorious sapping pleasure.

Shelly whimpered in pain beneath Erica. The dildo felt like it was shredding her rectum. But no, she didn't want Erica to go gently.

"Harder!" she moaned. "Pound my ass, you wimp!"

"Yeah, I'm gonna do just that, bitch!" Erica growled back and thrust harder.

Tears poured from Shelly's eyes. Tears that expressed her agony. Tears of sorrow. But most of all, tears of anticipation. She gritted her teeth, waiting for another dose of sheer ecstasy. Oh, it was vacuuming her away to nothing, but she was desperate to experience it again.

She came. She *went*. She felt herself *going*. Oh!—but the *feeling* of coming and going. No man had ever made her feel like this. And none ever would.

Erica pulled out of her anus. A sticky white paste spilled out from Shelly's ass—a mess of grubs pulped beyond recognition. (Most of the grubs now alive on the bed had escaped their bodies while they swapped places and exchanged the plastic phallus between themselves.)

Erica rolled Shelly over. "Now I'm gonna bang you face-to-face, slut!" She licked her lips. "You love that, don't you?"

"Yes, yes, yes!" Shelly whimpered. "Oh yes, yes, yes!"

But what she really wanted to say—no, to scream—was, "NO, NO, NOOOOO!" Beneath the endless arousal and craving, she felt only horror. Unspeakable horror. She was absolutely terrified, on a level she'd never experienced before. She didn't want to die. No, she didn't.

She remembered Craig. She longed for him now. Oh, she loved him. She really did. She'd never ever loved any guy in her life like she loved Craig. She wanted to marry Craig and be with him forever and forever and forever. But he'd never ever made her feel like this. Nothing on earth could make a woman feel like this. She *couldn't* stop feeling like this. Asking that of her would be asking too much of her. She wasn't going to stop feeling like this for anything or anyone.

"Give it to me!" she grunted at Erica. "GIVE IT TO ME, BITCH!"

The shadows on the bedroom walls dipped as if nodding in assent.

Erica began GIVING IT to her. Shelly helped out by rubbing her clitoris with both hands. Rubbing, rubbing, rubbing. Rubbing herself away. Erasing herself in orgasm.

In her horrified pleasure, Shelly regarded her lover's face as it came closer with each thrust. Erica's visage was almost a skeleton's now. Like she'd just been exhumed from a month-old grave. Her blonde hair was falling out of her skull as if she was undergoing chemotherapy. She'd lost two teeth, and when she drew her lips back over them, another tooth fell out of her mouth. Yet she couldn't stop making violent love to Shelly. The lust was a sickness in her, a disease reducing her to mere skin and bones.

But it was a disease that she loved.

Erica's blue eyes shone like a gas fire burnt in them. The maniacal fire of her lust affliction.

Shelly had no doubt that her own eyes glowed in exactly the same sick way. She rubbed her clitoris harder and harder. Instinctively, she knew that the orgasm coming was one to die for. But then, so had been the last orgasm she'd had. And she knew the one after this would be even more intense.

"Take it, take it, take it!" Erica yelled at Shelly, filling her rectum with the dildo.

Shelly TOOK IT. And as she did, Erica grunted like she was coming herself. Erica stiffened and let out a long howl. Her body no longer hers to control, her hips kept thrusting regardless, forcing the plastic phallus DEEP into Shelly's buttocks.

With rising dread, Shelly watched Erica visibly shrink as she came. The flesh sucked out of her face. Her facial skin pulled back taut against her skull and developed stretch marks. Death-camp Fashionista; just add lipstick and eyeliner.

Erica's neck collapsed inward. Her already collapsed breasts shriveled now to the size of unrolled condoms. The malnourished furrows between her ribs deepened. The flesh on Erica's arms sagged like handbags. Her fingers were skeletal linkages of bones wrapped in withered skin. More of her hair fell out. More of her teeth fell out. Now all her beauty was gone. She was no longer the gorgeous siren of yesterday, but tomorrow's withered hag. Old age come premature. Death knocking.

But her eyes glittered with eroticism. If death's dimming was in Erica's eyes, lust's light glowed even brighter in them.

The glow in Erica's eyes informed Shelly of the new truth of their shared existence:

Yes, Erica looked horrible now. She looked wasted and waiting for a coffin and the undertaker to cart her away. But . . . Erica was still alive and as long as she breathed, she would continue to make love to Shelly. She *had to* keep having sex with Shelly. She had zero choice in the matter.

Shelly was relieved. She felt exactly the same. She didn't want Erica to stop making love to her either. She climaxed like a bomb exploding. She felt herself 'reducing in amount.' Her molars all came lose at once. Before she could spit them out, a fresh ripple of orgasmic vaginal contractions struck her and she swallowed them instead. Her throat tightened painfully about the teeth as they tumbled down. It too was shriveling. Her voice box too. Soon she'd be unable to even gasp out her pleasure.

But it didn't matter.

Erica pulled out of her anus. Shelly lay gasping for a little while, staring at Erica's crotch. At the dildo smeared with her pubic and posterior blood. Herself, she felt ripped to shreds. But the pain was merely a gateway—the entrance to the orgasm.

Erica the Hag was breathing hard. Erica the Hag was now almost bald. Erica the Hag was now mostly toothless. Erica the Hag was now almost completely bones.

Shelly LOVED Erica the Hag!

Erica the Hag was pulling off the dildo harness. Shelly understood what that meant. It was her turn now.

Shelly took the dildo from Erica the Hag. She dropped it on the bed. She made a 'come here' gesture, then patted the bed beside her. "Bring your ass over here. I'm gonna fist you to ecstasy!"

Erica the Hag quickly lay down on her back. She grinned and another tooth fell out of her mouth.

Shelly rubbed her hand in the blood dripping from her anus to lubricate it. Then slowly, deliberately, she pushed the hand into Erica the Hag's anus. Erica the Hag moaned in pain as she was penetrated. Her ass began bleeding again. She grabbed the discarded dildo from the bed and sank it into her sex, doubling her agonizing insertions. She began thrusting vigorously into herself. Her withered hag face twisted up in pain.

Shelly forced her hand deeper into Erica the Hag's anus. Up to the wrist now. Several displaced maggots squirted out of the penetrated anus. Erica the Hag squealed in agony and fucked herself harder with the dildo.

Shelly laughed at the squirming grubs.

Then her hair fell out. A brunette spill onto the other young-old woman's ghastly-looking belly with its wrinkled skin.

Oh, I'm a hag too, Shelly thought grimly.

Again, that flood of desperate fear drenched her. She was about to die here. Nothing was worth that. Soon, very soon, both of their reserves of sexual energy would dry up. They would stop having orgasms and both give up the ghost. Leeched out, used up, finished. Wasted.

And then, this *thing* that was feeding on them—they both understood now that Daria wasn't a person in any true human sense— would simply move on to fresh victims.

To her, we're just meals.

Shelly the Hag thought this, and was terrified of her approaching fate, but there was nothing she could do to free herself. She didn't want to free herself.

"I've sold my soul to please my hole," she moaned. "My hole thinks it's worth it anyway. Way to go, hole."

She spat a loosened tooth down into her fellow hag's vagina, then really got to work on fisting her anus.

Beneath her, Erica the Hag hurt badly and came. And shrunk some more. And came. And shrunk even more.

The maggots squirmed happily around both women.

CHAPTER 29

Karen, Andy, & Craig

Karen reluctantly swung the black Chevrolet into the Crossway parking lot.

Andy pointed to the black/white squad car parked on the far right of the diner. "Well, Craig, I believe that more or less answers your recent question. It's not just us that can see this damned place."

Craig nodded.

"I'm relieved," Andy added. "If there's trouble here they'll be able to call for backup."

Craig nodded again.

"Where should I park?" Karen asked in a trembling voice.

"Between the Ford and the cops," Andy replied. (The other three cars—Craig's Ford, a brown Bentley Bentayga that had to cost almost as much as Andy's entire hardware store did, and a blue Volkswagen—had taken up all the parking space nearer the front entrance.)

Karen slid the car into the suggested space and stopped. Looking in through the glass, the diner seemed empty. No staff in sight. And no customers either despite all the vehicles parked out front.

The place sounded deader than a graveyard.

"Where is everyone?" Karen asked. "Andy, I don't like this."

Craig nodded yet again. His thoughts exactly.

"Alright," Andy said. "Everyone out of the car, but for the moment leave your guns behind. We might not need 'em. Let's first find out what the cops have discovered." He gestured right, at the police cruiser. One of the officers was napping in the driver's seat. "If the boys in blue see us all armed and dangerous, they might get the wrong idea 'bout what we're here for."

Karen said, "Honey, the damn place ain't supposed to be here. Who's gonna convict us of robbing a ghost café?"

Still, they left the guns behind. They got out and walked over to the police cruiser.

It was Craig who first noticed the blood pooled under the squad car. With the sun in the east, the cruiser was parked amidst shadows. Craig stayed where he was. He wasn't going near the vehicle.

It was Karen who first noticed that the officer in the driver's seat was dead. The man had a hole in his throat that would have admitted her fist if she'd felt inclined to shove it in there. She didn't, and stayed back from the car as well.

It was Andy, however, who noticed both that the police car was full of squirming maggots, and that there was another dead officer in the front passenger seat. This was because Andy was the only one of the three of them who dared walk up to the parked car and look inside it. (Craig had stopped ten yards away. Karen had initially stepped as close as eight yards, but then hastily retreated back to fifteen. She'd fished the car keys from her pocket and was dangling them on her index finger, ready to leap back into the front seat of the Chevrolet and drive them all the hell out of there.)

Andy made his jerky, broken-leg-in-brace walk the extra eight yards to the car and looked in through the windows.

Andy got a good look inside the police cruiser. He wished he hadn't.

The second cop had been ripped open from neck to groin in a long jagged cut. He'd half-slid from his seat down into the foot well. And . . . the grubs were inside him now feeding. The maggots were having a field day. They lay thigh-high on the dead driver. The parts of the cops visible beneath the maggots were just white bones. Even their uniforms had been consumed.

The squirming white lake of larvae extended all the way to the backseat.

As to where the maggots all came from, Andy decided the answer lay with the two takeout bags the driver cop had in his larvae-swarming lap. As to how/why the maggots were *eating* people, he had no answer.

Just managing not to puke, Andy stepped back from the car and turned to face the others.

"I think we're gonna need those guns after all," he said, his face white.

Craig and Karen didn't question him as to what he'd seen in the squad car. Both figured there was worse ahead waiting for them.

They unloaded the guns.

"I think we should just call the cops," Karen said nervously.

Andy flung a disgusted gesture over at the squad car. "Those *were* the damn cops."

"I think she means, call 911 and wait for reinforcements," Craig said. "I think she's right. Sounds like a smart plan to me."

Andy sighed. The two of them just didn't get it. "Man, you got your phone on you? Alright, call 911."

Craig dialed the emergency number. It didn't go. He tried again and again. He wanted it to ring. He willed it to ring. He was desperate for it to ring. He really didn't want to have to enter this damn Crossway Diner. Even up close to it one could see the black outline around its edges. This building clearly wasn't natural or normal.

And beyond that, they had to consider what had happened to the police officers. He didn't want that happening to him. But . . . Shelly and Erica were both inside the Crossway and he had to get them out.

He kept dialing. Finally he gave up.

"Nothing?" Andy asked.

"Yeah, nothing."

"I didn't expect there to be. You weren't listening to me when I told you what happened. I clearly said I couldn't call the cops."

"But you got through once . . ."

"Ten seconds. Then it cut out. And Piper said—"

"How 'bout if we drive down to the police station and make a report?" Karen suggested. The building's flickering edges were unnerving her too.

"They aren't gonna believe the Crossway just reappeared . . . out of nowhere."

"They'll believe . . . no, they'll come and investigate if we tell them we saw two dead cops in a squad car," Craig said.

Andy mused on this for few moments, looking over at the parked cruiser with its morbid content, then back at his two companions. "Yeah, that's true. But while we're gone, what about your girlfriend? And Erica? We can't just leave them in there. I say we go in now."

That got to Craig. No, they couldn't just trust the cops to carry out a rescue. Shelly might be in mortal danger. What if the police didn't arrive in time?

"You just wanna see Daria again," Karen accused Andy. Her voice was bitter.

He nodded. "Maybe."

"You're still pining for her after all this while? What about me?" Her voice conveyed her fear of threatened loss to him.

He looked kindly at her. "No, you've gotten it all twisted, baby. I don't want Daria back. I love *you* now."

She heard the honesty in his words. Her face showed signs of hope that he wasn't thinking of deserting a future with her for the past. "Then why do we have to go inside?"

"I want to stop this. Once and for all. It has to end and end now. Dead people coming back to life and killing the living? Hell no, I ain't havin' it. And if Daria's responsible, she's gonna have to stop it. I'm gonna ask her to stop."

"And if she refuses to?" Karen still remembered that 'warning' in the kitchen to lay off Andy. (She'd never told Andy about it, either.) "Daria always was stubborn."

Andy smiled at that. "Well then, I'll just have to find some other way to persuade her to stop."

Craig pointed towards the diner entrance. "Can we start, please? The longer we wait out here like this, the more I feel my courage draining away."

"Yeah," Andy said. Then he turned to his girlfriend. "Listen, Karen, I really don't think you should come inside with us."

"Why the hell not?"

"'Cos . . . well, remember how I promised your dad I'd never let any harm come to you? This sure looks like a source of harm to me."

She looked incredulous. "Huh?"

"Honey, now you just drive back into town like you just suggested, and find the cops and make that report. Bring 'em over here. Meanwhile, Craig and I will—"

Karen shook her head vehemently. "Forget it, Andy. Just goddamn forget it already. It ain't happenin' like that. Don't you dare patronize me! You're not leaving me out of this. If you're going in, I'm going in too."

Andy sighed. "Somehow, I just knew you were gonna say that." He winced. Damn, female jealousy was a curse.

He looked from Karen to Craig. "Alright, both of you two, remember it's *black magic* we're dealing with here. The honest-to-Satan real evil shit. Let's each do our best to not get killed in there."

He kissed Karen. "Just stay near me, right? And don't shoot Daria except she *really* pisses you off."

That said, Andy led the way towards the diner entrance. It was best they got a move on. He'd been standing too long on one spot already: his right leg was aching in its brace.

The seemingly empty building awaited them. Eerie and brooding. Spooky as a grave.

***

They stepped inside. Andy (still questioning the wisdom of his own courage) first; Karen (keeping as close to Andy as possible) in the middle; and Craig (praying they'd be in time to rescue Shelly and Erica) last.

"What the . . . ?" Karen instantly remarked. "How . . . ?"

"Never believe your eyes," Andy replied gruffly. "At least, not what they see from outside a ghost building."

"Yeah, I can see that," Craig added for something to say.

The diner interior wasn't empty like it looked from the parking lot. Not in the least. The ape-like Gorilla stood behind the service counter, and a waitress was carrying a drink over to a woman in the corner to their right. Well, it looked like a woman was seated there. She could just as well have been an aggregation of shadows.

Once past that surprise, the three entrants had a fresh shock. Over in the forward right corner of the dining room (the one opposite the shadows that might actually be a woman) stood a pool table. Andy and Karen remembered the pool table from two years ago; Craig didn't recall it from last night.

On the pool table, a beautiful blonde woman was having sex with an obese man. Violent sex. The pair were completely naked. The blonde lay on her back at the table's edge with both arms flung wide to her side. Her feet were up on the fat man's shoulders. He was thrusting relentlessly into her anus. Thrusting and grunting. Thrusting and grunting.

"Shit!" Andy said. "This is really bad." He looked at Gorilla. The giant shrugged back while whistling Glen Miller's *In the Mood*.

Andy looked back over at the pornographic corner.

The woman being sodomized on the pool table was gritting her teeth and squeezing her eyes tightly shut as if in extreme pain, but at the same time she was gasping in ecstasy.

"Harder!" she demanded. "Give it to me harder, TJ. I need you to fill me with your cock! Harder!"

TJ was clearly thrusting as hard as he could. His fat, hairy body glistened with sweat. The pool table shook with each forward movement of his hips. The couple looked like a grizzly bear having sex with a deer.

"Oh, oh—I'm cooommiiiinggg!" the woman screamed, arching her back off the table.

"I'm coming too, Poppy!" the man yelped, then stiffened like a board between her legs.

Alright, that's done then, Andy thought in relief. *Guys that fat usually can't go more than once.* He was aware that beside him, Karen and Craig were stricken speechless. Andy didn't blame them. He was speechless himself. He'd come in here to kick some paranormal ass if necessary. Not to watch a live porn show. He looked at his girlfriend. Karen was gaping with both eyes and mouth. She looked like she'd just found another reason to bolt from the diner. He now regretted not insisting she stay outside and go for the police.

Andy suddenly realized that something was wrong. The porno should have ended by now. But it hadn't. Once through the throes of their joint orgasms, 'TJ' and 'Poppy' had instantly resumed having sex. The sodomy on the pool table went on.

Poppy now began weeping copiously, gritting her teeth and screaming, "Stop, TJ, stop! Oh, I'm begging you, darling! STOP!"

"Hey, man, you heard the lady!" Andy growled, glad for a chance to interrupt the sexual proceedings. The sooner he got those two dressed again, the faster he and the others could get down to the business at hand. "Hey, you!—let the woman go!"

Andy took a step towards the pool table. His plan was to pull the large man off the beautiful woman. If the man didn't separate willingly, Andy was prepared to help him along with some shotgun butt to the head.

But then Poppy turned towards him and gasped at him through her outpouring of tears, "No, don't you dare stop TJ fucking me! Don't you dare come over here and disturb us, you crippled son-of-a-bitch! It's none of your damn business. He's my husband and I love him madly, and I want him to fuck me again and again and again till I die! I've just *got* to come again. I FRIGGING HAVE TO. Oh, oh, oh! Yes, yes. Shit—oh, it hurts so damn much, TJ! More! More! More!"

"Yeah, honey bun, take this hard cock until your ass explodes!"

Andy had already stopped dead at the unexpected rebuke. That 'crippled son-of-a-bitch' remark had hurt. He lowered his shotgun, turned, and gaped at Karen.

"What's going on here?" she asked before he could.

"I saw something like this yesterday," Craig explained nervously. "A young couple who began having sex in *that* corner." He pointed over to the corner with the woman of shadows. The waitress stood by the woman's table, her attention focused on Poppy and TJ.

"Hey," Craig whispered on seeing the waitress's face clearly. "I remember her from yesterday."

"Yeah, yeah, man," Andy said distractedly. "She served you your dinner last night."

"No, no!" Craig corrected quickly, his voice still low. "Andy, she wasn't a waitress then, she was a *customer*. She arrived here after we did and ordered dinner."

"She looks like a waitress to me," Karen said.

"I'm serious," Craig insisted. "Look at her face. She looks *upset*, like she's being coerced to do what she's doing."

Andy and Karen studied the waitress's face. It was either that or watch the couple on the pool table have their fresh set of climaxes, not recommended because Poppy had begun farting loudly around her rotund husband's erection.

So Andy studied the waitress's face. She was a slim mousy brunette. He decided Craig was right. The waitress was giggling as she watched the sex action, but under her mirth, he could see lines of fright. Or he imagined he did. She wasn't as entertained as she pretended to be, that was for sure.

For her part, Karen figured the waitress was merely a stuck-up bitch. Either that, or she was having an extra-bad day at the Red-Time-of-Month plaza. And where were Daria and the two girls anyway? That was what they were here for, not this porn show. She felt completely grossed out by the couple on the pool table. Not like she was a prude or any such, but it was just gross doing it in public like this. And the man was so large too.

She began worrying: *Why can't I see that woman in the corner clearly? Is that Daria over there?*

"We've gotta be really careful," Craig whispered. "I think this place exerts a kind of supernatural influence on everyone who enters it. If that's the case it might be able to control us too. We could easily wind up shooting each other."

Andy shook his head. "I don't buy that," he whispered back. "You were here too, weren't ya? You got out okay."

"With a kitchen full of maggots and . . ." All of a sudden, Craig's face turned pale. He looked really sick, like he was going to throw up. By slow degrees he got control of himself again, visibly forcing himself to swallow something that was coming up his throat.

"Andy, I think Craig's right," Karen agreed. "This building may be able to control us. It could even be why we've been standing in the same spot since coming in here. We'd best just start looking for—"

"Help us!" a loud plea interrupted. "Please stop this!"

They looked up from their whispering. The fat man—who somehow, inexplicably now looked thinner, as if he'd shrunk while they'd been huddled together—had an arm extended towards them. He looked horrible. The skin hung off his upper arm and in loose folds around his corpulent form, as if he'd once been even fatter but had lost weight in a hurry and now needed to have the extra-skin surgically removed. He really creeped Karen out. He reminded Craig of how Shelly and Erica had both looked thinner on their return from the ladies' last night.

"Help us!" TJ pleaded in a voice full of misery. "We can't stop ourselves! We can't stop screwing!"

"Yes," Poppy added. She was crying again. Her onetime perfect makeup was now a smeared mess on her face. "Something is making us keep having sex. It's killing us! Help us! Please, help us!"

This was news to Andy. "Yeah, sure, we'll help you guys. What're we supposed to do?"

But there was no reply to that question. At that moment, whatever evil force had the pair in its grasp once more exerted its iron control over both their wills. TJ's expression of terror altered into one of wrath. His eyes bulged out in rage, his nostrils twitched, and he slobbered at the mouth.

He shook his fist at them. "Don't you dare come any closer, assholes. Me and my wife wanna fuck in public, so that's what we're gonna do!"

With that, he pulled his penis out of her anus and shoved it into her vagina. He began slamming it violently into her.

"Yeah, baby!" his wife screamed. It was a bloodcurdling scream, one composed entirely of agony. And the expression on Poppy's face was once again a junkie's—that desperate craving for a fix which would let nothing stand in its way. And now, she too looked much thinner, her beauty reduced by several degrees, her skin stretched tight on her face, like she was in the early stages of becoming her own skeleton.

"Yeah, FUCK ME!" she screamed, sitting up to grip TJ's shoulders and throw her legs around his shrinking waist. Her obese husband began humping her again. Violently, bumping the pool table like he wanted to reduce it to firewood.

Sweat poured from her, streaming down between the vertical valley of her perfect breasts to the horizontal valley where their bodies met.

"OH MY GOD! I LOVE YOU! I'LL LOVE YOU FOREVER, TJ! I'M COOOOOMING! HARDER!" She began banging her fists on the pool table.

"YEAH, HONEY BUN! TAKE IT—I GOT A FRESH LOAD OF LOVE CREAM COMING RIGHT UP FOR YA!"

They stopped yelling and resumed grunting in unison, hog-like, eyes staring, lips snarling, muscles taut to the point of exhaustion. TJ was stamping his feet as he thrust; Poppy was kicking hers in unison and squeezing her breasts as though she wanted to burst them.

"Okay," Andy said, speaking to no one in particular, "I agree that this ain't anything natural." He looked grimly at the others. "Hey, I got a suggestion: how 'bout we just leave the lovers here to their family fun and go find the young women we're here to rescue?"

"Ask Gorilla where they are," Karen suggested, pointing to the giant behind the service counter. As far as she could tell, Gorilla hadn't moved an inch from his position since they'd entered the diner. She'd been doing her best not to look at him. Gorilla was a ghost. He was dead. She'd attended his funeral. Lots of other people had too. Karen was currently forcing intense suspension-of-disbelief on herself. It was the only way to cope with the situation at hand. At any minute though, that suspension bridge over her disbelief might crumble and she'd collapse into a shrieking bundle of terror. But not yet. None of this was in any way logical: Not the diner being here, not Gorilla being here either. And definitely not Daria Simpson apparently being alive and well in here too.

But, Karen figured, *if you can logically accept that you're somehow able to walk into a non-existent building, the rest comes easy.*

"Gorilla should know where the girls are," she repeated. "Ask him. He'll know where Daria is as well. Maybe she's in the kitchen."

Andy nodded. "Yeah, I shoulda done that when we walked in here. I should just've asked Gorilla where everyone was. I dunno what stopped me."

What else but this damn building? Karen thought.

Craig pointed to the waitress, who was now headed back their way. "I'll ask her the same thing."

"Yeah, you do that," Andy said.

Both men stepped away from Karen.

CHAPTER 30

Craig

Craig reached his objective first, mostly because the waitress was walking towards him.

She stopped when she saw he was about addressing her. She smiled her smile that wasn't exactly as smile. Her smile like the hounds of hell were on her trail.

He wondered what had happened to the previous waitress. *Is she dead? Is this one dead too?*

He caught himself. This woman standing in front of him most definitely wasn't dead. *She's here, ain't she?—flesh and blood? What put the thought of death into my head?*

But, yes, there was something morbid about this woman, something unwholesome under her everyday, lady-next-door surface.

"Hello, can I get you something?" she asked. Her voice was soft and pleasant. Even so, it held the same overtones of suppressed mania that her eyes broadcast.

"Hi," he said, raising his voice to be heard over Poppy and TJ on the pool table. "We're looking for my girlfriend Shelly and her friend. They both came here to—"

That was as far as he got. The brunette waitress had been carrying her serving tray under her right arm as she walked back to the corridor. Now, in a single fluid motion, she swung the tray up and swept it across Craig's neck.

The tray must have had a razor-sharp edge. It went into Craig's neck, deep through the muscles and blood vessels and nerves. As the metal opened up his neck, Craig had no idea what was going on.

He felt pain, pain, pain.

The tray exited his neck in a shower of blood. Thick crimson jets that squirted all over the waitress.

Craig stood with his hands clamped to his throat, trying to stop the red spillage. It was a wasted effort: the razor-edged tray had inflicted too deadly a wound. And with the muscles at the front of his neck separated and thus no longer pulling his head downwards, the wound yawned open. He couldn't cover it.

The blood spilled through and over his fingers.

He stared at the waitress and tried to speak. "Why?" he tried to say, but blood poured from his mouth instead. It was unbelievable, what she'd just done to him.

He could no longer turn his head. So he turned his entire body.

He stared at Karen

Fingers pressed to her mouth, Karen was gaping back at him.

Andy, about to pose his first question to Gorilla, heard Karen gasp. He turned back and gaped too. Andy raised his shotgun to shoot, but the murderous waitress had slipped behind Craig now.

Behind him, Craig heard Poppy and TJ grunting through another violent orgasm. Heard their expressions of intense lust, intenser pain, and the intensest of desperation.

He turned around to look at the waitress. "Why?" he tried to ask again, but this time not even blood exited his lips.

The waitress's miserable gaze apologized for her, pleading that she was merely carrying out a command. But he also sensed complicity in the woman. She enjoyed what she'd done. He was able to put his finger on it: she'd been hurt similarly, and now her satisfaction was in sharing the anguish of her own death with him.

By this time Craig knew he was dying. He felt death's grasp, ice-cold fingers squeezing him like he was a tube of toothpaste—forcibly ejecting his soul from his body. He also felt something else—another force sucking at him. This second force wasn't death. It was something much worse that death. The thing sucking at him—chewing on him like it was masticating food—was an unspeakable horror. The sucking/chewing thing obtained its nourishment from the *nature* of his death. Just like a vampire would have feasted on his spilt blood, this invisible creature—this monster he felt and sensed but could not see—was eating the *violence* of his passing. It was gorging itself full on the very atrocity of his dying so young, of his exceptional virility and potential going to waste.

It was then that he understood the truth about the waitress. She felt no malice towards him. She was merely a puppet, as much so as if she had strings attached to her. Also, she *was* dead. A walking corpse. As dead as he would soon be. The dark vitality that he sensed in her was merely the life of her puppeteer—the life force of the monster that had made her kill him and was now feeding on his death. The enjoyment of his passing that he'd sensed in her was a second-hand emotion, the radiation of another's pleasure through her.

He turned to Andy and Karen again. He couldn't blame them for looking so confused. In their shoes, he'd be just as confused. Andy still couldn't fire because the waitress was still hiding behind Craig. She'd dropped her razor-tray and was clasping his sides with both hands.

Karen was just staring in shock. She seemed to have forgotten she was carrying a gun.

Even though Craig hadn't been able to express his question to the woman who'd just murdered him, it was clear she understood. Maybe she'd read his lips, he thought. Maybe she was telepathic. Maybe the dead just knew things that the living didn't.

But, no, she hadn't understood him at all. She merely wanted to pass a final message to him. A message from the monster that owned her.

As Craig's mind shut down and he began slumping to the ground, he felt the waitress catch hold of him under the armpits and lift him upright again. Her lips pressed close to his right ear. He heard her, the last words he'd ever hear anyone say, in this or any other world:

"I think your death is delicious," Brie Becker whispered in his ear, speaking in another, far-longer-dead woman's voice. "I really do. It tastes exquisite. Now die for me, boy. Feed me!"

Craig died without understanding in the least what she meant.

CHAPTER 31

Daria

"I think your death is delicious," Daria Simpson whispered through the waitress's lips. "I really do. It tastes exquisite. Now die for me, boy. Feed me!"

He died. He fed her. His death was sweet on her tongue. The nasty manner of his passing tasted like ice cream. It tasted like chicken-fried steak. It tasted like honey. It tasted like a hotdog. The fastest food of all; yummy and also nourishing.

She licked him up, her molars grinding as she fed. She swallowed him down. He filled her with energy. He charged her like she was a battery.

Craig was very satisfying. But there were others to eat too.

And . . . Daria now felt very bothered. The man—the one she hated above all men on Earth—was now inside her building. Inside her. *She* was the building. The building was *her*. No more, no less. Everything was her now. Her original building was long destroyed; she had reconstructed this one from memory. Just as she had reconstructed her dead brother and the woman he loved from memory also. Gorilla, Helen, and now the reanimated Brie Becker—all three were merely extensions of herself. Detached additional limbs to do her bidding.

She watched the man.

She sensed the man. Why did she hate him so much? She began remembering. Long-lost images and scenes from her night of death filled her mind.

This HORRIBLE, NASTY, DISGUSTING man . . . his name is Andrew William Watson. Andy. Andy. Andy. He drives, no, drove a truck. He loved . . . he loved . . . he loved . . . me! ME? ME? He loved me?

And then the strangest memory of all touched Daria, along with a feeling she'd not felt since dying—love. She'd loved Andy too. She *still* loved Andy.

But he'd let her die and she'd vowed never to forgive him for that. *I'll never forgive ANDY for abandoning me . . . no matter what.*

Even the dead can know an overload of feelings. Particularly the 'empty dead'—those dead that sustain themselves solely by the draining of others.

Daria wept. She wept bitterly. She wept tears of rage and of heartbreak.

And while pouring out her heart to herself, for the briefest of moments she lost control of the world—the building—she'd recreated around herself.

CHAPTER 32

Shelly, mostly . . .

One moment, Shelly Parker knew she was dying and didn't care. The peerless ecstasy was sufficient compensation for her being drained away to nothingness.

The next moment, Shelly cared very much what happened to her. She didn't want to die. She wanted to live.

She was lying flat on her belly again, her eyes gaping open in orgasm. Erica was fisting her from behind, wrist-deep in bleeding woman-hole. They'd given up on the dildo. It was neither 'stretchy' nor 'immediate' enough. Fisting was a direct connection between them. It was also much more intimate; a true woman-to-woman penetrative experience.

Besides, persistent thrusting of the hips took lots of energy. Energy was something neither of them really had left.

Shelly was halfway through her orgasm when the change occurred. The bedroom shadows dimmed for half a second, and next thing . . .

The pleasure was all gone. All she felt between her legs was excruciating pain. Her sexual and excretory openings and passages felt shredded.

She howled with pain.

Erica abruptly pulled her hand out of Shelly's body. Shelly, no longer impaled, rolled over onto her back. She took one good look at Erica and began screaming.

Shelly wasn't screaming from pain, though she was feeling sufficient of that to justify her making a very loud noise. No, she was screaming because of how Erica now looked, which, by extension, was how she herself must now also look.

Erica (who was kneeling beside her) was no better than a living skeleton. A skeleton covered with skin. A skeleton with bloody hands that she was staring at with a dazed expression on her bony face. Erica's blue eyes were the only 'alive' part of her. The rest of her was totally 'granny.' Granny two steps from her funeral. Granny with her crotch so stained with blood that one could easily mistake her for a redhead. Appropriate because she hardly had any hair left on her head or elsewhere.

Worst of all, though, were the maggots crawling over Erica's legs as she knelt weakly on the bed. The maggots were all over the bed, squirming amidst the bloody sheets. As Shelly watched, Erica farted. Wriggling bloody larvae accompanied the evil-smelling gas out of her body. The maggots spilled from the cleft of her buttocks like she was full of them now.

Shelly screamed some more. Then she farted herself. She felt her well-stretched rear entrance widen more than was necessary to let mere gas out. She felt the maggots slither out of her backside and pile up between her thighs, the backed-up pressure of those exiting forcing those already out of her along like turds floating downriver. Some of the maggots began climbing her thighs. A few of them bit her.

Shelly stopped screaming and leapt to her feet on the bed. Her bones audibly creaked as she moved. She heard them. As she brushed the maggots off herself, she thought fast. Her mind was ringing bells of alarm. Completely vanished were even the memories of the ecstasy she'd recently felt. All that remained now was disgust. Disgust with herself and Erica: disgust at how disgusting they both looked now, all their youth and beauty leeched away to feed a monster posing as a woman.

Shelly looked down at herself. If anything, she looked worse than Erica did. Her arms and legs were mere sticks; flesh-tree branches with twig fingers and toes. (Both of her hands were red with Erica's vaginal and anal blood, and her previously brunette crotch was also a redhead's now, a messy crimson thatch with most of its hair gone.) Her belly was so sucked in, it seemed that she possessed no internal organs. She imagined she looked as near to total starvation as it was possible to get without actually dying. No, she looked worse than that. Anyone who looked as bad as she and Erica did should by all rights be dead.

She could feel in her mouth that she had no teeth left. Her gums were two rows of bleeding pits. Except for the molars she'd accidentally swallowed, her teeth were scattered all over the bed, mingled with Erica's similarly spilled dentition, and indistinguishable from those grubs that they'd mashed into the sheets during their infernal ravishing of one another.

But, impossibly, Shelly still felt *strong*. This wasn't a *vital* strength, however, but an 'emptying' one, a parasitic vigor that would enable her to keep having sexual intercourse until every ounce of 'her' had been used up.

Shelly understood that this was all Daria's doing: Daria had kept them both alive by her power, long beyond the point at which they should naturally have died.

Oh, but I'm done with sex now though. For a good long while. I'm so torn up down there now that I couldn't fuck even if I wanted to! And yet, while Daria had her hold on me, the hurting felt good. The agony was ecstasy!

She shuddered at the memory of how close to the edge she'd been, how close to taking that terminal plunge over death's cliff. She was glad too that now she'd see her darling Craig again. All of a sudden, the thought of losing him was the scariest thought in the world. She felt like she'd just recovered her sanity. *I was about leaving the man I love more than anything else behind? Abandoning the future we've been planning for ourselves? And for what? For at most two or three hours of mind-melting pleasure? I must've been crazy. I really must have been.* She looked at Erica. *We both must have been out of our minds.* It was an extremely sobering thought.

For her part, Erica looked utterly stupefied. Now sitting with her legs crossed, she'd begun mumbling like she was going senile, saying stuff that made no sense. She seemed not to know what she was doing here.

Shelly somehow got over her horror. This time when she farted, she didn't bother with looking down. She ignored the disgusting larvae plopping between her feet and spreading on the bed sheets. She focused all her energies on escaping from here.

She shook Erica. "Hey! Snap out of it! We've gotta get away from here!"

She shook her again, then a violent third time. "Erica, wake up, please! Something has broken Daria's control over us. We need to get away before she takes us over again!"

Erica slowly came out of her stupor. She nodded up at Shelly. "Yes, yes, let's get out of here!" she gasped. She raised a hand to her head and the rest of her hair fell out. Tears filled her blue eyes as she watched her hair fall in front of her face.

They didn't bother with their clothes. They left the bedroom naked. Outside in the corridor, they turned left and shuffled towards the landing. (Tellingly, and chilling in its implication, this time they heard no moaning or gasping from the couple who'd earlier been making frenzied, close-to-death love in one of the corridor's rooms.)

They reached the stairs and descended. Walking was excruciating because of the pain in their crotches, but the infernal strength Daria was giving them compensated.

Their progress was also helped by the fear they felt. Their terror propelled them onwards. They understood that they were fleeing for their lives. Gone for good was the delusion Daria had seeded in them, her lie that ultimate ecstasy was worth paying the ultimate price for.

'Gone for good' at least until Daria remembered them again and encouraged them to once more ravish each other.

They knew that if she took control of them again, they'd *want* to fuck each other to death. They'd do so with delight in their hearts. And they'd both love Daria while dying.

Now that their minds were once more their own, neither Shelly nor Erica loved Daria in the least. They feared her. They each dreaded her with all their being.

Daria was DEATH. She was DEATH of a kind neither of them had ever imagined DEATH could be. DEATH that you wanted to kill you. DEATH that *made you* want it to kill you.

Leaning on each other for support, they made it downstairs. Looking back up the stairs, they saw that along with a dripping of grubs they'd left two sets of crimson footprints.

"This way," Shelly directed, pointing along the lower passageway towards the dining room.

"No," Erica refused, restraining Shelly with withered and gnarled fingers. "The bitch is *out there*. I'm sure of it. If she sees us, we're done for." She farted, with the accompanying spillage of maggots.

"Okay," Shelly agreed, "we'll look for the back door." She figured Erica had to be right about Daria being out front. Of course they couldn't see around the corner, but what they could see of the dining room looked *corrupted*—the shadows that had been upstairs in the bedroom seemed to have moved downstairs now. The air out there seemed thick with evil. Like there were malevolent spirits swimming in it.

Erica gagged at the crawling larvae everywhere. "Shit—where are all these grubs coming from? I've never had worms in my life before and now this happens to me!"

"Let's just get out of here," Shelly wheezed. Her own belly was rumbling too, a larval-fart not far off. She was aware also that anyone seeking to track them down merely needed to 'follow the grubs' as it were. Like Erica, she didn't know where she was getting so many larvae to fart out everywhere. Each time she broke wind now, the maggots left her anus in a conical spray that spread over a wide area. Sometimes it was a wall-to-wall aerial bombardment.

She was disgusted with herself.

They turned and hurried off, two magically-aged old women, bony, withered and completely bald, both ceaselessly farting out a trail of grubs behind them as they tried to find an escape from the horror diner.

CHAPTER 33

Andy, mostly . . .

The madness continued. Poppy and TJ were still having sex on the pool table. Andy had lost count of how many times they'd each yelled "I'm coming!" since he'd been in here.

It wasn't irritating; it was scary. Both the husband and wife had now both shrunk to half their initial size. And Andy had worked out that each reduction in size coincided with their orgasms.

The formerly obese man was no longer obese. Except for his horribly sagging skin, he looked almost normal now. The beautiful woman too, was no longer beautiful. Orgasmic anorexia had leeched her looks from her. Most of her hair had fallen out. Only her breasts still maintained their exceptional shape. Which meant they were implants. Damn, Andy could practically see the silicone in them now. But if the woman shrunk any more her skin would surely tear and the implants pop out. Andy was certain of this: both of her breasts were already streaked with stretch marks.

And Poppy was coming again. And TJ looked like he wasn't too far off from shooting another load into her either. Andy hoped he never suffered from priapism like that.

That was happening at the far end of the dining room. Closer by—five yards from Andy—the blood-covered waitress was still hiding behind Craig's corpse. She had the dead kid standing upright—a postmortem shield. Andy was waiting for her to put Craig down, so he could blow her away. His knuckles were white on his shotgun from the tension.

But there was something else going on there that Andy didn't understand. There seem to be grubs in the wound in Craig's neck. Yes, he was sure of it, those squirming white things in the kid's throat were maggots. Yuck!

He turned to see how Karen was doing. He figured she was doing okay. She'd not yet bolted for the front door. He wished she would; then he'd be certain she was safe. Her face was white and drawn, and her eyes were large with fright. Her mouth was pruned-up like she would piss herself from fear. One hand gripped her revolver, the other gripped Andy. She'd anchored her nails in his muscles. She was standing almost behind him; as though he were her own human shield against the crazy waitress.

The crazy waitress now had Craig's gun.

Gorilla still hadn't moved from his place at the bar. Andy was relieved about that.

Then, the shadows in the far corner became a woman. The woman got up and walked towards them.

It was Daria.

Karen gave a little squeak of fright and clutched Andy's arm tighter. Now she made no pretense of not hiding behind him. She ducked behind him and peeked around his side to see.

Andy shuddered. A lump rose up in his throat and almost suffocated him with emotion. Yes, it was Daria. Daria, exactly how he remembered her. White silken hair, the slightly elongated face like she had some Indian blood in her, those rose-petal lips, those delightful eyes. She was wearing a gray dress that seemed stitched from shadows, a dress formed of darkness itself. She didn't walk; she *flowed* over the checkered floor as if the tiles were her feet.

Despite Karen's presence there, Andy wanted to hobble over to Daria. He wanted to take her in his arms, and kiss those perfect lips of hers and tell her how much he'd missed her. He wanted to weep on her shoulder and sweep her off her feet and . . .

He didn't, however. He couldn't. Something was different about this woman he'd loved and lost and now gotten back again. Something was very wrong with this Daria who was coming towards him. He felt repulsed by her. He felt like running away.

She'd almost reached them. She stopped in the puddle of Craig's blood.

"Hello, darling, I hate you," she said.

Andy studied Daria, wondering why he no longer felt like embracing her. She was smiling. She even had her arms outstretched to him in a gesture of welcome.

Then he got it: her eyes. Her eyes were different. Same color and shape; different person. He was suddenly back two years earlier, recalling those two pictures of Erin De Mornay that Xander Mood had shown him. This Daria reminded him of that long dead witch. This Daria had an aura of the forbidden about her. Not a black outline like the Crossway viewed from outside, but something worse. Something inherently nasty. A stygian interior rather than an ebon exterior.

"Andy, I hate you," she repeated. She'd dropped her hands to her sides again. She was still smiling.

"I hate you." Now the humor left her face. He saw only the darkest of animosities in her eyes.

He nodded back. She hated him now. He understood that: he'd hated himself too for not being able to save her. He still did. He had no idea what to say or do. He did nothing, said nothing. Karen was trembling behind him. He reached back and patted her arm to calm her. He wondered if he should just turn and walk away, forget the girls they'd come to rescue and get the hell away from here before they both wound up like Craig.

But there was something magnetic about Daria. Something malignly alluring. Something irresistible.

Over on the pool table, Poppy began shrieking again: "OH, FUCK, TJ, THIS FEELS SO MOTHERFUCKING FINGER-LICKING GOOD! GIVE ME THAT COCK!"

His attention shifted back to the couple again. The naked woman's feet were back up on her husband's shoulders. He was thrusting relentlessly between her buttocks. (Andy couldn't tell if he was in her vagina or anus.) He just kept pumping away like a robot. His mass of loose skin swung about, flinging drops of sweat everywhere. He looked like a giant scrotum.

"FUCK ME!"

And then, what Andy had feared happened: To a horrible tearing sound, the grossly overstretched skin on the woman's rib cage ripped open on both sides. Her breast implants popped out of her chest and slid sideways off her body. One implant wedged itself under her left arm. The other rolled right off the pool table. She shrieked at her pain and loss, then began coming again.

"OH SHIT, TJ! YOU'RE SO DAMN GREAT, BABY! FUCK ME, FUCK ME, DARLING! FUCK FUCK FUCK ME!"

Andy felt embarrassed for the woman. No wonderful breasts anymore—blood all over her chest—and still craving more violent sex? But her expression was desperately rapturous. She was clearly having the time of her life.

He looked back at Daria.

"I hate you!" she repeated.

He nodded again. This was getting tiresome. He figured he'd better just apologize and get it over with. If she still remained mad at him after that, then . . .

"Listen, Daria honey, I'm real sorry about what—"

"OOOOHHH, YES, TJ, YOU FANTASTIC STUD, FUCK ME HARDER. OH OH OH OH OH, I'M COMING!"

Daria's face squeezed up really ugly at the interruption. She turned to the waitress (who was still hiding behind Craig) and said, "For hell's sake, Brie, shut that bitch up!"

Brie dropped Craig on the floor. Then, carrying his gun, she walked over to the pool table.

Even before she'd reached the couple, Andy was cringing. "Oh no, don't!" he protested. "Don't you dare do it!"

But Brie *did*. With no fuss, she placed the muzzle of the revolver to Poppy's head and pulled the trigger. Once, twice, thrice . . . four times in all. Poppy had time for only the barest hint of shock and apprehension before her head exploded and her brains spilled everywhere.

TJ clearly thought Brie would murder him too. He threw his hands up to shield his face. But Brie showed no interest in him. Once certain that Poppy was dead, she turned and walked away, back to Daria.

Immediately Brie left the pool table, TJ resumed having sex . . . with his wife's corpse.

"I CAN'T STOP FUCKING HER! I CAN'T STOP FUCKING HER!" he began screaming. He looked over at Andy and there were tears in his eyes. Then he turned back to the pool table and began humping the corpse harder than ever. "OH BOY, THIS IS JUST SO FUCKING GREAT! YEAH! YEAH!"

Andy couldn't believe his eyes. *That man over there is having sex with a woman who's just had her brains blown out.*

Karen had cringed behind him on hearing the gunshots. Now, she peeked around Andy, took one look at the dead woman and accompanying necrophilia, and began puking everywhere.

Andy tore his eyes from the spectacle and gaped at Daria. "What did you do that for? What the hell did you do that for, woman?"

Daria was licking her lips and smiling. "Delicious. Just delectable."

"What are you ranting about?"

Her eyes glowed with evil satisfaction. "I feed on sex and violence, Andy baby. Sex and violence. That's all I eat now: raw pleasure and pain. It's ambrosial."

Karen nudged him and whispered, "She's nuts. Let's just get outa here."

"Yeah," Andy agreed, hardly noticing the thick vomit smell on her lips. "Yeah, screw heroics and rescuing anyone. Let the damn cops come mop all this crap up."

Karen still behind him, he began backing away to the front entrance. He kept his shotgun raised. He wasn't about turning his back on Daria and that insane waitress bitch who'd already murdered two innocent people.

"Stop!" Daria demanded. "I order you to stop. You don't dare leave my domain without my permission."

"Hell no, babe," Andy said. "I'm about to do my Elvis impersonation. Be-bop-a-lula and see you in Vegas, bay-bee—me and my darling here are leaving your building." He was glad of one thing though, a major side benefit of coming here to the Crossway Diner this Sunday morning: this trip had cleared up for him once and for all where his heart's allegiance lay—he loved Karen. Daria could go to Hell. She seemed to live there now anyway.

"Darling?" Daria's face twisted up in rage. "Did I just hear you say 'darling,' Andy?"

Oh fuck, Andy thought. *Don't tell me you dead chicks get jealous too?*

"You called Karen 'darling?' You nasty son-of-a-bitch." Her face was now purple with anger. "You disgusting piece of male excrement! And to think that I once loved you!"

Andy only half-heard. He'd stopped hobbling backward. "Karen," he whispered over his shoulder, his mouth dry, "what time is it?"

She looked over his shoulder. "It's . . ."

"No, no. Check it on your wristwatch."

"Oh."

He waited while she checked. "It's . . . it's . . . Andy, it's about the same time as we arrived here. Maybe two minutes later."

"Yeah," Andy whispered back, not taking his eyes off either Daria or the waitress. "It's still just seven fifty-eight. At first I thought that the clock had stopped. But it hasn't—the second hand's still movin'. Time seems to be standing still in here."

Crazy as it sounded to say, it was the only explanation that made sense to Andy. *Else,* he figured, *how come no one else has entered the diner in the past hour? Unless that past hour has really lasted only a minute or two?*

"Andy, what are we gonna do?"

"We play it cool, sweetheart."

"And then what?"

"Same plan as before. We're getting our asses outa here, right away."

"Forget that retreat plan of yours!" Daria snapped. "You're not going anywhere. You're mine, Andy, mine forever!!"

He frowned back at her. Surely this was overdoing things. But then, Daria always had been a little headstrong when she wanted something done her own way. "Look," he said, "let's all be reasonable adults and corpses here. You keep your ghost diner, and we'll drop in now and again for breakfast whenever it's in the neighborhood. How's that sound?" While speaking he was still stepping backward. But in addition to his bad leg hindering his motion (the brace wasn't designed with retreat in mind), the front entrance also seemed further away than it should be. He didn't dare look back at it though, that was the problem. He had to keep his eyes and shotgun focused on Daria and the waitress.

"Andy, the floor!"

He chanced a glance down. Shit! Now he understood why they weren't getting any nearer to the front door. The black/silver checkered floor was behaving like a treadmill under their feet, keeping them in place no matter how fast they moved.

"I told you you're not leaving," Daria said.

Andy took two steps back. The floor—just the portion of it he was standing on—slid forward and returned him to his initial position. Once he stopped, it stopped. His second attempt at retreating produced the same effect.

"We're trapped, Andy!"

"No we're not," he growled back. They were clearly in a tight spot here, but he refused to accept that they couldn't escape it. He wasn't concerned so much about himself as about Karen. He wasn't losing her the way he'd lost Daria two years ago. It was ironic that it was Daria herself who now posed the danger to Karen.

He considered Daria again. This was getting unnerving. Daria didn't seem in any hurry at all, that was the thing. She was acting like she had all the time in the world. Andy, however, doubted that was the case. She had to be concerned about people noticing the building. Particularly with those two cops dead outside in their car.

He peered out through the window glass. A red 18-wheeler was climbing the overpass. It was too far gone for him to alert the driver by firing a shotgun blast through the window.

"You can't shoot through my windows," Daria said.

He gave her his full attention again. "Alright, what do you want with us?"

She smiled bitterly. It was odd: she was human and yet nonhuman, inhuman. Herself exactly as he remembered her and yet at the same time someone entirely different.

If he needed any confirmation of that difference, all Andy had to do was look behind her, at the man screwing his wife's corpse over in the corner. (TJ Murphy had shrunken even further now, but was nonetheless still thrusting violently into Poppy's body. Every now and then he'd groan and ejaculate and shrivel up some more. Andy particularly hated looking at the twin tears in Poppy's chest where her breast implants had erupted out of her body.)

Or, Andy could look at Craig's corpse on the floor by Daria's feet, its throat slit in a way oddly reminiscent of a prostitute he'd known two years ago. (By now there was no mistaking the maggots spilling from Craig's throat and mouth for anything else.)

"I want you to stay here with me, Andy," Daria said. "Just like old times."

Honey pie, that is so, so not happening, Andy thought. But he played for time. There had to be a way to break her power over the building, he figured. Then they could escape. The outside world—the real world— was barely ten steps away. It had to be possible to reach it again.

"It ain't gonna work, Daria," he said. "You yourself just said that you hated me."

She licked her red lips slowly, her tongue a slug eating a perfect rose. "I'm prepared to forgive you," she said with a smile colder than the ice blocks in a igloo. "But only on the condition that you drop your baggage." She gestured dismissively at Karen, who was still standing behind him. "*She* has to go."

Karen emitted a low moan of terror.

"Go where?" Andy asked cautiously. "If you'll let Karen leave this place . . . yeah, okay, I'll stay here with you . . . O.K. . . . yeah, it's a deal." Hell no, he wasn't staying here with Daria and her crazy crew. It hadn't escaped his notice that Gorilla had remained frozen like a statue at the same spot for the past hour or so. And the waitress too was behaving more like a marionette than a human being. *No way am I ever lettin' that happen to me.* Once Daria took her damned control off the diner long enough to let Karen out . . . they were both gone from here already.

"No," Daria said. "Karen stays too. I want her as a pet. She can serve us." Her voice dripped with condescending nastiness.

"No," Andy said. "Even over my dead body that ain't happenin'. You can have me but not her."

Daria's eyes smoldered like coals. "I'll have you both anyway. And I'll have you exactly how I want you." She snapped her fingers at the giant behind the counter. "Gorilla, kill Karen!"

Gorilla immediately came alive and lumbered out from behind the counter. Andy spun to cover him with the shotgun. He almost tripped but he righted himself. "Yeah, come and get her, you overgrown son-of-a-bitch!"

"Get out of my damn way, cripple, before I knock you over like a bowling pin."

Andy stared at Gorilla. The right side of the man's head was bashed in, like someone had used a sledgehammer on it. His eyes were blanker than wiped-clean whiteboard. No expression at all on his face.

Damn, a fucking zombie.

"I'm warning you, Gorilla. You take one more step towards Karen and I'll let you have this shotgun between the eyes."

Then Karen shrieked "NOOOO!!" behind him and he forgot all about Gorilla.

He spun around and stared.

Shit.

While he'd been concentrating on Gorilla, and Karen had been watching *him*, the waitress had snuck around behind Daria. Andy was just in time to see her stab Karen in the belly for the second time. The waitress jerked out her bloody knife and prepared to stab Karen a third time.

Andy let her have the shotgun full in the face.

The weirdest thing happened then: the waitress melted. Immediately the gun blast hit her, she turned into a thick black liquid—dissolved like black candlewax—and flowed away into the floor. In a moment she was all gone. It looked to Andy like she'd merged with the floor's black tiles.

He grabbed Karen, who was bent over and gripping her belly. Blood had begun spilling from her mouth. More blood was trickling between the fingers clenched over her belly.

Andy felt cold fingers of apprehension squeeze his soul. *Oh no, not again. Not-a-damn-gain.*

"I told you, Andy," Daria said gleefully, cackling like a witch, "you're mine, mine—all mine and mine alone!"

CHAPTER 34

Shelly and Erica

Luck was on the girls' side in their escape quest. The diner's side exit was just a short distance from the stairs.

"There it is!" Erica yelped, pulling Shelly into the short passageway, at the end of which stood a cream-colored door through the inset window of which they could see the woods across the road.

They stared at the door. Freedom. They didn't dare believe that they'd made it. Actually escaped.

Behind them, and all the way back to the stairs, lay a twice-layered trail of farted-out maggots, more grubs than a human body could possibly contain.

"I'll be glad when this shit stops," Erica said wearily as she blew again, the grubs spraying from her behind like she was an aerosol can.

"Are you telling me?" Shelly asked. "We both need worm expeller." Her belly rumbled too and she exploded with her own blast of maggots. The horrible larvae swarmed around their feet and crawled up their legs and bit them. Both women ignored the maggots. The maggots didn't matter, just like it didn't matter that they'd both lost all their hair and teeth and looked like their exhumed great-grandmothers. (Their voices were now stuck in the never-never-pitch between teen-and-hag talk.) Hair could regrow and they could get dentures, and they could eat themselves back to health. Given time, their bodies would heal. Their front and rear crotch entrances would be as good as new again. Time. All they both needed was thirty-or-less seconds to reach the side door and then they'd have all the time in the world to recover from their ordeal.

The problem was that each expulsion of the maggots weakened them, so having both just farted, they had to wait several seconds before they felt strong enough to move again.

They leaned against the corridor walls, hoping they'd not have to 'evacuate' again soon. They stared at each other, holding in both their pain and their anticipation of freedom, an expectation even more painful than their torn loins.

But now the door lay just ahead of them. They'd made it.

"You ready?" Erica asked. "We better go fast, my tummy's already turning again."

"I'm as ready as a porn star on Viagra." As she'd been doing since they'd descended the stairs, Shelly concentrated on an image of Craig's smiling handsome face as a source of motivation. (But dammit, what the hell was he going to think when he saw her looking like this?) She winced. "Yeah, let's go before another bout of grub-poo stalls us here."

Hand in hand, they headed for the exit. Their bones creaking, their bodies trembling, insanely bright eyes staring from their wizened faces, they hurried as fast as they could manage for the side door, conscious that at any moment Daria might remember them and cast her spell of deadly lust over them again.

They heard Daria behind them when they were just four steps from freedom.

They froze. They wanted to push the door open and exit the building, but it was impossible now. Just like that, they were once more under Daria's power.

It felt so right, that was the thing. It really didn't feel wrong at all to be Daria's minions. Shelly's desire for her boyfriend instantly faded away. She found it utterly horrifying, how quickly and easily Craig and all her intense heartfelt longing for him suddenly became inconsequential to her.

Trembling, Shelly and Erica turned around.

Daria was walking down the passageway towards them. Her white hair like a wig made from snow. Her red lips like an ocean sunset. Her dark dress merged with the floor and the walls like it was made from overlapping shadows.

She looked hungry.

The mere sight of Daria immediately had Shelly and Erica farting from fear. Soon each of them was standing in an ankle-high pile of grubs. They held each other tight and shivered as she came closer.

Even with death at her doorstep, Shelly felt it was undignified to keep fouling herself like this. A fierce anger now mixed in with her dread of Daria.

"Hey, you evil witch, let us out of this damn madhouse of yours!" she growled.

"Yes, please let us go," Erica pleaded.

Daria frowned at them. She stretched out her hands and stroked their withered cheeks.

At Daria's touch, Shelly's rage faded and she began weeping like a baby. "Please, please, let us go. Please! We want to live."

Daria smiled. "I know. But I want you both to die. I enjoyed eating your sex a lot. Now I want to feed on your violence. What you two must do now is kill each other." Her smile broadened, revealing pointy teeth.

She drew her hands back from their cheeks. Each hand now held a knife.

She handed one knife to Shelly and the other to Erica. "Now, go on, darlings, feed me."

Unable not to, they took the knives from her. Both blades were identical: short and sharp.

"Kill yourselves, girls. Put the ends of your miserable lives to good use."

Her withered lips trembling, Shelly looked back at the exit door. *How can this happen to me right on the threshold of freedom?* she pondered.

But the next minute she answered her own question: *It's Erica's damn fault. If only the dumb blonde airhead hadn't kept up shitting grubs everywhere like she's a fly mother, we'd be free now!*

Anger filled her. Murderous rage like she'd never felt before. She pointed her knife at Erica. "This is all your goddamn fault, you stupid bitch! Because of you I'll never see Craig again!"

Erica was glaring back at her with similar unreasoning fury in her eyes. "No, you silly cow, this is *your* damn fault! If you hadn't insisted that I fist your pussy one more time, we'd have escaped from Daria by now."

"No, no, no, bitch! The reason we're still here is because you've got a slack ass!"

"It's slack because you were fisting it, you dumb heifer!"

"Who're you calling a dumb heifer!? Goddamn bug hive mother!"

Erica farted out a fresh complement of maggots. "How dare you, you cow!? I'm gonna carve you into steaks for Daria's kitchen!"

Shelly was about retorting to that when she felt a sharp, agonizing pain in her belly. *Shit—I ain't gonna fart now, am I?* She gaped down. What the fuck? Erica—that bald flatulent turd—had stabbed her. *She actually dared hurt me?*

"How dare you!?" she screamed, swinging her own knife up and down and burying it somewhere in Erica's scrawny chest.

"Fuck you!" Erica screamed back. She leapt on Shelly and swiped at her face. The knife tore out Shelly's left eye.

The blood and eye jelly spilling down her face only enraged Shelly further. She swiped back at Erica, but Erica had slipped away.

Erica ran over to the corridor entrance. There she posed in the doorway and pointed at Shelly and laughed and sang: "One-eyed cow! One-eyed cow! Boyfriend Craig won't want you now!"

Shelly clenched her fists in rage. She farted hard. "I'M GONNA KILL YOU FOR THIS!" she screamed.

She turned to Daria, who'd now moved to the side of the corridor to let them both by. "SHE BLINDED MY EYE! I'M GOING TO KILL THAT SLACK-ASSED PIECE OF FEMALE GARBAGE FILTH IF IT'S THE LAST MOTHER-GODDAMN-FUCKING THING I EVER DO IN MY LIFE!" she screamed at Daria.

"Daria nodded sagely. "Yes, *you are* going to kill her, and *it will* be the last thing you ever do."

"FUCK YOU TOO, DARIA! YOU GODDAMN BLEACHED-BLONDE CUNT! I HAVEN'T GOT TIME FOR YOUR TRANSCENDENTAL BULLSHIT! GET YOUR ASS OUT OF MY FUCKING WAY, BITCH!"

"Come and get me, one-eyed cow! You can't even see me now!"

Shelly staggered down the corridor. Ouch! The stab wound in her belly really hurt. She lunged at Erica, but missed and fell to the floor instead. Next, she felt a ripping pain across her back. Shit, Erica had got her again.

She played possum.

"Hey, co-ow, are you dead already!? Now there's a well-behaved cut of meat!"

She waited till Erica's feet were close to her head before striking. She got a good hit, deep into Erica's left thigh. Laughing, she jerked the knife up through the thigh muscle, all the way up from Erica's knee to her groin. Erica squealed like a stuck pig. Then, before Erica could escape, Shelly got her a second time. This time she cut her deeply across her left hand. She was delighted to see two of Erica's fingers fall to the floor. Food for the grubs.

Now it was Erica's turn to scream. She screamed long and loud. Backing away, she slipped on a pile of maggots and slid out into the main corridor. She fell down hard on her butt, gripping her wounded leg with her wounded hand. Blood jetted from the stumps of her missing fingers and dribbled from her thigh.

She glared furiously at Shelly. "I'm gonna kill you for this, heifer. You're T-bone steaks for real now!"

Shelly was back on her feet again. "Says who? You ain't got the guts! Ha ha ha! Yeah, look at you, you old withered hag, you really ain't got the guts—you've pooped them all out through that chasm you call an asshole! Fart ass! Fart ass!"

Blood streaming down both their scrawny bodies, they leapt at each other, each intent on murdering the other. They fought and farted and forgot Daria.

As if their having forgotten her was erasing her, Daria faded from view. She was licking her lips in intense pleasure.

Daria vanished. The squirming maggots remained. The maggots frolicked in the fighting women's blood. Soon, they had more to eat. Lots of sliced-off skin and flesh plopped to the floor around them.

CHAPTER 35

Andy, mostly

Andy heard yelling and screaming. Angry women sounds from far off. The noises were unimportant to him. With Karen wounded, Andy didn't have the time to care about anyone else's misfortunes.

Despite which, he looked up and looked around. Except for TJ still having sex with Poppy's corpse, the dining room was empty.

Where the hell did Daria and Gorilla vanish to?

It didn't matter none. He was relieved that the dead pair were gone. He returned his attention to his wounded girlfriend. It was time they left this evil place.

Karen straightened up painfully. Andy hated how she looked. She had blood all over her mouth and chin, and on her belly and thighs. He cursed the dead waitress. But had the woman actually died? Was she even alive to begin with? She'd become part of the floor. Not like Craig. Andy cast a regretful glance over at the young man, who now lay under a table with maggots bubbling from the hole in his neck.

Andy turned back to Karen. He stuck his shotgun under his left arm and began helping her toward the front door. Now that Daria was gone the floor had stopped acting like a treadmill. The front entrance was just ten yards off.

It was slow going. His bad right leg for one thing; Karen's belly wounds for another. She was staggering, hunched over and weaving left and right like she was drunk. Andy was scared, really scared she might die on him before he got her to a hospital. Her face was pale and her eyes weren't focusing right. There wasn't a lot of blood everywhere, but God only knew what that damn knife had sliced up inside her.

"Alright, baby, just take it easy now. We're almost there."

He tried to hurry her up, but she couldn't move any faster. Instead, she bent over and spat out a lot of blood.

Seeing the blood, Andy grew even more frightened.

"Please, sweetheart, don't you dare friggin' die on me now. I need you to look after me in my old age."

She swayed like she'd collapse and he quickly set her down in the nearest chair. He bent over her looking worried.

"I'm okay, baby," she said bravely, smiling and kissing him with bloody lips. Don't worry, darlin', I ain't about dyin' just yet. We've got loads more years together."

Though weak, her voice sounded strong. He was relieved.

"Okay," he said, "I ain't gonna rush you to get up again. But we've got to get away from here fast before Crazy Lady returns. And remember, you need a doctor."

While waiting for Karen to get some strength back, Andy looked around. He checked the floor to ensure that it was still behaving like a floor should. It was. Then, on a memory, he re-checked the clock over the counter. It was still stuck at 7:59 a.m. *Oh, so we've only been in here for three minutes? Yeah, right, and I'm Mark Zuckerberg.* He hoped that, even though they seemed to be making normal progress now, the damn clock wasn't slowing down their motion to the front door. He didn't want to be walking for two minutes that was actually two hours.

He peered outside. The sky was still stuck in early morning mode. Light blue, with some whites and greys colored in; the sun up there too somewhere.

Several cars passed, heading towards Conway. A gray pickup truck going the other way was halfway up the overpass. A woman on a green motorbike sped after the truck.

Andy was troubled by the fact that none of those passing seemed to notice the Crossway building. They couldn't all be out-of-towners, could they? (He still held to his original theory, that the diner was only visible to specific people: mainly those unfamiliar with this area and so unlikely to raise any alarm.) Or . . . was it that the Crossway had already begun to fade? That wouldn't be good at all—winding up trapped in this crazy dimension with his crazy ex.

Worst of all? If that happened, Karen was finished.

He was now also forced to accept something he'd been doing his best to ignore: the building was flickering. Every thirty or so seconds, the dining room walls, tables and chairs went out of focus around them like his eyes were bad. Then, just as suddenly, the blurred vista would normalize again.

Andy didn't think the flickering was a trick of the light. It had to mean that the building was becoming more insubstantial. They were definitely running out of time here.

He felt Karen tug on his sleeve. "Andy, let's go."

He looked down and gave her an enquiring glance. Face pale, she nodded back at him. He helped her up and they set off again. Five yards left. Soon they'd be out of this hellish place for good, and neither of them would ever have to see goddamned Daria Nicole Simpson again.

Just so long as Daria Nicole Simpson didn't come back before they made it outside.

The lady-noises sounded again. The sounds were faint but distinct. They were also slightly echoey, like the voices of people singing in a bathroom. One voice seemed to be yelling in triumph, the other in agony.

At that moment TJ also groaned: "Oh, shit! I'm coming! Oh, God, please help me stop doing this! Oh, oh, oh yeeeessss, Poppy, dead or alive, your ass is just so damn good!"

Andy filtered them all out of his consciousness. Step by step, the door was getting nearer.

"Go help the girls," Karen said suddenly. "Baby, go help them!"

Andy shook his head. "Forget it—I'm getting you out of here first."

"Andy, *please*. Look, I can make it to the door by myself." She tried to separate herself from him, but instantly slid halfway to the floor.

He strained and pulled her back to her feet. "For God's sake, Karen, let's just get out of this nutty place!"

She dug her feet in, refusing to budge even though the door was just two steps away. "Andy, they're still *alive* back there; that's the problem. We can't just leave them behind to die."

Andy wondered why Karen was being so stubborn about this. *Is the diner affecting her mind? Or is Daria doing it?* He stole quick glances around the dining room. Daria was nowhere in sight. He grimaced. *I didn't want Karen coming in with us in the first place, and now she doesn't want to leave either.*

He considered her suggestion. She looked strong enough to last a few more minutes. He could leave her in a chair and hurry to the back and see what was going on with Shelly and Erica. But what if Daria was back there with them? All he'd accomplish then would be to draw attention to himself and Karen again after Daria had apparently forgotten all about them. And he didn't want to leave Karen alone anyway. Definitely not in here.

"Please, honey, let's go," he said.

Karen shook her head at him. "No, Andy. You'll hate yourself forever if you don't help those girls. You know you will."

"I'll hate myself even more if *I do* go and you die as a result. I'm saving you first, *then* them. And that's only if this place is still here afterwards. No, don't argue."

He tried to get them moving the last few steps, but Karen held on to the final table and refused to let go.

It occurred to Andy then that blood loss might be affecting Karen's reasoning. Not enough oxygen was reaching her brain anymore. "Oh, alright, I'll go save 'em," he agreed quickly. "But only after I've gotten you outside the diner first."

She examined his face for a lie. "You sure, baby? I won't forgive you if you trick me on this."

"Yeah, yeah, I mean it," he grunted, and she could clearly see that he didn't want to do it, but he would because she'd insisted. "Yeah, O.K. Once you're safe out on the concrete where folks driving by can see you and fetch help, I'll come back inside again and go look for Shelly and Erica and get them out too."

She agreed to go then. Andy admired her stand but he felt it was kind of dumb to sacrifice yourself for others if you weren't Jesus.

A moment later, he realized that all their debate over escaping had been for nothing.

They'd reached the glass door. Andy reached out to push it open and the door vanished. They were standing instead in front of a black sheet of glistening darkness that forbade itself from being touched.

They both instinctively stepped back.

"Oh, Poppy, your corpse butt is so damn SHIT-ASSTIC!" TJ moaned behind them. "I'M GONNA COME AGAIN! OH, FUCKING SHIT!"

Andy, meanwhile, was staring at the fresh area of wall. The black sheet looked wet and sticky. It was in constant motion too, dripping from the ceiling to the floor. Though Andy knew it couldn't be wider than the thickness of the rest of the wall, he wasn't going to chance their stepping through it: they might just end up as part of the wall themselves. He had good reason to fear this: the black patch reminded him of the black liquid the waitress who'd stabbed Karen had dissolved into. He could also sense evil radiating from it.

He quit staring at the black patch. He understood that the front door's disappearance was Daria's doing. There was no point either in questioning how she'd done it. All that mattered was getting he and Karen the hell out of here.

He looked desperately around. Their exit would now have to be through the windows. They did also have both the building's left-side door and rear/kitchen exit as options, but neither was practically viable: Karen would never make it that far.

So a window then. He'd sit Karen down and smash one open with a chair, then they'd climb through.

He turned Karen away from the black portion of wall.

The full horror of their situation seemed to have just dawned on her. "Andy, what are we gonna—?"

Those were the last words she ever spoke to him. The black portion of wall solidified into Gorilla. Gorilla grabbed Karen, reaching down over Andy to do so.

"Help!" she gasped in fright.

Andy spun around. He froze for a moment, perplexed. Gorilla had become monstrous. The hands the dead man was holding Karen with were abnormal in both size and shape. Each was five times too large for his body and covered with rotting skin in which maggots crawled. The other major change in Gorilla concerned his mouth. His entire jaw had tripled in size now and was filled with metallic teeth, all of which seemed to be over a foot long.

Andy was still trying to retrieve his shotgun from the crook of his arm when Gorilla ripped both of Karen's arms off. Karen's arms separated from her shoulders like magic. Blood squirted and sprayed and Karen began screaming.

"NOOOOO!!!!!" Andy howled.

Gorilla flung Karen's arms away. One arm went over the service counter, the other shattered a window and streaked out into the parking lot. Before Karen could slump to the floor, Gorilla had grabbed her again and dug his foot-long teeth into the side of her neck. The teeth went in through one side of her throat and came out on the other. Her blood spurted up and filled Gorilla's mouth.

Karen slumped dead. More dead than a rat pulverized with a sledgehammer.

On Karen's death, madness filled Andy's mind. The noise of the man behind him having another necrophiliac orgasm filled his mind. Daria's disembodied voice filled the dining room and also seeped into his mind.

Daria was saying, "Delicious, Gorilla, just delicious. Oh, she's so tasty, so tasty. Andy's little bitch is so tastee!"

The madness held Andy captive. It paralyzed him. He stood with the shotgun half-lifted, staring at Karen's unbelievable death.

Gorilla let go of Karen. She remained standing for a moment, held up by the nine or ten teeth speared through her neck. Then, slowly, she slid off Gorilla's teeth and down to the floor. It seemed to take an eternity for the foot-long teeth to slide all the way out of her neck. Then her armless body fell to the bloody tiles.

Andy stared at Karen's corpse. The madness seeped out of his mind in little squirts. When he had enough sanity in his head again to finish raising the shotgun, he did so.

Gorilla was staring at him. Andy stared back. Gorilla kept staring at him. Andy aimed the shotgun carefully at Gorilla's head. Gorilla kept staring at him, his face sadistic and satisfied. Andy began shooting. **Boom! Boom!** Gorilla yelled in pain when his head exploded. Andy worked the shotgun slide like an automaton. **Boom! Boom!**

The noise and echoes of the shotgun blasts filled his head, forcing out the rest of the madness.

Andy fired and Gorilla fell apart. He didn't separate into flesh-and-blood though. No, like the waitress before him, he again became the black substance that had replaced the front door. He melted and flowed down to the tiles.

Andy stopped firing when Gorilla's remains also merged with the floor.

He looked down at Karen's corpse again. Karen's eyes were open, bulging with horror and agony. As Andy stared at her, the madness threatened to fill his head again, to shatter his mind into nice happy shards. He fought it off.

Somewhere in the building, he heard Daria cackling. Loud gleeful echoic laughter.

Alright, Andy thought, *this is about being settled in the only way it can be.* Daria spilling Karen's blood had seen to that.

With Gorilla gone, the front door had reappeared. Andy looked at it without interest. He knew that if he tried walking outside now, he'd make it without a hitch. He also knew that Daria knew he wasn't about leaving. And she was right. He wasn't going anywhere just yet.

He and Daria had business to finish here. Deadly business.

In a silence broken only by the grunts of the man fucking his wife's corpse, Andy began reloading his shotgun.

CHAPTER 36

Andy, mostly, again

Daria hadn't reappeared by the time Andy was through loading the shotgun. No problem; he would go look for her then.

He stared at Karen's armless body and wiped tears from his eyes.

Daria's laugher still echoed through the diner. The sound reverberated around him. The echoes felt like fists banging on the door of his mind, seeking entry into his head to steal his sanity.

Yeah, Daria, he thought back at her, *I'm gonna kill you, you crazy woman.*

Andy figured that Daria going all psycho had to be Xander Mood's doing: *You hang around crazy folks long enough and they'll infect you with their antisocial behavior.*

He cocked the shotgun, then turned and studied the two hallway exits from the dining room. The middle exit, the one between the counter and the drinks' fridge, led to the kitchen and back door. The one on the far left led upstairs and also to the side door. The angry female noises he'd heard had come from the left exit. Twenty-to-one, Daria was most likely over that way.

The female screaming and yelling had stopped though.

"Andy?" Daria was suddenly standing behind the service counter. She was holding up one of Karen's ripped-off arms. Andy stood frozen.

Daria pointed at Karen's corpse. "That makes two women now that you couldn't protect. So much for the power of love, huh?"

Enraged, Andy took his time raising the shotgun and aiming it at her. He however found it impossible to pull the trigger. "Why'd you kill Karen, Daria? She didn't do nothing bad to you." As he spoke tears filled his eyes.

"Because you're *mine*, Andrew." She locked her fingers with Karen's and swung the severed arm to and fro across the countertop, drawing a bloody semicircle on it. "Do you get that? You fucking *belong to me*. I don't play the love-triangle game."

"Not any more, I don't," Andy growled. He decided to just shoot her and get it over with. It wasn't murder—she was already dead. But once again, he couldn't pull the trigger. He tried hard to, but, though he hated to admit it, he still loved her. Even if now she was cold and heartless and deservedly belonged six-feet-under.

She laughed. She threw Karen's detached arm at him. He ducked. She vanished.

Andy kicked the arm away. Then he wiped his eyes with the back of his hand. He wiped the tears away. He wiped the sweat away. He wiped Daria away.

The spell was broken. Oh, he was so going to hunt her down!

"Hey! You over there!"

Andy turned towards the pool table. He'd forgotten TJ. The man had been there so long now, he'd become mental furniture.

TJ waved Andy over. "Hey, come here!" He was still thrusting away between Poppy's buttocks. He'd flipped her skeletal corpse over now and dragged it to the edge of the pool table. It looked like she was standing up on the tips of her toes and bending over the table. That was until one looked at her head. The back of her hairless scalp was just a massive hole. Poppy's shrunken face was acting as a paintbrush now, smearing her blood and brains over the pool table with each thrust of her husband's hips.

"Come here, man!" There was acute distress in TJ's voice.

Andy hedged about going over there. He was in a hurry to get started on hunting down Daria. "Me? You talking to me, man?"

TJ got angry. "Yeah, I'm talking to you, you meathead! Who the damn hell else is there in this room 'cept us two!" The insult was almost a parody of proper abuse. TJ's voice had lost all its vitality. It still held a thread of masculinity, but it was the masculinity of a teenage boy whose voice had just broken.

Andy went over. He made a wide detour around Craig's corpse, which was now covered with maggots. These maggots weren't any kind of normal—they'd eaten away Craig's clothes and were fast revealing his bones. Maggot-piranha more like.

Andy reached TJ. Andy was feeling nervous. More than just necrophilia had him uneasy here:

TJ now looked like some kind of crazy malnourished insect. Or like a turtle with a floppy pink shell. The once-obese man had shrunken to a skeleton now. This much was obvious from his head—all his hair gone, the skin drawn tight against a skull that seemed to have no muscles overlying it anymore, and eyes sunk deep in hollow bony sockets. (The man's eyes were what *really* worried Andy: they had an insane blaze to them, like dark pools of hellfire.) His skin, though, hadn't shrunk with the rest of him. It flopped over his bones like a huge bag. He looked like a melted pink candle. His penis was stiff and red as it stabbed back and forth into his wife's sex. His belly and crotch were smeared with excrement and his erection was red with blood.

Andy didn't speculate over whose blood that was.

Andy stood a good distance back from TJ, well out of touching range. He kept his shotgun at the ready too.

Andy looked at the wall, averting his eyes from the two skeletons having sex—the dead skeleton and the skeleton wearing the skin bag.

"Alright, I'm here," he said gruffly, trying to sound tough, though he didn't feel tough in the least. "What you want me for?"

TJ stared deep into Andy's eyes. Andy felt chilled; the desperation was back in the man's eyes now. And . . . TJ's teeth had all fallen out. A quick glance confirmed that Poppy too had lost most of her teeth before her murder.

"You gotta help me, man!" TJ pleaded. "I can't stop screwing Poppy! Please help me, man!" While speaking he didn't miss a single sexual stroke. His hips swung back and forth with a fixed rhythm, driving his erection in and out his wife's body.

Andy glanced at the dead vagina and quickly looked away again—it was a nasty sight: wet flesh peeled raw by excessive friction, cracked by too much stretching, and bruised almost black by repeated forceful contact with another body. During that glance, Andy also got a good look at TJ's erection. The skin of the man's penis was split in several places.

"Help me, man! I gotta stop! This shit's gonna kill me!"

Andy agreed that TJ had a good point there: if he kept shrinking at his current rate, he'd die. And die very soon at that. But . . . Andy didn't know what to do. He wasn't about to touch TJ, that was for sure. And it wasn't because the guy looked so horrible. Andy knew TJ was under Daria's control. He didn't want to fall into a trap and wind up bent over the pool table getting sodomized while all his teeth fell out too.

"I don't know what to do, man," he said. "What should I do?"

The deformed man looked confused himself, as if he'd only figured he needed to escape, but not thought of how it might be possible. Then he got angry again. "Just do something to help me, you asshole, or . . . or . . . or I'll take that brace on your leg and shove it up your crippled ass!" He grabbed his wife's shoulders and leaned over her, thrusting as hard as he could.

Andy scowled. *How come nobody thinks of me as 'physically-challenged' in this stupid diner? That's the third 'cripple' crack I've heard this morning.*

But Andy was seeing a pattern now. He could hear Daria laughing again, off somewhere out of sight. He was ignoring her as best he could, but her constant mockery was a rat gnawing at his soul. He sensed her goading him on, angering him towards acts of violence. The insults were all Daria too; she wanted him to feed her. But he wasn't going to. So far he'd killed two of her minions—Gorilla and the waitress—but neither of those two had been truly alive. If he lost his temper and killed this man here . . . it would be actual murder, exactly what Daria had in mind.

"Forget it, woman," he mouthed silently back at her. "It ain't happenin'."

She laughed. But he sensed disappointment behind her mirth. He listened, trying to hear fear in her laughter, fear because she knew he was coming after her for what she'd done to Karen.

But she wasn't scared. In her laughter he heard only her impatience for him to hunt her down.

Shit! For the first time since Karen's death, Andy began feeling really afraid. His rage cooled a little and he began thinking: *If she wants me to come after her—*

"Hey, asshole!"

Andy jerked out of his thoughts.

TJ was pointing past him. "Gimme that knife, you pansy!"

"Huh?" Andy turned. A hunting knife lay on the table behind him. He didn't recall seeing it there earlier. It had a red handle and a long sharp blade.

"I said—gimme that knife, you stupid crippled asshole!"

Andy glared back at him. This turtle-looking prick was starting to piss him off big time. He stared down at his shotgun. It would be so easy. All he had to do was aim at the man's five overlapping layers of gut fat and pull the trigger, and . . .

Then he saw through the angry haze. He frowned coldly. "Nice try, Daria, but it ain't gonna work!"

She didn't laugh anymore. He'd let her down.

"Well, what the fuck are you waiting for, asshole? Gimme the knife!"

Andy had a good idea that he knew what Daria's plan was: He'd give this crazy necromaniac guy the knife and the guy would grab him and stab him.

"C'mon, man," he said, "you know you don't really wanna do whatever it is you wanna do."

"Give me the damn knife, punk!"

The walls flickered again then. For longer than before. This time everything around Andy, TJ, and the pool table blurred out for a full two seconds before returning to normal.

Andy suddenly realized he'd been wrong. Daria wasn't interested in killing him. She was delaying him here so he'd not be able to escape before the diner vanished.

He needed to get a move on.

"Hey, you silly crippled shithead mofo, are you deaf too? Gimme that goddamn knife!" Flesh wobbling as he thrust relentlessly on, TJ was gasping fast again, like he was about to ejaculate.

Andy picked up the knife and handed it to TJ. He handed it to him blade first, so he couldn't immediately try to stab him with it. Then he stepped back quickly.

TJ's previous belligerence instantly vanished. He smiled at Andy. "Thanks, man!"

And, next thing, TJ jerked his penis out of his wife's gaping anus. He placed the knife's blade at the base of his erection. A tiny squirt of blood announced the blade's contact with his skin.

Now, he looked at Andy in terror. "Help me! I can't stop myself! The demon—she's inside my mind. She's making me do it!"

"Noooo, man! Don't you dare do that!" Andy yelped.

But it was too late. TJ was already slicing his own penis off. He looked horrified. Despite this, however, he finished the job of castrating himself. Three deep slashes later, he was holding his severed manhood in his hand. For a moment afterward, he looked really perplexed over what he'd just done to himself. Then the blood began jetting from his obscenely truncated crotch, and the agony hit him. His eyes widened in ghastly realization and he began screaming:

"NOOOOOOO! NOOOOOOO! NOOOOOOOOOO!!!"

Then, still screaming, he flung his severed penis across the room and began stabbing himself in the belly. More blood streamed out and ran sideways through the folds of his sagging skin. He stabbed himself and ripped himself open, and yelled and shrieked in pain till he collapsed dead on the floor beside the pool table.

Poppy's corpse was still posed over the pool table edge. A flood of maggots suddenly squirted out of her anus and poured all over her husband. The flood of the white larvae was endless, like a spillage of melted cheese. In a very short while the maggots had covered TJ's corpse and were feeding voraciously on it.

Andy bent over and vomited all over the table he'd taken the knife from.

Daria was laughing again. Loud delighted laughter like she was drunk at an office party.

The maggots were still spilling from the dead woman's anus. Like bleached toxic sludge they fell and squirmed and spread in a pale translucent pool of filth. Her husband's body was already noticeably altering in shape as the larvae ate their way into it.

The maggot-pool spread over the floor towards Andy's feet.

Seeing the grubs approaching him, Andy got out of there as fast as he could, dragging his bad leg behind him. Craig's corpse was already just bones, and the maggots that had been feeding on him had since crossed the room to begin stripping Karen's body bare of flesh and clothing. The grubs were eating Karen's head in fast-forward. What was happening there looked like a sped-up movie. The disgusting larvae stripped Karen's facial skin and muscles away as fast as if they were scalpels; they bared her skull bones as effectively as vitriol would.

Andy shed a lot of tears for Karen as he hobbled past her. It hurt him that he wouldn't even get her corpse out of this damned place to bury it.

Then he focused all his attention on Daria.

He was going to stop his ex, no matter what it took.

And if I don't get it done—if I fail? He shrugged. *Well, today's as good a day as any to die.*

***

The left corridor was strewn with more maggots. Andy winced. The damn grubs were everywhere, like the house was giant turd.

Alright, where the hell is Daria?

Since he'd left the dining room, Daria had stopped laughing. Almost like he'd left her behind to feed on the anguish of the dead she'd killed. Or was she incarnated in the maggots that were eating everyone out there?

Whatever the cause, she wasn't laughing anymore. He should have felt relieved, her mockery had been driving him nuts. But that wasn't the case. To Andy, losing her voice felt like losing an emotional anchor.

Shotgun at the ready, he stumbled along the corridor, dragging his bad leg along with him. He knew he was already surfing dangerously close to Crazy Reef, but he had to finish this thing. If he didn't, if Daria kept coming back year after year on her birth-and-death-day for more victims . . .

It didn't bear thinking about.

He reached the stairs. Here, a trail of bloody barefoot footprints joined the ubiquitous grubs. The red imprints were sparse but readable. The footprints led towards the back of the house. Andy figured they belonged to the two young women he'd come here to rescue.

Andy mused on the footprints. *Daria feeds on sex and violence? Follow the blood then.*

He kept going.

The bloody footprints turned off into the passage to the side door. Paradoxically, other footprints kept going towards the toilets. Holding the shotgun poised to fire, Andy peeked into the passageway. There was no one in there, just bloodstained walls, a shitload of grubs and two stripped finger bones a yard or so from his feet.

As he stared at the locked door (and the world beyond), the walls flickered again. This time they remained out of focus for almost five seconds. Andy felt like he was standing in the middle of a centrifuge.

The world normalized again, leaving Andy feeling like *he* was the centrifuge spinning around the walls. More Dizzy than if he'd been rocking with the Beatle's Miss Lizzy. Taking good care to keep away from maggot trails, he leaned against the right wall to steady himself. Staring at the floor, he now made proper sense of the red footprints:

Okay, now lemme get this figured out: two sets of prints lead inward towards the side door, and two sets—gotta be the same pair—walk back out again. Has to be Shelly and Erica then.

Only, from the smeared arrangement of the returning footprints it didn't look to Andy like the girls had *walked* out. It looked more like they'd *slipped* and *slid* out. He remembered the angry screams. *Were they fightin'?* He again looked down the passageway, the farther end of which had an almost wall-to-wall carpeting of maggots. At several points the girls' footprints clumped together, and then there was all that splattered blood on the walls to consider too. Indeed (he quickly noted this), the real bloodshed appeared to have begun here in this side passageway—the earlier footprints were merely sole ghosts prophesizing the violence to come.

Yeah, they must've been fightin' with each other. And to the death, by the messy looks of it.

He didn't ponder why the pair would be trying to kill one another. He already knew why: Daria.

Follow the blood. He set off for the back of the building.

Daria's voice began echoing around him. He looked around, but she was impossible to locate. It sounded like she was right inside his head:

"Oh, Andy, I love you, baby! I love your anger! It's delicious! Come and find me and fuck me and kill me! Yes, we'll be together. Together again. Come! Come and make me come and come in me! Oh, oh, oh, oh!"

She began gasping like she was having an orgasm.

Andy kept on walking. *Follow the blood. Even though the damn maggots have licked it all up.*

The maggot/blood trail led directly to the ladies' restroom. Now he was having to trample the damn grubs wholesale. They were crawling everywhere: on the floor, on the walls; even on the ceiling.

He hurried through the restroom entrance so they didn't start dropping on him. He shut the door behind him and looked around.

***

Andy had expected to find something horrible in the toilet. He found it.

Two women sat on the grub-covered floor, leaning against the outer cubicle wall.

One woman was dead, her body perforated by an uncountable number of punctures. The other was stabbing her corpse in a repeated, mechanical motion.

They had to be Shelly and Erica, Andy figured. But both were completely unrecognizable now—withered away almost to mere bone. Shriveled dry husks like corn forgotten in the desert sun. Neither had any hair left, just dry flaking skin on their heads, skin stretched to ripping point across their faces. Both women had knives. The dead woman's knife lay at her side in the lax grip of a right hand missing three of its fingers. (Neither woman had a complete set of digits anymore; the living woman gripped her knife between two fingers and a thumb.) Both scrawny bodies were covered with deep slashes. Half of the dead woman's left bicep hung down over her elbow like a bloody cut of meat. She also had a gory mess in place of her left eye.

Intent on eating her, the maggots were climbing up the dead woman and wriggling their way into her multitude of mortal punctures. Her killer kept stabbing her regardless, digging her knife as deep as she could into her chest, throat, and belly, grunting as she widened the holes she'd already made everywhere. The knife made a ghastly sucking sound each time it pulled out of the dead flesh.

Andy decided the surviving woman was Erica. The girls had come here to find a necklace, and this almost-corpse was wearing a gold necklace, one with a heart-shaped locket.

Taking care lest she stabbed him too, Andy shook Erica's shoulder. "Hey, Erica!"

She froze in her relentless stabbing and turned to stare at him. He found her stare unnerving. True, she was little more than a corpse now, but her blue eyes glowed with an unnatural light; the same unholy light that had shone in the eyes of the man who'd castrated himself; the same evil luminance that had glowed in that man's wife's eyes.

Erica grinned at Andy and he felt like entering the toilet and taking a long hard shit. What had scared him further wasn't her missing teeth;

it was how pleased with herself she seemed, as if killing Shelly was the high point of her life.

"I won," Erica announced in an old woman's voice. "I slaughtered the old heifer. The silly cow thought she was tough, but I was tougher. Ha ha!" She wheezed; her chest rattled like it was attached to a snake. "And I got my locket back, see?" She held the gold pendant up for Andy's appraisal. He saw too that she had a long, deep slash on the right side of her face; it ran from her ear down to her collarbone.

Andy nodded. "Listen, Erica," he said, "the house is fading. We've got to get away before Daria takes us both away to a very horrible place." He'd realized there was no time to both kill Daria and save Erica. Better he save Erica then. He'd promised Karen he would. Besides, Andy felt saving a life was always better than ending one.

Erica giggled. "Oh, but I don't wanna leave here, Andy. Daria is taking us all to SADE. It ain't a bad place at all. SADE is full of—"

Andy quit listening. The girl was clearly under Daria's influence. He'd simply drag her away. She looked too weak to resist.

"Come on!" he said, gripping her arm and starting to pull her to her feet.

He was prepared for her trying to stab him. He wasn't prepared for her simply shoving him away like he weighed nothing.

"Fucking leave me alone!" she screamed. "I don't wanna go nowhere with you!"

Andy prevented himself from falling by catching the edge of the nearest sink. He managed also to not drop his shotgun. His back slammed against the wall. He stood grunting from the impact and breathing hard.

"C'mon, Erica, let's get the hell out of here. We ain't got time to waste. Look!"

The walls had just blurred again. He and Erica and Shelly's corpse were inside what seemed like a giant spinning marshmallow. This time he shut his eyes. He counted to ten before opening them again. The toilet was normal again, pink stalls and white walls with maggots crawling everywhere.

A maggot bit his hand. He pulled the hand off the sink and flicked the damn grub away.

Erica got to her feet. "Goodbye, Andrew."

He watched her put the knife to her throat then slowly drag it across her neck, cutting deep into her flesh. There was less blood than he expected, just a few squirts.

Erica collapsed dead.

The crazy, entranced look on Erica's dead face was almost too much for Andy to bear. Still, he got a hold of himself. He had to stop this.

He turned to leave the toilet. He opened the door.

"Hey, Andy!"

At first he thought he'd imagined the voice behind him. It had been a whisper, and there had also been a weird creaking sound mixed in with it.

"Turn around, Andy!"

He turned around, dreading what he'd see.

It was the other dead girl, Shelly. She was getting to her feet. Denuded of all their flesh by the ravenous larvae, her legs shouldn't have worked. But somehow they still did. She stood there on those two red sticks of stripped bones and grinned at him. Erica had done a crazy hatchet job on her: she looked like a latticework of flesh. Some of the knife holes seem to run all the way through her body.

Andy didn't want any part of this. He began backing away out of the door.

"Wait!" Shelly commanded. She wobbled and her fleshless legs creaked like the mansion doors in a horror movie.

He waited.

"Daria says she hates you," Shelly said. "Ha ha ha ha ha ha ha!"

Shelly was still laughing when she exploded. She blew up like she'd been packed with dynamite. Chunks of her splattered the restroom walls and ceiling. Impossibly, the explosion amplified her laughter, so that even with Shelly scattered everywhere, Andy still heard her mocking him.

Andy wiped a smearing of Shelly's brains off his face. Staring at that pink mess on his hand, he was finally convinced of the folly of his hunt for Daria.

Propelled by a terror the likes of which he'd never felt before, Andy hurried out of the toilet. He felt like he'd just come to his senses. He wondered what insanity had possessed him to ever think he could take Daria on.

He cursed the irony of his life: a man couldn't run with a bad leg. And now he really needed to run. He went as fast as he could down the corridor from the toilets.

At the turnoff to the side door he hesitated a moment. The front door was open, this one might be locked.

A fresh blurring of the walls decided him. He'd better take this side exit out. If the door was locked he'd shoot the damn lock off. He turned into the side passageway.

"Where do you think you're going, you son-of-a-bitch? Running away again, are you? Leaving me to die again?"

Andy froze. Daria's voice was coming from directly ahead. But there was no one in front of him. The exit door wasn't covered with any black mess either, like had happened before Gorilla had killed Karen. Andy figured it was just scare tactics. He didn't have far to go to get out of here. He stepped forward again.

Just then, the walls blurred again. He shut his eyes while the world whirled around him.

When he opened his eyes, Daria was standing in front of him, blocking the way to the door. Daria was as gorgeous as ever: snow-white hair, rose-red lips, dawn-gray eyes; her pale face almost equine in its beauty; her perfect figure singing to his manhood.

On seeing her, his anger vanished and he felt like he was falling in love with her all over again. He wanted to grab her and kiss her. He wanted to make love to her and impregnate her. He knew it was crazy, but there it was. He knew she had to be controlling his mind for him to feel this way about her after all the evil things he'd watched her do.

She, however, was mad at him. "I just asked you where you're headed, Andy," she said in a quiet but enraged voice. He clearly heard the insanity in her voice, but found that he still wanted her. But how was that possible? He was terrified of her. He had to escape from her! This woman wasn't the woman he'd loved anymore. This one was a monster who'd killed everyone who'd entered her diner . . . she'd used them all up in sadistic games. For food.

But still, he couldn't help how he felt. He loved her. Being this close to her was even giving him an erection.

That's just sick, he thought. *Karen only just died and—*

He couldn't think too long, however. Daria grabbed him by the throat and began choking him. She leaned in close to him, so he could smell her perfume of roses and death.

"You promised to love me eternally, you jerk, but instead you let me die."

"It wasn't my fault!" he gasped. "It wasn't . . . !"

She'd lifted him off the floor now. His bad leg swung in an arc. His neck felt like it was in a noose. He figured she'd soon break his neck.

"It *was* your fault." She glared up at him. Intense hatred blazed in her eyes.

Andy realized that she meant business. His vision was already turning foggy from oxygen lack. *Hell no, sweetheart! I sure as hell am gonna die someday, but I sure as hell ain't dyin' like this today!* He rammed the shotgun into Daria's belly and pulled the trigger.

Boom!

Black liquid exploded from the rear of Daria's body. She, however, didn't seem to notice that he'd shot her, nor did she show any signs of pain. She kept staring up at Andy as she choked him.

Boom! Boom! Boom! Boom!

He shot her again and again, spreading black goop all over the corridor behind her. Looking down, he saw that her body was perforated with holes that dripped black slime. But she didn't care. He wasn't hurting her in the least. His efforts clearly amused her.

He was close to unconsciousness now.

The shotgun clicked empty. Daria's body repaired itself till she was whole again.

I'm fucked, Andy thought weakly. *I'm gonna die here.*

Then he heard Daria laughing. "Oh, Andy," she said, "can't you take a joke for once?"

"A joke?" he gasped with the last breath he could muster. "What kind of a sick joke is this? Daria, you're fuckin' killin' me!"

"I'm *not* killing you," she replied with grim emphasis. "I just want you to be unconscious when the building transitions back to SADE. That way you won't wake up crazy. We're leaving Earth now."

We're going to SADE? Oh shit! His mind was fading, and around them he could see that the walls had blurred again, only this time the walls weren't returning to normal.

She was still choking him. As he slipped into unconsciousness, he heard her saying: "See, baby, all this is me. See? I'm in control here now. The diner is all me. Yeah, Andy darling, Xander Mood was an asshole, but he sure taught me a lot about death and dying. Lots of really nasty things. And I'm going to share them with you, baby. I forgive you, baby. I really do."

She's forgiven me, Andy thought. *Why ain't I delighted to hear that?*

"Oh yes," Daria went on. "I love you again now, Andy. And I'm going to share everything I know with you. This time, baby, our relationship is really going to be 'till death to us part.' Only, you aren't ever going to die, so we aren't ever going to part."

No shit! Andy thought, and was out cold.

***

The Crossway Diner faded with them both inside it.

Big Dan Jenkins, a trucker driving down off the I-91 overpass, noticed the building vanish but thought he was hallucinating.

Big Dan decided to stay well away from drugs for a while.

EPILOGUE:
AN ARIA IN HELL

Andy, mainly

Andy sits in the darkness waiting. Despite what Daria promised, he isn't really sane anymore. But that isn't his fault. Where he lives now isn't a sane place.

So maybe he is still sane but SADE isn't.

Anyhow, it doesn't really matter now.

Andy waits. He's waiting for Daria.

It is now eight months since they both left Earth. They are married now. Xander Mood performed their wedding ceremony. The warlock now has horns and wings, and his body is hairy all over.

Daria was a gorgeous bride. Sexy, sexy, sexy. Andy had a hard-on all through their wedding ceremony.

Death attended their wedding. Death was a woman with a knockout body and a horrible, horrible face. Her nose was as big and veined as Andy's hard-on.

Andy waits for Daria.

In SADE, he and his wife live in a small stone house atop a tall, tall cliff. The cliff promontory hangs over an empty sea—a chasm full of monsters that swim in black air.

While waiting for Daria, Andy desperately tries to remember something bad. Something terrible that once happened to him. He feels troubled, but is uncertain what's going on. Andy is scared stiff. It's his usual frame of mind now. He's sure that if he can just remember the horror, it would end. But he can't remember a thing. So now he's perpetually scared.

If only he knew why he's so frightened.

Names occasionally come to his mind: Karen . . . Craig . . . Erica . . . Piper . . . Shelly . . . Poppy . . . TJ . . . Brie. But the names mean nothing. 'Karen' is the name he most remembers, but content-wise, it's like the others—a vacant house, an empty box. He's decided that Karen must have been his mother's name. A really nice woman she must have been too for him to still remember her.

Or maybe Karen never existed. Most likely, all the names he thinks he remembers are merely expressions of his madness. His psyche playing tricks on him.

He's scared, that's the thing. Really terrified. But of what?

Daria isn't the problem. Andy is certain of this. Daria always tells him how much she loves him. "I love you, baby," she says. "Don't worry about the past and the bad times. Everything is fine now. I'm gonna be a good woman to you now. The best woman ever. I'm gonna treat you really wonderful."

Andy takes her at her word. He has no reason to disbelieve her. Besides, Andy loves Daria too. He LOVES her more than life itself. She's the center of his world.

Besides which, Andy is crazy now anyway. So maybe he's just scared of recovering his sanity and then going mad again from what he'll remember happened to him before he and Daria eloped over here.

Andy's right leg still hurts sometimes. Like today. It's why he's not outside with his lover at the moment, hunting down some little SADEish critter for their dinner.

Daria will soon be back home. Andy can't wait to take her in his arms again.

They might even retire into their bedroom and make love. Daria likes lovemaking. She really enjoys it, even though she's eight months pregnant with Andy's baby.

Despite his terror and worries, Andy smiles as he thinks of their baby. It'll be nice to be a father; he's always liked kids.

He grins broadly.

Their kid isn't going to be any kind of normal though. Both Andy and Daria know this. Their daughter or son (they just call it 'it') is going to have six or seven or eight arms and legs and whole lot of needlelike teeth. Really long teeth, like knitting needles. More eyes than normal too. Also, it is going to grow up really, really fast, and then it will leave home into the void, where it will begin relentlessly seeking an exit to the human world so it can feed on human sex and violence like its mom does.

And once baby number one has left home, Andy and Daria will make another monster child with an excess of arms and legs and an insatiable desire for human lusts and passions.

And after that one they'll make yet another, and another, and another. On and on and on.

Daria and Andy are going to keep on making monster kids endlessly. Forever. They've both agreed on that.

So, see, Andy's really scared now, but he's also in love, and he's really, really, really happy, though it's a 'scared madman' kind of happy.

Andy grins. He can hear Daria outside now, her soft fast footfalls on their front walk. He can also hear the miserable moanings and pleadings of whatever it is that she's caught for their dinner.

Andy gets up. Dragging his bad leg after him, he walks to his front door to welcome his wife home with a loving kiss.

The End.

ABOUT THE AUTHOR

Wol-vriey is Nigerian, and quite tall.

He believes there actually are things that go bump in the night.

He writes horror fiction—for adults only, please. And also some surrealist stuff.

Wol-vriey blogs at: *http://oddityfarm.wordpress.com*

WOL-VRIEY
BIZARRO AND TRANSGRESSIVE FICTION

BOSTON POSH (BUD MALONE #1)

In 2028 AD, the USA is a nation ravaged by hungry dragons and dinosaurs. In Boston, Massachusetts, private eye Bud Malone is hired to rescue a kidnapped heiress. But nothing is as it seems.

Malone works to unravel a tangled web involving Boston Chinatown, a 200-year-old woman with a 9-year-old body, white robots, a human-liver-eating psychopath, a golem, a porcelain dragon, and a snake goddess with a crush on him. There's also a woman obsessed with chicken sex. Then Malone meets Posh Lane, a gorgeous call girl who's desperate to quit her pimp.

Romantic sparks ignite between Posh and Malone, but Posh's past suddenly catches up with her in a BIG way. To save Posh, Malone agrees to run a quest for Earth's new rulers, the Forks. But, Malone has no idea that agreeing to the Fork's odd request will send him on the weirdest trip he's ever been on in his life.

BOSTON CORPSE (BUD MALONE #2)

MAGIC CAN BE MURDER! - Drag queen Lucy Tang is back in Boston, and is hell-bent on settling her vindetta against casino owner Sookie Ling. And suddenly, Bud Malone, PI, has the case of his life to resolve.

When Boston's robot police force are baffled by a mind transfer case, they come to Malone for help. The one person who can likely help Malone out here is the witch Soledad Bathory. But Soledad seems to know a lot more than she's telling him. It's a case not made easier when Malone meets Soledad's beautiful cousin, Josephine 'Slave' Bailey. Slave has her own plans for Malone, most of which involve teaching him BDSM and making him her new Master.

Oh, and Rick Rogers owes Sookie Ling a whole lot of money, a gambling debt that's going to be literally Hell to pay!

BOSTON CORPSE - Not your average detective novel!

Burning Bulb
PUBLISHING

WOL-VRIEY
BIZARRO AND TRANSGRESSIVE FICTION

BOSTON LUST (BUD MALONE #3)

"Bless it, Father, for she has sinned."

Seven murdered gay women, all their bodies completely drained of blood. All also with large parts of their bodies dissolved away like acid has been pumped into their veins.

Bud Malone has to find the female vampire preying on Boston's lesbian population.

Then Malone meets the beautiful Trudi Carmen and the case gets even more tangled. Trudi needs Malone's help in recovering a ring that's gone missing. But how in the world is one little black ring related to either the dead women or their killer?

Resolving this case will lead Malone deep into Lucy Tang's legacy—The Abstracta. And then to the city of Genesis.

Boston Lust—Just when you thought Bean Town was safe to visit again.

HELL DANCER

Six people find themselves trapped in Detention, a nightmare realm where the demonic Schoolmaster is hell-bent on reforming them . . . until they die.

Porn superstar Venus Deluxe came to Springfield, MA to party, and next found her life hanging by a thread. One wrong answer will mean her death.

Suspended BPD detective Tanya Rockford was trying to stop one kind of violence, but found a terrifying another. With her and her companion's lives hanging in the balance, it's going to take all of her courage and resourcefulness to escape this hell she's stumbled into.

Porn stud Chad Cannon has made a career from his ten-inch penis. Here in Detention, however, it's his brains that matter. He'll soon be hoping all the pot he's smoked over the years hasn't completely messed up his memory.

The three students, Sherri, Jordan, and Mike? They were all just in the wrong place at the right time. Will anyone survive Detention? The evil Schoolmaster doesn't plan on letting that happen . . .

Burning Bulb
PUBLISHING

WOL-VRIEY
BIZARRO AND TRANSGRESSIVE FICTION

VAGINA MUNDI

Rachel Risk is a professional thief with super-strong hair that can stretch like tentacles to manipulate objects. Ashley Status has both a digitally augmented brain, and 'muscle-purses' in her arms and legs in which she stores inflatable objects—cars, guns, rocket launchers, etc.

When Raye is framed as the fall girl in a jewel robbery, the pair flee Chicago's vengeful robot gangsters and take refuge in the Hotel Bizarre, where the gorgeous 'vagina singer,' Femina, is performing for a week.

But the Hotel Bizarre is even stranger than its name suggests, and very soon Raye and Ash are involved in an deadly adventure, a struggle for survival the likes of which they'd never imagined possible—with loads of deviant sex, drugs, music, and violence at every turn. And just what is the old woman in the skin desert really doing with all those cats glued to her walls?

VAGINA MUNDI—a Bizarro Hymn in praise of WOMAN!

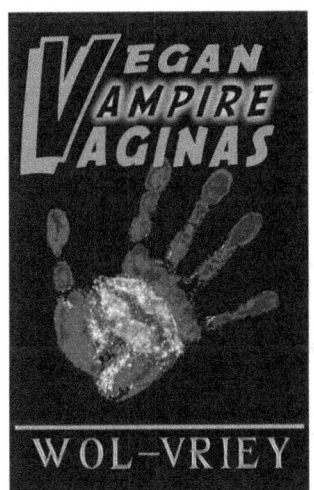

VEGAN VAMPIRE VAGINAS

The biggest bank heist in US history. And Tom Palmer can't remember pulling it off. And no, this isn't your standard case of amnesia. After a one-night-stand gone horribly wrong, Boston salesman Tom Palmer wakes up with a vagina implanted in his left hand. Then his day gets worse.

Tom is transported across space-time to a nightmare version of Boston, one where the Bizarro virus has transformed half the population into cannibals. Worst of all, Tom discovers that in this new Boston, he's the infamous gangster Pussypalm, wanted for robbing the Federal Reserve Bank of Boston a year ago. He also learns that the vagina in his hand is prophetic, i.e. it talks . . . after sex.

With 130 people left dead during his bank heist and six billion dollars missing, Tom knows he's living on borrowed time. It is in his best interests not to remember anything. Because once he does . . .

Burning Bulb
PUBLISHING

WOL-VRIEY
BIZARRO AND TRANSGRESSIVE FICTION

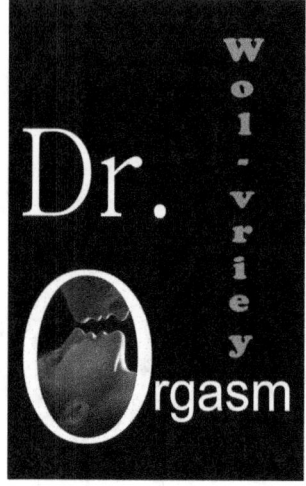

Dr. Orgasm

Courtney Taylor is young, intelligent, beautiful, and successful. She also has a boyfriend who loves her deeply. The problem is, no matter what Courtney does, she can't climax during sex.

When Florence Rigid's communist forces destroy the city of Metaphor, Courtney and her friends Teresa, Highball, Miki, and Heather are cast into the midst of a quest to find the only person able to save the land of Innuendo—Dr. Carol Orgasm, wanted by the communists for developing the O-Pill, a wonder drug that grants women sexual ecstasy on demand.

The communists will do anything to get their hands on the O-Pill and prevent its reaching the millions of Innuendo's women. But Courtney desperately wants that pill too. And so it's now a race between Courtney and the communists to find Dr. Orgasm first.

And Courtney has no choice but to win this race. She must win it: For her own orgasm . . . and for the freedom of female sexuality everywhere.

PUSSY TRANSMISSION

Pussy Transmission were the most decadent Pop Art ensemble of the 90's. Led by the beautiful painter Isis Lynch, the trio revolutionized the art world. Then suddenly, without explanation, Pussy Transmission vanished into historical obscurity. Now, twenty years later, three women come to Lynch Place. Lily and Nina are journalists desperate to interview Isis Lynch. Raven, on the other hand, wants to find her boyfriend, who's gone missing inside Isis's house. Raven's worried—she's heard that Pussy Transmission broke up because Isis began dabbling in black magic . . . with devastating results. All three women will shortly wish they'd never left home. Particularly once the rats in Lynch Place start warning them that they're going to die . . . and Raven meets Betty Butcher, the bouncy supernatural psycho who's intent on chopping her into bits. Pussy Transmission, Baby! Just because . . .

Burning Bulb
PUBLISHING

WOL-VRIEY
BIZARRO AND TRANSGRESSIVE FICTION

VEGAN ZOMBIE APOCALYPSE

In the post-apocalypse worlderness, zombies rule the earth. They're allergic to meat, and brains literally make them explode. Zombies now eat blood potatoes, parasitic tubers grown in the flesh of humancows corralled in maximum security farms. Two fugitives meet in the ancient ruins of Texas. The first is Soil 15-f, a womancow who's escaped her farm a week before she's due to be killed and her blood potato crop harvested. The second fugitive is Able Kane, former head necros food technician, now sentenced to death for heresy. But Soil is no ordinary humancow.

Unknown to herself, she's the vegan zombie agricultural revolution, and the zombies desperately want her back. And the necros equally desperately want Able Kane dead. He's fled with a forbidden discovery which will reshape the world for the worse if used. And Able is just hardheaded/misguided enough to use it.

MELANIE NEMESIS CATCHPOLE

In Springfield, Massachusetts, Melanie Catchpole is hired to fetch back a magic teddy bear worth millions of dollars from a warehouse across town. Problem is, the warehouse is down in Springfield's O-Zone-that totally weird sector of the city where Bizarro fell to Earth. The 'O' is a fairytale land, a place where dreams and nightmares literally live and breathe.

Worse still, the gingers—mutant cannibals—prowl the O. The gingers have already eaten everyone else Melanie's employers sent to get back the magic teddy bear.

Accompanied by the handsome but ruthless Doug Fisher (who she finds sexy but doesn't dare entrust her heart to), Melanie enters the O-Zone. Melanie and Doug are instantly caught up in an adventure they'd never have believed credible even if written as fiction . . . and Melanie's used to experiencing the very weird as the norm.

And now, additionally, there's a mystery to unravel: What does the dark, freezing-cold being called The Fixer want with Mary, the barkeep's daughter?

Burning Bulb
PUBLISHING

WOL-VRIEY
BIZARRO AND TRANSGRESSIVE FICTION

BIG TROUBLE IN LITTLE ASS

From Bizarro master storyteller Wol-vriey comes a truly weird western tale that will leave you awe-struck and on the edge of your seat...

In the town named Little Ass, tight-assed prostitute Rosa overhears a gunslinger's plans to assassinate rancher Edison Bennett. Once the badass Bennett learns of the plot, he ensures there'll be hell to pay for any attempt on his life!

Yes, it's going to take all of gunslinger Jude's shooting prowess, his eclectic collection of strange firearms, a trusty horse that requires an owners' manual, and the help of the lovely and invigorating Nell (who's EXTREMELY odd when the going gets weird), to survive the Bizarro hell that Edison Bennett unleashes in order to hold onto the land that he'd stolen from Madam Zizi.

BIZARRO 101 (A BASIC PRIMER)

Welcome to the strange place:

A collection of 37 flash fiction stories designed to introduce one to the Bizarro/New Weird Genre.

Weird, dreamy, nightmarish, absurd, sad, surreal, humorous . . . this collection of tales is all this and more.

***

"This primer is the very essence of any and all styles and types of Bizarro writing. Wol-vriey collects, distills, and bottles up these 37 tiny stories for your sensory enjoyment. This is an absolute must-read for anyone new to the genre, because it demonstrates the scope of what Bizarro is, and what it can be."
        –Teresa Pollack, Bizarro commentator and blogger

Burning Bulb
PUBLISHING

WOL-VRIEY
BIZARRO AND TRANSGRESSIVE FICTION

GIRLS ARE NOT SMILING

Welcome To The Road Trip From Hell

Pagan is demon-possessed.

Lori is suicidal.

Britt is just terminally pissed off.

Meet three young Boston women on the run from the law, each with problems that will fuse into more than the sum of their individual parts, becoming a holocaust of sex and violence and terror, a literal rain of blood and horror and gore and evil.

And if that wasn't already bad enough, Pagan's pet demon is slowly transforming her into something both unspeakable and unholy. Truly, these girls aren't smiling.

BLUE NIGHTMARES

Consummate EVIL is coming. It is relentless and unavoidable. It is Blue.

Jessica Schreiber is seeing things. Very horrible things. Since arriving in Raynham for what should have been a relaxing vacation, she's been seeing *The Big Blue*.

Jessica is smelling things too—dead and rotting things that she can't see. She is sure those dead and rotting things are dead people. Lots of dead people.

Jessica's worst nightmares will soon become her reality. Her reality will soon become a terrifying nightmare.

The tentacled residents of the House of Death have a lot that they wish to show Jessica Schreiber. They have a lot that they wish to tell her. But will she survive long enough to learn their lessons?

Burning Bulb
PUBLISHING

WOL-VRIEY
BIZARRO AND TRANSGRESSIVE FICTION

BRAINCHEW

It was supposed to be a simple jewel heist, but it went badly wrong. Chuck got shot and died.

Lance hid his friend's corpse in the Pleasant Street Cemetery. But that was a big mistake—there was something undead, something extremely hungry . . . something eXXXtremely horrible, buried in the Pleasant Street Cemetery.

And Lance had just woken it up.

They called the monster Brainchew because it ate brains. Human brains. And it preferred those brains fresh from the heads . . . of the living.

And now it was awake again, Brainchew planned on feeding big-time tonight. Oh hell yes, it did.

BRAINCHEW 2: OUT OF THEIR HEADS

After Tiff Hooper recognizes Josh Penham, the man who abducted her and kept her in his basement and abused her, she brings her three friends to Raynham for a night of well-deserved revenge on him.

Only things don't go according to plan.

It is never a good idea to leave a corpse in Raynham's Pleasant Street Cemetery. You run the very real risk of awakening what lies underground there. And that thing—Brainchew—is more horrible and more evil than anything the average mind conceives of even in its worst nightmares.

Brainchew is back! And this time the monster is extra-hungry. But there are plenty of delicious human brains about tonight, and Brainchew intends to eat them all before dawn.

Burning Bulb
PUBLISHING